PRAISE FOR ANDREW M. GREELEY

"FATHER GREELEY WRITES WITH PASSION AND NARRATIVE FORCE." —*Chicago Sun-Times*

"HE HAS MASTERED THE ART OF SUSPENSE."
—*Arizona Daily Star*

Happy Are the Peace Makers . . . a Blackie Ryan novel. A beautiful widow is suspected of murder. Bishop Blackie Ryan is the only man who can resist her charms . . . and solve the perfect crime.

"GREELEY UNCOVERS THE PASSIONS HIDDEN IN MEN AND WOMEN." —*UPI*

"READERS WILL NOT BE DISAPPOINTED, FATHER GREELEY IS A GOOD STORYTELLER."
—*Minneapolis Tribune*

"A MASTER!" —*Cincinnati Enquirer*

Continued . . .

ALSO BY ANDREW M. GREELEY

FICTION

An Occasion of Sin
Death in April
The Cardinal Sins

The Passover Trilogy
  Thy Brother's Wife
  Ascent Into Hell
  Lord of the Dance

Time Between the Stars
  Virgin and Martyr
  The Angels of September
  The Patience of a Saint
  Rite of Spring
  Love Song
  Saint Valentine's Night

The World of Maggie Ward
  The Search for Maggie Ward
  The Cardinal Virtues

Mystery and Fantasy
  The Magic Cup

The Final Planet
God Game
Angel Fire
Happy Are the Meek
Happy Are the Clean of Heart
*Happy Are Those Who Thirst
  for Justice*
Happy Are the Peace Makers
Happy Are the Merciful

SELECTED NONFICTION

The Making of the Popes 1978
The Catholic Myth
Confessions of a Parish Priest
How to Save the Catholic Church
  (With Mary G. Durkin)
Religious Change in America
The Bible and Us (With Jacob
  Neusner)
God in Popular Culture
Faithful Attraction

WAGES OF SIN

ANDREW M. GREELEY

JOVE BOOKS, NEW YORK

While the culture of the Archdiocese of Chicago is accurate, none of the clergy or hierarchy are based on actual people.

This Jove Book contains the complete
text of the original hardcover edition.
It has been completely reset in a typeface
designed for easy reading and was printed
from new film.

WAGES OF SIN

A Jove Book / published by arrangement with
Andrew Greeley Enterprises, Ltd.

PRINTING HISTORY
G. P. Putnam's Sons edition published August 1992
Jove edition / October 1993

ISBN: 0-515-11222-4

A JOVE BOOK®
Jove Books are published by The Berkley Publishing Group,
200 Madison Avenue, New York, New York 10016.
JOVE and the "J" design
are trademarks belonging to Jove Publications, Inc.

PRINTED IN THE UNITED STATES OF AMERICA

10 9 8 7 6 5 4 3 2 1

Of a much richer life the merest hint
A story is only an invitation
A slight tale told with no deep intention
Save that your life not heedlessly be spent;
Of whom you might be a modest revelation
Another world temporarily lent
To seduce you gently from your daily bent
And entice you with its fascination.

Do not ask for moral speculations,
This is the storyteller's sad lament,
Nor rules nor advice nor regulations
For these needs other worthy folks are sent
And honored at academic convocations—
I'll sell you only illumination!

*Hell is where we wake up dead
And realize how much life we had
And didn't use.*
  —Richard Shelton

Hell, my dear lady, is not loving any more.
  —Georges Bernanos

Every shutting up of a creature within the dungeons of its own mind is hell.
  —C. S. Lewis

The wages of sin is death, but the grace of God is everlasting life.
  —Rom. 6/23

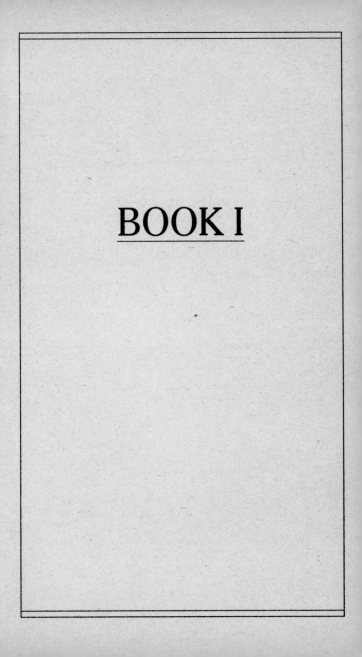

BOOK I

1

"He takes her away from me. It's night and we're lying on the beach towels in each other's arms. Then the mists roll in, dark red mists, and they flow all around us. There's a burst of light. He appears, laughing hysterically. She goes away with him . . ."

"Of her own volition?"

"I don't know!"

"To make love with him?"

"I don't know!"

"Is it your mother or the girl that he takes away?"

"I don't know!" His voice caught in a quick sob. "I don't know!"

"I see." The woman inclined her head, a nod of acceptance, not agreement. "You've had this dream often?"

"I don't know." He hesitated. "I was never conscious of it before . . . yes, I suppose I've had it many times . . ."

"I see," she said again.

"He's ruined my life and he's continuing to ruin it," Lorcan rushed on, making a fool out of himself. "He'll do something terrible before he dies."

"You seem quite sure of that."

In her black business suit and plain white blouse and behind granny glasses, the woman was attractive, sympathetic, and damnably perceptive, a mature, sexually alluring Mother Superior. His sudden dependence on her embarrassed him though her warmth reassured him.

He wished nonetheless that he dared to glance at his watch to see how much time was left in his fifty-minute hour. He was already a couple of hours behind his daily schedule, printed out that morning, as every morning, by the implacable Sidekick program on his Compaq 386/20 computer.

"Something happened on that beach thirty-five years ago. If I don't find out what it was, he'll use it against me. . . . Do I sound paranoid?"

"You sound hurt."

"When I told him that Marie was marrying Maura Meehan's son, he threw back his head and howled with laughter. I'm familiar with that laugh; it means trouble for me."

"You've been competing with him all your life?"

"I've won. I've beaten him at everything, but it doesn't do any good. Even my kids admire him more than they admire me."

He had never said those words to anyone. Having said them, he was ashamed of his childish hatred. In fact his kids really did not admire their grandfather more than their father. They only seemed to some of the time.

His outburst did not seem to shock the doctor.

"He's been a lifelong rival?"

Do all women analysts have such softly erotic voices or is it part of this one's bag of tricks?

"By his choice." He choked back his tears again. "I've always loved him."

"Deep ambivalences," she said with a hint of a smile.

Lorcan—the Norman-Irish version of Lawrence, he often explained—understood the psychiatric process. He was supposed to fall in love with his therapist, work out his relationship with her, and then reorganize his life—maybe even fall in love with a woman again. He did not fully trust the technique. He would not lie defenseless on a couch while a woman coolly and clinically evaluated him.

Never.

Doctor Murphy was a lot like Maura—well, a lot like the woman he imagined Maura had become.

"Most of the time I don't pay any attention to him. He's an old man, the past is the past. I tell myself I've forgiven and forgotten."

"Yet at critical times, all the old conflicts resurface?"

No, she was not quite Maura. She was as objective and intelligent as Maura, but not distant, reserved, icy.

"He'll ruin the wedding."

"Have you ever experienced these premonitions before?"

"They're *not* premonitions. I'm not psychic. I don't believe in that stuff. It's nothing like that. I'm certain that he'll try some trick because I understand the bastard."

Then the tears came, raging torrents of them.

"I was a real ace in Korea," he sobbed. "I shot down five MIGs. He spent his war sitting on his fat ass. The first thing he said when I came home was that shooting down Chinks didn't count."

The woman listened silently.

The enormity of what he had just said stopped his tears. "That was a childish, petulant comment," he moaned. "I'm sorry."

"Lorcan." She smiled gently. "You comprehend the rules of this game we're playing. In my office there are no childish remarks."

His tears abruptly turned to laughter. "Good God, I'm a classic case, am I not?"

"Whether it's good or bad to be a classic case," she said soothingly, "will have to wait till our next session. I'm afraid our hour is up."

"Fifty-minute hour." He stood up, eager to escape, yet also reluctant.

"That's right, Lorcan. A fifty-minute hour."

The client is more interesting than most—a vigorous, handsome, successful, charming man, a certified member of the Chicago elite. Your witty Irish male as business celebrity, a kind of Donald Trump with a self-deprecating grin.

Broad shoulders, flat stomach, dancing blue eyes, thick blond hair mixed with silver, a heartthrob for the fixated adolescent that lurks within most women.

His wife left him a couple of years ago, I gather, to "be her own person." That even did not drive him into my office, although he seems to have struggled to save the marriage—as men do under such circumstances, usually when it's much too late. He has not mentioned that trauma to me. Rather he fixates on his relationship with his father.

Apparently his unresolved childhood Oedipal conflicts are still a very serious problem for him.

There are memories in his unconscious, deeply disturbing memories, which are threatening to explode.

What kind of repressed memories reduce a man like Lorcan James Flynn to tears?

We shall see.

Outside on Michigan Avenue, across from the Doral Plaza, Grant Park looked cold and naked against a dark and glowering sky. Lorcan Flynn drew a deep breath. The session had been strangely exhilarating, like confession forty years ago when he was a teenager worried about sins of the flesh. This time it was different, however: not only would he admit his darkest thoughts, he would begin to understand himself. He would amend his life, straighten out his fouled-up relationships with his wife and his father and his brothers and his children.

After confession, you had to have a firm purpose of amendment.

He would probably continue the sessions with Doctor Murphy. He would not, however, tell her how much she reminded him of Maura.

2

"I'll write the autobiography," Lorcan Flynn conceded to his son, Patrick, as he pried open an oyster shell, "but I won't stretch out on her goddamn couch."

"Come on, Dad." Patrick Michael Flynn II, M.D., glanced up from his clam chowder. "You're a sophisticated man of the eighties. You know better than that. Anyway," he grinned mischievously, "Mary Kate Murphy usually has her way."

"You didn't tell me she was so sexy."

"Thought I'd surprise you. . . . If she had been doing training analysis five years ago, I would have signed on with her." Pat grinned at his father. "I'm sure the atmosphere in her office must be conducive to self-disclosure."

Named after his grandfather, Pat Flynn had inherited the old man's heavy black hair and beard and nothing else. A young man who might, if he was lucky, stretch to five feet eight inches, Pat had the shrewd, darting eyes and dark skin of a professional gombeen man. In an earlier era he would have been a bartender or an undertaker with shady connections or a precinct captain with lots of clout. Possibly all three combined. In a more recent era he might have been a senior police detective or an able criminal lawyer and sometime president of the Bar Association or possibly a canonist at the Chancery Office. Now, so far had the Irish come, he was a psychoanalyst-in-training at the Chicago Institute of Psychoanalysis.

"I feel like an idiot dredging up childhood memories at my age in life," Lorcan confessed. If he was frank enough, he hoped he might coax his son into saying something about his problems that he did not intend to say. It was, he realized, a vain hope—Pat was far too astute to be tricked.

"It can't hurt, Dad." He smiled and stroked his carefully trimmed black beard thoughtfully. "Besides, there can be pleasant aspects of working out transference with Mary Kathleen. She's a Freudian all right, but a highly eclectic variety. She makes up her own rules as she goes along and gets away with it because she's so successful."

They were eating lunch in the hallowed oak dining room of the East Bank Club, a place where employees and members alike treated Lorcan Flynn with only slightly less reverence than the Pope merited in Vatican Palace.

"I suppose"—Lorcan sighed heavily—"she might help me to cope with women a mite better."

Pat raised a thick eyebrow as he began to work on his tuna salad. "That's not why I recommended her, Dad; I actually believe cross-sex therapists from the same ethnic background are normally the most effective."

Lorcan often wondered whether he had ruined his relationship with his own son as the old man had with him. How did Patrick II rate him as a father? Maybe he didn't hate him the way Lorcan hated Patrick I. There were times when Lorcan got the impression his son thought of him as nothing more than a harmless fool.

Lorcan had tried to avoid the mistakes his father made. He praised everything Pat did. He encouraged all his decisions. He approved of his friends, his loves, and especially his wife, that red-haired leprechaun Maureen—though that wasn't too hard. He never made fun of him. Yet he wasn't sure that they were friends. He had given his son the paternal love and approval he himself had never received, but somehow Patrick seemed not to need any of it.

"I don't exactly consider myself a success with women," Lorcan said. "Maybe fifty-five is not too old to learn."

As they talked, Lorcan was watching a woman eating lunch across the room, a lawyer whose first name was Linda and whose last name he did not remember. A woman in her early forties, she was slim, handsome, intense. His imagination, acting on its own initiative, was removing her charcoal suit and pink blouse, gently and tenderly indeed but also firmly.

"Come on, Dad! Women adore you. My wild Irish rose of a wife tells me that if I live to be a hundred I won't be 'the foine Christian gentleman me Old Fella is.'"

In his mind he had undressed every attractive woman he had encountered since the Archdiocesan Matrimonial Tribunal had mailed him a Decree of Nullity, thus annulling his marriage of thirty years. The top had exploded off the bottle in which he had stored his sexual desires.

Lorcan toyed with his fruit salad. "I didn't do all that well with your mother."

Across the room, Linda was aware of his interest, flustered by it, and also flattered.

"Look, Dad." Pat put down his fork and leaned across the table. "You know as well as I do that Mom just didn't want to be married anymore. You did all you could to save the marriage."

Pat and his sisters, Elizabeth and Marie, had not chosen sides when their parents' marriage collapsed. Lorcan did not expect them to, although he was delighted that Marie, still in college at the time, chose to accept his custody and to make her home with him during vacations. Yet why couldn't they give a hint that they did not blame him?

"At the end, sure," he said to his son, "when it was too late. I never saw it coming."

"Don't blame yourself," Pat said judiciously as he resumed his assault on the tuna salad. "Some relationships are not meant to go on for the whole of life."

"I suppose so. But I've never been too good with women."

"Who says so?" Pat demanded.

"Grandpa, for one."

Pat snorted. "No one takes him seriously, Dad. You know that. It's all talk."

None of Lorcan's children sensed the depth of the lifelong conflict between their father and their grandfather. Dorothy hadn't seen it either: "He's a nice old man, dear. He doesn't mean a thing with those crazy comments of his. It's all for laughs. Why do you have to be hurt by them?"

Fair question.

"I guess I'm kind of unsure of myself."

"That's natural, Dad. You've suffered a severe trauma. You should grant yourself time to convalesce from it. That's why you're in a no-lose situation with Mary Kathleen. She can only help."

It was at Patrick's suggestion that Lorcan had decided to seek an annulment of his marriage. "It's over, Dad. Face it. Write finis. Put closure to that part of your life."

"Easy to say," he had replied gruffly.

"I understand." Pat had touched his shoulder. "You loved her once as much as I love the Maeve."

Dorothy had asked for the annulment at first; then, when he agreed, she turned against it. "You've always wanted a chance to marry one of your bimbos, haven't you?"

There never had been any bimbos. Given his failures to sustain relationships after their divorce, there were not likely to be.

"Well, I'm glad you got off on the right foot with Doctor Murphy," Pat continued. "It won't in all probability be a long-term, classic analysis. She's quite flexible. Did she mention self-hypnotism yet?"

He shuddered. "No, and I won't ever mess with it if she does. . . . Tell me again—why am I doing this?"

Patrick played with a piece of unbuttered rye bread. "Because you aren't able to sleep at night without a prescription, because your famous Sidekick schedule, which has made you the most efficient man in the western world, no longer works, because you have strange, obsessive forebodings, and because you asked me whether it would be a good idea to talk about these with someone."

"That's an accurate replay, Doctor." Lorcan laughed. "Though I didn't use the word obsessive."

"I'm your son." Pat stabbed a large slice of tomato with his fork. *"Not* your therapist. So I won't try to diagnose you."

"But you suspect that my youngest child's marriage coming a couple of years after divorce as I move into the wrong side of fifty-five has caused me to become fearful about my own mortality."

"You read too many books." Pat skewered an avocado slice and grinned again. "What interests me is the chance that these fears are related to the fact that your daughter is marrying the son of your old sweetheart."

Those shrewd dark eyes flicked across Lorcan's face.

"I haven't thought of her in years, Pat."

"Marie says she's quite a knockout."

"That doesn't surprise me. She was also a distant, reserved, almost impassive young woman."

"Marie agrees with that, 'sweet but kind of quiet' were her exact words as I remember them. . . . Was it an, uh, intense relationship, Dad?"

"Hmnn . . ." He tried to look away from the pliant Linda. "Oh, sorry, Pat, I was remembering about those days. A lot of it's kind of hazy. I came down with meningitis about the same time. What was your question?"

"Were you really in love with Moire Halinan?"

"Maura Anne Meehan then. . . . Were you in love with Irene Gallagher?"

"For a couple of days. But I was eighteen and you were—"

"Twenty-three—and not as mature as you were at eighteen."

"Pretty immature, huh?"

They both laughed.

Nonetheless, Lorcan's head began to ache. While he remembered the incidents of that horrendous summer, there were gaps in his understanding of what they meant. Presumably Doctor Murphy would pry those secrets out of him.

And thus prepare him to meet Maura again, a prospect which he both dreaded and eagerly awaited.

"Your feelings were intense then, weren't they?" Patrick probed delicately. "Did you think about marriage to her?"

"Sure, who doesn't at that age in life? Still, I can't say my heart was broken when she left for New York."

That was an accurate description of how he felt when he had come out of his fever and his parents had told him that she had left Chicago. Couldn't blame her, all things considered, was what he had said to his brother Hank.

Why then did he have such an odd reaction when young Rob Halinan had said, "I think you knew my mom long ago, Mr. Flynn, Maura Anne Meehan?"

Why was he so angry at her?

He had covered up nicely, as he always did when caught off guard. "The most beautiful girl on the beach. I'll look forward to seeing her again. Marie, you're lucky to have such a fine future mother-in-law."

"She's still beautiful," her son had said fervently.

"You better believe it. Awesome," Marie had agreed.

Why do I hate her after all these years? he had wondered. *Nostalgia over a lost love is one thing, but why so much rage?*

Why do I sometimes feel that I ought to try to stop the marriage, even though Rob is a nice young man and perfectly worthy of my daughter?

Why did Dad laugh the way he did when I told him about the marriage?

As Patrick and Lorcan left the grill of the East Bank Club, Lorcan stopped for a word with Linda Henry and introduced Patrick to her.

"We'll have to have lunch someday soon, Linda," Lorcan said.

"Wonderful!" Her face had turned pink and she was obviously disconcerted by his invitation, not the reaction one would expect from a highly professional and very successful estate planner.

"I'll give you a ring."

"I'll be waiting."

"Pretty woman," Patrick observed in the elevator.

"I guess so."

"Nice tits."

"Patrick!"

"As the Woman says, if you deny you noticed them, you should have your hormones checked."

"The Woman" was Patrick's wife, Maeve.

"I suppose," he said sadly.

"You charmed her."

"Did I?"

"You sure did . . . will you call her?"

"I don't know. Maybe."

"The Woman thinks you should marry again."

"Irish matchmaker."

"Will you?"

"Probably not."

They walked off the elevator in silence, Lorcan still picturing Linda Henry's admittedly pretty breasts.

"You'll be on the couch tomorrow?" Pat asked as they rode down the elevator in the East Bank Club.

"No way."

"Bet?"

"Fifty bucks!"

"You're on!"

3

"B each towels?"

Doctor Murphy sounded surprised.

"Beach towels, big ones, the towel on the left is red and white stripes and the towel on the right is blue and white."

"Fascinating . . ."

He was lying on the couch, just as his son had wagered he would.

When he entered the office, Doctor Murphy had pointed at the couch, her gesture half disarming plea, half gentle command.

"I'm losing a fifty-dollar bet to my son," he had said with a sigh as he stretched out.

"I'll make sure he splits the fee with me."

"That doesn't seem to be a professional remark for an analyst—too flippant."

"Only if the analyst"—she waved her hand—"is not Irish."

That settled that.

Now, relaxed on the couch, he was more at peace than he had ever been in his life. I might just stay here, he thought to himself, forever. He had returned once more to the dream. This time he told her how important the beach towels were in the dream.

"Exciting, terrifying, stimulating, threatening."

"I see. . . . Are there people in it besides your father and the girl?"

"People?"

"Surely the drama must have its cast of characters?"

"I guess it must; but I never remember them."

"Just the striped towels?"

"There may be people hovering in the background, shadows."

"I see. Is it day or night?"

"Both. I mean, it's night but the sun is out."

"Pardon?"

"You said I should try to describe how it felt. It's kind of silent and secret like night but there's a bright light like the sun."

"Indeed. . . . Is the dream erotic?"

"Powerfully. When I was married I would wake up from it wanting to make love."

"Did you?"

"Not very often. My, uh, wife did not like me interrupting her sleep."

"Your father is definitely in the dream?"

"Yes . . . no . . . I don't know. Sometimes he is and sometimes he isn't."

"The girl who was your lover?"

"I'm not sure. . . ."

"Did you not make love with her on the beach towels that summer?"

"I'm not sure."

"Not sure?" Her tone was incredulous.

"I wanted to, oh, how I wanted to. I may have. It's all a jumble. I was coming down with the fever. I may have made love to her. Or I may have dreamed it. Or I may have raped her. I've always feared that."

"Raped her?" Her tone was even, with no judgment. "Is that very likely?"

"My images are of violent sex."

"On the beach towels?"

"I don't remember." He became aware that he was sweating profusely.

"Violent sex is not the same as rape, Lorcan."

"I understand that now."

"There is a certain amount of violence inherent in the activity, even if one engages in it with tenderness and affection.

"What did the young woman say after you recovered from your illness?"

"I never spoke to her again."

"Isn't that unusual?"

"I guess it is. Maybe I'll ask her when she comes to Chicago next week."

"You're looking forward to that encounter?"

"Not particularly."

Mary Kathleen's eyes narrowed.

"All right—I am looking forward to seeing Maura." With a mixture of anger and hope and fear, he did not add.

"To determine whether the love can be renewed? And we want the truth, Lorcan. I am not one of your children whom you can dodge."

He felt tears sting his eyes. "I don't want to have any illusions."

"Naturally a successful, efficiently scheduled man like you would want to be free of illusions."

"You're being sarcastic."

"You bet," she said crisply. "So you blame your father for losing this young woman?"

"He made fun of her when she was absent and flirted with her when she was present. . . . I haven't thought of her much in the last thirty years."

"Yet the engagement of her son to your daughter was traumatic, was it not?"

"That means she's deep in my unconscious?"

"I have problems with aggressive male patients who dabble in psychiatry books; they move much too rapidly. They jump at conclusions—logical conclusions perhaps, but ones that do violence to the richness of unconscious symbols that lurk within them."

"Macho clients?"

"Your word. We can argue about it on Monday, because I see that our time is up."

The patient is an excellent prospect for treatment. He is not unintelligent, honest according to his own lights, and determined to be good at the business of being a patient—typical behavior of an assertive, aggressive, and well-educated male patient who has been good at everything else in life, except possibly marriage.

Lorcan James Flynn does not seem to have a long history of conquests and does not, like most such men, feel the need to claim successes with women.

He does not remember whether he made love to this Maura person for whom I have so quickly become a surrogate.

He admits that he was not successful with his wife.

He does not, however, link these seeming failures with women to his resentment toward his father. Surely he realizes that possibility.

What am I to make of the mixed symbols of the year 1954? Lake and explosion, water and fire—obvious sexual symbols if one wishes. Blended with a terrifying and destructive reality.

The beach towels certainly embrace us with warmth when we rush out of the water, envelop us so to speak, veil us in delicious comfort. Possibly that is a womanly metaphor. Beach towels as lover?

There is something sinister lurking deep in the unconscious of my stalwart, resourceful patient. That's more raw Irish-witch intuition than therapeutic insight. Something terrible happened as he was coming down with his deadly fever.

Why are the beach towels so important in his symbolic memory?

An east wind was sweeping in off the Lake, and a nasty rain was slashing at the faces of pedestrians when Lorcan Flynn left the 30 North Michigan building. Automatically he turned up the collar of his Burberry trench coat as he walked north to the East Bank Club and lunch with his Uncle Rory.

He scarcely noticed the rain; pictures of Maura flooded his imagination: aloof, remote brown eyes, exquisite facial bones, tall grace, smooth dark skin, lips surprisingly eager, glorious breasts. In his fantasies Maura was as vivid as though he had embraced her yesterday instead of more than

three decades ago. In his mind he easily confused her with
Doctor Murphy.

Had they known one another? They were about the same
age. Both had spent summers in the Dunes.

What did that matter?

Marie had said repeatedly that her love's mother was,
"like totally gorgeous, Dad. Really."

Lorcan's imagination had spun out of control at that
observation. He had lived long enough to realize that erotic
appeal came in far more than the proverbial fifty-seven
varieties. A striking woman who has just turned fifty might
be infinitely more enticing and more rewarding than a child
in her early twenties.

As he rode up the elevator to the East Bank Club, his
graphic image of Maura somehow blended into the taste of
raspberries, the attraction of the East Bank Club.

He would have to ask Uncle Rory about the explosion.
Hank too when he saw him tomorrow.

Maura had loved raspberries, too, had she not?

He couldn't quite remember.

Lorcan thought back to those days of summer in 1945—the
summer of his father's return from the war. He was fourteen
years old then; a big clumsy kid who nevertheless had led
the Saint Ursula basketball team to a regional championship. He hadn't seen his father in four years. He barely
remembered the man. Lorcan had been only seven years old
when his father enlisted in the Army Air Corps back in
1939. In his absence, Pat Flynn had become larger than life
for young Lorcan. Lorcan's mother had told him at least
once a day what a great man his father was. His younger
brother Hank had warned him that when their father came
home he would put Lorcan in his place. His Uncle Frank,
the priest, repeatedly told him what a fine Catholic layman
his father was. His Uncle Rory reminded Lorcan that he
had a big pair of shoes to fill. The people in the parish
repeated stories of his athletic prowess, his successes on the
Board of Trade, and his capacity to consume beer and
entertain parties all night long. He was a legend in the minds
of everyone who knew him, family and friends alike. In

retrospect Lorcan realized what a small world this was; but it was the only world he'd known at the time.

Of course, Lorcan realized, his father was not quite a war hero. At the time, his hero worship of the man was so great that he glossed over the fact that eye trouble had grounded his father upon his arrival in England and that he had never flown a combat mission.

Strictly speaking, Pat was entitled to wear his battered flyer's leather jacket with the Eighth Air Force shoulder patch and silver wings. Colonel Patrick Michael Flynn, A.U.S., was a pilot until bad eyes forced him to become a supply officer. The ribbons on his jacket were good conduct and campaign ribbons, but they seemed impressive, especially when he also sported his floppy pilot's cap.

Lorcan had been and still was a model-airplane freak. Back then, he'd been a purist. He started with a sixteen-inch block of balsa and carved it to precise shape—the beginning of his dilettante interest in sculpting. He made himself a detailed scale model of the B-17H, complete with the nose and tail turrets that were not on the early versions. He painted the camouflage with loving care and added the various insignias with a perfectionist's concern for accuracy. It was a fine piece of work.

His father, devil-may-care war veteran in full uniform, returned to the adulation of his family. He smothered Lorcan's mother with kisses, swung Hank in the air, then firmly shook older Lorcan's hand. "Gosh, buster, you've grown up, almost as tall as I am. I bet if you work at it, you might end up a pretty fair basketball player."

Lorcan tried to tell him that he'd be a starter on Saint Ignatius's freshman team and that Saint Ursula had won its regional. But his father wasn't listening.

Days later, when Lorcan told him again, he asked, "Only regional, buster? That's not much. Why didn't you win city?" and "Ignatius? That's a sissy school. Why aren't you going to Saint Justin's?"

That comment notwithstanding, that same day Lorcan dragged his father to the basement of their family's brick bungalow and showed him his B-17H. Pat Flynn considered it carefully, nodded as if in approval, then began his critique.

"Not bad, buster, not bad. I used to make these things when I was a kid too. You're pretty good at it. But you have to learn to do the details right. What's worth doing at all is worth doing well, never forget that. You got some paint? Good. First thing we do is paint out these stars. You did right by not putting the red circle in them, but they're too big. We didn't need them that big, everyone knew a B-17 was American. Not like the ME-109 and the P-51, which looked a lot alike. See, you can paint in smaller stars, maybe about two-thirds as big. Then, we didn't have squadron numbers over there. Toward the end of the war we didn't have to hide our aircraft on the ground from enemy bombers because there weren't any left. So you could paint it aluminum if you want, though that's not necessary. And these guns are too big. They look like small cannons, not fifty-caliber machine guns. Here, let's just knock them off and glue on these toothpicks and you've got it pretty near right."

Lorcan watched in horror while his father defaced his treasure.

After Pat Flynn went upstairs whistling the Air Corps song, little Lorcan smashed the model into a thousand pieces.

4

"Thirty-four years, Lorcan," Uncle Rory wheezed. "It was thirty-four years ago."

Rory Flynn was a lawyer, a fussy, bald bachelor with a narrow, sad face that suggested a perpetual complaint against the injustices of life. His shifty eyes hinted that he was working on several devious plots to fend off the conspiracies which raged around him.

"I still want to know what happened."

Lorcan was eating his second serving of raspberries, available for dessert at the East Bank Club every day because of a bequest from a raspberry-loving member.

Rory glanced around nervously, and his voice sank to a whisper as it often did when he was about to say something he felt was portentous.

"Leave it alone, Lorcan. For God's sake leave it alone."

Rory, whose appetite for military service had vanished when the North Korean armies struck south across the 38th parallel, had been Lorcan's lawyer for a few years in the late fifties. He was not a very good lawyer. When Lorcan shifted his major accounts to a couple of big Loop law firms, he left Rory sufficient business to keep him alive and in his carefully tailored three-piece suits and expensive cigars.

"Why did they die, Rory? Who killed them?"

"Why is it so crucial now?" Rory removed a cigar from his inside jacket pocket with respectful care and then jabbed it back in as he remembered that Lorcan did not like anyone smoking at the lunch table.

"Marie is going to marry Maura Meehan's son, that's why."

"That's not a good idea." Rory waved his small hand with its carefully manicured fingers as though he were on a board which passed judgment on family marriages. "I've told you repeatedly that it's not a good idea."

There was not much dignity left in Rory Flynn's life, so Lorcan permitted him the conceit that he was a senior counselor in the family whose advice was almost law.

"Your brother agrees. However, Rob and Marie have made up their minds. . . . I want the whole story."

"Made up their minds?" Rory jabbed the air angrily. "What do you mean, made up their minds? You hold the purse strings, don't you? Tell them they don't get any money. That'll stop them pretty damn quick."

"They're quiet kids." Lorcan pushed aside the empty raspberry dish and promised himself that he'd swim a few extra laps at the East Bank Club after lunch. "But they're not about to change their minds for me or for anyone else. Anyway, what reason could I give them?"

"He's Maura Meehan's son. Isn't that a good enough reason?"

"What's wrong with Maura Meehan?"

"You don't want to know, Lorcan. Believe me, you don't want to know."

So it went with Uncle Rory. You danced around a subject for hours and never moved an inch. Not until you delivered the ultimatum which hinted that his retainer might be in danger.

"Cut it out, Rory. It wasn't an accident."

Rory sputtered. "Sure it wasn't an accident. A lot of people went to a lot of trouble to cover it up. You know that."

"I don't know that or anything else. I was in the hospital, half dead with meningitis."

"Damned convenient time to get sick if you ask me."

"How was Maura involved?"

"You know the answer to that one."

"Damn it, Rory, I'm tired of this game. Tell me what happened. Now."

"OK, OK." His voice sank to a whisper. "Do you mind if I have another drink—just a small one?"

Lorcan signaled the waiter and ordered a Courvoisier on the rocks for his uncle.

"Let's have it," he ordered when the waiter had brought the drink.

Rory glanced around anxiously and rubbed the big diamond on his right hand.

"I don't know it all, Lorcan. Honest, I don't. Your father and Father Frank and Father Gregorio, God be good to them both, and even Hank were the ones who took care of it. Old man Meehan was on the take from everyone. The rules were different in those days. He was an embarrassment to lots of people. Dick Daley wasn't mayor yet and the gray wolves were running loose in Chicago—"

"Get to the point, Rory."

"Yeah, yeah," his uncle whined. "Give me a chance, will-ya? Like I was saying, Meehan was in bed with the Mob and with real estate people who were using Mob money. They say he was close to a bunch of guys who were smuggling money and guns to Ireland. Joe was on the intelligence committee in Congress, you know. Maybe he was trading on a few secrets, nothing important really."

"When he was supporting Senator Joe McCarthy's anti-Communism?"

"Joe Meehan was a hundred-percent American patriot." Rory snorted indignantly. "Don't you ever forget that."

"The same Mob people who later killed Father Gregorio?"

"Don't ever say that, Lorcan," his uncle spoke solemnly. "Father Gregorio was killed by a black mugger."

"That's not what the police thought."

Gregorio Sabatini was a darkly handsome priest and confidant of Lorcan's mother. Father Frank, Lorcan's father's brother, never liked Gregorio. A cabin hunter, he had said, preying on the rich people whose money belongs to their parish.

Gregorio was the perpetual Provincial of his order and had been the patron of Lorcan's brother when he entered the Order of Saint Justin—O.S.J. Now Edward, sleek and smooth himself, was the General of the Order.

Sometime after Edward had gone off to the seminary, 1959 or 1960 perhaps, the police had found Gregorio's body in an abandoned apartment building in Englewood. There were rumors of financial scandals and Mob revenge—though the Outfit did not usually kill priests.

The official version was that Gregorio had been mugged while on a sick call. However, as a cop had said to Lorcan years later, muggers don't usually garrote their victims.

Did Edward remember anything about the explosion? Did he remember Maura? Lorcan resolved to ask him the next time he returned from Rome.

"Father Gregorio was a good priest," Rory persisted. "Even Father Frank thought so."

"Go on," Lorcan demanded, knowing that Frank Flynn had thought no such thing and had always lamented that the Justines had "stolen" Eddie from the Archdiocese.

"Well, see, there were lots of people who might want to put Congressman Meehan down. They didn't much care whether they put down the rest of the family at the same time."

"A wife and two teenage daughters—"

"The kids were ugly little brats, the wife was a bitch."

"So put them down too?"

"I'm saying that if they were in the house when it blew up, it didn't make much difference."

"And Maura?"

"She didn't count. She was a nothing."

"So she wasn't involved at all?"

"I didn't say that. All I said was that no one cared about her one way or another. Her parents were dead, she didn't have any money. She was a nothing. Afterwards she came into a little money, just like you did."

There was a touch of resentment in Rory's voice, as if he believed that Providence had been unjust when it arranged for Great-Aunt Marie's bequest to Lorcan.

Maura's background had been obscure. She had lived with her uncle and aunt since she was an infant. Her parents were dead, it was said; no one seemed to know who they were or where she came from. She had ducked direct questions when Lorcan had asked them. Occasionally she hinted that she had not lived all her life in Chicago.

Had there been a hint of California? Something about redwood trees?

"So I understand. . . . Who blew up their house?"

"Whoever lit the match."

"Cut it out, Rory." Lorcan sighed. "Do I have to ask who opened the gas jet?"

His uncle fidgeted on his chair and glanced around the almost empty dining room.

"I don't know the answer to that question, Lorcan. If I did, I'd tell you. Whoever did it was acting on orders."

"Whose orders?"

"Take your pick."

Lorcan surmised that Rory hadn't the foggiest notion who gave the orders. It was imperative to his self-image that he pretend to the inside story, to be the trusted confidant of the movers and shakers.

"Someone murdered them, and there was a cover-up.

Dad and Father Frank and Hank and maybe Father Gregorio helped in the cover-up?"

"You didn't hear it from me, Lorcan. Don't tell your father I breathed a word. Anyway, there were others involved too. The big guys."

"Who?"

"Take your pick."

So Rory didn't know which big guys either.

Later, at the corner of Michigan and Wacker Drive, Lorcan watched the snow-laden clouds glide across the sky. The wind had shifted. It was racing down the Chicago River toward the Lake. He was on his way to the East Bank Club for a swim.

If there had been a cover-up of the Labor Day, 1954, disaster, his family had been quite incapable of engineering it by themselves. His father and his brother and his uncle were small-time operators at the most, real estate speculators, occasional commodity speculators, maybe dabblers in dubious highway-construction contracts. In the world in which they grew up they were thought to be major political and commercial powers; in reality they were hangers-on at the far fringes of power. No, there was no way they could have pulled off something like the Labor Day disaster without big-time help. They couldn't simply have been very lucky. They had to have acted on the orders and under the protection of someone else. Maybe they didn't even know who the "big boys" in this particular episode were. Not all of them were bright, but they were smart enough not to ask questions.

Rory knew a little more than he had admitted, but not a hell of a lot more. Lorcan knew his father wouldn't tell him a damn thing. Hank? He'd have to scare him a lot more than he had scared Rory to get a word out of him.

Inside the East Bank Club Lorcan found an empty phone booth and called his office in the 180 North Michigan Building.

"Lorcan Flynn and Associates," said Mary Murray, his longtime and totally loyal assistant.

There were, of course, no associates. Lorcan ran his empire with the help of Mary and various professional firms in the Loop. Very few people had an idea of the extent of all he owned. The common consensus was that he owned a lot and that what he sold was invariably worth more when he parted with it than it had been when he acquired it. Lorcan got right to the point, explaining to Mary what information he needed to obtain. She did not ask why he wanted to see newspapers from 1954. Perhaps she already knew. He added that perhaps Mr. Rooney could stop by on Tuesday morning before his doctor's appointment.

Lorcan trusted Mary Murray more than any being on the planet. Half the time it seemed she could read his mind. Naturally he had told her about his series of sessions with Dr. Mary Kathleen Ryan Murphy. The woman was uncanny, he reflected as he hung up. To lose her—not that the prospect seemed likely—would be more traumatic than having lost Dorothy.

Lorcan bumped into Cindi Horton outside the phone booth. She was still glowing from her workout.

"See you tonight, Lorcan?" Her brown eyes shone expectantly.

He had almost forgotten their date. Tall, blond, willowy, and luscious, Cindi was an anchorperson on Channel 4. She was young enough to be his daughter, only a year or two older than Patrick.

"Pick you up at six-thirty?"

"Fine. I'll rush home from the program and be ready for you."

They were going to a black-tie benefit dinner—he didn't remember which worthy cause. Cindi had invited him.

In the shower later he wished that it might be possible to live the rest of his life without women. Enter a monastery perhaps.

How much simpler, he reflected, *life would be if women were not so damn attractive.*

Back in his home on Astor Street, a glass of Bushmill's Single Malt (Green Label) in hand, he read Ed's most recent newsletter, an undisguised plea for money. Probably it was very effective with the elderly Catholics who were the principal targets of Ed's fund-raising.

"Father Ed Reports," the title said. Smooth desk-top

publishing. Ed's picture next to the title. "A darling priest," his admirers would say.

He reached for the phone to call Ed in Rome. Maybe he did remember Maura Meehan. As he punched in the number, he remembered that it was probably midnight in Rome and hung up the phone.

Then he tried to write a poem while he waited until it was time to pick up Cindi. But his poem was not about the anticipation of meeting an alluring blonde for an enchanted evening. Rather it was about a perhaps imaginary woman on the beach.

> *A square of pale silver on the beach*
> *Blue lights dancing in the Lake*
> *White foam gently touching the sand*
> *A meteor trace across the sky*
>
> *Pebbles cool and firm against my toes*
> *The wind a ghost against my face*
> *The distant hum of traffic on Highway Twelve*
> *Secret whispers hovering in the air*
>
> *The dipper pouring Bailey's Cream*
> *With the Perrier of Aquarius*
> *Into a goblet of Irish crystal starlight*
> *And stirred with a solitary moonbeam*
>
> *A Haydn sonatina floating free*
> *The barest breath of laughter*
> *The rustle of fabric soft and silken*
> *Footsteps quickly passing by*
>
> *Alone*
> *No one else*
> *Only fleeting images*
> *Nothing real*
>
> *Incense of lilac blossoms*
> *Mixed with barbecue and beer*
> *And dead fish and suntan cream*
> *Somewhere a whiff of inexpensive scent*

Perhaps a melancholy sigh
Or maybe a mosquito buzz
A firefly moment
In which a hand imagines that it holds a hand

Nothing real

A light caress
A brush of lips
An insubstantial embrace
A hint of naked breast

All quite unreal

Silence and solitude,
Like the distant galaxies
Only romantic fantasy
On a so soft and sweet spring night

Maybe

Maura!

He threw his pen aside in frustration. He was not quite the renaissance man *Time* magazine had made him out to be back when he had served as a U.S. representative to an international trade meeting in Geneva. He was only partially worthy of the epithet—more for his sculpture, he felt, certainly not his poetry. Only a few people were aware of his incarnation as Alex Stone, the name he had chosen to keep his identity as a financial wizard separate from his artistic life. And although lately Alex Stone had been attracting decent notices—Lorcan was, in fact, in the process of correcting galleys for a book on Alex Stone's work—what Lorcan Flynn was feeling more and more like these days was not a renaissance man but a mere jack-of-all-trades, master of none.

5

"**S**o you took that anchorwoman with the big tits to the fancy dance last night?" his father demanded.

"A hospital benefit ball is hardly a fancy dance," he replied, sighing wearily. Would the game never end?

Dad prided himself on his ability to trace Lorcan's every move. Lorcan patiently tolerated his father's need to feel omniscient.

"All the big-time people were there. . . . Did you bang the woman?"

Pat Flynn delighted in language which made his son wince. The best way to respond to him was not to react to him.

"Of course not," he replied, hardly telling the full truth.

Doctor Murphy would ask why he had not told the truth if he admitted this mental reservation to her—a confession he had no intention of making.

"You never did have any nerve with women, did you?"

Lorcan and his brother Hank were paying their weekly Saturday-lunch visit to their father, a routine established in the last two years after Pat Flynn (Colonel Pat Flynn as he liked to be called—in imitation of Colonel Harry Crown) had been confined to his Sheridan Road apartment overlooking Lake Michigan. Lorcan paid for the care of a patient housekeeper whom Pat alternately harassed and charmed—characteristic behavior in his relationship with women.

At eighty he was still erect and striking, an Irish veteran who might have stepped out of one of the pictures of the Royal Hospital at Kilmainham: thin white hair, red face, cherubic blue eyes, ramrod back despite the withered legs which had been paralyzed by his stroke. He was always clean-shaven and well barbered and smelled of expensive male cologne. His mind was still reasonably sharp, some of the time anyway. He read the papers—*Sun Times, Tribune, Investor's Daily, Wall Street Journal,* though not the *New York Times,* and watched Cable News Network all day. He did not begin drinking till four in the afternoon—faithful to his fiercely held principle that you weren't a drunk if you could hold off till four—and then drank himself to sleep every night.

He hinted in conversations about his big investment coups, sometimes to hassle Lorcan, on whose financial support he was totally if ungratefully dependent, and sometimes, Lorcan suspected, because he had come to believe in them himself.

If he was grateful for the Saturday visit and lunch, brought in by an expensive caterer, he never admitted it to his sons.

The walls of the apartment were plastered with faded photos of World War II planes, paintings of air combat, and framed newspaper headlines. Models, made long ago, littered every flat space. A tattered flying jacket with the Eighth Air Force insignia and a pilot's floppy cap were tossed casually on a chair from which they never moved—save for the times that Liz and Maeve had donned them.

By now Pat Flynn believed that he had flown on the disastrous Schweinfurt raids. He told stories to his grandchildren about the raid which sounded like the accounts that Lorcan had read in histories of the air war—histories which Pat could have read too.

"You take your brother here." Pat waved an emaciated hand at Hank. "He knows how to treat women. You keep your wife in the kitchen, fat, happy, and pregnant, and you enjoy your dollies on the side. Isn't that right, Henry?"

Hank blushed. His one success in life was his marriage. Joanne, his wife, was a bit plump perhaps, but she was a competent nursing supervisor at West Suburban Hospital and a skillful mother to their four kids. Hank's fidelity to her was unwavering.

He sighed. "I don't have any dollies, Dad."

Hank was a younger version of Uncle Rory—with long

hair and a bushy mustache, but the same darting nervous eyes and the same beaten lapdog expression. Long ago Lorcan thought it might be possible for him and Hank to be friends. But he was unable to break through Hank's blend of diffidence and resentment toward him. Nor was he able to forget the years of humiliation during which his father held Hank up as a model of success, the real man among his sons.

"Keep telling her that, kid." He chuckled. "That's the way to do it. At least you enjoy life, which is more than your brother does. Hell, he's as much a celibate as Father Ed."

Rarely did anyone in the family hear from brother Ed, save for a rare hasty call to Lorcan, usually from an airport lounge on one of his frequent mysterious visits to the United States. Almost always the purpose of the call was a request for money to aid a good work of the Order. He seemed to feel that he had nicely calculated how much Lorcan could and would give and never went beyond that calculation.

Ed erred on the side of conservatism. Lorcan would have cheerfully given his brother at least twice his average request—not because he liked Ed all that much—frankly, he didn't really know him—but because he liked the Church. Ed had always been such a silent presence in their household.

Their sister, Eileen, named after her mother, the youngest in the family, had been anything but silent. She was the only one among them who openly rebelled against Colonel Pat Flynn. She had moved to Seattle after graduating from Saint Mary's of Notre Dame and promptly married a Notre Dame lawyer—to escape, in Lorcan's judgment, from Dad's stern and capricious supervision as soon as she could. She and her husband had three kids and seemed happy when Lorcan visited them last year on his way to Tokyo—happy and delighted to see Lorcan. The sole communication between her and the family was an exchange of Christmas cards.

"I hated him, Lorcan," she had said of their father when her husband was out of the room. "I can't remember not hating him."

"Me too," he had muttered.

Her pretty blue eyes had widened in surprise. "You loved him more than the rest of us, Lorcan. And he thinks more of you even if he can't tell you that."

His father wore a flannel shirt and a sweater and a robe over his chinos, even though it was warm in the apartment. He won't be with us too much longer, Lorcan thought with a catch in his throat. Maybe I should try to straighten things out between us. He knew, however, from the failure of many past attempts such a reconciliation—or whatever it might be called—was long since impossible.

"You gonna keep after the bitch with the big tits, Lorcan?" Having discovered that this subject offended Lorcan, his father would pursue it relentlessly. "She's probably after your money."

"Probably," Lorcan agreed.

"Sure, she's a looker all right, but their looks go quick when they're that fat."

Mom had adored Pat Flynn with an absolute and unswerving loyalty, even in her later years, when he was irritable most of the time. Lorcan never knew if the man had remained faithful or not. His talk might have been just talk.

However, the bastard had not wept a single tear at her graveside when she was buried there on a cold winter day after three months of painless wasting in the ravages of liver cancer.

"I told you that you never should have married Dorothy Kramer, she was a piss face from the word go. But, hell, I can't say I blame her for getting out. You never did know how to keep a woman in line, did you? I mean, they want to be kept in line, don't they, Hank?"

The same old words were recited as if they were brand-new revelations. They were repeated with high good humor, so no one could say he really meant them. Hank always laughed on cue. Lorcan simply would not reply—if he could manage to hold his tongue.

So it went, Saturday after Saturday, over steak and mashed potatoes and peas and carrots with red wine that his father drank like water and chocolate ice cream for dessert.

"Did you go back into the market this week, like I told you to?" Dad tilted his head, as if he were certain that the answer would be a disappointment, another revelation of cowardice.

"Not as long as the Fed is raising the discount rate."

"Short-term." His father waved a translucent hand. "There's no inflation danger."

"Greenspan thinks there is."

"He's wrong, mark my words. You're missing a big opportunity by not jumping into the market now."

"Maybe."

Lorcan dreaded the Saturday lunches—at which he always ate too much—but he would fly back from Washington or Tokyo or Rio to make them if he could.

His father never mentioned it when he missed a Saturday—by definition the lunches didn't make any difference to him.

He asked careful questions about Hank's kids. Despite his failing memory, he remembered that the oldest, a daughter with an MBA, was having a hard time finding a job, and that the youngest, also a daughter, looked like a merit scholarship winner.

"Elizabeth came home from Tufts this weekend, Dad," Lorcan said when the catechism about Hank's kids was finished. Dad never asked about his kids.

"Yeah, like I told you, it's a mistake to waste money on teaching a woman that kind of stuff."

Liz, his middle child, was the most carefree of the bunch, with madcap Irish flair inherited from her grandfather. Once the latter had turned speechless with rage when she put on his cap and jacket and pretended to be a World War II bomber pilot. She laughed at his anger. "Come on, Gramps, loosen up! You laugh at us!"

Liz didn't much care. Whatever the old man felt, she was amused by him. Liz was a tall, slender, black-haired girl with wild wit, enormous energy, and a first-rate mind. At Tufts she was following in her father's footsteps in the study of international economics.

"I'm gonna sit in that chair you vacated at Loyola," she would say to Lorcan, grinning impishly, "and not the one you funded either."

She was the one of whose love he was most confident.

The lunch ended unpleasantly with old Pat Flynn's mouthing off about the upcoming election. As usual he was long on passion and certitude but short on facts.

"I hope I don't end up that way," Lorcan murmured as they rode down the elevator. "It must be hell to be old."

Hank glanced at him, a quick look which disclosed nothing.

"I'm not so sure, Lorcan. He's happy. Same old bullshit. A lot of people that are younger wouldn't mind trading with him. Whatever you say about Dad, he sure knows how to live. I've never seen anyone who can squeeze so much out of life."

"Are you in any trouble with this latest FBI scam?" Lorcan asked casually, perhaps too casually.

The government had put two of its agents on the floor of the exchanges with tape recorders. Scores of traders reportedly had made incriminating statements. The FBI was more like the KGB every day, or the Gestapo.

"Nah." Hank dismissed the scam with a toss of his head. "I talked to those guys once or twice but I never said anything they could use. You gotta be careful on the floor, like Dad always said. Don't trust anyone."

Not even your relatives.

As the elevator door opened on the ground floor, Lorcan asked the question he had been planning all morning for that moment: "What happened that summer at the Lake, Hank?"

Hank jumped at the question and walked out the elevator without answering.

"What summer?"

"The summer I came home from Korea."

"That summer."

"Right. Mom was sick." Henry wouldn't look at him. "She'd been in and out of the hospital a couple of times. Her usual spells."

"What spells?"

That his mother had been in the hospital was a surprise to Lorcan. No one had mentioned it to him when he came home from Korea. She had not been well and it made sense that her doctor might have put her in the hospital.

"You know, anxiety, that sort of thing."

"No one told me."

"You never asked."

That was how it had always been. Lorcan was expected to ask whether his mother had been in the hospital. It was his fault for not asking, not their fault for not telling him.

"I wasn't talking about Mom." He tried again. "I meant the night the house burned down."

"Why ask that now, Lorcan?" Hank said cautiously. "Let the dead bury their dead, like the Bible says."

"My daughter is marrying Maura Meehan's son, that's why."

They walked out onto Sheridan Road. A fierce wind was sweeping down from the north. Snow flurries were already being whipped around like whip cream froth. Three inches accumulation by night. The promised warming trend had been postponed.

"What's that got to do with it?"

"I want to know what happened that summer!"

"You were well rid of her, Lorcan. She was a creep. . . . The cops said it was an accident. What more do you need to know?"

They bent against the wind and walked north on Sheridan Road.

"You don't think it was an accident, do you, Hank?"

There was a moment of hesitation and another quick glance. "What I think doesn't matter. Look, let Maura come to town for the wedding, whenever it is. Then let her go back to New York or wherever it is she lives. There's no reason to open that can of worms again. Forget it."

A long speech for Hank. They turned the corner and hurried to the shelter of the parking lot where they had left their cars—Hank's Mercedes, Lorcan's Mustang. They shivered as they waited for the cars.

"It has always bothered me. What happened on that Labor Day day, Hank? I want to know. I have to know."

Hank stared at him again, astonished by the intensity of his emotion on a subject about which they had not talked in more than thirty years.

"You don't want to know. Believe me, Lorcan, you don't want to know."

Just what Rory had said.

Lorcan gave the parking lot attendant a twenty-dollar bill for both their cars and waved off the change.

"It was a long time ago, Lorcan," his brother said softly, almost sadly. "Don't open it up again—for the love of God don't open it up again!"

"Why not?"

Hank hesitated. Then he whispered so the attendant who had opened the door of the Mercedes would not hear them.

"If you must know—and I won't say another word no matter what you do to me—the reason *for you* not to open it up again is that there is no statute of limitations on murder."

6

"**B**each towels!" Liz pondered the new painting in her father's study. "I like it. I *like* it! It's not like what you usually hang in here, Dad. Too bright. Too realistic. You're normally into the dark, heavy, abstract, crack-of-doom, day-of-apocalypse stuff."

His second child stood in front of the new painting, tumbler of Bushmill's Single Malt in her hand, head cocked to one side, finger under her chin.

"I saw it in the window of a gallery over on Huron the other day," he explained, trying not to slur his words. "It struck me as the perfect painting for a cold week in February."

He had been sitting in his study, brooding and drinking whiskey in preparation for bed. Earlier he had called Cindi Horton and cancelled their session for the afternoon. It would be inappropriate for them to begin their work with his daughter loping around the house.

"Yeah." She nodded and sipped a minute amount of

Bushmill's. "Maybe you're entering your bright phase. On the whole that would be an improvement."

For her supper with her mother, she'd worn light blue slacks and a matching sweater—simple, elegant, and expensive.

"How was Mom?"

"She was Mom." Liz shrugged her shoulders and flopped into one of his leather easy chairs, gracefully as she performed even the most casual actions. "You know Mom. . . ."

When she had bounded into the room and found him with the whiskey, she had grabbed the bottle and a Waterford tumbler and poured herself a large drink. "I hope you don't mind. Green Label is not a graduate-student drink."

"Help yourself," he had said, hoping she would not notice how many sheets he was to the wind.

"Did she seem happy?" He persisted in his cautious probing of her dinner at Dorothy's apartment, two blocks away on North Dearborn Parkway.

"Manic, maybe." She gestured with her drink. "Not happy. I can't remember Mom happy. She's beginning to realize that being your own person means being lonely. She'll never admit it, though. Drinks a lot. Nothing as good as this."

"She's not seeing a therapist?"

"Mom? You gotta be kidding, Dad! No way. There's nothing wrong with her, to hear her tell it. . . . Now, look, she's not coming back, not ever. She's burned too many bridges. So there's no point in waiting for her."

"It doesn't seem right, her living two blocks away."

Liz shrugged her fluid shoulders and draped a long leg over the side of the chair. "Maybe not, but that's the way it is. You should stop drinking yourself to sleep at night and find yourself another woman."

"Liz!"

"I'm sorry, Dad, it's true." She sank deeper into the vastness of the chair and pondered thoughtfully the dark mystery of her drink—straight up, naturally. How else did one drink Irish whiskey? "How much of this darling liquid, to quote our beloved Maeve, have you gurgled down tonight? A quarter bottle? More than one glass gives me a headache. A woman might be more expensive and more trouble, but she wouldn't give you hangovers."

"What would you have thought if you burst into the house this morning and found me in bed with a naked woman?"

She considered the issue carefully. *"Well . . .* I'd have been astonished, to be honest. Then, on reflection, I'd have been delighted—always assuming that she was the right woman—and I'm sure you'd demonstrate good taste." She sat up straight and leaned forward in the chair, tumbler in both hands like a prayer book. "I'm confident you'd make a good choice."

"I thought I did once."

"Dad." She frowned impatiently. *"That* was so long ago. You must stop blaming yourself. You did your best. Life goes on."

"I wonder."

"Look, Mom may be lonely but she'd rather be alone. She doesn't need a man, she doesn't want a man. She's finished with men. You're lonely and you don't want to be alone. You're losing your mind in this great big old Edwardian house all by yourself. You're not finished with women, even if you think you are." She grinned crookedly. "So find yourself a woman."

"I'm afraid I'd be gauche in a relationship with a significant other. I'm too old-fashioned."

"You are *not* old-fashioned," she declared fiercely. "So marry this hypothetical woman if you want. After I approve of her, naturally."

"That goes without saying." He laughed. "I wouldn't dare to do anything else."

"Right!" She uncurled herself and stood up. "Even a few sips of Green Label loosens my tongue. I'm sorry if I was out of line."

She bent over to kiss him goodnight.

"You're never out of line, Liz."

She bolted out of the room the same way she had entered, a filly bounding through life.

How did we manage to produce such a carefree daughter?

he wondered as he picked up the bottle to pour himself a nightcap.

A woman, he thought, *would be more fun than this.*

He placed the bottle back on the desk and put the cap on it.

What went wrong between Dorothy and me? We are at the time of life when we should be enjoying our children, all three a delight in their own way, and our grandchildren, and each other. Now we're separated by two blocks of February ice and millions of light-years of alienation.

The house had been a cause, or perhaps merely an occasion, of their breakup. Dorothy had grown weary, she said, of their home in Evanston. It was too old, too dirty, too depressing, and too hard to keep clean despite the servants he hired to help her. Moreover, it was too far from downtown Chicago, where the children lived. He had dutifully begun the search for a house by himself, since she was too busy to help. He had found the old Astor Street mansion the first day of his quest. Though it needed a lot of work, it was one of the most beautiful Edwardian homes on the Gold Coast.

Dorothy had loved it at first, bubbling with enthusiasm at all the improvements they might make. As the remodeling dragged on for over a year, she had lost interest in it and left the decisions to him and the designer—a Ph.D. from Chicago Circle specializing in the restoration of old homes.

When they finally moved in, Dorothy had been querulous. "You really made an awful mess of it, didn't you, Lorcan? It's dark and ugly and depressing."

"It's authentic, dear."

"Who wants to live in a museum that looks like a prison?"

The house may have been too perfect a restoration. Every carved molding, every panel, every chandelier, every drape, every staircase was a minutely executed restoration or reconstruction of turn-of-the-century opulence—with modern electric circuitry and plumbing fixtures added.

"I'm afraid an attendant will tell me not to litter," Dorothy had complained.

Nor had she approved of the pool in the basement. "I

smell chlorine every hour of the day and night. I'll never set foot in it."

She never did.

Lorcan glanced at the note pad next to his private phone. He had scrawled Maura's number when he had learned it from the Huntington, Long Island, information earlier in the day. *Why not call her?* he'd asked himself. Surely their children's engagement warranted renewed communication. What could be more natural than a call?

Shouldn't she have called him?

No, the first move was his.

What did he honestly expect to hear when he called her? Surely any connection they'd once shared had long since died. It was sheer wishful thinking on his part to suppose he could resurrect a late-adolescent crush. That acknowledged, it was with hope that he began to dial Maura Meehan Halinan's number.

As the phone rang, Lorcan recalled the surrealistic images of the days when the fever had begun its attack. What happened? Why did she leave?

He hung up the phone and slumped in his chair. For the second time in as many days he burst into tears.

"Maura, Maura," he had groaned, "how did I ever lose you?"

Then he had reached for the bottle of Green Label.

Later that night, after Liz had gone to bed, he stood staring at the number on the scratchpad. Again he reached for the bottle.

Before he filled his glass, he crumpled the note and threw it into the fireplace's flames.

7

"T is your man, the frigging little Bishop," Maeve Anne O'Leary Flynn exploded in a stage whisper which might have been heard half a dozen pews away—and was designed to be so heard. "He'll never make it to the pulpit this time at all, at all."

She sighed a loud Irish sigh which would have convinced even a specialist that she was about to come down with an acute attack of asthma—and would also have wakened any dead that might have been buried in the Cathedral crypt.

Maeve, the wife of Lorcan's son, Paddy, was a shrewd little West of Ireland Gypsy woman with flaming red hair, dangerous green eyes, and as quick a tongue as Lorcan had ever heard. Her claim to Gypsy ancestry, Lorcan suspected, was part of the Maeve's carefully calculated act, a persona she could hide behind when she felt shy or fragile in the company of "yanks," or as she called them, "your highly civilized yanks."

Maeve was a passionately dedicated wife and mother, a first-rate specialist in neonates, and an instantly beloved friend, no, co-conspirator, of her sisters-in-law.

She also worked overtime at impressing and pleasing her father-in-law, who, as she had commented in another stage whisper, "is a terrible powerful man, isn't he now?"

She was certainly clever enough to have discerned early on that she could wrap him around her little finger. Nonetheless, she kept up her act to amuse him, quite possibly for the same reason that Lorcan was still in the finance game—"for the sheer bloody hell of it, Old Fella!"

Outbursts of near obscenity in the solemnity of Holy Name Cathedral amused the Old Fella, so what the hell!

"Shush, Maeve." Liz giggled. "You'll embarrass us all with your shanty-Irish ways."

" 'Tis no fault of mine," she whispered back, "that I never used inside plumbing till I was nineteen."

More giggles from the Flynn family.

Maeve had somehow won over Dorothy, who had dismissed her before the marriage as "uncouth." Lorcan often wondered which of her many masks the wee Gypsy woman wore for her mother-in-law.

The Flynns were gathered in a pew two-thirds of the way back on the left (or Epistle as it used to be) side of the Cathedral—a discreet place for prominent, not to say noisy, people.

The Maeve had manipulated the seating arrangement in the pew so that Lorcan was surrounded by herself and Liz. On Maeve's left were her sons, two frighteningly well-behaved pre-school urchins named Diarmuid and Conghor (Dermot and Conor or more frequently "Derm" and "Con"), and beyond them the boys' father, who was responsible for their continuing good behavior at Mass.

"I'll look out for the Old Fella, poor dear man, and you watch the brats."

At the far end of the pew she had stationed Marie and her Rob in their own private world where they could hold hands during the Mass—or Eucharist, as the modern term seemed to be.

As penance for his various sins, Lorcan had risen early, worked out on the Nautilus for a half hour, and swum for an hour. The exercise cleared away his headache but made him sleepy. He would have just as soon fallen back into bed as join the family at the ten-thirty Mass.

But as he looked down the pew, he was glad he had come. Not everything was right in his life, yet he ought to be grateful for his family.

What was left of it.

Marie, blond, diminutive, sweet, looked like a serious sixteen-year-old with her pug nose, her smooth skin, and her clear, innocent eyes. She was the kind of young woman who made you wonder whether her mother knew she was out as late as she was. Powerful intelligence lurked beneath her seemingly naive exterior. At twenty-four Marie already had an M.S. in computer science from MIT and was working on a doctorate.

Dorothy had always resented their youngest child, insisting that she was spoiled and sullen. But Marie seemed to have survived her mother's dislike. In fact she seemed unaware of it.

In Rob Halinan, Marie's beloved (met at the Old Saint Patrick's "World's Largest Block Party"), Lorcan could see no trace of his mother, as best as he could remember the Maura of long ago. Rob was a slim, freckle-faced young man with sandy hair, unassuming gray eyes, and a winsome smile—every pastor's favorite altar boy, just as Marie might be every pastor's favorite assistant sacristan. He was as quiet and dreamy as Marie. They were two young people who did not quite live in the same anxious world as the rest of humankind.

Was he a reflection of his father? Was that the kind of man Maura had married? Surely she would have been happy with such a man. He had died in a collision with a light plane, flown by a drunk, which had wiped out him, his DC-9 crew, and all twenty-nine passengers as he approached the runway on Martha's Vineyard in broad daylight.

Bishop John Blackwood Ryan, Ph.D, pastor of Holy Name Cathedral and adviser to Cardinal Sean Cronin, his eyes blinking behind thick glasses, had finally, with the assistance of a careful acolyte, found his way to the pulpit.

"Thank you, Fiona." He bowed to the acolyte, who blushed and giggled. "I am persuaded," he began, all sign of ineffectual confusion swept away as soon as he opened his mouth, "that we are stuck with an adolescent God. She is in fact a teenager, a couple years older than the inestimable Fiona. As to the question of whether She, God that is, not Fiona, will ever grow up, I regret to have to report to you on this Lenten Sunday in February that such an eventuality seems most unlikely."

The congregation sniggered, accustomed as it was to Bishop Blackie's (as parishioners usually called him) offbeat beginnings. Then they settled back to see what rabbits he would pull out of the hat this Sunday.

Lorcan had been daydreaming during the Gospel reading, about the full, cream-colored breasts and raspberry-red nipples of Cindi Horton, and did not remember the reading. Thus he was unable to link the image of a teenage girl God with the liturgy. It probably didn't matter. Literalism never stopped Bishop Ryan.

"I argue this position based on the observation that no one in our experience is more exuberant, more energetic, more playful, more outrageous, more fanciful, and more excessive than young women of our species."

Maeve nudged him with her elbow and began to giggle uncontrollably, wee hand over her face.

"Succinctly, who is more inclined in our experience to show off than a teenage girl person? Who, it might be added, has more reason to show off?"

He nudged the Maeve back. She doubled up in an effort to suppress her giggles. Her husband, a responsible and serious professional man, seemed to be smiling proudly.

"How, gentle souls, can we avoid the conclusion that Our God is an exuberant and incorrigible show-off? Consider the wild variety of species that inhabit our tiny speck of solar dust. Consider the inordinate and totally unjustified number of solar systems and galaxies, black holes and quarks, protons and weak forces, great attractors and star clusters which constitute the universe as we know it. Who could possibly deny that this display is excessive?

"An exercise, I insist, in adolescent excessiveness.

"This adolescent God of ours knows more math than the brightest of our mathematicians—an allowable phenomenon. Surely, nonetheless, it was immoderate to design our universe so it fit formulae which the mathematicians are only now deriving. I put it to you, that is like an adolescent saying, 'I know more than you do, nah! nah!'

"Moreover, I understand that the world operates according to the principles of quantum mechanics, which no one really comprehends and which are highly uncertain anyway. If quantum mechanics and statistics are not a hilarious and indeed atrocious joke of a comic God, they seem utterly pointless."

Lorcan wondered how many in the congregation had

caught the priest's witty allusion to Heisenberg's Uncertainty Principle.

"I am told by astronomers, a species of scholar whose erudition awes me, that it is likely that our universe is one of millions and perhaps billions that this youthful comedienne has fashioned so that by laws of chance one or many of them (who knows) would eventually sustain rational life.

"I have the image of Herself playing with a cosmic matchbox, striking one match after another and clapping Her hands joyously when one of Her many big bangs actually produces a cosmos on which in due course playmates for Her, a crowd with which She can hang, will come into existence.

"How can we possibly deny that this is the kind of fun and games we expect of adolescents and especially adolescent women?

"Will she grow up? Will she mature? Will she settle down and 'act right'?

"It is dangerous to make predictions about God. Yet I can observe that She's had an eternity to mature and shows no signs of doing so. It's probably too late.

"I'm engaging in God talk, as you doubtless perceive, metaphorical approximations which give us a hint of Who God is and What She wants. My metaphors, however, are not exaggerations. Quite the contrary, they underestimate the exuberance of our excessive, playful, and show-off God.

"It has been remarked by those who must deal with young women on a full-time basis, their mothers to be blunt, that I cannot possibly be comparing God to young persons who desperately lust for an expensive new dress and then, upon finding in the mall—the normal habitat of such beings—that it has been marked down, promptly lose all interest in it."

Knowing laughter—from the mothers of such young women.

"Metaphors are not strict comparisons. Nonetheless I insist that such behavior, trying as it is to those who must tend to these charming if on occasion feckless creatures, does represent an unpredictable exuberance which may be revelatory.

"I suggest to you that reflection on this image of our ever-youthful God, a God for whom it is always spring, and early spring at that, might just see us through to the end of a Chicago February.

"In the name of the Father and of the Son and of the Holy Spirit."

Fiona, the inestimable and faithful acolyte, appeared to lead the Bishop back to his presidential chair.

Maeve Flynn, who had stopped giggling and had been listening intently to the homily, led the congregation in applause, a common phenomenon in the New Church which nevertheless always shocked Lorcan. Nonetheless, he joined in.

Before Mass, he had decided that he could not receive Communion because of his sins on Friday night. He would remain in the pew to supervise the punks who were too young to have made their First Communion.

After the homily he changed his mind. The teenage God of whom Bishop Ryan had preached would have already forgiven whatever he might have done that was sinful— including his fantasies during the Gospel.

"You've never had teenage daughters, Bishop." He shook hands with the Pastor in the bitter cold after Mass. "So you don't know the downside. Still, it was a great homily."

The Pastor was wearing an Aran Island sweater over his clerical shirt, a Chicago Bulls jacket over that, a Chicago Bears cap, and fur earmuffs, surely a Christmas present.

"How wise of God to protect such from a parent like me," he murmured. "Ah, I see that the inestimable Liz has returned from Tufts, filled with knowledge about Gini curves and other magical indicators."

Liz poured out the story of her semester thus far and promised she'd be back in Chicago again to vote on election day. Like most women of every age, she thought Blackie Ryan was "cute." Even "adorable."

"Brunch at the yacht club." Blackie lifted an eyebrow. To consume the admirable Beth's superb pastry. "Do they let Gypsy women in there, Doctor Flynn?"

"Itinerants is what they call us now, your reverence."

"More properly, 'Traveling Folk.' "

"Jaysus," Maeve whispered as they piled into her husband's BMW, "your man got me that time, now didn't he?"

Although Maeve was a wee bit old to be a teenager, the idea that she might be a hint of what God was like lifted Lorcan's spirits on that cold, dark Sunday in February.

Monroe Harbor was frozen solid, a haunted ghost of the blue waters and white ships which filled it on a summer day. The clouds were rushing by so low that one could not see the Adler Planetarium and Northerly Island at the other end.

Inside the Yacht Club, however, there was light and laughter and champagne and sweet rolls and Beth's pastry and bacon and other such indulgences which Lorcan did not permit himself during the week.

"Did I ever show you my mother's picture, Mr. Flynn?" Rob asked him as Lorcan nodded with a touch of guilt at the waitress who offered him more champagne.

"No." Lorcan put aside his third sweet roll to look at the wallet picture, trying not to seem hasty. "Yes, you and Marie have told me the truth, she is a handsome woman indeed."

"She spells her name M-o-i-r-e now. That's the Irish way. Actually, it's a Gaelicized form of Marie or Mary, so my wife and my mother will have the same name. Does she look like she did when she was our age?"

"Five years younger than your wife-to-be, as a matter of fact, Rob; and, yes," he lied, "she's just as I remember her."

"Lemme see! Lemme see!" The Maeve almost jumped over the table to peek over his shoulder. "Jaysus, Robbie, she's gorgeous. I should be after looking so good when I'm forty! . . . Con, stop taking Derm's cake or I blister your behind! I don't want you gossons shaming your grandpa in this terrible nice place. . . . We have to get to know the poor woman better, don't we, Paddy? Don't we, Old Fella?"

"I'm sure we will, Maeve."

The young gossons—the proper word for them, Lorcan had learned—continued to fight over the piece of cake, oblivious to their Old Gal's dire threat. He didn't correct her estimate of Maura's age, more than ten years too generous. Maeve knew that.

Back in the quiet of his Astor Street home, Lorcan tried to write a sonnet based on the Bishop's sermon. Better poetry than booze—though Liz would probably say that neither was a substitute for a woman.

> *That God exists the world is not a proof*
> *But a metaphor for who She really is,*
> *An unrestrained adolescent, showing off,*
> *An excessive, exuberant, playful whiz,*
> *Determined gamester with the quantum odds,*
> *An ingenious expert in higher math—*
> *This frolicsome and comic dancing God*
> *Is charming and just a little daft.*
>
> *Will God grow up? Will She become mature?*
> *In the creation game announce a lull,*
> *Her befuddled suppliants assure*
> *A cosmos that is quiet, safe, and dull?*
> *Can God be innocent of romance?*
> *No WAY! On with the multi-cosmic dance!*

The sonnet also kept his mind off the letdown he had experienced when he had seen Moire Halinan's picture. She was a strikingly beautiful woman doubtless. But he could find no memories in his head to compare with the face in the picture.

His longings from the past were for a woman he could not remember.

He dozed off, dreamed of beach towels, and woke up to the sound of the phone.

"Is it yourself?"

"Praise be to all the saints in heaven, woman, who else would it be?"

"Well, would you be after knowing that poor dear Rob's mother is coming to town next week? Doesn't she have her own quality typesetting business? And aren't they having a convention here in Chicago at your Chicago Hilton? And shouldn't we meet her now, and herself one of the family almost? And haven't I set up a dinner at the Cafe Twenty-One on the Thursday night before your man wins the primary? And am I not calling you to make sure you can come?"

"Are you asking me, woman, or telling me?"

"Wasn't I just after telling you?"

"Were you now?"

"Wasn't I?"

"I give up, Maeve, you win."

"Ah, aren't you a grand man altogether?"

"Would you be saying so, now?"

"Wasn't I after just saying it?"

As he hung up, he wondered whether the family suspected that he and Moire, as he must think of her now, had been in love.

Probably not. They saw her only as a beautiful woman for a lonely man.

Not as nubile perhaps as Cindi Horton.

Yet . . .

It would be an interesting dinner.

The Maeve, shanty-Irish biddy that she was, would see to that.

He no longer felt sleepy.

8

Lorcan quietly reviewed the copies of newspaper articles the resourceful Mary Murray had collected at his request. They didn't reveal much, except perhaps what the public had been willing to swallow at the time.

CONGRESSMAN DIES IN DUNES BLAST
GAS LEAK SUSPECTED

Congressman Joseph J. Meehan (D, Illinois) and his family were killed this morning in a predawn explosion at their summer home in Long Beach, Indiana. The Congressman, 45, his wife Jane, 40, and their daughters Janet, 16, and Constance, 14, were all killed. A niece, Maura Anne Meehan, 18, survived the blast.

A neighbor, Colonel Pat Flynn, told authorities that the explosion occurred at 4:35 in the middle of an early morning downpour. "I thought it was the loudest firecracker of the weekend," Flynn said. "It knocked me out of bed."

The Meehan home was completely destroyed and several nearby homes incurred minor damage. Michigan City (Indiana) firefighters said that only the early morning downpour prevented the fire from spreading to other homes.

"The whole beachfront could have gone up," said Fire Chief Metro Hohlman. "We were lucky."

Chief Hohlman refused to speculate about the causes of the fire. However, sources in the Michigan City Police Department ruled out foul play.

"Someone must have left the gas jet on in the kitchen," one source said, "and then they closed the windows when the thunderstorm began. All it took after that was a match."

Congressman Meehan had represented the South East Side Second District for four terms. He won the seat for the first time in 1946, shortly after his return from naval service in the Pacific during the war. He served on the Labor and Government Operations Committees and on the Investigations Subcommittee. Although a Democrat, he was an enthusiastic supporter of Senator Joseph R. McCarthy (R, Wisconsin) in the senator's anti-Communist crusade.

A devout Roman Catholic, Congressman Meehan was active in Church philanthropy, and especially in the work of the Justine Fathers. He was a member of the advisory board of St. Justin High School, from which he was graduated in 1920.

He was also active in civic affairs in Chicago and in Irish-American activities. It was rumored that after his re-election this autumn he would seek the Democratic Committee post in his Tenth Ward. A group of committeemen who had opposed the election of County Clerk Richard J. Daley are thought to have been grooming Congressman Meehan as a replacement.

"It's a tragic loss for all Chicagoans," Mr. Daley said

this morning. "We'll pray for the repose of his soul and his wonderful family."

The late Major Timothy Meehan was the Congressman's brother. Mrs. Meehan is survived by her sister Henrietta Crawford.

Funeral services for the Meehan family will be held at Saint Kevin's Church in Chicago on Monday at 10:30. Visitation will be at Clarke's funeral home on 103d Street from 2:30 Friday.

FOUL PLAY RULED OUT IN CONGRESSMAN'S DEATH GAS LEAK SAID TO CAUSE BLAST

The LaPorte County Coroner today concluded his investigation into the death of Congressman Joseph Meehan (Dem, Illinois) and his family on Labor Day with a verdict of accidental death.

"It was a typical holiday tragedy," Coroner Arch Klink said. "People are so busy enjoying themselves that they forget the precautions they would normally take. An open gas burner, windows closed because of a thunderstorm, someone strikes a match and we have a tragic end to four wonderful lives."

Asked about rumors of possible organized crime involvement, Coroner Klink replied that such stories were completely unfounded. "The Congressman was not on the Sub-Committee investigating crime," he said. "There is no justification for such silly rumors or any of the others flying around. The Meehans died a tragic and unnecessary but accidental death."

Reached on the telephone, Henrietta Crawford, the late Mrs. Meehan's sister, withdrew her earlier charges that her sister had been murdered. "I was understandably upset," Mrs. Crawford said. "I couldn't believe my sister and her children had died so suddenly. I have no reason to question the Coroner's verdict."

Mrs. Crawford is the wife of John J. Crawford, vice president of Southeast Side National Bank and Trust.

DID BRITISH AGENTS KILL CONGRESSMAN?

Were Congressman Joseph Meehan and his family willfully murdered by agents of Her Majesty's Government? Did the long arm of the English Secret Service slip into Long Beach, Indiana, on the morning of Labor Day and blow up the Congressman's home with his family in it?

The official story is accidental death, a "typical" summer tragedy. Many Chicago police officers, to whom Joe Meehan was always a loyal friend, remain unconvinced. "They finally got Joe," said one officer. "And out of town where we couldn't do anything about it."

"The Chicago Irish Republican" is not convinced the Congressman's death was an accident. Almost alone in the American Congress, Joe Meehan was a supporter of freedom for the whole of Ireland, including the occupied six counties in the north. He was unswerving in his opposition to British occupation and to the puppet free state government in Dublin.

His death pleased many tyrants in Westminster and many traitors in Dublin Castle.

We say to those who loved Joe Meehan and love the cause for which he stood that he did not die in vain.

Lorcan set the copies of the articles down on the desk before him. Thirty-five years after the fact it was tougher to say that Meehan hadn't died in vain. But more to the point, was his death the tragic accident the mainstream papers and authorities made it out to be? What exactly had led up to that deadly Labor Day explosion? Did Lorcan really expect to find an answer after all this time?

9

"I'm not altogether sure, Lorcan, whether you are admitting sorrow for your transgression or boasting of your achievement."

Wishing that Doctor Murphy did not sound so much like a Mother Superior, he squirmed on the couch. "I'm not altogether sure myself, Doctor."

"I see."

"She offered to come home with me. I didn't see how I could refuse without hurting her feelings."

"Ah. You're telling me she seduced you?"

"If she did, I certainly didn't protest. . . . She was so lovely . . . and so, well, so frail."

"I see. . . . She sexually harassed you?" A light touch of irony, perhaps even of sarcasm.

"Doctor Murphy, the mere existence of women is a sexual harassment for men."

He heard a soft chuckle. "You protest the way the species has been designed to reproduce?"

"No. I'm merely trying to say that—"

"You never had a chance?"

"I never wanted a chance."

"I understand."

"It was violent, more so than ever before."

"Oh."

"I didn't hurt her," he added quickly.

"I would not have expected that you did, Lorcan."

"I astonished her, I guess. As far as that goes, I astonished myself. She seemed to enjoy it once she got over her surprise. Heaven knows I enjoyed it."

Truth be told, Lorcan was afraid of the man who enjoyed Cindi Horton Friday night. He certainly wasn't inclined to tell Doctor Murphy about him.

"Indeed. Not like with your wife?"

"Certainly not. A wife is different."

"How so?"

"Well, most wives are. . . . I don't know that. My wife was. The way men talk, their wives seem to be cold too. Dorothy would have been disgusted and angry."

"But not Ms. Horton?"

"Not at all. Scared maybe at the beginning, content later."

"Dream sex?"

"Male fantasy sex . . . under the beach towels too."

"What?"

Finally he had shocked her.

"We made love, the first time, on a leather couch in my

office, under the painting of beach towels that I bought last
Friday."

"Why?"

"Why I bought the painting or why we made love?"

"Why both?"

"I was showing her the house. I guess the painting turned
me on. I became . . . well, implacable. Terrified her at first.
Terrified me too."

"Terrified, yet you were both pleased, were you not?"

He gulped. The woman understood too much. "Yes," he
agreed weakly. "All my fantasies were realized."

"And you had purchased the painting to facilitate fantasy
lovemaking on that leather couch?"

He had not considered that possibility. "Perhaps I did.
I'm frightened. Terrified."

"A pleasurable fright?"

"Kind of . . . I'm not sure what I might do next."

"Assault women on the street?"

"Certainly not!"

"I note that our hour is finished."

"Just when it's becoming interesting."

"So they all say."

*The patient is in deep water, a symbolic statement
which even a crude and mechanistic Freudian like
myself can acknowledge. Poor Cindi Horton, to
continue the metaphor, is further adrift than she
anticipated. She rather likes it for the moment, but
will most certainly have second thoughts.*

*My patient is a throwback to an Irish king or
Viking warrior or a renaissance explorer. No
wonder his father found him threatening. Presently
it is beyond his imagination that he can be anything
more than thoughtful, respectful, and loyal. He
surely possesses those virtues; however, they make
his fearsome hunger all the more dangerous because
they render him all the more appealing.*

*He speaks very little of his mother. I permit him
to escape from that responsibility. Not, however, for
much longer.*

> *Thus far in life he has been constrained in his avaricious appetites by his ethical principles and his Irish inhibitions. When his wife left him, she unintentionally liberated him from much of both. He is quite properly afraid of the primal man who is trying to escape.*
>
> *He is in serious trouble.*

Lorcan Flynn leaned against the bank building and watched the huge snowflakes dance hypnotically as they fell to the sidewalk in front of him and began to accumulate. It would be a big storm today, five or six inches. He tried to breathe deeply to restore his balance and confidence.

The damn woman had picked him apart. Worse, she had offered him no reassurance and no encouragement. She knew damn well that he would continue to ravage Cindi and she did not warn him against it. It was sinful and it was dangerous. The affair would hurt them both if it went on.

Doctor Murphy wants to find out more about me and Dorothy. I won't talk about it. That's not part of the problem.

What would have happened if I had tried to make love with Dorothy the way I did with Cindi on Friday night?

The thought was absurd, but he pursued it nonetheless. Curiosity, he told himself.

On the couch under the painting in broad daylight.

She probably would have fought him. Pushed him away.

Maybe not. Maybe he could have soothed her, calmed her down, won her with the power and the depth of his love. Maybe if their sex life had been better—for both of them—they wouldn't have drifted apart.

For a moment Lorcan imagined trying unrestrained passion with Dorothy even today. The picture had a certain perverse appeal.

A few drinks in her and it could be done. *When she'd had an extra martini or two during the last years, I occasionally had pleasure with her. Real pleasure. It took the drink to loosen her inhibitions.*

Lorcan contemplated the process of such an entrapment and seduction. It would not be without its pleasures. Maybe after that they could try to patch up their marriage.

But even as he tried to imagine such a seduction's successful results, he knew that it would never come to pass. With determined resolve he decided to end this ludicrous reverie.

He struggled away from the bank and trudged south on Michigan Avenue. He'd gone as far as Monroe Street when he realized the East Bank Club was in the opposite direction. He'd have to hurry if he wanted to get in his exercise before his appointment with Dinny Rooney. And then there was that call to Rome. . . .

10

"Looks pretty suspicious to me." Dennis Rooney rubbed the Xerox copies of the three articles with slender fingers. "Nothing more than this, huh?"

Lorcan nodded. He hadn't been able to reach his brother Edward. A cleric speaking broken English with a strong Italian accent had told him that "Father President" (as the General of the Order was now called) was out of Rome, on a special mission for "santo padre." That was always the explanation for Edward's absences from Rome. For all Lorcan knew it might be a valid excuse, but he did not altogether trust Edward.

"That's all we could find, Dinny."

"Yeah. It was a lot easier to cover up in those days. No pushy TV anchorwoman with microphones and cameras." Dinny's voice was always flat and unemotional, like a cop's, even if his carefully manicured hands were not cop's hands. "Maybe it's better now, though."

"Depends on whether it's us or them covering up."

"So what do you want me to find out?"

Dennis Rooney was the top private investigator in town, a lawyer, a former police captain who held an M.A. in criminology. He looked like a prosperous banker—broad, solid shoulders, dark blue three-piece suit, carefully trimmed silver hair, rubicund face, innocent blue eyes. If Mike Casey had been made police superintendent a few years back, Dinny would have become his top deputy. But Mike had been passed over for political reasons and took up painting. Dinny set up his own agency.

Lorcan Flynn would not have hired anyone else; his philosophy about professionals was that you hire the best—after you make sure that they really are the best.

"I want to know whether there was a cover-up, why there was a cover-up, and who did it."

Dinny nodded. "The works."

"Right. We won't worry about price."

His innocent blue eyes twinkled. "Naturally."

"Naturally."

"It's been a long time, Lorcan."

"I'm aware of that."

"You can't tell what worms we might dig up if we go messing with the stones." He flicked the papers in his hand. "Your father might be involved."

"I understand. . . . You won't learn anything from him, by the way; his memory isn't what it used to be. Moreover, even when the memory was good, he could keep his mouth shut tighter than most men."

"Refresh my memory. Who was Tim Meehan? War hero?"

"An Irish nationalist. He went to Ireland in '46 after the Army discharged him. Joined the IRA and disappeared. His body was found later, riddled with bullets. Or it was said that it was his body. Anyway, he was never seen again."

"I remember now. Might not have been dead after all?"

"Probably not anymore. Nothing was ever heard from him again."

"Is this Henrietta Crawford still alive? Her husband died about ten years ago, as I remember."

"She is. She's a couple of years younger than my father. Lives in a retirement community in Arizona."

"You know there's no statute of limitations on murder?"

"Sure. It was thirty-five years ago. The killer or killers are probably dead too. We all die eventually."

"Yeah. So I understand." He considered the copies of the clippings again. "You were there when it went down?"

Lorcan nodded. "I'd just been discharged from the Air Force and was getting ready to attend Notre Dame in the fall."

"You don't remember what happened?" Dinny frowned. "How come?"

"I was coming down with epidemic meningitis, a really bad case. I had a high fever. In all the excitement of the holiday I guess no one noticed, myself included. The world was a blur for the next couple of weeks. I almost didn't make it."

The innocent blue eyes pondered Lorcan thoughtfully. Dennis Rooney did not ask and would not ask why it was suddenly so pressing that an ancient mystery be solved. If Lorcan wanted to tell him, fine. If not, it was his money that would pay for the investigation.

"This Maura Meehan." He touched one of the copy sheets. "Is she still around?"

"She left for New York shortly after the explosion. She inherited a bit of money from the Meehans. She married an airline pilot who died in a crash at Martha's Vineyard. Maura Halinan now. Actually, she now goes by the name Moire. She owns a quality typesetting company in Huntington, Long Island."

"Yeah. . . . Kind of strange that Joe would have left money to her."

"She might have been the sole surviving relative."

"Whose daughter was she? Joe's only sibling seems to have been his sister."

"I noticed that too."

"Will she cooperate?"

"Hard to tell. . . . And, Dinny, her son is engaged to my younger daughter."

"No kidding? That makes it kind of interesting, doesn't it?" He touched his tie clasp.

"There was—and is—a mystery about her origins."

"Uh-huh. You've seen her since then?"

"No. . . . She'll be in town next week for a trade convention."

"You want me to talk to her?"

Lorcan hesitated.

"Let's find out something more about her background before we make a decision about that."

"Was she the kind who might blow up a house for money?"

That's the troubling question, isn't it? Might as well face it.

"I didn't even recognize her in the picture her son showed me."

"People age . . . or do you think the woman in Huntington is someone else?" His blue eyes twinkled again. "That would be a nifty twist."

"No, it's Maura Meehan. I found summer pictures in one of my mother's scrapbooks. She's still quite striking. I'd forgotten what she looked like."

"Uh-huh." He touched the tie clasp again. "You didn't answer my question."

"I was trying to think about it. . . ." He rubbed his forehead as he grasped for images out of the past. "She was kind of deep and quiet; maybe reserved is the right word. It was hard to tell a lot of the time what was going on in her head."

"In my experience with four daughters who were that age, one of whom still is, there is often nothing going on in their heads."

"Sons too."

"Even worse." Dinny grimaced. "Were we ever that age, Lorcan?"

"I was flying an F-86 over the Yalu at that age; there wasn't much in my head either—or I wouldn't have been there."

"Maura Meehan, if that's her name?"

"She was smart. Loved to talk about books. Also she was perceptive; never missed a thing. You couldn't tell what she was thinking, but she was thinking, all right."

"Uh-huh. Get along with the rest of the family?"

"She seemed to be a kind of baby-sitter for her cousins. She was a freshman at Saint Xavier College, the old place on Cottage Grove. The kids were brats, gave her a hard time, but she seemed able to laugh them off. No, wrong word. She didn't laugh much."

"Intriguing young woman, huh? So she might have opened the gas burner?"

"She might have done anything, Dinny. Yet she didn't seem cruel, or mean, or hateful."

"You gonna ask her about it?"

"Maybe."

"Should I talk to your uncle and your brother? And Father Ed?"

"I've already tried to pry something out of Rory and Hank." He hesitated. There was no point in hiring an expensive investigator unless you told him everything—even if you were Irish and laid it out for him in thin dribbles.

"Yeah?" Dinny prompted him.

"Hank wouldn't tell me anything. He reminded me, as you did, that there's no statute of limitations on murder. Rory was more loose-lipped. He suspected a cover-up in which my dad and Hank and Father Frank, my uncle, were involved. Maybe Father Gregorio too. You might remember him. He was the priest that the Outfit had killed about thirty years ago."

"Garrote job?"

"Right . . . Rory's guessing mostly, I think."

"Uh-huh." Dennis Rooney stood up. "Speaking of Father Frank, your other brother, the Jesuit—"

"Ed. He's a Justine, not a Jesuit. Saint Justin High School."

"Yeah. How old was he then?"

"Eight years younger than me. He's forty-eight now."

"So he would have been, what, in the middle teens?"

"Thirteen, fourteen. Quiet, studious kid. Kept out of everyone's hair."

"You haven't talked to him?"

"No. I don't see him very often. He's stationed at the Generalate in Rome."

"Might be a good idea, sometime along the road, you or me find out what he remembers."

"Sure."

Dinny put the papers in the inside pocket of his jacket. "Fascinating case, Lorcan. I'll stay in touch. If you want to call it off anytime, I won't be surprised or offended."

"I understand." Lorcan helped him on with his cashmere overcoat.

"Incidentally," Dinny added, "were you in love with that woman? Maura, I mean."

"I was just out of the service and she was beautiful. I thought I was in love."

"Yeah, I understand."

Do you really? Lorcan wondered as he returned to his office, glancing at his watch to see how far he had slipped behind his schedule. The sessions with Doctor Murphy were wrecking the precision of his daily routine.

Back in the office he tried to catch up with his battered schedule. He read the newspapers, made a couple of calls to brokers, phoned the housekeeper to make sure his father was all right, and corrected the galleys for the catalogue from his last exhibit. Images of Cindi were not far from his mind, teasing, tempting, promising.

He stopped his work to reconsider what he had done by turning Dinny Rooney loose. What possible good could come from turning up the rocks under which worms might be lurking? Were not Rory and Hank right and, by implication, Dinny? Was it not better to let the dead bury their dead?

Moire, am I doing all this for you? Do I want to clear away the past so I can finally claim you for my own? Did I make love to you that night, perhaps on beach towels? If I did, how could I forget?

We have much to settle between us, Moire Anne Meehan Halinan; I won't admit this to myself an hour from now, yet I am determined to settle it before summer comes.

Checking his watch, Lorcan banished all thoughts of Moire and returned to his work. He couldn't maintain his schedule if he wasted time indulging in daydreams about the women in his life, past and present.

On his way back to Astor Street, head bent against the wind and the storm, he stopped at Bloomingdale's to make an expensive purchase.

11

"Are you really Alex Stone?" Cindi Horton asked.

Lorcan was working feverishly with his molding clay, like a demented craftsman who had a few hours to finish his task.

"Who told you that?"

"I heard someone around the studio mention it."

"I confess I'm guilty. I try to keep my two identities separate."

"It's strictly off the record," she said.

She wasn't joking. She was standing on a platform, naked save for a towel around her loins, yet she was still a journalist. Everything was on the record unless she said otherwise.

When she arrived for this posing session soon after the Six O'clock News—with the warning that she must be back by nine for the Ten O'clock News—she had been understandably tense.

"I've never done this before," she had said, fretfully brushing the snow from her mink coat.

"Nothing to it, really. It's up to you, Cindi. If you don't want to . . ."

"I *do* want to," she had protested. "I'm just a little queasy. Can I have a drink?"

"Certainly." He had led her into his study. "Bushmill's Green Label?"

"On the rocks. Make it a double. Call it Irish courage for a WASP."

Under the circumstances he had decided that it was imprudent to tell her that it was uncivilized to drink Irish whiskey any other way save straight-up.

"Here we are."

"Thanks." She drank a large gulp. "Hey, you micks

know how to make good whiskey! Where has this been all my life?"

"We're good at a couple of things, not many but a few."

"Tell me about it." She had taken another healthy nip. "All right, how do we do this?"

"Well, I had a studio built upstairs with no windows, only a big skylight. When you're ready, we climb the staircase to the third floor and then the spiral staircase to the attic—or ride the elevator if you want. There's a small room next to the studio where you can hang your clothes and leave your jewelry. There's a washroom attached. I left a robe in there for you. Then you come out, at your leisure remove the robe, stand on the platform, and we begin work. Sound OK?"

"Well, I'm scared but game. Not as scared as my first time on Channel 4."

She had finished her drink in a single huge gulp and stood up. "OK, let's go."

Later, when she had come out of her dressing room in the pink silk kimono he had bought for her at Bloomingdale's, she had seemed quite relaxed.

"Lorcan, this is beautiful."

"I'm glad you like it. The model is worthy of her robe."

"It's for me?" she asked, perhaps too quickly for good taste.

"Certainly."

"The next step is that I remove it and we begin work, right?"

"Whenever you're ready."

"I'm ready." She had shrugged out of the silk robe and folded it carefully on a chair. "Let's go; I have to be back by nine-thirty at the latest."

Not so ready that she had failed to tie the towel precariously around her hips.

Lorcan threw himself into his task with furious energy. As he had told Doctor Murphy, the task was erotic, yet not related to lovemaking, not when he was working. Cindi was beautiful, all right. Tall, slim, with long, lovely legs, sallow skin, slim hips, tiny waist, marvelous breasts, and short blond hair. Yet in his studio he saw her with clinician's eyes, the way he imagined an M.D. would—aware of her possibilities for lovemaking, but for the moment with those possibilities bracketed as he pursued other and more urgent tasks.

Unbidden thoughts of Maura—Moire—came to his head.

Had he ever seen her naked? If he had, why couldn't he remember?

That's when Cindi asked about Alex Stone and thoughts of Moire waned.

"Will I be in a gallery someday—and a book?"

"Not if you don't want."

She considered the possibility for a moment. "I wouldn't mind. What you're doing fascinates me."

Was she thinking of a special on sculpting? Or maybe a five-minute feature?

It wouldn't surprise him. Perhaps even an account of the experience of being a nude model. Geraldo material.

"Thank you. How are you doing?"

"It's funny. I felt awkward at first, then I began to relax. Now I admit I kind of like it. Maybe I'm an exhibitionist at heart."

"I think all people— We can remove this?" He reached over and eased the towel away from her loins.

"Sure." She gulped. "You look at me so intently," she said. "Like you are absorbing all of me."

"That's the way Alex Stone works. . . . Does it bother you?"

"No . . . not exactly. Not any more than you bother me all the time."

"All the time?"

"You're a fierce man, Lorcan. I've never known anyone like you. So intense. . . . I like that. I like it a lot. Yet it scares me, too."

"Maybe Alex Stone is scary; Lorcan Flynn is utterly harmless."

He paused in his work to phone the limousine service which he patronized and part of which he owned. They promised him a limo at nine-fifteen.

"You won't have to wait for a cab."

"You think of everything." She sighed admiringly, stirring her breasts and sending a shiver of need through Lorcan's body.

At eight-fifteen he put down his trowel, laid aside the mound of clay, and begin to wipe his hand. "You look tired. It's time to stop."

"I never thought posing in the nude could be exhausting." She sighed. "Fun all right, more fun than I expected, but exhausting fun. Thank you."

"It will be easier the next time." He held the silk robe for her to put on and eased it over her shoulders.

As he was walking with her to the car, the snow still biting at his face, she pecked him again on his cold cheek. "Do you want to work after the news broadcast? I'll be through at ten-thirty."

It would ruin his schedule for the evening. He was already too far behind for the day.

"That's a good idea. Once I'm into something I like to finish it as quickly as I can."

She sniggered and squeezed his arm. "That's not true in every respect, Lorcan. I've known you to take your sweet time."

12

Lorcan's thoughts wandered back to his days in the Air Force, to his very first mission. He remembered having the MIG in his gunsight. He must have thought briefly about killing another human being. The enemy MIG was about to zero in on Lorcan's squadron commander. Lorcan pressed the button on the top of the control stick of his F-86. The MIG blew apart. In a few more seconds, a parachute appeared. Somewhere in Russia, Lorcan remembered thinking at the time, a young woman had narrowly escaped widowhood.

Back then, Lorcan and his fellow pilots were convinced that the pilots were Russian. Some claimed to have heard Russian conversations on their radios. Lorcan was never certain of the rumors. How would any of them have been able to tell Russian from Chinese? Voices on the radio waves were so choppy. Besides, it didn't seem reasonable that the Russians would try out their pilots, their tactics, and their planes on the U.S. forces.

Lorcan's squadron commander had sounded pretty casual for a guy who'd just had his life saved. "Charley leader to Charley Two. Thank you Charley Two. That fellow almost had me."

"There's another one coming out of the sun for you," Lorcan had replied in the same level, controlled tone. "I'll dispose of him too."

Lorcan was covering his squadron commander the way their tactics dictated a wingman should. That commander had, however, taken the risk of plunging into a dive, thereby putting too much distance between their two planes in violation of all their rules. It was a dangerous lapse when the wingman was a kid still in his teens out on his first mission.

The second MIG was at the far range of his weapons. Lorcan would have time for a quick burst before the Russian fired at the Major, possibly leaving an American widow.

Beneath the ice-blue sky, North Korea and China were a blanket of winter white. The Yalu was a strip of black cutting between the mountains. No matter what happened, U.S. planes were not to fly across it into China.

In those days wingmen didn't have all the fancy electronic firing mechanisms they have today. Lorcan had had to hold the plane steady and wait till the MIG touched the crosshairs of his sights, and then squeeze the firing button gently and pray. Pray for what? Lorcan had wondered at the time. To kill a Russian kid still in his teens? To save his commanding officer, a man he didn't like? To do his job well? Lorcan squeezed the trigger. The MIG started to shiver and smoke. The pilot abandoned his chase and tried to bring his plane under control.

Lorcan could have fired a second time to make sure of his

kill. But he didn't. The Major was safe and the Russians would never be able to use that plane again. Even so, Lorcan kept after him just in case. A few seconds later the Russian gave up and ejected. *A wise move,* Lorcan had thought.

To this day Lorcan wondered if the parachuting pilot had waved at him as he descended. If there was a heaven, as Lorcan suspected there was, maybe the two of them would compare notes one day.

"Thank you, Charley Two," his commander said over the radio. "I guess you're my good-luck charm."

"Yes, sir," Lorcan had replied tersely.

That had been the only lick of gratitude Lorcan had received. Back in Japan, the commander chewed him out for "not finishing off the bogey."

Lorcan hadn't paid attention to him. Nobody took that CO too seriously.

The Eighth Army had been pushed back from the Yalu by a "surprise" Chinese intervention in the war. Dumb Doug MacArthur had overextended his lines and spread them all over the vast mountainous area between China and Korea. The U.S. forces had pulled themselves together in the midsection of the country, had given up Seoul (for the second time), and had then recaptured it. Then it was the Chinese turn to be overextended. Long-range U.S. B-29 bombers had been assigned the task of "interdicting" the Chinese supply lines. Like the B-52s which were supposed to do the same thing later in Viet Nam, the planes were not designed for such tasks as knocking out bridges and rail lines. However, they turned out to be quite good at it. Then the MIGs showed up north of the river, darting across to shoot at the bombers, then scooting back to their sanctuary.

The MIG-15s had probably been a bit quicker on the turn and on the dive than the F-86s. They had, however, a disconcerting habit of falling apart in their dives. The MIG pilots were not protected with as much armor as the U.S. planes were. If Lorcan's second kill that morning over the Yalu had been flying a Sabre, he would not have had to eject over the mountains of North Korea; he could have flown home.

In the end, the U.S. won the fight with the MIGs. It was one of the great, classic victories in air war—for whatever that was worth. U.S. forces swept them out of the skies with practically no losses. By the time Lorcan's tour came to an end, the MIGs were rarely crossing the river.

The occasional footnote in history books states that the U.S. won because its pilots were better trained. Lorcan was always amused by such statements. He had barely finished his advanced flight program when he was put on a DC-6 and flown to Anchorage, then Japan. The day after he'd arrived, still confused by jet fatigue—it wasn't called "jet lag" back then—he was piloting a Sabre across the Sea of Japan.

Just what he was doing there, he sometimes wondered to this day. Ostensibly he'd gone to earn money for his college education. Yet Notre Dame had offered him a basketball scholarship, and his father had never threatened to withhold tuition money. So just why had he gone? Oh, it hadn't been an uncomfortable war for him, especially when he considered what the troops on the ground had been going through. Lorcan's base in Japan had been heated in the winter and boasted a swimming pool open in the summer. The food had been good, the quarters had been clean, and if he'd been interested there were willing Japanese prostitutes.

Lorcan's family was not poor, not even during the Depression. His grandfather had been a police captain, a lucrative trade in those days. Pat Flynn had been raised in a nice home on Parkside, just off Washington Boulevard, then an elite neighborhood in the Austin district of Chicago. Lorcan's mother had come from Saint Lucy's, north of Lake Street, behind the old Austin Town Hall. Not much of either community was left now.

Neither was Lorcan's family wealthy, although many of his classmates in grammar school had thought so when Lorcan was enrolled there. By their standards, perhaps they were. To this day, Lorcan only thought of his family as being comfortable.

Lorcan's father had not joined the Air Corps when Hitler invaded Poland in 1939 because he didn't have a job. He'd flown small planes all through the thirties—despite his wife's terror of them. When he did join, the Air Corps promised that he would be a flight instructor in the Chicago area—or so he'd told his wife. For years Lorcan had nursed his own suspicion as to why his father did eventually sign up. He had it figured that his grandfather had gotten his father out of some scrape, with the proviso that Pat Flynn enlist.

So just why had Lorcan chosen to go into the Air Force? Certainly not in exchange for his father's having gotten him out of any scrape. If Lorcan were ever in such a scrape, he could probably only count on his father to push him still deeper.

The only thing Lorcan could state honestly about his motives was that at the time, he had had something to prove. To himself? To his parents? That he couldn't say. But, for however unsure he was about this part of his past, he was equally sure that it had nothing to do with his current emotional difficulties.

For his success on that first mission, Lorcan was awarded a DFC—no thanks to his commanding officer, but through the efforts of another CO who'd heard about his performance. He had a second DFC to his credit by the time he returned home at the end of his tour of duty. So it was with some irony he occasionally reflected that his father was the one with a reputation as a war hero while his own war efforts went unsung. But Lorcan only ever noted this irony privately. If no one knew of his distinguished war record, it was because he kept such a lid on it himself.

Lorcan's last couple of missions should have been routine. The MIGs were rarely crossing the Yalu by then, and he flew too high for the North Korean and Chinese antiaircraft.

On the return from his penultimate flight, his Sabre flamed out over the Sea of Japan, which was something a Sabre rarely did. The plane tumbled into a dizzying spin while Lorcan tried frantically to restart the engine. He wasn't conscious of experiencing terror at that moment; there had been, as he'd later told his crew chief, no time to be frightened. The ocean spun up toward him like a merry-go-round at Riverview.

Lorcan was not quite touching the whitecaps when the engine finally kicked in. The altimeter was reading 1500 feet when he at last regained control of the aircraft and leveled off.

Lorcan hadn't slept that night or the next. Or the night after. He'd twisted and turned through the night. When he closed his eyes, he saw the ocean rushing up toward him.

On his last mission, a couple of MIGs wandered across the Yalu. Lorcan let one of them sneak in behind him. The MIG's cannon shells ripped the rear of his plane to shreds. Lorcan should have crashed. Somehow he didn't. He slipped away from the Russian in a long dive, smoke trailing after. Maybe the Russian had thought he was going in. But then Lorcan pulled up and headed south. The Russian didn't bother to give chase; by then Lorcan's wingmen were giving him a belated hard time. But that probably didn't prevent the Russky from claiming a kill back in Manchuria.

Lorcan had heard stories of men dying on their last missions. He had a crazy thought as he limped back toward South Korea that he might be the first one he knew who died that way.

He made a wheels-up landing when he couldn't get the gear to work, touching down on an emergency field outside of Taegu in South Korea, then walked away from his plane. The men who had watched him land had cheered.

Lorcan had gone so far as to wave and give them the thumbs-up sign. Later, in his quarters in Japan, he'd collapsed. His pals had wanted to call in the medics or a chaplain. He had only wanted to get the hell out of Japan and never fly another plane again.

The Air Force made him an instructor at a base in Texas. Most of his work there was on the ground. When he did go up in a jet trainer, he was terrified, though as far as he knew, not a single one of his students ever knew.

Lorcan hadn't flown a plane since then. He wasn't afraid of being in a plane, he just didn't want to fly one.

To that day, he still had nightmares. All those near escapes in the war seemed to have concentrated in the image of the sea spinning ever closer to the sound of 20mm shells tearing into his aircraft and the screech of metal against a runway, the same screech he'd heard as he'd skidded to safety in Taegu.

Lorcan had to admit, he'd returned home something of a basket case. At the beginning of the summer, the meningitis epidemic of '54 wasn't his problem so much as his own wrecked nerves.

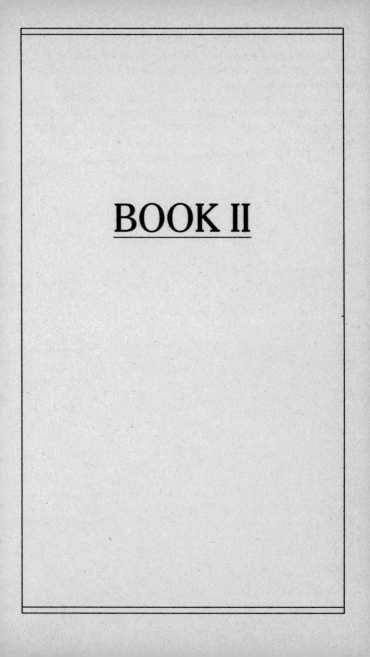

BOOK II

BOOK II

1

"W hy don't you want to talk about your mother?"
Doctor Murphy was annoyed with him, as if she
sensed his amusements with Cindi Horton the night before
and did not approve of them.

"There's nothing to talk about."

"You were your father's rival for her affections, weren't
you? Of course there's something to talk about. Or is it the
rivalry and not her affections which is crucial in your life?"

Lorcan squirmed uneasily on the worn leather couch.
Mother Superior sounded like she might order him out of
her office and send him to Monsignor.

"She was a sweet, pretty woman—fragile, easily hurt, and
easily healed. Affectionate, shy, kind."

"Your mother or your wife?"

"Did you ask about my wife? I thought you said my
mother. The same words could apply, I suppose."

"And they're virtually the same words you used the other
day to describe your new friend, the anchorwoman, were
they not?"

"No." He felt shamed. "She's very different from Mom
and Dorothy."

"I should play the tape for you?"

His face flamed. "That won't be necessary. I'll take your
word for it. What's wrong with a man falling in love with
someone like his mother?"

"Nothing is wrong with it so long as he understands why
he is doing it and that no real woman can live up to his
mythic image of Mom. Suppose you tell me how your sculpture model is different from your wife—besides being
younger and more sexually pliable."

"You fight dirty."

"Naturally."

Lorcan was dead tired. He and Cindi had both overslept, pleasantly exhausted from their night of activity. He had worked on the statue until midnight. Then they had devoted themselves to a wondrous sexual orgy, including a gambol in his basement pool at three in the morning. Their continual lovemaking made him feel guilty even though he kept telling himself that he was a free man—not only in the eyes of the state but the Church as well. Even so, it was difficult not to feel such unmitigated pleasure wasn't somehow illicit. Sexually, Cindi couldn't be further from Dorothy. It was as if the two were not simply of different generations but different species. And now the ineffable Mary Kathleen Ryan Murphy, M.D., was asking him to spell those differences out for him.

"I'm not sure what you mean, Doctor Murphy," Lorcan said evasively.

"I do *not* mean that she may be more sexually experienced and responsive than your erstwhile wife . . . such variations are merely the result of changes in fashion. Certainly you will be able to engage in activities with her at which your wife would have been aghast. It does not follow that she experiences any more fulfillment, much less that she is free to act as your sexual equal."

"I don't know what you mean."

"Some women do things with men, whether in bed or on the tennis courts or wherever. Others permit men to do things to them. I submit that you have chosen the latter in your life. Clearly that is the sort of person your mother was—otherwise she would not have tolerated the absurd male power games you and your father played."

"That's pretty blunt."

"I judge bluntness to be appropriate."

"Maura wasn't passive," he said defensively. He had dreamed about her during the night. And of the beach towels.

"You lost her . . . and did not pursue her, is that not true? You were angry at your mother, weren't you? In fact you still are, although the poor woman is long since in her grave."

"Why should I have been angry at her?"

"Because she preferred your father to you . . . or seemed to."

"I was angry at him."

"Did not that hide your real anger toward her?"

"You're the psychiatrist. You should know the answer to that."

"Come on, Lorcan, if you intend to distract me, you must do better than that."

"Maybe I was angry at her."

"Still are?"

"Maybe."

"And your wife?"

"I loved her," he sobbed, still somehow enjoying the shouting match.

"You are angry at her because she dominated your relationship with her passive-aggressive behavior, behavior similar to that of your mother."

"What do you mean by that Freudian gobbledygook?"

Mary Kathleen sighed.

"How did you handle your adjustment difficulties, your disagreements, your conflicts?"

"We compromised, like every married couple does."

"For example?"

"Well, she didn't like trips to Europe, so I went by myself on business."

"Go on."

"She didn't enjoy Washington, so I stayed out of government. A good idea anyway."

"And?"

"She didn't like expensive foreign cars, so I didn't buy Jaguars or Mercedes."

"And she favored very modest sex and you went along?"

Doctor Murphy was triumphant—a lawyer who had won her case.

Trapped. He wanted to deny it, but after last night how could he?

"I guess so."

"You guess so?"

"All right, damn it, *yes!*"

"What did she give up by way of compromise?"

He searched for an example. "Well, we stayed in the house on Astor Street, which she thought was more a museum than a home."

"And?"

"Well . . . I'd need time to think of others."

"So compromise meant that you sacrificed?"

"I wouldn't say that."

She erupted in fury. "Damn it, man, that's exactly what you said. You've given me cases where you made the sacrifice for her. That's how you perceive the nature of the marriage, not only deep in your unconscious but on the surface. You perceive yourself as the holy Christian martyr who gave up his own legitimate wishes for the good of his marriage."

He paused, trying to arrange his thoughts.

"Answer me!" she demanded.

"Don't I get a chance to think?"

"No! I want your feelings, not your carefully arranged seminar presentations!"

"I feel very angry."

"At me or her?"

"Both!" he bellowed.

"That's better!"

"I never did anything to hurt her—or my mother either."

"Of course not, except smother them with your patience and kindness, your thoughtfulness and your power."

He imagined her leaning toward him and jabbing her finger in his direction.

"Huh?"

"Women scare you, Lorcan James Flynn, scare the hell out of you."

"Any man in his right mind is scared of women."

"I don't mean that kind of fear." She sighed loudly. "I mean your own special fear, which is less of women than of your anger toward them."

"I see."

"No, you don't—and don't try to fend me off by premature closure."

Doctor Murphy glared at him. "Now, why don't you

admit that you are too much for your wife, were probably too much for your mother, and most likely will be too much for the anchorperson?"

"What do you mean?"

"It's a difficult task to be married to a renaissance man, more so when his tastes in women do not incline him to search for a wife who could engage in healthy competition with him. Such a man needs to lose to his wife as often as he wins. Moreover the outcome of their games ought not to matter after the game is over."

"I don't compete with women."

"You harness your anger and your propensity to violence with tenderness and concern. For most women that is a devastating combination of characteristics in a man. You are the kind of man women seek in their fantasies and fear in real life."

"Oh . . . is that good or bad?"

"Either and neither, depending."

"Oh."

"Living with a tightly scheduled renaissance man who is tolerant of your failings and patient with your aggressions would make any woman feel like real shit."

"I'm not a renaissance man."

"The hell you're not—your father was alleged to be good at everything. So you set out to be perfect at everything, even patient with passive women."

"Cindi isn't passive."

"Nonsense. You find much of her appeal in her innocence, her need for protection from a world which is much crueler than she understands."

"Well . . ."

"You enjoy your poetry and your sculpture and your business ventures and your political activities. Others benefit from them too. Perhaps you even like the efficient schedule which has become a corset around your existence. There's no need to abandon any of the things you enjoy. Perhaps some loosening of the corset is in order. The subject of our sessions is how the competition with your father for your mother has introduced an unnecessarily compulsive dimension to your life and work and your relationships with women."

"I delight in loosening corsets."

"There are none left to loosen, probably a net improvement for women, though perhaps there was also some pleasure in having them unloosened by a man, which is neither here nor there. . . . Do you accept my summary?"

"It's a reasonable summary. . . . We're winding down now?"

"I watch the clock, not you, Lorcan Flynn."

"I should have found a renaissance woman?"

"It might have helped. A woman who was in some rough sense a match with you, a woman who felt little need to compete with you save for the fun of it, and a woman who would not lose herself when she tried to share life with you."

"There aren't many such around."

"Thousands, especially in our ethnic group."

"I never found any."

"You didn't look. Or rather, perhaps, you couldn't."

"Maybe Moire would fit the job description."

"Would she?"

"Competition didn't bother her. She found it amusing, maybe even enjoyed it. I almost said that she laughed at it, but Maura didn't laugh all that much."

"You remember that about her after all the years?"

"I hadn't thought of her attitude toward competition for a long time . . . it kind of jumped back into my memory."

"I see."

"She was a great second baseman, one of the best I'd ever seen."

"What?"

"Well . . . second base in softball—sixteen-inch Chicago softball, 'indoor' we often called it because the game was played indoors in K.C. gyms and national guard armories before basketball was invented. It was—"

"Yes, Professor Flynn."

"All right—I met Maura for the first time at a Long Beach/Grand Beach softball game when I came home from Korea. They didn't let girls play much in those days. She was too good to pass up."

"Good field, no hit?"

"Good both. . . . Funny, I forgot completely about soft-ball."

"Was she better than you were?"

He paused and tried to remember.

"She claimed she was. I told her I'd just come home from the war and was out of condition. She said the war had been over for a year. We played on the same team. She was damn good."

"Interesting."

"I'll see her Thursday night."

"What?"

Lorcan was pleased to surprise the uncannily prescient doctor for a change.

"She'll be in town for a trade meeting. Maeve—my crazy daughter-in-law—set up a dinner for the six of us."

"I see; how convenient. . . . And I also see that our hour is up."

> *The patient is quick-witted. He grasps my theory more quickly than most would. It does not follow that he understands in any depth the mother-father-self triad which has shaped his character and personality for weal or woe—or that his mother is more the problem than his father.*
>
> *I will not dismiss him as a patient until he takes the initiative. No harm can come from continuing the sessions indefinitely. Money will certainly not deter him.*
>
> *What will this mysterious Moire be like, this woman of the beach towels?*
>
> *I daresay I will find out in rich detail.*

2

The FBI ruined his afternoon schedule.

"A young man and a young woman from the Federal Bureau of Investigation, Mr. Flynn."

"FBI?" He looked up with a jerk of surprise from the galleys of his book. "Damn!"

If he did not finish the galleys soon, he would never catch up with his schedule. He couldn't rush through them. Proofreading was something you had to do right.

"Should I show them in?"

He hesitated. Perhaps it was a security check on someone that pious phony George Bush was trying to appoint to public office.

"Did they call for an appointment, Mary?"

"No, sir."

"Then it's one of their traps. I'll talk to them."

He put on his jacket and strode into the outer office.

The young couple rose as if on command and held out their IDs.

"I'm Special Agent Foster." The woman smiled appealingly. "My colleague is Special Agent McGrath. We're with the government and we'd like to ask you a few questions."

Handsome young people. A woman who looked like a model, a man who could have played linebacker for the Bears. The bastards, a perfect trap.

"I respectfully decline to speak with you," he said. "I suggest you contact my attorney, Mr. Laurence F. Whealan of Whealan, Bishop, and James."

"Just a few questions," Agent Foster pleaded. "We'll only take a few minutes."

It was an old government trick: you walk into an office for a friendly conversation, ask a few questions, catch the victim in a lie, and charge him with perjury. The scam was a simplified version of the technique by which the IRS had put Governor Otto Kerner behind bars. Lorcan had no idea what the scam on him was. He had broken no laws. However, Donny Roscoe, the United States Attorney for the Northern District of Illinois, and Maynard Lealand, the Special-Agent-in-Charge of the FBI, could investigate and indict anyone they wanted. The two were desperate to snatch headlines away from Rudi Giuliani, the Attorney for the Southern District of New York.

"I respectfully decline to answer any questions. Once again, I refer you to my attorney, Mr. Laurence Whealan."

"We'll stay until you agree to answer our questions," Agent McGrath sneered. "We have a right to ask them."

"And I am exercising my right to refuse to speak with you. Moreover, I am also exercising my right to ask you respectfully to leave my office."

"We have our orders not to leave until we talk with you." McGrath had been cast as the tough guy in the team.

It was like a scene from a crude film, or a TV program that was a send-up of *Miami Vice*.

"I respectfully point out that I could consider you to be trespassers in my office."

"We don't scare that easily, Mr. Flynn." The young man was overplaying his role.

"Once more I warn you, with all due respect, that you could be considered to be loitering on my property without my permission. Ms. Foster, you're a lawyer, I presume—would you recite the appropriate paragraph from the criminal code for your colleague."

Furiously angry, Lorcan turned on his heels and walked into his office.

"Ms. Murray, would you please call Larry Whealan for me."

"Yes, Mr. Flynn."

With FBI loitering, you became formal in the office.

"Larry? Lorcan Flynn. Two of Maynard's storm troopers are here in my office wanting to ask a few questions. I told them to see you."

"Respectfully, I presume?" Larry chuckled.

"With utmost respect. I also warned them that they were loitering on my property."

"You intend to have them arrested?"

"Damn right!"

"Now, Lorcan, calm down."

"Calm down, nothing! They have no right to threaten me."

"You haven't done anything wrong."

"That doesn't mean that our government can't harass me for years."

"Maybe they want you to testify against someone else."

"Then subpoena me in the proper way."

"OK, Lorcan, I quite agree, Donny and Maynard figured they could spring a trap on you. Dumb trick at this stage of the game, but they're both dumb. They want more headlines from their CBOT and MERC scams, and you'd give them headlines."

"Fine. I'm about to call Maynard and tell him to call off his coyotes. If he doesn't I'll phone the Central District Police Station. I have friends over there who'd like nothing better than to book a couple of FBI people on loitering."

"Warn them once again," Larry murmured. "And call me afterward so I can share in the fun."

Larry had played the part of the good lawyer who counseled his client to prudence, well aware that it was a waste of time.

Lorcan strode back in the office. Both the agents jumped to their feet.

"I am warning you for the final time that your continued presence in my office after I have asked you to leave is a violation of the law. I am prepared to take appropriate action."

"We have our orders, Mr. Flynn." The young woman looked miserable. She would look even more miserable before the day was out.

"Very well."

"Did you sleep with Cindi Horton last night?" she asked as Lorcan wheeled to return to the inner office.

Ah, the sucker question. They've been watching me. If I denied it, they would arrest me for perjury.

Slowly, carefully, controlling his temper, he turned on the woman.

"Agent Foster, I repeat my respectful response: all questions may be properly addressed to Mr. Laurence Whealan. And I repeat my warning. You're guilty of trespassing."

Back at his desk, he phoned the FBI and demanded Maynard Lealand. As he waited to penetrate the government phone bureaucracy, he reflected that if Maynard wasn't an idiot, he would not be available for Lorcan James Flynn. However, idiot that he was, the Special-Agent-in-Charge would not be able to contain his curiosity.

"Maynard Lealand," a heavy voice finally spoke to him.

He's been practicing in front of a mirror to look and sound intimidating.

"Lorcan James Flynn, Maynard. Two of your jackboot types are in my office. They refuse to leave. I have warned them as I am warning you that they are guilty of loitering and trespassing. I ask you once, and once only, whether you will speak to them now on my phone and instruct them to leave. Yes or no, Maynard?"

Silence.

"Maynard?"

"They are carrying out orders."

"Thank you, Maynard."

He then called the Central District Police Station at 11th and State. His friend was in and delighted at the prospect.

"How far should we go, Lorcan?"

"Read 'em their rights, cuff 'em, book 'em, print 'em, put 'em in your bullpen. I'll be over later in the day to file a complaint."

"Sock it to them, huh?"

"Absolutely. We'll continue the case indefinitely to make them sweat for the next year."

"You're a dangerous man, Lorcan James Flynn."

"These are dangerous people."

While he was waiting for the cops, he wondered about Hank. Could this visit be connected with Hank? He phoned him at his office. Not there. The Board was closed. He called Hank's home in River Forest. Joanne, sounding distraught, answered.

"Hi, Jo." He switched on the charm. "Sorry to bother you at this hour of the day. Is my brother home?"

"I'll get him."

Had she been crying?

"Hello, Lorcan." Hank spoke like a man the world had been persecuting.

Instead of warning him that the FBI was on the prowl, Lorcan decided to assume that his brother already realized that.

"What's going down, Hank?"

"They came early this morning, woke us up, identified themselves as FBI to Joanne, who answered the door. They asked her if I was home. What would any wife do under the circumstances? She said no. They arrested her for perjury, slapped the cuffs on her, and dragged her off to the car. In her robe and nightgown. She was hysterical. The kids that are home were sobbing and shouting. I had to agree to go downtown and talk to them."

"You *had* to?"

"What was I going to do?"

"Call your lawyer. No grand jury in the country would indict a woman on such a perjury charge."

"Joanne was *hysterical.*"

"It sounds like she wasn't the only one. What did they ask about?"

"Mostly about your business affairs." Hank gulped. "They wouldn't believe that I knew nothing about them."

Damn good thing for me you don't, Lorcan thought.

"You had a lawyer present?"

"No. I didn't feel it was necessary."

"Next time, Hank, do me a big favor and call your lawyer. Send me the bill."

"All right, Lorcan. I'm sorry."

"Why didn't you warn me? There are two of them in my office laying for me."

"I was afraid you'd think I'd let you down."

The remark was typical of the mix of resentment and diffidence which for decades had stood as a concrete wall between Lorcan and his brother.

"From now on, call me as soon as anything happens.

They're fishing and they're lousy fishermen, but they're dangerous."

"I will, Lorcan, I really will. I promise."

Unless Joanne is hysterical, Lorcan thought ruefully.

"Thanks, Hank. I'll ask Larry Whealan to talk to you about the details of their questions."

"Very general, Lorcan. Very general. . . . I'll talk to Larry of course."

"Thanks, Hank. . . . And, by the way, were the two that cuffed Joanne named Foster and McGrath?"

"Yeah, I think so. Good-looking girl and big guy?"

"Right . . . well, they're about to be cuffed themselves. Tell that to Joanne if you think it will make her happy."

He drummed his fingers on his desk, glanced longingly at his galleys, and phoned Larry Whealan again. He described briefly the new FBI scam.

"They've done that on some other traders the last couple of weeks. Totally ruthless. The media haven't touched it because the reporters don't consider traders to be sympathetic people."

"Hence not possessors of the rights of all Americans. By the way, Donny's gumshoes have been trailing me."

"Yeah? You sure?"

"I'm sure."

Whealan was not about to ask how he knew. "They're out to nail you, Lorcan. Or maybe to trap someone else through you. Be careful."

"I sure will. . . . My dear brother says that the questions were general."

"He doesn't know anything about your business, does he?"

"Not a thing."

"They're fishing, Lorcan."

"Just what I told Hank."

He was about to call Dinny Rooney and ask him to put a shadow on the shadow, when Mary Murray came into his office, slightly flustered.

"There are four police officers outside, Mr. Flynn. They are having a verbal altercation with the FBI people."

"I would imagine they are."

"Is there a problem, Sergeant?" He stuck his head into the outer office.

"Yes, sir, Mr. Flynn, sir," said the massive black officer. "We have a complaint that some subjects are loitering in your office. Are these the subjects?"

"Yes, Sergeant, they are."

"We're law-enforcement officers!" Agent McGrath shouted.

"I don't believe, Sergeant, that law-enforcement officers are immune from the law, are they?"

"Certainly not, Mr. Flynn, sir."

"Good. I'll ask Mr. McGrath and Ms. Foster once more to leave my office quietly."

"We have our orders," the young woman snarled. "We're staying until you answer our questions."

"Do your duty, officer."

"I'm afraid that if you don't leave, it will be necessary to charge you with trespassing."

"We don't leave."

The kid was young and inexperienced. Probably had just passed her bar exam. Didn't know what to do, so, fearing Maynard's contempt, she was digging in her heels.

"You'll press charges, Mr. Flynn?"

"Certainly, Sergeant."

The cop read them their rights. The two young G-persons listened in disbelief. No one did that to them.

"Officers, arrest these two trespassers," the sergeant ordered solemnly, a black pope issuing a bull of excommunication. "If they resist, it may be necessary to handcuff them."

Resist they did. Agent McGrath shoved the officers aside and tried to break for the door. His South Side Irish self rose to the surface. It would be a brawl.

The struggling men knocked over two vases, both of which shattered, spilling flowers and water on the floor. Inexpensive vases. Then they collided with one of Lorcan's pieces, an abstract Madonna and child, and shoved that over too. The young woman, wrestling with the black sergeant, kicked a hole in the fabric of the easy chair on which she'd been sitting.

It would be necessary to inventory the damages for the trial.

"I'd say they're resisting arrest, Sergeant."

"They sure are, Mr. Flynn, sir." The black cop was struggling to fasten cuffs on Special Agent Foster. She kicked and punched and screamed.

"Let go of me, you fucking pig!" she bellowed.

"You heard her say that, Ms. Murray?"

"I certainly did, Mr. Flynn, sir."

"Disorderly conduct, officer, and malicious mischief, wouldn't you say?"

"Sure would." He gasped as the young woman jammed an elbow into his stomach.

The cop shoved Agent Foster against the wall and tried again to lock the cuffs on her wrists.

Then Agent McGrath made a terrible mistake.

"Take your hands off her, fucking nigger bastard."

All movement in the office ceased. There was a moment of dead silence.

"Special Agent McGrath," Lorcan intoned, "you just ended your career as a G-man."

Agent Foster was sobbing hysterically now, all fight gone out of her.

McGrath had collapsed as the enormity of his failure penetrated his thick, shanty-Irish skull. The cops had to help him walk out of the office.

"I'll be down later to fill out a complaint, Sergeant."

"Yes, sir, Mr. Flynn, sir." The cop seemed undismayed by the racial slur. He realized what the young creep had done to himself.

Lorcan was not finished. He dialed Channel 4. "Cindi, I have a story for you. The Chicago police just arrested two FBI agents on the charge of trespassing in my office. I refused to answer their questions unless they spoke to my lawyer first. They refused to leave. I summoned the police, who asked them to leave and then arrested them. There was an altercation." He glanced at Mary Murray, who was still smiling. "Considerable damage was done to my office, and the male agent called the arresting officer a black bastard, a 'fucking nigger bastard' to be precise. . . . I figured you might like it. . . . Naturally I'll go on camera. . . . Thanks, Cindi."

"That'll be the end of them, won't it, Lorcan?" Mary Murray began to pick up the pieces of the broken vases.

"It will indeed."

Lorcan lifted his Madonna. Fortunately, bronze didn't break.

Still high on the heat of battle, Lorcan charged into his inner office and reached for the phone to call Larry yet again.

"Dear God, Lorcan." Larry sighed. "They ran into a juggernaut, didn't they?"

"It'll be on Channel 4 news tonight. We'll throw Maynard and Donny for a big loss."

"They'll be permanent enemies, Lorcan."

"So what? They are anyway. They'd cut open my chest cavity and eat my still-beating heart if it would earn them thirty seconds on the Ten O'clock News."

"You're absolutely right."

"Get them before they get you."

"In dealing with the U.S. government, that's a reasonable assumption . . . you've been careful so far. Continue to be careful on camera and at the station."

"Sure."

"I'll be there just to make sure."

Lorcan hadn't expected that.

"Good idea."

One last call before he tried to calm down and glance over a few more pages of galleys before he went over to the police station.

Next he dialed Dinny Rooney. Dinny picked up on the second ring and listened without comment to Lorcan's story.

"Yeah," he said when Lorcan was finished. "I bet the guys had a good time. They hate those arrogant FBI fuckers." Of course Dinny would view the whole event from a cop's perspective.

"We'll string out the fun for them."

"I don't imagine they'll continue the tail. We'll watch you just in case."

"Thanks, Dinny."

Lorcan wondered briefly if he should tell Dinny about Agent Foster's question about Cindi. He decided there was no good reason to do that.

"Yeah. One last thing, Lorcan. Hank doesn't have any dirt on you, does he? Like out of the past?"

"Nothing, Din, absolutely nothing."

After he had hung up, Lorcan stared at the galleys, searching for a lingering memory. He couldn't find it.

He tried another call to Rome. Padre Eduardo was still on a papal mission. No, the voice at the other end of the line did not know when he would return.

Lorcan rose from his desk to put on his overcoat. That's when he remembered.

It was the tone in Hank's voice when he had warned him about the statute of limitations. The tone had seemed strange then. Almost as if it were an accusation. With his coat half on, half off, Lorcan slumped back in his leather chair.

Dear God, they wouldn't try to accuse me of murder, would they?

Then Lorcan James Flynn had an even more terrible thought: *I was delirious that night. I might have done almost anything. Including murder.*

3

"Jaysus, Lorcan, I'm worried about this frigging dinner."

"Who is calling, please?" He put his hand over the phone and winked at the delightfully undressed Cindi Horton. "My mad daughter-in-law."

Cindi, still happy over her scoop on the arrest of the FBI agents, grinned back at him.

" 'Tis meself, who else would it be at this bloody hour of the night?"

Maeve was in one of her hyper/hyper states, a condition that amused her husband.

Everything she did amused Patrick Michael Flynn II, M.D., the more outrageous the better. Probably that was the reason that Maeve was so often outrageous.

Well, if Paddy—Maeve's nickname for her husband had become official for the rest of the family when she was around—was the descendant of a father and a grandfather who married passive-aggressive women, at least he himself had not made the same mistake.

"What is your name again, young woman?" His eyes roamed over Cindi as she talked. She turned away shyly.

"I'll not listen to your guff, Old Fella. I'm trying to tell you that I'm worried about the dinner with your old flame from Long Island."

He almost asked what old flame and then decided that such a question would not amuse Cindi.

"What's the problem, Maeve?"

"The proper arrangements for driving her to the Cafe Twenty-one."

"Can't she take a cab?"

"Jaysus, Lorcan, she's marrying into our family, we gotta treat her right."

"Her *son* is marrying into our family, Maeve."

"Isn't that what I was saying? Sure, can't you have one of your frigging limousines pick her up?"

"Sure, why not?"

"Would you ever mind doing it this way?" Maeve was now wheedling him, the warrior queen turned fishwife. "Could you not pick up poor Robbie and then the two of you collect his mother at the Allerton?"

The Allerton? A nice place with a fine restaurant, but hardly a luxury hotel. Kind of far from the Chicago Hilton, where her meeting was. But then she had always been careful with a dollar, hadn't she? Another bit of memory clicked into place.

"If you think that best, Maeve. You're the boss."

I must get rid of you, Maeve. I'm losing my mind.

"Promise you'll act right."

"When haven't I?" His other hand traced a path to Cindi's loins. She arched her back gratefully.

"This is different."

"I promise."

"Thanks, Old Fella." She chortled. "Sorry for calling so late, but you have nothing to do at this hour of night, do you?"

"Nothing at all."

Cindi tried to maintain the pretense that she was still posing for a statue.

Lorcan quickly disabused her of that notion.

Later, when he had soothed her into a satisfied sleep, he continued to sit up in the darkened bedroom, listening to the distant traffic on Lake Shore Drive.

He was indeed a violent man, violent and angry. The violence in his office earlier in the day had made him positively high, just as he had once gotten high on the thrill of battle in Korea. But even in Korea he hadn't the heart to pursue an enemy to the death so long as he'd disarmed him. For years he had taken that as a sign of an essentially passive nature, but the good Doctor Murphy had disabused him of that myth once and for all. The propensity for violence was there, all right, right beside his propensity for tenderness.

Could it be possible that under certain circumstances he could be capable of murder?

For the first time in his life, Lorcan was not confident that he could say no.

4

All this focus on the past led Lorcan to try to remember the first time he'd ever met Maura Meehan. She'd been leaning on a baseball bat, drinking a can of beer.

Her pose, her red and gray uniform, her cap—all said she was a softball player. But even in the baggy uniform, her shapely figure was clear.

"What are you?" Lorcan asked. "Bat boy? Mascot?"

"Second baseman," she replied.

Lorcan was incredulous. "Why?" he couldn't help but ask.

She cupped the beer can in her hands. "Must be kind of good at it if they let me play, huh?"

"I would think so." What else could he say?

She was sweating, her face was dirty, her uniform ragged, her cleated shoes badly scuffed. She was a real, serious softball player. Yet there was a whiff of scent on her, and her brown ponytail was tied with a red and gray ribbon.

She was tall, at least five nine, maybe a half inch more, and shapely. Her face was full, even round. Not beautiful maybe, but haunting. She was serenely self-confident. From the start, Lorcan knew he'd never met anyone like her before.

"Do you object to girl softball players?" she asked. Somehow she made it sound like a genuine question instead of deliberate banter.

"Not if they're good at it."

She lifted her shoulders ever so slightly, giving him a brief hint of luxurious bosom. "They say I'm all right."

"In many different ways."

She raised an eyebrow. "Oh?"

"I'm Lorcan Flynn."

"Lorcan James Frances Flynn. The war hero. I know." She was not making fun of him, merely stating facts.

"No hero."

"Two DFCs."

"Who told you?"

"Your kid brother, Ed, who adores you."

"I'll try to remember that. You do have a name, don't you?"

"Maura Anne." She placed the beer can carefully on the Grand Beach park bench—at the corner of Perkins and Royal—and began to swing her bat in a most businesslike fashion.

"Maura Anne with no last name?"

"Maura Anne Meehan." She tilted her head over the bat, a hint of defiance, as if to say, *Do you want to make something out of who I am?*

The game started. She was the leadoff batter. She hit the first pitch, a solid ground ball between short and third. Then she raced down the first-base line at an alarming speed.

"Nice hit," Lorcan yelled.

She tipped her cap in solemn response.

"You got more conversation out of her in a few minutes," Jeff Carey murmured, "than the rest of us have all summer. She plays ball with us and ignores us the rest of the time."

"Must be my Air Force windbreaker."

The next two hitters popped up.

"You're the batter," Jeff told him. "Let's see you bring her home."

"Not a bad idea," Lorcan replied. He was already in love.

Lorcan doubled to right center. The third-base coach waved Maura Meehan home, probably a mistake. Lorcan pulled up at center.

Lorcan watched Maura charge down the third-base line, wondering whether she would try to knock over the Grand Beach catcher. Instead, as the short center's relay raced her to the plate, she slid in and hooked the corner of the plate with her cleated shoe.

Everyone cheered.

"Nice hit," she yelled at Lorcan as she dusted off her trousers.

He tipped his cap to her just as she had to him.

Their team won the game. Lorcan couldn't remember by how much. But he did recall that Maura got a hit each time she went to bat.

"I'd like to know you better, Maura Meehan," Lorcan said as she was unlacing her cleats.

She glanced up and considered him carefully with her astonishingly soft brown eyes. "Would you?"

"Yes."

She stopped her work with the shoelaces to give Lorcan her full attention. "I might like that too," she said cautiously, her eyes never moving from his face.

"A movie tonight?"

"A date with a second baseman?"

"Not at all."

A frown crossed her smooth, high forehead. "Oh?"

"With a leadoff girl."

She smiled then. Maura Anne Meehan didn't smile much, but, when she did, she lit up the whole world.

"All right," she said simply. "I'd like that."

Lorcan's eyes grew moist as he remembered that long-ago day. How could he have let a woman like Maura Anne Meehan get away from him?

5

"I have news about your friend Moire Halinan, as she calls herself now." Dinny Rooney's pink face was expressionless. "She's a strange one, Lorcan. Impressive and strange."

"Good news and bad news?"

An English priest had called from Rome to tell him that his message had been relayed to "Father President" and that "Father President" would be in touch with him as soon as possible.

"I guess, though I'm not sure which is which. You'll have to figure it out yourself."

"Let's have it," Lorcan said.

"First, she's an upstanding citizen of Huntington, Long Island, active in civic affairs and faintly liberal Democratic politics, a bit to the left of Geraldine Ferraro."

"No more left than we are."

"No more left than Rich Daley, huh?" Dennis Rooney smiled enigmatically. Every white cop in town and many of the black cops would vote for the State's Attorney next week. "Here's a few newspaper clippings. They like to put her picture in the local paper, understandably, I guess." He passed a stack of copies across the desk to Lorcan. "She runs a classy, well-respected union firm and is admired by her employees. No current or remembered past romantic links. Rejects passes and propositions firmly and definitively. Says she will not consider remarriage till her younger child is raised. The kid's in college now. . . ."

"I see."

The pictures of Moire Halinan were of a beautiful woman he might have once known. It was difficult to link her with the images that had flooded back into his memory last night when he began his story of her in the memoir. *Why must we grow old?* he wondered. *Why must we forget our first loves?*

In one of the pictures, a charity swim meet, Moire was wearing a swimsuit that suggested her figure had resisted the assaults of time. Lorcan could not take his eyes off the picture.

"Strictly a legitimate and respectable upper-middle-class suburban matron," Dennis Rooney commented. "Better-looking than most, and tougher emotionally than most. Nothing unusual, right?"

"You picked up your information in a hurry."

"Could be that one of my sources was impressed by her."

"Natural enough." Lorcan placed the clippings on his desk.

"The other side of the coin is that we found the adoption records. She is, according to the records, the daughter of

Teresa and John Meehan, deceased cousins allegedly of old
Joe Meehan. She was born in Lakeland, Florida, on June
14, 1937. So she was seventeen the summer you knew her,
right?"

"I thought it was eighteen. It doesn't matter."

"There's only one thing wrong."

"That is?"

"The records are counterfeit."

"What?"

"There's no record in Lakeland of any such birth. The
photostats of her birth certificate are copies of a carefully
constructed fake, for which there is no counterpart in the
Lakeland vital statistics office. Someone went to a lot of
trouble to give her a Meehan family link which probably
didn't exist."

"Why would anyone do that?"

"Beats me. All the possible perpetrators are either un-
known or dead or possibly both. I can't see a way to find
out."

"I told you she was evasive about her background.
Maybe she didn't know."

"Or maybe she did know and didn't want to talk about
it. . . . You heard that she inherited money from the Meehans at the time of their death, didn't you?"

"Yes."

"That's what she's told her family and friends in Long
Island. Her alleged parents were killed in an auto accident
while on a vacation in California. Joe Meehan and his wife
adopted her. When they died they left money in their will for
her, money that her parents had left to the Meehans to
provide for Maura. That's how she managed to graduate
from Hunter College. Does the story sound reasonable?"

"Not if you stop to think about it. Not unless her parents
were planning to die."

"Precisely. It's the kind of story you hear at a party and
you don't question—not unless you're a suspicious cop.
Anyway, there was no mention of her in Joe Meehan's will.
All the money went to the Justine Fathers."

"To the Justines!"

"Right."

"It doesn't follow that she didn't believe the story. The question now is where the money came from."

"Yeah. Incidentally"—he passed a copy of a document, dirty and gray, across the desk to Lorcan—"here's her parents' death certificate—Alameda County, California, January 10, 1940."

Lorcan glanced at it. "Fake?"

"You bet."

They were both silent for a moment.

"Could Tim Meehan, Joe's war hero brother, have been her father?"

"I thought about that. In 1937, when she is alleged to have been born, Tim was sixteen years old and a student at Delasalle High School. It's not impossible, but unlikely."

"Unless she was born several years later."

"Did she seem to be fourteen or fifteen to you that summer?"

He hesitated, trying to remember.

"At times she seemed wise enough to be much older than her eighteen or nineteen years. Other times she was just a kid. Not a fourteen-year-old, though."

"It's a possibility to check out. I'm not sure we can find out. Let's see, Tim was born in 1920. That would make him a little under seventy today. There should be some of his classmates from D still around. We'll find out if he had a way with the girls back then. Later on he certainly had that reputation."

"What do you make of it, Dinny?"

"Craziest thing ever. Whole new mystery within a mystery, know what I mean?"

"Yeah."

"You'll be seeing her soon?"

"Tonight. At the Cafe Twenty-one East, with my family. She's in town for a trade show."

"I dunno, Lorcan. You're the boss. Logically there may be no connection between her mysterious origins and the explosion back in '54. Yet two mysteries, kind of at the same place and time, look suspicious to me."

"Can you find out more about her?"

"I can try. Won't be as easy as this stuff." He gestured at

the clippings from Long Island papers. "No promises.
. . . We're not making any progress with Henrietta Crawford."

"Why not?"

"The first time I talked to her on the phone she said that
she tried her best at the time of the funeral and no one
wanted to listen to her. Now, she says, she isn't interested
anymore."

"Yeah?"

"She added that the government had hidden the truth
then and would continue to hide. Sounded bitter."

"She say which kind of government?"

"Hung up on me when I asked her. Hangs up now when
I call her. I think she won't change her mind. I think we'd
better leave her alone. Like I say, it will be hard from here
on in."

"I understand." Lorcan rose from his desk chair. "I want
no stone unturned."

Dinny Rooney grimaced at the cliché. "Like I said before,
no matter what worms might lurk under them?"

"No matter what worms might lurk under them."

Dinny nodded. "You're the boss."

6

Dinny's visit brought up more thoughts of the past.
Lorcan remembered how much his family had dis-
approved of that first date with Maura Anne Meehan. Lorcan had been twenty-three at the time. He was a major in the
Air Force reserve with a hundred combat missions under his
belt, yet his parents believed they could tell him whom to
date.

"She's cheap and common," Mom said. "A tomboy.
Trash."

"You'd be making a real mistake getting involved with her," Dad warned.

Hank was no better. "She puts out," he sneered. "If that's what you're looking for, you can get it there. I don't imagine she'll be as good as your Japanese whores."

Only Eileen was on his side. "I think she's neat," nine-year-old Eileen protested. "All the kids say she's fun."

"You don't know what you're talking about, kid," her dad dismissed her. "If you act like that bimbo when you're her age, I'll tan your behind."

Ed did not look up from the book he was reading.

It was a typical conversation in the Flynn household at that time. Lorcan came out of the Air Force to find his mother more querulous, his father more irritable—if that was possible—Hank more mean-spirited, Ed more bookish, and little Eileen more rebellious.

Lorcan was tired of these dynamics. Except for Eileen, he was tired of the personalities. He could hardly wait to escape through college. In the meantime he did his best to keep silent. But that night he was pushed to the limit.

"I didn't have any Japanese whores, and the guys on the softball team tell me the exact opposite, Hank. I'm taking her to the movies and that's that."

His mother left the room in tears.

"You stupid little bastard," his father exploded at Lorcan. "Now look what you've done to your mother."

"Look what Mom's done to yourself," Lorcan fired back. "I'm old enough to make my own decisions."

"You're not old enough to know shit from Shinola."

"I'm old enough to have flown a hundred combat missions while you sat behind a desk during your war." With that, Lorcan stormed out of the house.

They fought the rest of the summer about Maura. The scenario changed after Lorcan brought her to the house a couple of times. His father did a turnabout and flirted with her—as he did with almost all visitors who wore skirts. Lorcan's mother pointedly ignored her. Maura must have been sensitive to the reception she received at the Flynns', but if she was, she said nothing about it. Occasionally she would smile at one of Pat's tasteless efforts at gallantry.

Whatever her thoughts, she never said a word to Lorcan about them.

The night of their first date, Maura wanted to walk to the theater on Franklin Street, so she and Lorcan left his secondhand Studebaker in the driveway at Long Beach. She was wearing a modest apricot-colored sundress and matching ribbon. Her legs, now revealed as sensational, were brown and bare; on her feet were businesslike sandals, designed for beach walking. At the ball field she might have seemed a tomboy. Now she was a lovely young woman. Lorcan observed that she had slender hips, a tiny waist, and marvelous breasts, a Greek statue in a sundress perhaps, although the Greek models had more ample rear ends.

Maura Anne Meehan did not ask Lorcan about Korea or Japan or about his plans for Notre Dame. Nor did they discuss Saint Xavier College or her mysterious past—everyone in Long Beach seemed to know that there was something unusual about her background. Rather, they talked about books. They both were, they discovered early and to their mutual delight, addicted readers.

The old section of the beach area, where Long Beach merges into Michigan City, dates back almost to the Civil War. The old homes are small and close together, a hodgepodge of different styles and no style at all. Now they say that Sheridan Beach, as it is now called, is considered picturesque. Then it seemed merely rundown, dilapidated. Lorcan recalled vivid memories of them walking down the streets of Sheridan Beach, hand in hand, bathed in red and gold sunlight, as they talked about books they both had read.

They discussed the current picks avidly. Forty years later, Lorcan couldn't name a single one, but he knew their passion had been sincere. No doubt they covered *The Adventures of Augie March* by Saul Bellow, which Lorcan hadn't liked, *Battle Cry, The Light in the Forest, The Bridges at Toko-Ri,* Faulkner's *A Fable,* which neither of them could understand.

What Lorcan did remember was the movie they saw their first night together. For him Audrey Hepburn in *Roman Holiday* would always mean Maura.

They walked all the way back to their homes on the

deserted beach under a three-quarters moon, hand in hand. For much of the walk they were quiet, content with each other's presence and the touch of their hands, happy with the certainty that they were both falling in love.

"You'll be fine, Lorcan James Flynn," Maura said at last, breaking the silence. "Don't worry." Her fingers touched his cheek in an airy caress.

"If you say so, Maura Anne Meehan. If you say so."

"These are bad times, but they'll go away."

No one had said that to Lorcan since his return, yet instantly he recognized them as the words he needed to hear.

"I hope so," he said at last.

Then she kissed him, a firm, determined, unabashed kiss—what one would expect from a firm, determined, unabashed woman.

"Wow," was all Lorcan could manage.

"First time," Maura said proudly.

"First time you've been kissed?" Lorcan could hardly believe it.

"Of course not. I've been kissed by boys a lot of times. That was the first time I kissed a boy. Except you're a man, not a boy. Well, you're a mixture of both, which makes you cute."

In response, Lorcan kissed her. And Maura kissed back.

So the love affair started under the light of a three-quarters moon on Duneland Beach in the summer of 1954.

The summer was idyllic until its culmination. It seemed impossible that such a blissful season could end so abruptly and inauspiciously, but by its end Lorcan was in St. Anthony's Hospital and Maura was attending a funeral, then heading for New York. They hadn't seen or spoken to each other since.

How could it have ended thus? Although they'd never spoken of it, Lorcan felt that a marriage between them was understood. It was only a matter of time. Now Lorcan regretted not having said more. If only he could go back. Turn back the clock. He would have handled those events of late summer so differently.

7

"Y ou resented your father's attentions to your sweetheart?" Doctor Murphy was in top form.

"There was something vile about his approach to her, snide, insinuating."

"Sexual?"

"He seemed to be implying that I was a kid and he was a real man and that she would find what she was looking for in him and not in me."

"I see. . . . How did she react?"

"Maura was unfailingly polite. She didn't encourage his phony gallantry. Neither did she discourage it. Her reactions were always difficult to read, even on the softball field."

"Did you speak to her about your father?"

"No."

"Why not?"

"It didn't seem worth mentioning when I was with her alone. There was so much else to talk about."

"Yet on several occasions you were close to striking your father."

"Yes. . . . There was nothing Maura could do to stop him."

"I understand. . . . Does your son, do you think, object to your flirtation with his wife?"

Lorcan felt as if a Zulu warrior had implanted a spear in his belly.

"What?"

"I have been led to believe by your remarks that you flirt outrageously with her."

"No way!"

"You tolerate her flirtation with you. It's the same thing isn't it?"

"It's not flirtation. . . ."

"Maybe that's what your father thought?"

"It's different."

"How?"

"I don't demean Paddy, uh, Patrick."

"Maybe he thinks differently."

"I doubt it."

"Have you asked him?"

"No!"

"We tend to imitate behavior patterns across generational lines, Lorcan."

"I'll ask him to make sure."

"Relationships between sexes within families are intricate and complex and have different meanings in the contexts of different family cultures."

"I'm not trying to take Maeve away from Paddy. I couldn't if I wanted to."

"Would not your father have said the same thing?"

"He might have said it, but he would not have meant it. He did want to take her away from me. In the end he did."

"You're blaming him for your loss of her."

"Yes, goddamn it!"

"What proof do you have?"

"It was what he wanted to do. When I was sick, somehow he did it."

"He prevented you from phoning her when you recovered?"

"No," Lorcan admitted lamely. "I guess not. Funny, I never thought of phoning her. Probably because she didn't write me or phone me when I was sick. I assumed she lost interest."

"That doesn't sound like a very bold lover to me."

"I wanted to forget about the summer and continue with my life."

"What was there to forget, other than the tragedy of the home explosion?"

He clapped his hand to his forehead. "I can't remember."

"That suggests that you did an excellent job of forgetting, doesn't it?"

I displeased my client because I did not show proper interest either in his two memoir segments about his former sweetheart or in the pictures of the woman that his investigator (a good friend, I note, of Mike the Cop and hence of integrity beyond question) had collected.

She is certainly a striking woman. I should look that way when I am her age—which is what I am now!

She does not look like a romantic in these pictures. Quite steely-eyed and realistic, I would judge. She has made her own way in the world successfully without parents and eventually without a husband. Obviously she experiences no need to remarry or she would have done so.

A husband, particularly one as much a bull in the china shop as my patient, would probably disturb the tranquil and orderly private existence she has constructed for herself. Men, she might well feel, and not without some reason, are messy.

On the other hand, someone who played second base on a boys' softball team in 1954 had to have a certain amount of romantic impulses in her character.

She and I must have crossed paths at the dances and the beach parties in those days. I can't quite recall her even when I look at her pictures, save for a vague impression of brown ponytail and red ribbon.

Red and gray ribbon; and pain in her eyes.

8

Moire was not in the lobby of the Allerton Hotel. Lorcan had dashed in from the limo, shivering with the subzero cold, and run up the stairs. Blowing on his fingers, he glanced around the second-floor lobby, gray walls, art deco mirrors, comfortable chairs, more charm than hotels which charged twice as much. A nice place, indeed; yet no Moire. He saw no one who looked remotely like her.

The Maura of 1954 was punctual.

Had she run away again?

He began to search for the public phones.

Maeve had called him earlier in "a great, terrible dither." Everything had to be rearranged because Rob had a late-afternoon conference. "Would you pick herself up first and then your man over at Arthur Andersen?"

"It does not seem to be an insurmountable problem, Maeve. Remember that we're dealing with a middle-class matron from the suburbs, not a reigning monarch. She may just possibly be out of her class in a limousine and the Twenty-one East."

"Haven't I seen her picture, Old Fella? And isn't the fear on me that we'll be out of our class?"

"Maevie, you'll never be out of your class."

He looked around the lobby once more. Still no sign of his "date." He would call her room before he called Maeve. He strode over to the reception desk to ask where the house phone was.

"Lorcan?" A soft voice by his shoulder, like a breeze rustling trees after a summer storm has ended.

"Moire?" She had been standing next to him all the time, perhaps laughing to herself at his frantic search.

She brushed his lips with her own. "You seem to have recovered nicely from your illness."

"Illness?"

"Meningitis, wasn't it?"

She was disappointing, as he feared she would be, an ordinary woman, bundled up in a long tan down coat, a big plaid scarf, and a matching ski cap pulled down over her ears. Her face beneath the cap was a mostly unlined face certainly, but not that of a striking beauty.

"It's been a long time, Moire."

"It has."

"Rob had a meeting. We'll pick him up on the way to the restaurant."

"Fine."

"The car is outside." He took her arm and led her down the steps to the ground floor. "You didn't need to bundle up like that. We'll be delivered right to the door of the restaurant."

"I've just walked back from the Hilton. I've never been so cold in all my life. I'd forgotten what Chicago winters were like."

"All the way from the Hilton?"

"There's no pool in this hotel. I figured that I'd better get some exercise so I could eat the food at your fine restaurant with less of a guilty conscience."

The driver opened the door of the limo for them. Lorcan ushered her in.

"I have a pool at my house. You're welcome to use that anytime you happen to be in Chicago."

"I'm afraid that would prove a serious temptation for me. I hate meetings where I can't swim."

What did she mean by "temptation"?

Dummy—all she meant was that she would be tempted to accept my hospitality.

"Or you could use the pool at the East Bank Club on my account. It's an interesting place."

"I've been there; it's the largest singles bar in the world."

She pulled off her ski cap as the car started and shook her short brown hair, tinged with gray.

Lorcan realized that his first evaluation had been inadequate. Her face was as arresting as it had ever been—calm, elegant, a face from a renaissance painting, with mysterious, gentle brown eyes and touched by the slightest hint of makeup. You had to study that face a bit to recognize how stunning it was. Despite its apparent deviation from the ordinary norms of beauty, and despite the hints of soft flesh around her neck, once you had given yourself over to meditating on the magic of her face, you found yourself constrained to interpret it as beautiful in its entirety, if not in all its details.

"You didn't answer my letters." She put the ski cap in her pocket.

"Letters, Moire? When did you write? The mail delivery in Chicago has been bad for the last few days because of the tieup at O'Hare from the blizzard."

"I mean the letters I wrote in September and October of 1954." She considered him candidly, as she had done often that summer.

"I never received them, Moire. Never." His gut knotted. "I would have certainly replied. I wondered why you didn't call or write."

"I called four or five times my first week in New York. Your mother said you were too sick to talk and she would give you the message. You could return the call, she said, when you felt better. She was insistent the last time that you would call me. So I prayed for you."

"They never told me, Moire. As God is my witness they never told me you called or gave me your letters."

"You don't have to swear an oath for me, Lorcan. I'll accept your word."

"But why . . ."

"Hush." Her gloved hand touched his. "It was done so long ago."

"Our lives might have been different."

"And our two beautiful children would not be marrying one another."

She had been more serene than most in 1954. Now serenity had captured her soul. "You accept it easily, Moire."

"Not so easily, Lorcan. I am as cross as you are. What good does it do to let anger dominate you?"

"I was sorry to hear about your husband's death."

"Thank you, Lorcan. Do not be too sad. We were happy together. No true happiness is ever lost permanently."

The limousine crept south slowly, trapped in an icy Michigan Avenue rush hour. If they were late for supper Maeve would have a fit.

"Our happiness that summer?"

"It, too, will last forever in the mind of God. . . . I hope you don't think I've become a pious old woman. Although I really believe what I said, I'm not at all devout."

"We have a priest in Chicago—rector at the Cathedral as a matter of fact—who compares God to a teenage girl."

"This priest I should like to meet."

"I'm sorry," he said, changing the subject. "I didn't explain the plan to you. We're picking your son up next. My daughter-in-law, Mad Maeve, is in a dither because we weren't able to fetch him first. She'll be in a worse dither if we're late."

"You did explain. . . . That young woman I have talked with on the phone. I can hardly wait to meet her."

There was an awkward pause. Lorcan's brain raced furiously. Who had confiscated the letters? His father probably, goddamn him.

"You're separated from your wife?" she asked politely. "I'm sorry to hear that."

"Divorced and annulled, against my wishes. Dorothy didn't want to be married anymore. You'll meet her at lunch tomorrow. Maeve didn't think it would be good for the two of us to be at the same table. It will be hard enough during the wedding in April. I'm afraid she doesn't much like me."

"I hardly know what to say." She weighed her words judiciously, as he suspected she always did. "You would be too much of a challenge for many women, Lorcan. That was clear even thirty-five years ago. Not that you would make explicit demands on them to keep up with you. Quite the contrary. They would make the demands on themselves in your name."

"That's what my shrink says."

"Shrink?"

"Psychiatrist, psychoanalyst. One Mary Kathleen Murphy, M.D."

"She's one of the Ryans, isn't she? Just my age? Very able, I would imagine?"

"Very. Her brother is the Cathedral rector I spoke about. Johnny—or Blackie as they call him."

"I remember him from the Dunes. Cute little dickens."

"That's what most women say."

"I like your Marie. She's a perfect match for my Rob. Sweet and gentle and smart."

"I like him too. I'm sure they'll be happy. They'll both always be innocents, God bless them."

"God protect them."

The limo pulled up to 33 West Monroe. Rob bounded out and into the car. He and his mother embraced.

Lorcan, conscious that his hands were sweating, tried to order his thoughts. His sweetheart of long ago had matured into a wise and gracious woman, almost too imperturbable. On the other hand there were hints of wit that she had not displayed in 1954.

Fortunately for all their sakes and for the peace of mind of that promising young neonatologist, the three of them arrived at the 21 East Hotel on time.

They rode up the elevator to the second-floor café. "It's small," Lorcan apologized, "but it has a charming view of Rush Street and Bellevue Place and the food is superb."

"I'm sure it will be wonderful. Your wee Irishwoman would not have chosen anything else."

Rob dashed ahead of them to peek into the dining room in hopes that his love was already there.

Lorcan helped Moire off with her coat at the check booth near the elevator. It took great self-restraint not to gasp.

Moire Halinan was dazzling. She wore a dark brown suit with a beige turtleneck sweater, a small string of pearls around her neck outside the sweater, and gold swirls as earrings. No other jewelry. She needed little adornment and knew it.

"More beautiful than ever, Moire," he whispered, wanting to kiss the back of her neck.

"Thank you, Lorcan." She flushed at his compliment.

"You haven't changed much either. Still the winsome mix of boy and man. The picture on the cover of *Time* didn't do you justice."

He kissed the back of her neck.

"My," she said, turning away, still glowing. "More romantic than you used to be."

She seemed neither pleased nor displeased.

"Couldn't resist it." He tried to laugh easily. "You're so lovely."

"Mostly genetic luck and a couple of unintentional good habits. A few years ago my daughter got on my case. Obligation to take care of what God had given. I'm a pushover for any appeal to God, as you've guessed already. So now I'm a physical-fitness freak like women a couple of decades younger than I am."

"I hope you keep it up."

"Oh, I will. I'm addicted now. I feel so much better at the end of a day when I've worked out."

"As I said, you're welcome to the pool and Nautilus at my house anytime you're in Chicago."

They were at the entrance to the restaurant. She turned to inspect his face. He smiled at her.

"You mean that, don't you, Lorcan? It's not a pro forma invitation, is it?"

"Certainly not."

"How about tomorrow? Your delightful daughter-in-law promised me she would show me your house."

"Did she now? Ah, the woman will be the death of me, won't she ever? . . . Sure, Moire. I'd be delighted."

"Good evening, Mr. Flynn." The maître d' welcomed him with a handshake. "Good evening, madam. Mr. Podesta is in California at the present; he said to give you his greetings. He hopes that you and your party enjoy the dinner."

"I'm sure we will. Give my best to Bob. Tell him I'm sorry we missed him."

"Your party is already here. They've just arrived. You're at the corner table by the windows."

If the little scene with the maître d' impressed Moire, she did not show it. Probably she expected that he would receive such greetings from owners of hotels. Maybe she would have been surprised if there had been no such greetings.

They entered the dining room. The others rose enthusiastically, Rob's arm around Marie. Maeve's eyes bulged when she saw Moire.

Lorcan felt every eye in the dining room turn to watch him and his companion—mostly, his companion. Moire herself seemed immune to the attention, either unaware of it or, more likely, accustomed to it.

Maeve had arranged the seating so he was on one side of Moire and Paddy on the other side, with Maeve herself directly across the table from her. Outside, an occasional pedestrian hurried down Bellevue or Rush, eager to find shelter from the cold.

"Ah, sure," Maeve began, her brogue thicker than usual, "won't you be after comparing this little place with all your grand restaurants in New York and us not able to compete with them at all, at all?"

"Huntington is not Manhattan, Maeve, my dear." Moire smiled and illumined the whole dining room. "It's simply a suburban American town. I'm fortunate to make it to Midtown a couple of times a year. I'm afraid that my suburban manners will embarrass you sophisticated urbanites."

Maeve's facial expression changed five or six times in less than a second—and raced through as many shades of red. "Ah, sure, isn't yourself that must have swallowed the Blarney stone instead of merely kissing it?"

"I'm afraid I've never been to Ireland." Moire was solemn, serious again. "I hope to go there after my daughter graduates, with her if she'll have me."

"The Irish don't have to kiss the stone," Paddy observed, "to be full of blarney."

"That they don't," Lorcan concurred. "And that includes Irish-Americans, even if they live in New York instead of Chicago where they belong."

"It's always nice to come here," Moire agreed, betraying nothing.

Today or tomorrow he would have to ask her about many, many things. She must remember what happened the night of the explosion. He would have to find out what she knew—and what she knew about her own origins.

Maeve decided tentatively that she liked Lorcan's old sweetheart. Shrewd fishwife that she was, however, she wanted to be certain. So, over the white wine and the salad (with house dressing), Lorcan's daughter-in-law administered her quiz. How did Moire earn her living, what were her future plans, did she go to church, what books did she read, did she approve of psychotherapy, how often did she come to Chicago, what kind of home did she live in, what were her attitudes toward feminism, did she like Woody Allen films, did she care about the National Football League?

Maeve may have felt that her quiz was subtle and indirect. In reality her questions were as blunt and direct as a sex survey.

Thus she asked, "I suppose a gorgeous person like yourself would have all kinds of gentleman friends, wouldn't you now?"

Lorcan winced. Paddy grinned. Marie and Rob smiled gently.

"I wish I could say that I did, dear." Moire was undisturbed. "Admirers are pleasant until they think they have the right to become importune. I'm afraid I've earned a reputation for dismissing them at that point. Such a reputation discourages others."

"Sure, you wouldn't be opposed to them altogether, now would you?"

"Not the right one."

Lorcan waited for the smallest sign that she had glanced at him. Alas, there was none.

"And you're in the printing business?"

"Typesetting and layouts actually." She reached in her purse and removed a pack of business cards. "Special designs for quality advertising and similar tasks. Mostly done by computers now . . . that's what the meetings this year are about. Soon all my staff will be able to work at home."

She passed the cards around the table.

The cards were foldovers, light blue with dark blue type: HALINAN DESIGN.

"Very elegant."

"Show them your personal card, Mom," Rob spoke up eagerly. "That's really sensational."

"Rob!" She was mildly flustered, quite mildly.

"Please, Moire," her future daughter-in-law begged. "It's wonderful, and poor Maevie will die of curiosity if you don't."

The second set of cards were off-white, her name, HALI-NAN DESIGN, and business phone on front, and a color photo on the inside fold—Moire radiant in an off-the-shoulder evening gown.

"Glory be to God!" Maeve erupted. She was mortified by her outburst but Moire did not give her time to be embarrassed.

"I'm afraid I've become vain as I've turned into an old woman. . . . Actually it's a sample I use to show clients the kind of work we can do for them. I don't have the nerve to give it to more than a few friends."

Lorcan put his card in his wallet. He wished for an enlargement.

Maeve propped her picture up against her coffee cup and turned to questions about Moire's political attitudes. When she finally paused for breath, the older woman launched a counteroffensive. "You're a medical doctor, like your husband, are you not?"

"I am." Maeve's green eyes glittered suspiciously.

"A psychiatrist too?"

"Ah, no, I'm not cut out for that kind of work at all, at all. I'm one of your neonatologists. I take care of the wee, wee ones."

"How exciting!"

" 'Tis fun, all right enough. . . . Now why would you be after asking?"

"I was thinking"—Moire tasted a small sip of the Chardonnay—"that your wonderfully expressive face might disconcert a psychiatric patient and enchant the little children."

Paddy coughed and almost spat out a mouthful of wine. Lorcan grinned broadly. Even Rob took his eyes off Marie long enough to chuckle.

The Maeve knew she'd met her match. She reached across the table and squeezed Moire's hand.

"Sure, woman, now haven't you done me in altogether? The wee wee ones can't really see me Gypsy face, but they can hear me singing to them, which I do all the time."

"Will you sing one of your lullabies for us? Softly so it won't embarrass your celebrity father-in-law?"

Did she have the same grace in 1954? Lorcan wondered. *She must have. I was too inexperienced to notice.*

Maeve glanced at her husband and at Lorcan, seeking approval. Patrick smiled. Lorcan said, "Ah, now, woman, would I be after trying to stop you from entertaining our guest?"

So Mad Maeve sang, softly and shyly, two wonderful Gaelic tunes, the sort that would assure peaceful sleep for anyone who heard them. A couple of millennia of Celtic warmth absorbed their table. The people at the next table smiled their approval.

"They're so beautiful, Maevie," Marie said, tears in her eyes. "I hope when Rob and I have babies you'll teach them to me."

"All in good time, isn't it?" Maeve beamed contentedly.

Lorcan saw a tear or two in Moire's eyes.

"I've often thought," she murmured, "that the experience of cradling and being cradled is one of the clearest hints we have of what God is like. That's why the Christmas scene and Madonna art are so powerful."

The piety is new. She didn't like to attend Mass in the old days.

"Dad has a lovely bronze abstract Madonna in his office," Paddy said. "He's really not bad at sculpting. He's probably a better sculptor than he is a poet, though the poetry is good too."

Moire was melting hearts and loosening tongues. Patrick never complimented his father on his hobbies.

"I'd pretend I'm surprised by his renaissance activities." She said it with a perfectly straight face. "However, I did read the cover story in *Time*. I'd like to see the Madonna someday."

"I'm sure we could arrange that. . . . Rob, I want to ask

you about one of your mother's secret sins. Does she still play softball? The first time I met her, she was leaning on a softball bat and drinking beer from a can. Classic tomboy!"

"She sure does." Rob grinned proudly. "We try to keep it a secret because we're ashamed of it. She and my sister are on the same women's team. They won the park district championship last summer. 'The Halinan Type' they call it, red and gray uniforms. She still drinks beer too, corrupting the young."

"Only at the games, dear," his mother said amiably. "I'm afraid I've lost a step or two in thirty-five years, Lorcan. My eyes aren't as good as they used to be either, despite my bifocal contact lenses."

"Not Chicago indoor?" Lorcan asked.

"Twelve-inch. I'd rather play sixteen-inch—I could see the ball when it was pitched instead of guessing where it was."

Over the raspberries and cream—and Moire had, indeed, liked raspberries in 1954—Maeve led the discussion about plans for the next day. She and Marie and Moire would eat lunch with Dorothy in the Zodiac Room at Neiman-Marcus. Then Moire would return for her final meeting at the Hilton. Maeve would collect her at the hotel in "one of the Old Fella's limos, faith, doesn't he have a whole fleet of them?" and deliver her to the house on Astor Street. Lorcan would join them, drop Maeve off at Children's Memorial Hospital, and escort Moire to O'Hare.

"Sure we can't let the poor woman go up to that awful place by herself, can we now?"

"It might interfere with Dad's schedule." Paddy's eyes twinkled mischievously.

"I've taken cabs up there many times by myself," Moire insisted placidly. "There's no need to escort me."

"Don't we know you're able to provide for yourself?" the red-haired Gypsy woman insisted. "But aren't you after being almost family now? Don't worry, the Old Fella has nothing to do with his afternoon anyway except making more money, and he already has enough of that."

"Really, Lorcan." Moire turned to him. "It's not necessary."

"If you ride in one of my fleet of limos, woman, we make the arrangements."

She nodded in acceptance of his rules. "I won't try to break your rules. . . . You did mention your pool and exercise room." She hesitated. "But I wouldn't want to intrude."

"Ah, it would be no intrusion at all at all," Maeve insisted. "I'll collect you at the Hilton an hour earlier. 'Twill be no problem. I could do with a bit of a swim myself."

"Lorcan?"

"I'd be delighted to have you, Moire. I can show you the museum in which I live."

So it was arranged.

Lorcan found himself alone with Moire in the car which was to bring her back to the Allerton, another nice touch of Mad Maeve's. She was bundled up again, unlike Lorcan, who rarely wore overcoats if he could avoid them.

"It's a short walk," she had protested. "I could use the exercise after that sumptuous meal."

"The wind chill is forty-five below. Do you want me to be in even more trouble with my mad daughter-in-law?"

"She's an adorable young woman. Does your other daughter—"

"Elizabeth, Liz."

"Is she as good friends with her as Marie?"

"Co-conspirators."

"How wonderful. You have a family of which to be proud."

He wanted to say something about Dorothy and lunch tomorrow, to warn her, to defend Dorothy, to apologize, to explain Dorothy's dislike for Marie. No adequate words came into his head.

Instead he returned to her lost letters.

"When my mother died, she left a dozen or so cartons of pictures and souvenirs and memorabilia. I've been meaning to catalogue them. I'll search for the letters."

"Why, Lorcan? What good would it do?"

"I'd know what happened to them."

"Would it make you happy to be certain that your mother intercepted my love letters?"

"They were love letters?"

"Of course," she said promptly. "What else would they have been in those days? Can't you let the dead bury the dead?"

There were many questions to be asked and answered. But not tonight. Moire was tired. So was he.

"Did you not say that no happiness, once enjoyed, is ever lost?"

"I did. I also said it survives in the mind of God, not in our efforts to apportion guilt for the past."

"I will think about it."

He walked up the stairs to the Allerton lobby with her, and at the elevator door extended his right arm around her and kissed her, gently but firmly.

"You're dazzling, Moire."

"Thank you, Lorcan." She leaned against his arm for a moment—an appetizing hint that someday she might capitulate to him. "I worried about what you would be like. Foolish. You are as good and as kind as you always were."

"Thank you, Moire."

The moment ended. She slipped away. "See you tomorrow."

He looked at his watch. Tomorrow was only an hour away.

Later that night Lorcan had trouble falling asleep. His head was full of visions of the current-day Moire as well as recollections of the past. How could her letters have been kept from him? Who had intercepted them back in '54? Like everyone else—Rory, Hank—she seemed to want to forget the past.

Lorcan wondered how she found him now. Was he very different? Could she still find him attractive? As attractive as he still found her? That kiss in the lobby had been disquietingly ambivalent.

He struggled for memories of that softball championship game played the Sunday of Labor Day, 1954. He could picture Moire on second base. Breathing deeply, breathing deeply, she is triumphant and eager. Lorcan can't fathom whether or not he's made love to her.

His father is in the stands. So are Hank and a silent Edward. No sign of Eileen—but she may be there. Lorcan steps to the plate. The first pitch is coming; it's low and outside, but Lorcan is determined to swing. He does. It's a hit. The ball sails high—possibly a foul.

But no, it's fair. An easy home run. His team wins the game. Moire hugs him, pulls away, then squeezes him again. . . .

Lorcan rolled over. Was he truly remembering the past or creating new fictions? It was tough to say. But for once one thing seemed clear: he never assaulted her on those beach towels. Their love was peaceful, idyllic. Not desperate. They thought they had all the time in the world.

Lorcan was certain of one other thing: something went wrong the night their team won the softball championship. Whatever it was, it succeeded in keeping him and Moire apart for thirty-five years. Lorcan wondered if there were a way for him and Moire to find love now without digging up the past—a past that no one seemed to want to review. Yet even as he entertained the thought, he knew he'd find no peace, and no happiness, until he discovered just what had transpired that Labor Day weekend thirty-five years before.

9

"Kill someone?" Doctor Murphy was astonished at his question.

"Yes."

"And not remember it?"

"Yes."

"What makes you ask the question?"

"You said that I was a violent man whose anger is sublimated into tenderness."

"Not once, not once, in all my years of practice, have I used the word 'sublimate.'"

"Well, you know what I mean."

"Tell me what I know that you mean, Lorcan."

"My anger toward women, particularly toward my mother, is checked by tenderness. Hence I am a violent man and a tender man; women, especially, uh, weak women, find that attractive. Fair summary?"

"Fair summary. Do you accept its validity?"

"As a working hypothesis. . . . My question is whether the tenderness mechanism could fail and I could do serious harm to someone. Maybe even kill them."

"A woman?"

"Maybe. Or a man."

"Let's take the first case. Have you ever hurt a woman physically?"

"I don't think so."

"Or a man?"

"No. Except maybe in the war. . . . I've felt like it often."

"That does not count."

"So?"

"I would say that your fail-safe system works pretty well . . . even those unfortunate government agents who made the mistake of crossing you are likely to be let off the hook, perhaps before they ought to be."

"What if I were sick, delirious, out of control? Might I have done something terrible and then, uh—I don't know whether you use the word—repress it?"

"You worry that's what might have happened?"

"It's a possibility."

"The woman would know about that night, would she not?"

"Yes. Might I have blown up the house in a mad delirium and then forgotten about it?"

"I can't rule that out as a remote possibility, Lorcan. It is, however, most unlikely. In altered states we rarely do that which we wouldn't do in the state of ordinary consciousness."

"Why have I forgotten so much?"

"That worries you?"

"Yes, it worries me. What happened that Labor Day morning?"

"You don't remember?"

"No."

"Presumably the woman does?"

"Yes."

"You will ask her tomorrow?"

He did not want to answer that question.

"Lorcan?"

"I don't want to ask her. However, I will. I must know."

"Would she be as relaxed with you as you describe her to me if she thought you had done something terrible?"

"No."

Nor would she have written him love letters, but Lorcan wasn't prepared to let Doctor Murphy know about them.

"Then it's safe to ask her?"

"I guess so. . . . Could I have amnesia?"

"I think that highly likely—what we call local amnesia— the result of strain, sickness, and trauma."

"It could last this long?"

"It's possible, certainly. Normally it's short term, but there are some exceptions."

"That's a relief."

"Perhaps. In any event we can talk more about it on Monday morning and about your developing relationship with the woman."

"If it develops at all this afternoon."

"Yes. If it does. . . . And now I note that our hour is over."

"Thank you, Doctor Murphy. You've been a big help."

Five will get you ten that my patient will not ask her about their final weekend together. There's something he saw or heard that night that he doesn't want to see or hear ever again.

10

Lorcan picked up the report Dinny Rooney had sent him. He had to hand it to Dinny; not only was he thorough, he was quick. Lorcan read through the document a second time. Going through the first time, he'd been too anxious. This time he didn't want to miss a word.

DENNIS ROONEY AND ASSOCIATES

FROM: D. Rooney
TO: L. Flynn
SUBJECT: Conversation with Captain Miles O'-Rourke of the Michigan City Police Department (Retired)

We've had good luck on the Michigan City front. Captain O'Rourke is an old friend and associate of my colleague Michael James Vincent Casey. He was only too prepared to talk at great length about a wide variety of problems of police procedure "with a friend of Commissioner Casey."

With his permission I have had his conversation transcribed and his signature to it notarized.

Thus it becomes an affidavit. I take it that this is a reasonable precaution since we are dealing with a matter which could at some future time lead to legal action.

In this report I digest our conversation. Should you wish the entire transcript I will be happy to provide it.

Captain O'Rourke was a patrol officer in Long

Beach at the time of the Labor Day explosion. He was involved in the investigation in a lesser capacity. His tone of voice and facial expressions as we discussed that matter indicate that he still finds the suppression of the investigation's findings on the order of nebulous "higher authority" quite distasteful.

The Captain is a large man, well over six feet tall, not exactly obese but overweight and bald. He has consumed prodigious amounts of beer through the years, an accomplishment to which he added while we talked. I am saddened to have to report that he talks and acts like a stereotype of a southern sheriff on a television program. He is, however, both by his own claim and by general reputation, an honest cop.

I should note that I have edited obscenities out of this digest, perhaps curtailing the verbiage by one half in so doing.

R. You worked on the Meehan case when you were a young patrol officer.

O. That I did, that I did. It left a bitter taste in my mouth, let me tell you. Those crooks upstairs were covering up.

R. Which crooks?

O. You were never sure which crooks. Word came down from the chief that they wanted to wrap it up. He gave the impression that he didn't like it any more than we did. He had his orders too. You knew better than to ask the chief who gave those orders. Meehan being a politician, I assumed that it was other politicians who gave the orders. Can't prove it.

R. The official coroner's report was that the explosion was caused by a gas leak set off by an unintentional spark.

O. There was no gas leak. Hell, the gas pipes were still intact after the explosion.

R. Colonel Pat Flynn reported a gas smell.

O. Pat Flynn was a clever so and so. Real charmer. War hero, I guess. A hundred missions over Germany, something like that. You had to work at not believing him.

R. He was lying about the gas smell?

O. I don't know that. You sure smell something when a house blows up in the middle of a rainstorm. Flynn wasn't telling us everything he knew. Some of what he was saying was certainly not true. Maybe he was part of the cover-up. A fella like Pat Flynn tries to deceive sometimes because it's in his interest to do so and sometimes because it's in his nature to do so, know what I mean?

R. You encounter people like that in investigations.

O. You sure do.

R. What did cause the blast?

O. Explosives, high explosives.

R. Someone planted them?

O. Nah! they were in the basement of the house all along. Not a lot, but enough to destroy the place and the people in it.

R. There were high explosives in the Meehan house?

O. Yeah, maybe fifty, a hundred pounds. And the BARs.

R. BARs?

O. Browning Automatic Rifles. A lot heavier than the things they use today, AR-15s, Uzis, stuff like that. Your BAR is a big bulky thing—about thirty of them in crates, next to the high explosives, right alongside the furnace.

R. The furnace was on?

O. Nah, it was a real hot weekend.

R. Ammo?

O. You'd expect that, wouldn't you? But there wasn't any. Weapons without ammo, doesn't make sense. If there had been ammo a lot more people might have been killed.

R. Anything else?

O. You mean military stuff? Nah.

R. It would have been a sensational case.

O. Sure would. That's why they closed it down, I guess.

R. The four victims were killed in the explosion?

O. Or by the collapse of the building on them. The Congressman and his wife died instantly or almost instantly—the stuff was right under their room, blew them to pieces. For the poor kids it might have taken longer—suffocation and internal injuries. They were dead for an hour at least by the time we were able to dig them out.

R. What ignited the explosive?

O. Heat.

R. Heat?

O. Yeah. It was volatile stuff, the kind that blew up on you if it got hot enough. There must have been a fire first. We couldn't find any trace of someone starting it. No gasoline can or anything like that. Not that there was any systematic search. A guy from the F.D. told me that he thought it was deliberate but they wouldn't let them search for evidence.

R. Might have been an accident, though?

O. Sure, but then why cover up?

I can't determine yet what to make of any of this. Even in those days it took a lot of clout to cover up a killing that big. Execution-style murder of a congressman's family followed by an explosion of hidden high explosive and the subsequent discovery of thirty automatic rifles.

We are in deep waters, Lorcan, real deep.

11

"I t was a frigging disaster." Maeve sounded like she was in tears. "A total disaster."

"I expected it might be."

"Before it was over, Dorothy had too much of the drink taken, Marie was in tears, I was in a terrible dither, and Moire was angry."

"Moire angry? At whom?"

"At Dorothy for being such a fool!"

Maybe I should have eaten with them after all. I'd like to have seen Moire enraged.

"What went wrong?"

"Well, doesn't Dorothy treat Moire like she's some kind of lower-class trash? You know the snob game she plays, although she isn't real good at it. All her friends that she has to invite to the wedding, as if she'll have anything to say about it. 'Your friends are welcome, too, my dear,'" Maeve mimicked her mother-in-law, "'if they can afford to fly in from New York, although they *might* feel out of place.'"

"She must have been drunk when she did that."

"I suspect she was after having a few to give her courage before we met, poor woman."

"How did Moire react?"

"That wasn't when she got mad. It was when Dorothy went after you."

"She would do that."

"You bet she would! First she pretends that she'll be running the wedding. Marie and Liz are doing it, er, with a wee smidgen of my help. Marie won't let her mother anywhere near the arrangements. After today she doesn't even want her to be at the wedding."

"I can understand that."

"Well, Marie's in tears and I'm steaming, but holding my big country-girl mouth shut, and Moire is being her usual calm self. Then Dorothy, poor woman, starts blaming you for all the trouble they're having about the wedding plans."

"I would have expected that, too."

"Then she tells Moire that she's the lucky one for not having a husband to mess up her life."

"Oh, my God!"

"Moire takes it for a while. Then, very quiet-like, she says, 'Dorothy, I miss my husband very much. He was a wonderful man. Women who have husbands may not understand how lucky they are, particularly when they're good men like your husband is.'"

Lorcan was stunned.

"You still there, Lorcan?"

"I am. Then Dorothy runs sobbing to the women's room, right?"

"Sure, you've seen the film already, haven't you? Marie goes after her. Moire and I are alone and she doesn't say much. She's not sorry for what she's said at all. Then Marie comes back. Her mom, she says, has taken a cab home. She thanks Moire for sticking up for you and bursts into tears herself. Her mother, she says, will try to ruin the wedding like she's tried to ruin everything else in her life."

"And?"

"And Moire puts her arm around her and says that we, meaning herself and meself, won't let her do that. So Marie dries her eyes and we have chocolate cake for dessert."

"Sounds delicious."

"And I'll be after picking her up and bringing her by your house at three-thirty."

"Will you now?"

"We will. . . . Don't put me on, Lorcan!"

"Would I be putting you on?"

"Answering the questions with questions is my game."

"Fair is fair, isn't it now?"

"'Tis *not*. . . . Isn't she a grand woman, Lorcan?"

"Who?"

"Moire, who else? I'd kill for a body like that, I really would."

"I doubt it, Maevie."

"I would, I really would. . . . Lorcan, I'm not at all sure I should be saying this, but maybe you and the pretty widow lady might pick up where you two, er, left off, if you know what I mean. You are, after all, a free man."

Lorcan said nothing.

"You're thinking I should be minding me own business, aren't ya?"

"Did I say anything?"

"Na, but I can hear you thinking it. I'll keep me mouth shut now that I've spoken, Lorcan. I won't be pestering ya when I bring Moire by."

"See you at three-thirty," Lorcan said.

Maeve sighed. "Three-thirty it is."

12

Salad tray in one hand and two Pepsi bottles in the other, Lorcan waited for the elevator door to the swimming pool to open.

"Anyone for lunch?"

"Hurry up! We're both perishing with the hunger," Maeve shouted, signaling that there were no reasons of modesty to prevent him from entering the pool.

"Avocado and shrimp salad, with dressing made in the establishment, and two Diet Pepsi's with lime. At your service, mesdames."

"Didn't I tell you, Moire, that he was a useful man to have around?" Maeve, in a white bikini that was little more than symbolic, lunged out of the pool, wrapped herself in a huge towel, and dove at the table where Lorcan had placed the lunch and was beginning to arrange the dishes, silver, and place mats.

"He has improved a mite with age, Maeve." Moire

emerged from the pool more gracefully. "I'll grant you that. Did you really make the salad, Lorcan?"

Her form-fitting one-piece suit was technically more modest than the Maeve's skimpy costume. It left no room to question, however, the authenticity of her figure. Moreover, the suit revealed sufficient cleavage to make an ordinary healthy man gulp.

So Lorcan gulped. And stared.

"I did really make the salad. I had a hunch certain people might be perishing with the hunger and themselves just after having eaten lunch. The shrimp are frozen, I hope you don't mind. Also, since herself has to watch the wee, wee ones, she can't have any of this. However, because neither you nor I are working or driving, we can share this." He ducked back into the elevator and brought out an ice bucket with a bottle of white Châteauneuf du Pape.

"I really can't, Lorcan," Moire, huddling under her towel, protested. "I really can't."

Then, after he had filled her glass, she picked it up. "I can't, but I will."

"I thought you might."

She raised the glass with one hand and adjusted a strap on her swimsuit with the other. "Superb, Lorcan."

"I'm glad you like it."

"Your health, Lorcan. Yours and all your remarkable family's—in-laws not excluded." Gravely she toasted him as he poured a glass for himself.

Maeve was wolfing down her salad and guzzling Diet Pepsi. "I don't even want to smell the piss-ant stuff," she insisted. "You're trying to tempt me so they'll fire me from that uptight Protestant hospital."

Earlier, Lorcan had admitted his two guests to the house on Astor Street, hung up their coats, and conducted them to the pool.

"You won't join us, Lorcan?" Moire lifted an eyebrow.

"The pool will be crowded with two people. Besides, filled with virtue, I did my exercise this morning. . . . Moire, I have no doubts about you because you're facing an airplane dinner tonight. Maeve, would you prefer cafeteria food at the hospital a little later or my shrimp and avocado salad?"

"Don't say no, darling," Maeve had begged Moire. "Sure, ain't I perishing with the hunger?"

"Curiosity alone would prevent me from saying no." Moire had smiled for the second time in her visit, illumining the pool area, which, despite powerful lights, always seemed dark and morose.

"Enjoy yourselves," he said.

"We'll try our best."

She took off her suit jacket and hung it on a hook on the wall of the pool—a movement that briefly etched her breasts sharply against the fabric of her gray sweater.

Light-headed, Lorcan left them in the pool while he attended—briefly—to business and to the lunch he'd just so happily served.

"It's wonderful wine, Lorcan. I'll sleep all the way home to New York, which is most likely a good thing."

"I tell the Old Fella he should be buying his own corporate jet to fly us around in. He could pilot us himself."

"It'd require hundreds of hours for me to qualify as a pilot of a multiengine passenger aircraft, Maeve. It wouldn't be worth it."

"You haven't flown, then, since you left the Air Force, Lorcan?" Moire studied him intently, as if she were trying to figure him out as much as he was trying to understand her.

"Not much desire to do so, Moire."

"Still see the Sea of Japan spinning up at you?"

"Did I tell you about that?"

"The night we won the softball championship."

"Sea of Japan?" Maeve was chewing vigorously on a mouthful of avocado and shrimp.

"I had an engine flame-out there during the Korean War, Maeve. No big deal."

"Did you crash?"

"I'm here, am I not?"

" 'Tis true," she said, refilling her glass.

"To answer your question, Moire, I dream about it occasionally. I could fly a plane if I had to. I did for a year in Texas after my hundred missions. But I'd rather have someone else fly for me."

"Well." Maeve continued to demolish the salad. "I always say that if you can afford to buy a private jet, you can afford to hire a pilot to fly it for you."

"You need a copilot too."

"What's one more salary?"

Lorcan could certainly afford his own jet. There was just too much of the Saint Ignatius graduate in him to justify such conspicuous consumption.

Moire ate her salad and drank her wine with more grace than her newfound friend but no less determination. Her soft brown eyes continued to absorb him. A hint of amusement seemed to glitter in the depths of those eyes. Had she looked at him that way long ago?

"You'll have to meet me brats, Con and Derm, when you're next in town, Moire," Maeve babbled on, fearful of lulls in the conversation. "They're not bad as little punks go, not at all."

"Actually," Lorcan corrected the record, "they're well-behaved gentlemen, particularly given their antecedents."

"I'd like to meet your grandchildren, Lorcan. I'm sure they're a great joy to you. I'll admit I'm looking forward to my own."

Lorcan was mesmerized. The more time he spent with her, the more he wanted to spend.

"Why don't you get dressed, Moire," Maeve said. "Let himself show off his home. I'll try to do more of next week's exercise."

"When you're ready, ride up the elevator to one," Lorcan directed as he gathered the remains of their lunch. "Turn left, and at the end of the hallway you'll find me hard at work on my Compaq computer."

"A 386/20?"

"Naturally."

"That way he can carry it around." Maeve tossed aside her robe and dove into the pool. "And look important," she sputtered as she came to the surface to finish her sentence.

Lorcan smiled and left the pool.

Less than ten minutes later he heard the elevator grind and chug as it labored upwards. A few moments later Moire entered the office, hair plastered flat against her head, ra-

diating freshness and vitality and the smell of shower soap.
Once more she took his breath away.

He almost embraced her passionately. Almost.

"Thank you, Lorcan. It was wonderful. I fear it was
presumptuous of me to take you up on your offer, but I'm
glad I did. Your house is quite—"

She stopped midsentence when she spotted the Beach
Towel painting on the wall.

"How lovely. Powerful colors." For once she seemed
disconcerted. "Is there any special symbolism in them, Lorcan?"

"I saw the painting in a gallery over in Suhu—that's the
Superior/Huron Street art district."

"Yes, I know."

"It seemed the perfect thing to brighten up this room."

"It surely does that." She continued to stare at the painting. "Does it remind you of the towels we used at Long
Beach that summer?"

"Should it?"

She turned away from the picture and considered him
again. "Maybe. It certainly brings that memory back to
me."

She paused, expecting him to comment.

Lorcan felt he was missing something. Moire knew what
that painting signified and he didn't. If he asked her, they'd
begin to talk about what happened that night.

Instead of probing further he said, "I'm finishing up the
galleys for the book they're making from the catalogue of
my last exhibit."

"Alex Stone's last exhibit," she said, but Lorcan could tell
her thoughts were still on the painting.

"How did you know that?"

"From Maevie, who else?"

They both laughed.

Dutifully Moire inspected the galleys. "Nice typeface.
Quality company. And, Lorcan! What wonderful work! Is
it all yours?"

"Afraid so."

"Congratulations." She leafed through the pages. "So
you did study under Mestrovich after all."

"I did. I'm sure the poor man wouldn't like the work I'm doing now."

"It's outstanding, Lorcan." Her voice caught. "I'm proud of you. . . . Do you have a studio in the house? May I see it?"

"It's the high point and the finale in the tour."

Having suspected that she might want to see his studio, he had tucked away the unfinished clay of Cindi in the adjoining room and locked the door. But on second thought, why not show it to her?

They talked about families as he showed her the house.

"Your children certainly adore you, Lorcan. You're lucky. It doesn't always end up that way. I haven't met Liz yet. Maeve says she's the worst Lorcan-worshiper of them all."

"Do they like me, Moire? Sometimes it's hard to tell. When this divorce hit me, I didn't know where they stood."

"Dorothy doesn't seem to get along with Marie." It was a flat statement of fact and a reference to the luncheon for which he was unprepared.

"That goes back a long time. A third child was her idea, though God knows I was happy about the prospect. It was a difficult pregnancy, however, and a painful delivery. Dorothy always seemed to hold it against her."

"Marie is a sturdy young woman, although you wouldn't perceive it at first. She'll be all right."

"The trouble with being a parent is not so much the deliberate mistakes you make as the unintentional ones."

"I quite agree. I've worried a lot myself. I never had proper parents, as you remember—I don't even have pictures of them. The Meehans were nice to me most of the time. I was brokenhearted when they died so horribly. I've been afraid that I didn't have any models of what a parent should be."

"You seem to have done very well."

"Tom did very well. I'm not so sure about myself. . . . Oh, what a lovely bedroom! You have fabulous taste, Lorcan, in interior design as well as in salads and wine."

The wine was making his head spin and was threatening to loosen his tongue. The presence of Moire in his bedroom sent a thrill through his entire system.

"The Ph.D. decorator was the one with the taste in these rooms. It's a reconstruction from the original. Edwardian is back in fashion."

Her breasts, outlined by the soft gray fabric of the turtleneck, were in easy reach of his eager fingers.

They went into the bath with its wide and deep bathtub which one ascended by steps. Cindi would be in it tonight if there was enough time.

"That's not Edwardian."

"Hollywood fantasy modern."

"Dorothy didn't like it?"

"She was horrified by it."

"Poor woman."

Lorcan was thinking how much he'd like to love Moire in that tub every night for the rest of his life.

"You must have been lonely in New York." They strolled out of the master bedroom suite and back into the corridor.

"At first. The Hanlons—you remember them, they had lived in Chicago and moved to New York but kept their home in Grand Beach—invited me to visit them after the funeral. Their daughter Anne is my age. I wanted to escape from all the ugliness and suspicion. Then your Uncle Rory flew down with the check from the Meehans' will. I realized I could pay for college myself. The Hanlons invited me to stay on. I still miss Chicago sometimes. My daughter, Josie, is very close to her brother. I wouldn't be surprised if she settles here after she graduates."

Lorcan was tempted to suggest she join them.

Just then he realized there was something strange about what she had just told him. Uncle Rory had never been Meehan's lawyer! There was something funny here. Moire didn't realize it and never had. Otherwise she wouldn't be mentioning it so casually. Well, if the money was not Meehan money, whose was it?

"Uncle Rory is still alive. So's Dad."

"Yes, Marie told me. Still the comedian and the cutup, I suppose, even at eighty?"

"I've never found him all that funny, Moire."

"Still? I remember the awful rivalry between you and him. I thought it would diminish with time."

"I love him, Moire. I've always loved him. My kid sister Eileen says I love him more than any of the others do. Maybe that's true. But he's set up barriers that I can't break through."

"What a pity. For both of you."

They were climbing the spiral staircase to his studio. Lorcan could only think how much he loved Moire. Why were there barriers between him and those he held most dear?

He began vowing to speak his mind to her before she boarded that plane for New York. For the moment he decided to stick to his father. "I'll confess I suspect he intercepted your letters and wouldn't permit Mom to tell me about your phone calls."

"Really?"

"I'll never be able to prove it. As you said last night, I should let the dead bury their dead."

"You should."

They entered the studio. "It's kind of small," he apologized. "I'll expand it if I become more serious about the work."

"It's lovely. What wonderful light from the skylight! And your work . . . !" She touched his uncast clay of a modern *pietà*. "You really must cast this, Lorcan. It's special."

"If you say so."

"All your work"—she wandered about the studio admiring the little pieces he had scattered in the room, mostly unfinished—"is abstract?"

"No . . ." He hesitated. "I locked up a work in progress in case Maeve was part of the tour. Despite her language, she's a bit of a puritan."

"I'm not so sure about that."

He opened the door to the adjoining room and carried the unfinished Cindi out to the cold glare of the February sun, streaming through the skylight.

"Oh, my! I'll say that's not abstract! How exciting! Lorcan, it's the best piece here. I like it better than any of those I saw when I glanced through your catalogue."

"You surprise me."

"She's quite sweet, isn't she? Young and innocent and not exceptionally sexy despite her cute little body." She laid her hand on the statue's flank. "You worry about what will happen to her. If you're me you almost want to pray for her. Superb vision, Lorcan, superb."

If Moire wondered about the model, she didn't say.

"Thank you. I'm glad you like it."

"I must see some of your poems before we ride to the airport. *Time* was correct. You are a renaissance man."

"You make me blush."

"That makes you even cuter."

"That makes me blush even more."

Lorcan wanted to take her in his arms that minute.

"Do you remember the clay you did of me at Long Beach?"

"I did a model of you? Not like this!"

"Oh, I suspect you thought about it! I sure did. It was a bust of me in my softball shirt, my cap pushed back on my head. You made it in the boathouse. I thought it was splendid. Do you still have it?"

"I don't remember it, Moire," he said miserably. "It's one more memory that the fever seemed to have wiped out."

He pushed the button for the elevator. It groaned in protest and began to chug up from the first floor.

"A lot seems to have been wiped out."

Lorcan wanted to ask what she meant by that, but he couldn't bring himself to.

Instead he said, "I'm sure it disappeared by the time the doctors released me from Saint Anthony's. Whoever destroyed your letters must have destroyed it."

"I'd find that harder to forgive, Lorcan. The letters were from a silly teenage girl with a crush. The bust was a beautiful effort by a young artist with promise."

"Someone didn't think so." He ushered her into the elevator.

He should offer to do another one now.

In the elevator, he longed to kiss her, yet he couldn't bring himself to make a move.

Instead he led her back to the office, printed out copies of the latest poems for her, found Maeve, and escorted both of them to the waiting car.

They dropped Maeve off at the hospital and struggled

through the rush-hour ride on the Kennedy Expressway in silence, both of them dozing from the wine.

He asked her none of the questions that churned in his head.

She took his hand into hers just as she had at Sheridan Beach.

Lorcan felt sure that if he took her into his arms and kissed her then, she would be his. He just knew. She was his for the taking. They could make love that night. Dinner and a room at the O'Hare Hilton. They could start over again. Turn the clock back.

Despite Moire's protests, Lorcan escorted her to her gate at United Terminal B, carrying her bag.

He brushed her lips as she prepared to board—coach class.

"It's been truly wonderful, Lorcan. I'll admit I was nervous about meeting you again. I ought not to have been."

"We'll see you after Easter at the wedding," was the only reply that would come from his dazed brain to his clumsy lips.

13

Colonel Pat Flynn's temper was exceptionally vile. Lorcan judged that his father was slipping more each week. As he slipped, his resentments became more wicked. Even granted that slow deterioration, he was in a wretched mood today, a caricature of one of Charles Dickens' contentious old men.

"I hear that whore was in town this week," he began.

"Who was that, Dad?"

Lorcan had resolved to maintain his patience, no matter what his father said. Dad was an old man who could not be blamed for his prejudices and malice.

"That one you screwed in the Dunes when you came home from your phony war, the one from the wrong side of the Meehan bed."

"Moire."

"Yeah. Did you screw her?" His father's eyes screwed up in a gleam of intense animosity.

"No, Dad. I did not. She's not a whore, either. She owns an elegant typesetting business."

"A whore's a whore, no matter what else she does. What's she in town for this time?" Pat Flynn licked his lips, relishing Lorcan's discomfiture. Hank seemed amused too.

Same old stupid game.

The cold spell had slipped away to the east to be replaced by a surge of warm air from the Gulf. Sheridan Road was slushy from a rapid thaw. The sky over the lake was heavy with rainclouds. Lorcan preferred the cold. It did not pretend to be anything else but vicious.

"She came for a meeting of a trade association. Presented a paper, I understand, on the use of computers in high-quality typesetting. Since her son and my daughter Marie are marrying one another after Easter, my daughter-in-law organized a dinner for her."

"Yeah? I hear she was rude to your wife!"

So that was one of Pat's sources. Dorothy through Joanne.

"I wasn't at that meal."

"Didn't I tell you to stop that wedding?"

"They're both of age, Dad." He continued to be patient. "I have no control over their marital decisions."

"You're the girl's father, aren't you?"

"You were Eileen's father and you couldn't stop her marriage."

"I don't want you ever to mention that slut's name in this house!" His father pounded his withered legs. "Not a word about her, do you hear?"

"Yes, Dad."

This was a new rule. Eileen's name had rarely come up in their conversations. Lorcan had not mentioned his last visit to her in Seattle because the result would have been an unpleasant outburst. However, she had never been placed under interdict before.

"You hold the purse strings, you can stop the marriage if you want to."

"They both have excellent salaries, Dad. If I tried to deny them any money, they'd simply go ahead without me."

"That's because you're weak, always have been, always will be."

"Dad has a point, you know," Hank joined in, eager as ever to put Lorcan on the defensive, especially eager this week when he had betrayed Lorcan.

"Oh?"

"Maura Meehan was never much." Hank soothed his big mustache with delicate care. "I couldn't tell what you saw in her that summer. . . ."

"Good second baseman."

"Yeah, well apples don't fall far from their trees, you know. Blood tells in the end."

"Perhaps it does at that. Good luck to you in trying to control your children's lives, Hank, when they decide to marry. Whether you like the intended one or not, you're stuck."

"Not if you're tough with them, like Henry is," his father sneered.

Henry was a pushover for his children. Fortunately, Joanne was made of sterner stuff. The four children had a fair chance of amounting to something. Dad would never oppose the weddings of Henry's children.

"I don't like that ugly little daughter-in-law of yours either." Dad continued to beat up on him. "Her brogue is phony and she shows no respect."

Lorcan rolled his eyes.

"Just keep her away from here," his father continued. "That's all I ask. She makes me want to vomit."

"She hasn't expressed any desire to come here, Dad."

"And I see that our nigger mayor has caught up with your dumb-dumb friend, Mr. Little Smart Ass, Fancy Pants Daley."

"That's not the way I read the polls."

"Whaddaya think, Hank? You always understood politics better than lunkhead here."

"I think Gene Sawyer will pull it out"—Hank's fingers

continued to stroke his mustache like he was preparing to
make love to it—"Dad, just like you do."

For as long as he could remember Lorcan was baffled
when Henry would revel in his father's approbation as the
smarter and more manly and more successful of the two of
them. How could such patently absurd praise cause Henry
for a moment to forget where he really was in life?

Lorcan decided to stick to his vow to keep his cool.

"Well, we have our fifty-dollar bet, Dad. We'll see next
Tuesday night who wins it."

"Damn right we will." Pat Flynn downed most of a glass
of red wine. "This time I'll make you pay up, too. I won't
let you welsh like all the other times."

"You do that. . . . Incidentally, Ed is flying in tomorrow
for a meeting at the Provincial House. I'll be taking him to
the Daley party on Tuesday."

"Who?" The old man frowned in displeasure, wine drip-
ping in tiny rivulets from the corner of his mouth.

"Father Ed, your third son."

"Oh, that holy joe bastard. Don't bring him around here.
I got sick of him a long time ago. Spent all his time sucking
up to Father Gregorio. Guy runs off to the seminary because he likes little boys instead of little girls. Ain't that true,
Henry?"

"I wouldn't be surprised, Dad. He never did date."

Ed had dated all through his senior year at Saint Justin's.
They're both sick, Lorcan said to himself. *At least Dad has
the excuse he's senile. What could Hank say to explain himself?*

"He's highly thought of in the Order."

"Bunch of faggots. . . . Ed's no more a man than you are.
If you were a man you would have screwed that whore."

Lorcan should have figured his father would circle back
for another swipe his way.

Lorcan's patience had worn thin. Fortunately, a couple
of minutes later, their father threw them out.

Hank and Lorcan rode down in the elevator in silence.
Lorcan knew there was no point in losing his temper with
poor Hank. Hank treated lunch with their father as a different reality from the ordinary world. He did not expect

and would not permit himself to be held accountable for anything that he might have said in Dad's world of surrealistic lunacy.

Dad did say that Moire was an illegitimate Meehan. Was that merely his venom or was there a hint of truth in it?

"Thanks for talking to Larry Whealan," Lorcan finally said to Hank as they walked out onto Sheridan Road.

"Yeah, like I told him, it was all pretty general. They don't have anything on you. Just looking. I understand they're furious about what you did to those two kids, though."

"I'm delighted to hear it."

"Limo today?" Henry stared at the waiting stretch Lincoln.

Lorcan usually drove to lunch at his father's to avoid hostile comments about his limos—which cost less for a year than did the depreciation on Hank's Mercedes.

"I have a meeting downtown with clients from out of town. I don't want to be late."

"Well, make another million on them."

"I'll try."

"You do that."

"By the way." Lorcan had a sudden idea. "I noticed that Dad said that Maura was an illegitimate Meehan. Did he mean she was Joe's daughter?"

"How should I know?" Hank shrugged indifferently, averting his eyes. "Maybe she's Tim's daughter, the guy the English killed in Ireland."

"He would have been only sixteen or seventeen when she was born."

Hank continued to study the clouds sweeping past Sheridan Road toward the Lake, lovingly stroking his mustache.

"They said he had a way with the girls. It's too late to find out—and why bother, anyway?"

"Yeah, you're probably right." Lorcan paused. "They said Joe Meehan left her some money, didn't they?"

"That's what everyone said. . . . It was a long time ago."

The driver of the car opened the door for him. Lorcan prepared to enter. He turned to Hank, as if he had an afterthought.

"As a matter of fact, there was no bequest to her in the Meehan will."

"Yeah?"

"So the money Rory gave her when he went to New York to visit her must have come from someone else."

He paused long enough to see the astonishment and fear on Hank's face, not long enough, however, for Hank to be able to reply.

The driver closed the door. Hank continued to stare, mouth hanging open under his huge mustache.

Lorcan decided to call Rory as soon as he could find a phone. That should stir the pot.

14

He should have been reviewing his Alex Stone galleys, but Lorcan was becoming increasingly preoccupied with questions raised in his sessions with Doctor Murphy.

Specifically, he was trying to focus on his images of his mother. Of his whole family, why was she the most indistinct figure of all? Whatever her failings, Lorcan remembered her fondly. Yet the more he thought about her, the more he realized there were really two different mothers he knew. The first mother was affectionate, warmhearted, fun to be with—the mother he had known his early years before his father's return from the war. The second mother materialized after Lorcan returned from the war. This mother was a dowdy, disheartened, querulous woman, old before her time.

As Lorcan tried to recall that summer of '54, he found the mother who emerged in his memory astonishing. What had happened?

She bickered constantly with her children, complaining endlessly about their refusal to help keep the house clean.

The house was not disorderly as summer houses go, and she was responsible for much of the disarray herself. Her half-empty coffee cups and cigarette butts littered the house. Her stacks of unsorted laundry were heaped high on the dining room and kitchen tables.

Father Gregorio was around a lot. Dad didn't like him, but he didn't protest. The priest seemed to calm Mother down.

Lorcan was amazed to recognize the degree to which his family had disintegrated—particularly his mother—that particular summer. How could he have forgotten that? Despite the perennial problems of his father's irritability and Hank's resentment, the family Lorcan left after high school graduation was a happy one.

The family he returned to was not happy. At first he had assumed that the problems were simply anxieties he'd brought home from the war. Then he realized that something had fundamentally changed in his absence.

His mother had openly wept at his departure. His return found her nearly somnolent. She seemed more concerned with the clutter in the house than with Lorcan's rejoining the family. Lorcan cleaned up after his mother in an effort to appease her. He collected her coffee cups and cigarette butts, doing his best to relieve his sister, Eileen. As the only other woman in the household, much of the housework had fallen to her.

For all his efforts, Lorcan still found himself judged harshly. No wonder he sought solace in Moire's arms! And, of course, his mother found room to complain about even this innocent attachment.

In her last days, when she was dying of liver cancer, she remained bitter to the end. Her last words to Lorcan were recriminating: "I hope you realize how much I'm suffering."

Lorcan was amazed that he could ever have forgotten all this. What was wrong with him? In desperation he decided to call Eileen. She was the only one he could trust to shed some light on his ill-remembered past.

Eileen was glad to hear from her older brother, even if she was a little surprised by the hour of his call. Lorcan asked after her children and was delighted to hear of their latest triumphs in school. Then he got to the point.

"I don't remember Mom much before you went away," Eileen said in answer to his question. "I have the impression that she was happy when I was five or six and then changed. I don't recall what happened, if any one thing did happen."

"What was her problem in later years, Eileen?"

"Problem? It was obvious, Lorcan; she was a neurotic hypochondriac. Quite sick, poor woman, I mean quite sick in the head. She got her kicks from changing symptoms and medicines and doctors the way other women change their clothes. Poor thing, I should feel sorry for her now. But Dad blamed me for so many years for Mom's 'problems,' as he called them. It's hard to work up the sympathy."

"What went wrong, Eileen?"

" 'Midlife crisis' we call it these days, don't we? Fear of old age, disappointment with your life, emptiness after your childbearing years are over. Common enough symptoms, Lorcan."

"Nothing out of the ordinary?"

"Well . . . Dad was a problem, as you know."

"How?"

"You mean you didn't know he played around? He had the hots for every attractive woman he saw. Some of them thought he was a charming flirt. They soon found out differently. He was quite incapable of the singleminded loyalty Mom received from you. You were her favorite, naturally. Maybe when you went away to war there wasn't enough simple affection left to sustain her. Does that sound possible?"

"Not impossible."

Lorcan felt his sister's psychological sophistication implied that she must have had long-term therapy. It seemed to have worked for her.

"How bad was Dad?"

"Not as bad as he liked to pretend. He talked more than he actually misbehaved. Mom saw more rivals than there were. Naturally she couldn't admit any of this to herself. So she turned to pills and doctors."

"The bastard!"

"You know what I think of him. Still, I wouldn't blame him altogether. Mom became hard to live with. They slept in separate bedrooms as long as I can remember."

Lorcan had never noticed. Or rather, he had never permitted himself to notice.

"It scares you that the same thing could happen in our lives."

Lorcan and Eileen talked more, but Lorcan was eager to get off the phone and digest all Eileen had said. Eileen seemed to sense this. After warm goodbyes were exchanged, Lorcan hung up the phone.

Not for the first time, he felt haunted by the parallels between his mother and his wife. Dorothy had long been convinced he was often unfaithful. Even an apparition from God would not have changed that conviction. Yet, for all her certainty, so long as they were married, he'd never once strayed.

He wondered if his mother had been comparably deluded. Was history doomed to repeat itself generation after generation?

BOOK III

1

"Would the poor woman have had to remove her clothes to make her message clear to you?"

"Doctor Murphy!" Lorcan attempted to sound shocked.

"You admit that all the signals of readiness, even eagerness to renew your relationship after three and a half decades, were there and you ignored them?"

"Not completely. I gave a few responding signals."

"Faint ones; the least you could do and still be civil."

He sighed. "I didn't see it that way while it was happening. I was trying to be considerate."

"And you sent the poor woman back to New York wondering whether she had made a fool of herself?"

"I lost my nerve."

"Ah, now we finally hear the truth. . . . You would never have married her in the nineteen-fifties, you know."

"Certainly I would have married her," he erupted, now goaded beyond endurance. "I loved her!"

"I'm not sure young people that age know what love is. You would not, however, have married her. You didn't pursue her after your illness; you didn't seek her out in later years; you married someone as different from her as a woman could be."

"There weren't any others like her."

"Forceful, self-possessed women? Come now, Lorcan: River Forest, Long Beach, Notre Dame abound with such women."

"She scares me," he confessed. "I love her but she scares me."

"Then and now?"

"Then and now."

He had never considered that possibility before. Yet it was evidently the truth.

"Lorcan James Flynn, successful financier, acclaimed sculptor, albeit under a nom de chisel, closet poet, international trade expert, friend of the mighty and the famous, habitué of Kup's column—afraid of an upper-middle-class suburban matron? Lorcan, you've got to be kidding! Why are you afraid of her?"

"I wouldn't be free anymore." The sentences tumbled out. "I'd have to give up my schedule. My life wouldn't be my own. I'd have to do what she wanted."

"Because you really don't want to share your life with a woman as an equal."

"What can I tell you?"

"I'm sure I don't know. I can tell you, however, that our hour is up."

"I'll do better with her the next time," he said as he struggled off the couch.

The patient progresses. He is, for a patient, especially for a male patient, remarkably honest about himself. Some of his honesty results from a desire to please me, but that is not unsatisfactory in the present phase of the relationship.

If it were not for the mystery of the death of his neighbors, I think we would continue to make excellent progress. There is, however, something quite sinister about that affair. His family, to put the best possible interpretation on them, were and are weird. His father, uncle, and brother sound like certified bastards. They were up to something that night. He may have been the victim or the intended victim. It worries me.

I will probably try to talk the patient into hypnosis first. He will resist the suggestion. However, if he actually intends to join forces with the suburban matron, he might as well become accustomed to taking a risk when a demanding woman suggests it.

I confess she sounds thoroughly admirable in his

*version of her. If she is the person he thinks she is,
he will never have a thoroughly peaceful day for the
rest of his life.*

*I must resist my propensity to be a matchmaker.
That is not appropriate behavior for a therapist.
Under ordinary circumstances.*

In his office Lorcan dictated a memo to the law firm that
was handling the contracts for his potential venture with
Japanese partners in the manufacture of computer chips. It
would take a long time for the Japanese to make up their
minds. Too bad for them if they blew this chance. Lorcan
would send them a contract before the week was over just
to nudge them a bit. If he had to adjust to their mentality,
they damn well better accustom themselves to his.

"Ms. Horton on the phone, Lorcan," Mary told him.
Lorcan was relieved there was no judgment in her voice.

"Have a nice weekend, Cindi?"

"Dull. The snow was melting. I'm on assignment and in
a rush. Are we on for tonight? Tomorrow night I'll be busy
with election coverage."

"Naturally! Same time?"

"See you then! 'Bye!"

He had forgotten about her completely. His dreams Saturday and Sunday had been filled with Moire. Moire on the
beach towel. Moire in his studio. Moire in his life now.

"A call for you, Mr. Flynn. He won't give his name.
Sounds odd."

Lorcan did not ordinarily take such calls. This time on
impulse he picked up the phone.

"Lorcan Flynn."

"Yeah, I figured it might be."

A muffled voice with perhaps a bit of burr in it.

"Who is this?"

"I hear you been asking questions, you and that ex-cop
friend of yours."

"Who is this?"

"If you know what's good for you, Flynn, you'll forget
about the whole thing."

2

"**M**aura Meehan?" Edward Flynn's lean and handsome face creased in a thoughtful frown. "I don't think so, Lorcan. Who was she?"

"I dated her back in 1954. At Long Beach—after I came home from Korea."

Edward shook his head. "I was only a kid then."

Edward was a half foot shorter than Lorcan. He was a silver-haired, polished ecclesiastic in a tailor-made Italian suit and handmade shoes. When he spoke, he spoke with the authority of someone preaching from a pulpit.

"She played second base on our softball team."

"I'm sorry, Lorcan. It was a long time ago."

They were standing in the Crystal Room of the new Fairmont Hotel on the shore of the Lake, awaiting the appearance of the candidate and his family. There wasn't much doubt about the outcome of the election. With an eye toward better ratings, some of the TV reporters and news anchors, Cindi included, had tried to persuade the citizens of Chicago that a 7-point Daley lead in the final polls made the race a dead heat. They'd succeeded, briefly, in rousing public interest. But now it seemed clear Rich Daley would win by 10 or 12 points.

The group in the stylish Crystal Room, maybe fifty or sixty strong, were technically members of the "finance committee"—contributors, friends, old allies, an occasional cleric. A buffet heaped with food stood in the middle of the room, and a bar with a substantial supply of liquor was conspicuous in the corner, although the Irish who were present were nursing their drinks very carefully.

The Crystal Room was a transition point between the "family suite" somewhere else in the hotel, where the candidate, his family, and his closest advisers awaited the verdict, and the victory-party throng assembling downstairs in the grand ballroom.

Before Lorcan could probe Ed's memory further, Cindi appeared on the TV monitor Lorcan had been watching. "On the basis of its exit polls, Channel 4 has declared that Richard M. Daley has won the Democratic nomination by a margin of eight percentage points."

The rest of her report was drowned out in applause and cheers.

Once the cheering had abated, Lorcan turned to his brother.

"About Maura: her son, Rob, and my daughter Marie—that's the youngest, I think you've met her—will be married the week after Easter."

"That's wonderful." Ed smiled again. "A fascinating twist, isn't it?"

"We'd like to have you officiate."

"If I'm free I'd be delighted. I have so many responsibilities—the Order and now the Pope assigns me an occasional little task." He waved a deprecating hand. "My life is not really my own. Never has been, I guess."

"She lived in the house next door—the Meehans. They were the family who died in the explosion when I was coming down with meningitis. Don't you remember that?"

"I remember the explosion." Ed caressed his drink—Campari and soda. "Why is it so important after so many years?"

"I might have married her if I hadn't got sick."

The candidate and his family entered the room to tumultuous applause. When he came over to them, Lorcan introduced Ed as his brother, a Justine father from Rome.

"Thanks for coming, Father. It's a long trip from Rome."

After accepting Lorcan's congratulations, the victor moved on. Lorcan was more interested in his talk with Ed. He picked up where they'd left off as soon as the new Democratic candidate left them.

"Considering what happened to my marriage, Ed, I may have made a mistake by not marrying her." He hesitated. "She's a widow now and still very attractive and engaging. Maybe I'll undo the mistake."

"Really?" Ed seemed uninterested. "That might not be very wise. At your age in life."

"I've had a hard time accepting the annulment business. In my gut I feel that Dorothy is still my wife."

"It was a marriage, Lorcan—not, however, one of sufficient maturity to be a sacrament. It was certainly not your fault . . . and you should not be holier than the Church."

Liz sailed by and placed glasses of Bailey's Irish Cream in their hands. "Mr. Daley said I could come and work for him when I graduate! Isn't that wonderful!"

"Wise choice on his part."

"Ed, do you remember the night the house next door blew up? It's all a blur in my head."

Ed sighed. "It was, as I have said, a long time ago. I was reading on the porch, as usual. There was a party next door at the Meehan's. Mom and Dad were there. They came home early. I'm afraid Mom had too much to drink, as she often did in those days, poor woman. She was fighting with Dad. As usual he didn't fight back. I didn't pay much attention to it. Hank was out drinking with his boorish friends. I don't know where Eileen was. I went to bed early. I was awakened about three o'clock by some disturbance on the beach in front of our house. I didn't wake enough to know who was there or what was happening. Then I fell back to sleep till the explosion. I remember bouncing out of bed and thinking it was the end of the world. The thunder was right above us, lightning was crackling all around, the rain was pouring down, and the house next door was blazing like a bonfire. . . ."

Ed Vdrolyak, Democrat turned Republican, was on the TV monitor now, claiming victory in his write-in candidacy for the Republican nomination, a position from which he might spoil the Daley bid in the general election in April.

Ed continued slowly, as if he were struggling to open up the file cabinet of his memories.

"You know, I do remember that night," he said slowly. It seemed as if the act of speaking was bringing it back to him right then and there. "There had been some strange men around Long Beach the week before, maybe three or four of them. Not part of the regular community at all.

Renters maybe or visitors was my first impression. They seemed to watch everyone closely. They asked a lot of questions, casual seeming. No one else noticed, I guess. At the end of the summer, who cares about visitors who are a little peculiar? Anyway, they disappeared after the explosion. Then the FBI arrived asking their own questions. They were especially interested in the strangers. It was all very odd."

"Did they talk to Mom and Dad?"

"They talked to Dad. For a long time, I think. He seemed excited to be the center of attention."

"Father Gregorio was there the day after the explosion, wasn't he?"

Edward's face went blank. "I'm sure he was not."

"What was the story behind him, Ed?"

"No story, Lorcan." Ed turned away. "He was a wonderful priest who died a martyr's death serving the poor."

Ed's tone said that there would be no further discussion of Gregorio Sabatini.

Later, in the grand ballroom, when the candidate made his victory announcement—and his sleepy younger daughter charmed everyone—Lorcan pondered the new information. Nothing fit together yet. He would pass it on to Rooney the next morning.

As he rode next with Ed to the Justine House, near Lincoln Park, he asked one final question. "Did you ever have any sense as to who the surviving girl's parents were?"

"You mean who do I think your Maura's parents were?"

Lorcan nodded, but added, "I'm not sure she was ever mine."

For the first time Lorcan wondered if Ed was holding something back.

"At the time, no," he said finally.

"Later?"

"One of Ours—a Justine, I mean—told me years later that a most generous contributor to our work had borne a daughter out of wedlock. She was grateful to us for taking care of the woman at some time in her life when she needed help—we acted as couriers to bring her money, I believe. The mother watched her daughter from a distance but thought it wise not to identify herself. From the description of the time and the place, it seems to me now that the girl might well be your Maura."

"This was common knowledge?"

"I was not told it in confidence. The woman did not make any pretense about the fact that she had borne a child out of wedlock. It is not, however, part of her public image either."

"Can you tell me her name?"

Ed hesitated. "You would tell your Maura?"

"No."

"Very well, then. As I think about our little conversation this evening . . . it's pure speculation on my part, but your Maura might well be the woman in question. Our benefactor is Mrs. J. Keeley Allen."

"Betty Allen, a *grande dame* of Chicago society—with lots of hints of a busy past swirling around her silvered head!"

"Yes."

"I'll treat it as privileged information."

"I'd appreciate that."

Lorcan marveled at the possibility that Betty Allen was Moire's mother as his limo brought him back to Astor Street. Could be. How had she become part of the Meehan family? And why?

It was a long shot. Probably not true. Why would the Justines have used Rory as a go-between? And why the Meehans?

Why would Ed, who at first denied remembering Maura, ultimately recall so much? He must have been well aware of who Maura was at the beginning of the conversation, but for some reason had wanted to avoid talking about her. He had become forthcoming only after Lorcan mentioned Father Gregorio.

Edward had revealed Maura's presumed origins to steer his brother away from something else, no doubt. Something that was important to the Church or the Justines or both.

In good conscience Lorcan felt he could not mention his lucky break to Dinny Rooney. He'd have to explore it himself. He had promised Ed he would consider the information privileged.

Well, we won tonight, he mused as he walked up the sidewalk to his house. Five weeks to the general election, the first Tuesday in April. On the Saturday before it, Marie and Rob would be married.

He hoped to clear up the mystery before then.

3

When Lorcan got back to his office, there was another memorandum from Dinny Rooney awaiting him.

DENNIS ROONEY AND ASSOCIATES

From: D. Rooney
To: L. J. Flynn
Subject: Conversation with Sister Mathilda Miller, O.S.F.

Sister is presently the administrator of St. Anthony's Hospital. She is a comfortable, smiling woman, of about our age, of obvious competence and charm. She wears a veil with a gray dress, though her shoes and the dress say "nun" so clearly that the veil is not strictly necessary.

While I would not want Sister angry at me, I regret that we are not producing nuns like her anymore. Everyone loses as these women slowly disappear from the Church.

I had dropped into her office because I was looking for records from thirty-five years ago to check on your illness. It had occurred to me that someone might have wanted you to be sick. I admit that I am following hunches and instincts as well as pursuing other leads.

She assured me that the records from that era

no longer existed. "Sister used to throw them out every three years." She smiled at the memory of "Sister," whoever that might have been. "She said once they paid their bills there was no need to keep their records. Now it's all on computer."

I told her about the patient in whose illness I was interested.

"Oh—I remember him very clearly. Isn't he someone important now? Wasn't his picture on the cover of *Time* a few years ago? I must check to see if he's on our benefactors' mailing list."

She made a note on the pad. A concession to human frailty I would not have expected of a sister in the days when we were in school.

If you receive one more appeal for funds, Lorcan, you will know whom to blame.

"How sick was he, Sister?"

"He was an extremely sick young man, Captain Rooney. I had finished my novitiate and was a student nurse. Most of the students were home for the weekend. Since I was a sister I was at the hospital in the emergency room. When they brought him in, I didn't think he would live. I've never seen anyone with such a high fever. We didn't have all the wonder drugs then that we do now. He was allergic to penicillin, so they couldn't give him that. The doctors were angry at his parents for not bringing him earlier. They said he'd been sick for a couple of days."

"I see."

"He seemed to be such a nice young man. Handsome and very thin. His little brother—I understand he's a priest now—told me that he had been a flyer in the war."

"How long was his life in danger?"

"Almost a week. It was a very bad case. Nowadays we'd have the fever under control in twenty-four hours. He's fortunate to have survived."

"The doctors kept him here for a long time?"

"Let me see. Well, I remember visiting him in

his room and joking with him. He was so sweet, such a nice young man. Sister wouldn't have approved if she'd found out . . . a couple of weeks, I'd say, Captain. Doctor wanted to watch for a relapse, and he really didn't trust the young man's parents. There was something else. . . . Oh, yes, they lived next door to that poor family that was blown up on Labor Day—by the crime syndicate, everyone said. I suppose that's why his family didn't notice how sick he was."

"Was he delirious when they brought him in, Sister?"

"Out of his mind, Captain. I remember it quite clearly because the things he said were so wild. I'm sure the poor boy had not been rational for at least twenty-four hours."

"Would it be foolish for me to think you might have remembered what he was raving about?"

"Well, let me see. It was the first case of high fever I encountered, so he made a strong impression on me, poor young man. He seemed to be convinced that some girl, his sweetheart I imagine, was being threatened in some way. He was trying to defend her. And he was very angry at his father too, furious at him. Threatened to kill him. Shouted at some people that weren't really there."

"Did you ever meet the sweetheart?"

"No, I didn't. Sister said that she came by one evening at visiting hours after he was out of danger, but his family wouldn't let her see him. I always thought that strange."

I had her statement notarized too, Lorcan, although I can't see any immediate use for it. Based on Sister's account, I would say that it is not strange that you do not recall the events of the twenty-four hours before the explosion.

You were out of your head with the fever.

4

"T im Meehan, they said, was a grand fellow." Dinny Rooney, in a dark brown banker's suit today, handed a manila folder across the desk. "I take it, Lorcan, you know what that means on the South Side?"

Outside the window of his office, snowflakes lazily drifted toward Michigan Avenue—occasional lake effect snow flurries, they had said. In Chicago winter did not give up easily, not even a mild winter like this one. Nor did the cold virus which had taken possession of Lorcan's body and threatened to remain till the day after the last judgment.

"About the same thing it means on the West Side, Dinny. He was a fine athlete, a great singer, a prodigious drinker, and had a powerful effect on both men and women."

"You got it."

"I ought to know: my father was a grand fellow in his day."

Lorcan glanced at the file. Not all that thick, and the last clipping from 1950. The grand fellow—Tim Meehan—would have been thirty then if he had lived that long.

The first clipping bore the headline

MEEHAN LEADS CARAVAN TO PLAYOFFS

Running, passing, and kicking, Tim Meehan, Mount Carmel's brilliant single wing, led the Caravan by Saint George this afternoon, 28 to 7. The Caravan thus earned the right to play Austin in the Kelly Bowl at Soldier Field next Saturday. A crowd of 103,000 is expected to attend the game.

Meehan scored two touchdowns, passed for a third, and blocked a kick to set up the fourth score.

"Nineteen thirty-seven? He was only a junior."

"They lost in the Kelly Bowl. Austin chased them out of the park. Meehan was still the hero." Rooney touched his Celtic cross tie clasp. "He was perpetually the hero, win or lose. The next year they came back and beat Fenger. Tim scored the winning touchdown in the last five minutes of the game."

"Impressive."

The next clipping was from the Metropolitan Section: Timothy Meehan had been elected outstanding senior at Mount Carmel in 1938; and after that a Sports Section clip announced that Tim Meehan planned to attend Notre Dame the coming fall.

In the picture which accompanied the Metro Section piece, Tim looked like a healthy Tyrone Power—pale skin, thick black hair, bright toothy grin, dancing eyes.

"Nothing about Notre Dame?"

"He was thrown out the first year. Drinking. Automatic expulsion in those days. Now they serve booze at class breaks."

"Not quite," Lorcan said with a laugh. "Times have changed. . . . Where did he go to school after he left Notre Dame?"

"He didn't. He was smart but he didn't like school much and he was tired of football. He also wasn't good enough to be first-string for the Fighting Irish. If he wasn't the top man, Tim Meehan didn't want to play. Someone with a lot of clout, maybe Captain Flynn, your grandfather, wangled a job at the Sanitary District—which meant Tim was paid for not working. He sang in a bar on Fifty-fifth Street."

"My grandfather?"

"He was a close friend of Meehan's father, who was also a police captain. When your father was looking for a home in the Dunes, he called the Congressman in search for a place. It turned out that there was a home right next door. Your parents became friends with the Congressman and his wife after they'd moved in. Renewing an old family relationship. Or so the people from Long Beach I interviewed tell me."

"Meehan's father didn't have any clout?"

"Not much money either, Lorcan. I hope it won't offend you: he was an honest cop."

"I have no illusions, Dinny, about my grandfather."

The next stack of clippings were announcements of Irish entertainments on the South Side—former Mount Carmel football star Tim Meehan would lead the singing.

"Kind of a frivolous life, wasn't it?"

"The Depression had returned with a vengeance. No jobs for young men with college degrees, much less someone with only a high school diploma. The economic situation worried the responsible folk. For Tim it was a wonderful excuse for not working. He sang, he drank, he wenched, he laughed, he picked up his Sanitary District check, he enjoyed himself."

"Wenched?"

"I realize that it's unusual for a Chicago Irishman: women found him irresistible. He was good-looking, funny, charming. They fell all over themselves fighting to jump into his bed, mostly women older than he was. Mind you, he was only nineteen or twenty at the time."

"Gigolo?"

"Maybe he took money from women, know what I mean?"

"He could be Maura's father?"

"Does he look like her?"

"Not in the least."

"We're not making much progress with the ordinary routine of investigations, Lorcan. I figure now's the time to look at some far-out possibilities."

"I agree." Lorcan looked at another clipping.

MOVIE CONTRACT FOR FOOTBALL STAR

"Well!"

"That was an exaggeration. He did have a screen test. They decided they had enough crazy Irishmen in town: Cagney, O'Brien, that bunch. He flunked. The legend is that he was drunk during the test."

"A grand fellow!"

"You got it. . . . By then the government was expanding the military because of the war which the American people tried to pretend wasn't coming. Tim won the draft lottery and was snatched out of his bar and sent to Fort Benning."

"Combat Infantry."

CARAVAN STAR COMMISSIONED

The article was from a neighborhood newspaper. The picture showed the same wicked smile, this time under a military cap. Lieutenant Timothy Meehan was quoted as saying, "Now let's get this war over with and get on with the serious business of life—in the bars on Fifty-fifth Street."

"Not exactly a patriot." Dinny sighed. "Yet, oddly, a man of courage and a crazy kind of integrity. Tim had more to him, if you're to believe the folklore, than the devil-may-care rake of Fifty-fifth Street revealed. The people that remember him will still tell you that he was twice the man his brother was."

"And an Irish patriot?"

"Unreflective like most of them, then and now. The English didn't belong in Ireland. Why were we preparing to fight England's war? Throw the bloody limey bastards out. Tim wasn't much for books or serious thought."

"He was only a kid."

"You were devouring books in Japan at the same age."

"Jesuit training."

"Tim didn't get into combat until the autumn of 1944. Led a platoon through the Hürtgen Forest. Silver Star for gallantry. They invented war for guys like him. The ultimate turn-on."

"A war lover?"

"Read that big feature piece in the *Trib*. That'll give you some idea of the kind of man he had become."

CHICAGO HERO LAUGHS AT GERMAN ARMY

Paris. February 15. Captain Timothy Meehan, Mount Carmel football great and now a war hero, laughs at the German Army.

"The Krauts are overrated," says Meehan, who won the Distinguished Service Cross for Heroism during the Battle of the Bulge in December. "We'll polish them off in another couple of months and then deal with the Japs next summer. It's a cakewalk from now on."

That sort of talk is what one expects of recruits and perhaps of newly arrived G.I.'s at a replacement depot. One hears it less often from a combat veteran, particularly one who has fought in some of the toughest battles of the war and has been wounded in action.

"I can hardly wait to get back up to the front," Meehan said during a recent interview here in Paris, "I'm fine. It was only a flesh wound in my shoulder. I want to be there when we finish off the Krauts."

His contempt for the German Army seems well founded. During the surprise German attack in December at St. Vite, Meehan's platoon, most of them recent recruits and replacements, kept a German armored column at bay for more than twelve hours. Then Meehan led his men off into the snow to join forces with another outfit and stop the Germans again.

The ingenuity and initiative displayed by American junior officers during these critical days are credited with slowing down the headlong German rush toward Antwerp.

"I didn't do any more than a lot of guys did." Meehan shrugged his shoulders, much thinner now than when he shredded the Fenger line in the 1938 Kelly Bowl.

Once the war ends, will Meehan return to Notre Dame, where he was a promising reserve quarterback before he enlisted? Or will he play pro football?

"I don't know," he says. "I don't mind saving the English in this war. They're our allies, even if they're lousy fighters. After this is over we should throw them the hell out of Ireland."

"He held up an armored column for a half day with a few riflemen? He deserved more than the D.S.C. Yet a wee bit daft, as Maeve, my daughter-in-law, would say."

"By then, certainly. Look at the picture. Closely."

In his Ike jacket and garrison cap, Tim Meehan at first glance didn't seem much different from the outstanding senior seven years earlier. But, on closer examination, Lorcan noticed that his face was leaner and his eyes shone with a manic glow.

"Ever see pictures of Doc Holliday?" Rooney asked.

"He had TB." Lorcan became the automatic pedant. "That's why his eyes seem to shine."

"Yeah, but Tim Meehan didn't have TB. He had a worse fever. He'd fallen in love with killing and war."

"And thought that he was invulnerable?"

"Sure sounds like it. It was said that his men loved him. He took crazy chances, but there was no one like him at slipping out of tight corners. The legend back on Fifty-fifth Street is that they would have given him the Medal of Honor if he hadn't pissed on George Patton's fancy boots in a latrine on the Rhine."

"Apocrypha!"

"Probably. . . . Look at the last clipping."

It was only an inch and from a back page.

WAR HERO BURIED

Major Timothy Meehan, football star at Mount Carmel and hero of the Battle of the Bulge, was buried last week in Holy Sepulchre Cemetery. Major Meehan died in Ireland in an auto accident. He is survived by his brother, Congressman Joseph Meehan of the Second Congressional District. Father Gregory Sabatini, O.S.J., recited the private requiem mass for Major Meehan. He played on the famous 1937–1938 Mount Carmel championship team.

"Not much, is it? Dead football star and dead war hero. People forget quickly."

"By 1950 we had a new war. No one was interested in Ireland, especially not the Irish-Americans who were busy catching up from the Depression and the War. I guess you know about that. They found his body in a car in a lake, a bullet in his back. He had been in the lake for a long time. Sealed casket."

Lorcan leafed through the papers. "Quick end to what might have been a brilliant life."

"Those kind of guys don't last long, Lorcan. The cocky, fast-talking young cop who nails two, maybe three coke-heads with guns blazing at him. Thinks he's immortal. Next time he catches an automatic weapon blast in the gut. Tim Meehan's life would have been short, war or no war."

Lorcan studied the photos carefully and wondered again whether he was looking at Moire's father. If Tim was her father, a lot of pieces would fit together.

"Is he really dead, Dinny?"

The cop squirmed in his chair. "Argument against: no positive identification on this side of the Atlantic. Argument for: he was, like you said, a little daft. Even if he cooked up a scheme to fake his death, he would have got himself killed for real long since then."

"Seems reasonable."

Lorcan considered the last picture again. No physical resemblance to Moire. Maybe, however, the kind of handsome guy that a young Betty Lyndon would have found attractive in a bar on Fifty-fifth Street fifty years ago.

"You wonder," Dinny said, "what the point of this file is—other than that he was a brother of the Congressman who died in that blast?"

"Yeah."

"The gunman that killed him, or claims to have killed him, lives in Chicago. Goes to Mass every morning."

"Ah?" Lorcan sat up straight and leaned forward. "Who is he?"

"His name is Eammon Rafferty; he lives up in Jefferson Park and owns a small bar. He's about sixty now and has a young family—five kids. He doesn't dare return to Ireland since there are people there with long memories, and a lot of questions the Special Branch would like to ask. There were other deaths besides Tim Meehan's that he evidently claims credit for."

"Still active?"

"A small band of IRA immigrants, people who left Northern Ireland thirty or forty years ago to escape prosecution or reprisals, have set up a loose and informal organization to keep the fight on this side of the Atlantic alive. The group is mostly talk, but it does collect for Noraid and organizes demonstrations when the Irish ambassador comes to town. Although the Lads in the current IRA don't pay much attention to them, they take the money offered."

"They don't sound too dangerous," Lorcan commented.

He sensed that Dinny Rooney was building up to a dramatic dénouement of his story. Like all Irishmen, Rooney had that kind of flair.

"The Chicago Police Department has more crucial tasks than keeping an eye on this band. However, there is one informant who keeps my former colleagues on the force posted on what Rafferty and his band are up to."

"Oh?"

Dinny touched his tie clasp. "That source tells me that Rafferty and his bunch are greatly upset about my investigation. They don't want the Meehan case reopened."

"The phone call?"

"They want to scare you off."

"Then we must be getting warmer."

"A lot of crazy things were happening that summer at Long Beach, Lorcan."

"I missed them all. . . . Well, if these folks are worn-out revolutionaries from the past, they can't be too dangerous."

"I'm not so sure." Dennis Rooney sighed. "The Lads only kill people intentionally. These guys can do it by mistake."

"I'll keep that in mind. One more thing, Dinny. I want to find out all I can about the Order of Saint Justine and their late Chicago provincial, Father Gregorio Sabatini. His name keeps coming up."

"I thought you might want more on him."

5

"Donny Roscoe says he's prepared to nail you on a murder rap unless you cooperate with him."

"What?" Lorcan moved the cup of hot coffee away from his lips and placed it back on the saucer.

They were eating breakfast, two days after the primary, in Larry Whealan's office across from the Merchandise Mart, overlooking the Chicago River. Pale sunlight flickered on and off the water as clouds alternately revealed and hid the river.

A note had come to his house by messenger proposing the breakfast meeting in Larry's office. "Don't phone me, even if you can't come," the note had ended.

Uneasy about the cloak-and-dagger atmosphere, Lorcan suspected that the FBI was trying a new tactic. But a murder charge?

Whealan ran a hand through his thick, wavy brown hair. "I encountered your good friend and mine, Maynard Lealand, Special-Agent-in-Charge of the Federal Bureau of Investigation's Chicago office yesterday on Wacker Drive. Lealand made out as if our meeting was a chance encounter, but really he'd been lying in wait like some clumsy sheriff planning an ambush."

"Same old inept gumshoe."

"He talked around the subject at first. I'll spare you the details. It boils down to this: they gave your brother Henry immunity in their investigation of you. Henry didn't have much—Maynard just about admitted that. So they sweated him and he came up with a story about an explosion you caused thirty-five years ago—the one that blew up a congressman—"

"The late Joe Meehan, Second District. Labor Day, 1954. Also his wife and two daughters."

"Hank has apparently told them that you turned on a gas jet and tossed a lighted match through a window. Some love motive. You confessed it to him and his father and they covered up for you."

"I see," Lorcan said, trying to take this in.

"Now Maynard admits that even if there is no statute on murder, it's pretty late in the day." Larry lifted a glass of orange juice. "On the other hand, your being a celebrity, the prosecutor down in LaPorte County might want to have a go at you. Can't tell, says Maynard, what would happen in those circumstances—small town, local jury, big man from out of state."

"And your reading?"

Whealan shrugged his broad shoulders. "They have good lawyers in Indiana, too. Henry would make a lousy witness. Your lawyer would eat him alive. It'd be a lot of trouble and distraction, but chances are you'd win."

"Chances are . . ."

"I can't give any better odds once there's a jury of your peers making a decision."

"I see."

"Anyway, Maynard says he's willing to forget the indignity to his young colleagues and advise Donny Roscoe that there isn't sufficient evidence to turn over to LaPorte if you help them in an investigation in which they're engaged."

"So . . ."

"Precisely. They sweat Hank to get at you, and then you to get at their real target."

"Who is?"

"Who are. The various and sundry members of the Allen family. From old J. Keeley Allen on down. You've done business with them, I take it?"

"A couple of local industrial-development projects. They're into saving the City. I happen to agree with the goal, although they're stodgy in their methods. What do Donny and Maynard have on them?"

"Maynard was very vague. Probably that they're big names and lots of TV appeal. Have they done anything illegal in their work with you?"

"Definitely not. As far as I know, they're straight as a plumbline."

"So what should I tell Maynard?" Larry Whealan's eyes narrowed.

"They want me to commit perjury against the Allen clan?"

"They want you to testify against them. They don't absolutely require perjury. That's optional."

"Fuck 'em. And you can tell Maynard that in so many words."

Whealan grinned and helped himself to a sweet roll. "I figured you'd say something like that. Nine chances out of ten, they're bluffing anyway. . . . Do you want to tell me about that explosion?"

"Not much to tell. I don't think I set it off. I had a fever of 104.9 at the time. Meningitis. I almost died."

"I wonder if Hank told them that. He's a real son of a bitch, Lorcan. You do know that, don't you?"

"Always has been."

"Maynard says that Henry confesses to terrible guilt feelings because he's covered up for so many years. You can almost hear him saying it at a press conference."

"Typical, I'm afraid. . . . I've had Dinny Rooney looking into the explosion the last week or so. The son of one of the survivors is marrying my younger daughter. I wanted to clear it up for my own reasons. Can I tell Dinny about Roscoe's scheme?"

"You sure can. But don't call him or me from your office. Maynard has you bugged. Hell, Lorcan, you're a dangerous criminal."

"Let me make sure I understand this. They're really after the Allens. . . ."

"I have a hunch they were after you first. They couldn't find much in your tax returns or your records so they leaned on your brother, hoping he'd provide them with dirt. Because you're smart, you never tell Henry anything. So they write you off. Then Henry cooks up this murder story. It's not too good because the trial won't bring Donny or the Bureau much publicity. If LaPorte doesn't bite or if you're acquitted, they look real bad. So they decide to use this charge of Hank's to browbeat you into giving them one of the biggest financial names in Chicago."

"This is the United States of America, isn't it, not the Soviet Union?"

"When dealing with the United States Attorneys and the Bureau it's hard to tell. . . . A lot of us didn't realize ten or fifteen years ago that what they did against crooked politicians and judges and Mafia bosses they could do to any of us. Otto Kerner's freedom was our freedom. When Jim Thompson rode into the state house on the bodies of politicians convicted this way, he rode in on all our bodies."

"And we ignored him or cheered for him," Lorcan said bitterly.

"I'll be candid." Larry shoved his teacup away like it was

a temptation. "The odds against an indictment are high, and against a conviction astronomical. The odds against unfavorable publicity which can hurt you and your family are much lower."

"All the more reason"—Lorcan stood up—"to find out who really did kill those four people."

"Way to go!" Larry rose too and shook hands firmly. "You might have Dinny Rooney get in touch with me. I know some people in the prosecutor's office in LaPorte. They won't be particularly eager to play horsey for Donny Roscoe's Lady Godiva."

"I'll call Dennis from an outside line as soon as I figure he's in his office."

As he walked down Wacker Drive toward Michigan Avenue, Lorcan thought about his children, about Maeve and the wee punks, about Rob and the family he and Marie wanted so desperately. They would be the real victims of Roscoe and Lealand and the media ghouls who feasted on the bodies of such victims.

He phoned Rooney from a public phone on Michigan Avenue. The ex-cop listened attentively.

"Lorcan, they're out of their fucking minds!"

"Which won't prevent them from going through with their plans."

"Yeah. Did you tell Whealan about Captain O'Rourke's affidavit?"

"I forgot about it."

"And you forgot about Sister Mathilda's testimony too, I suppose."

"I did indeed."

Lorcan winced at the realization that the reason he had neglected to tell Larry about either was because he was half afraid Hank might be telling the truth.

"If your brother is telling people that you lighted that gas jet, he's going to have to explain how you did that with a hundred and five fever and how come it was high explosives which blew the Meehan house apart. They haven't got a thing on you."

"I guess they don't." But somehow Lorcan did not feel reassured.

After speaking with Dinny, he decided to give Larry a call to fill him in.

"You forgot to mention those two facts, Lorcan?" Larry asked after Lorcan had filled him in about the high explosives O'Rourke believed were the source of the blast and his own ravings as remembered by Sister Mathilda.

"It was early in the morning, Larry."

"Well, that settles it. There's no case against you."

"Will you go to Maynard with the facts?"

"If we did that, they'd just persuade your brother to change his testimony. No, we'll wait till they leak the charges to the press. Then we call a press conference and cut the ground out from under them before they call their press conference."

"Trial, conviction, and execution by press conference, huh?"

"That's the way the game is played these days. The TV people want drama for the evening news, Donny and Maynard want to see their pictures on the tube, and the public figures that if people weren't guilty they wouldn't be charged. Not what James Madison had in mind, is it?"

It was Lorcan's morning off with Doctor Murphy. He would have liked to talk to her about this latest development. He needed a woman's sympathetic ear.

Cindi?

He'd have to warn her that it was off the record.

Moire?

Maybe he could call her.

"A call for you, Lorcan," Mary Murray said, greeting him at the door to his office. "Won't give his name. Sounds like the same man as before."

Lorcan frowned and picked up the phone. "Lorcan Flynn."

"If you don't want anything to happen to your grandsons, you'll stop asking questions."

"Fuck you," Lorcan replied and slammed down the phone.

Mary Murray winked at him.

He went into his office and punched in Dinny Rooney's number.

"I'm calling from my office, Din, so I assume we have Maynard's gumshoes listening in. Someone just made a threat on the phone against my grandsons. I want everyone to know that I hold Maynard and the Bureau responsible. Would you put guards on the whole family for me? And we have a wedding coming up for which we'll need security."

6

C indi's head rested submissively on his chest.
    "I didn't want to fall in love with you, Lorcan. I couldn't help myself."

She snuggled closer to him, like a little girl seeking comfort from a powerful father figure.

Cindi had learned earlier in the day that she had placed second in a race for a network anchor job in New York. She had managed to keep her emotions under control until she arrived at his house. Then she had collapsed into tearful hysteria. She needed reassuring love. Lorcan was the designated lover to provide it.

She had absorbed him like a sponge needing affection. Although Lorcan realized that if she had won the job in New York she would have left him without a backward glance, he had been happy to oblige her need for love.

His hand rested in the small of her back. "Feeling better?" he asked her.

She sighed happily.

He leaned over and kissed her.

"I have to be at the studio in ten minutes," she murmured lethargically.

"Let's go, then." He climbed out of bed and lifted her to her feet. "Can't have the anchorwoman coming in late, especially when she is as radiant as you are."

"I'll come back after the program if you want me to," she said meekly.

"By all means. We have work to finish."

"Not just work"—she put her arms into her coat, which he was holding for her—"I hope."

"Maybe a bit of play, too."

She rushed down the sidewalk to the waiting limo.

It won't last, he told himself sadly. *It can't possibly last.* But he knew he would find her tough to give up.

What did his schedule call for during the interlude in which she was at the station?

He walked wearily back to his office and turned on the computer. The Sidekick program told him that in the interlude between the seven-thirty entry dubbed "Cin" and the ten-thirty entry with the same name, there was a nine-thirty entry: "continue search."

He groaned. No wonder he hadn't remembered. The schedule demanded that he return to searching his mother's collection.

No rest for the wicked.

7

His conscience still gnawing at him, Lorcan Flynn opened another carton of his mother's memorabilia. He was finding this a depressing, melancholy search.

Over the past few days he'd been allocating what free time his Sidekick schedule permitted him to exploring the cartons in the basement storeroom next to the swimming pool.

Now, after another depressing Saturday lunch with his father, Lorcan had returned to his task of preventing the dead from burying their dead. At the lunch, Hank had been particularly prickly and contentious, perhaps preparing himself for an assault on his betrayal of his brother. But Lorcan would not give him the satisfaction of a complaint.

Dad had attacked Moire and Lorcan's children through

the whole meal. Lorcan had fended him off. He was in a no-win situation. If Pat Flynn angered him, then he lost, and if Pat Flynn attacked his family with impunity, he lost too.

His one victory came when Dad sneered, "Well, don't expect me to show up at that wedding. I'm not giving it my blessing."

"I don't think they planned to ask for your blessing, Dad."

So now, with the solace of a large Waterford tumbler of Bushmill's Single Malt, Lorcan was back home again poring over his mother's effects. There was a baptismal picture of Eileen Marie McArdle Flynn. Whoever could have guessed that her life would end so bitterly. His mother had saved little after the summer of 1954—some pictures from his and Hank's weddings, ordination, and first Mass remembrances of Edward, a photo of young Patrick in the arms of another laughing girl, her disliked daughter-in-law, Dorothy.

Nothing of Eileen, her only daughter. Mom and Dad had attended the wedding in the grotto at Notre Dame under protest—they hated Eileen's husband for vague, unspecified reasons. After the wedding there had been almost no contact between mother and daughter. Sometime later, Mom must have gone through her souvenirs and systematically removed every trace of Eileen.

Her daughter had flown in for their mother's funeral, only to be verbally abused by her father the first night of the wake, indeed to be blamed for her mother's liver cancer.

She did not stay for the funeral Mass. Rather she flew back to Seattle the next morning.

The phone in the pool area rang. Lorcan sighed, picked up his tumbler of Irish, and walked into the next room.

"Lorcan Flynn."

It was Maeve, a welcome relief after so much melancholy.

"Are you all right now, Old Fella? Aren't you sounding a little bit weird, if you take me meaning?"

"An afternoon watching college basketball on television and my usual weekend weirdness."

"*Well,* I'm calling about this friggin wedding of yours."

"I'm not marrying anyone that I'm aware of, Maeve."

"That's another matter altogether. 'Tis your daughter's wedding I'm in a dither about."

"God forbid."

"The immediate problem is what to do with the groom's mother, poor dear woman."

"She is of an age to take care of herself, Maevie."

" 'Tis not the point, Lorcan James Flynn, and you know it."

"Ah, woman, would you stop blathering like a cow with loose bowels and in the name of all the holy saints above tell me what the point is!"

"Not bad, Lorcan, not bad at all at all. Keep working at it and you may be as good some day as my Da is. . . . The point is that we can't put the poor woman up in a hotel, can we now?"

He should have seen it coming.

"Maeve, the new Four Seasons is on Michigan Avenue, it has a splendid view of the Lake, it's a three-minute walk from the little Bishop's Cathedral, and it is one of the great luxury hotels in the Western World."

" 'Tis a heartless inhuman place to be alone all by yourself."

"I'm sure Mrs. Halinan has stayed in hotels by herself many times."

"Not when her son is after getting himself married."

"And her daughter will be with her."

"A poor slip of a girl, not out of university yet."

"What would you propose, Maeve? I am, so to speak, putty in your hands."

"Pure blarney, Lorcan. . . . Anyway, what I'm after suggesting, as you well know, is that we put Moire, the poor dear thing, and her daughter, Josie, up at your place. Sure, aren't you after having more guest rooms than you ever use, and won't Liz be home for the wedding and won't Marie herself be staying there for the last few nights?"

Lorcan sighed. "Tell me, have you cleared this scheme with the two women of the house?"

"Liz and Marie, is it now? Weren't they after insisting I call you and suggest it, meself being in charge of arrangements in a manner of speaking?"

"Then it's fine, Maeve. I'll be happy to have Moire and Josie use the guest rooms. I'll leave which rooms to you as the Great Arranger."

Maeve seemed delighted having pulled this off. Lorcan couldn't resist teasing her.

"Maeve, I can practically hear you beaming."

Maeve giggled and they exchanged farewells. Then Lorcan turned his attention back to his search.

He was shocked in his exploration of her memory boxes at how much of the material pertained to him. There were more stacks labeled LORCAN in a flowing, feminine hand than for the other children put together—coloring paper from primary grades, spelling tests, term papers, report cards, honor certificates, his boyish and reassuring letters from Korea.

Yet she did not seem happy when he had returned. Although he had been the great pride of her life, she seemed so dissatisfied with him from 1954 to the end of her life sixteen years later. What had he done—besides growing up?

Then he found the letters.

She had buried them under a stack of Long Beach pictures from 1951—the year that Dad had bought the house. She had bound them with a rubber band and had slipped under the band a label: LETTERS FROM MAURA ANNE MEEHAN TO LORCAN, SUMMER 1954.

Lorcan sat down heavily on the beach chair which he had dragged from the pool area to the storeroom. If she had intercepted the letters, why had she bothered to save them? And why label them so neatly?

He considered the stack. Six letters. The envelopes were addressed in the perfect Palmer Method scroll taught in Catholic schools in those days. Maura surely received A's from many nuns for her penmanship.

Suddenly presented with these missives from the past, Lorcan wasn't completely sure he wanted to read them. He held the packet in his hand. Moire herself had said he ought to let the dead bury the dead. Perhaps he should. But what if the letters contained a clue to the mystery of the explosion that Labor Day weekend?

He removed the rubber band. It broke in his fingers, worn

out like he was from the years. He counted the letters and glanced at the postmarks—six of them arranged according to date. Mom had kept a neat record.

Oyster Bay, Long Island
September 10, 1954
Darling Lorcan,

I hope you're feeling better. Before I left for here, I peeked into your room at the Hospital. Sister said I could look for just a moment. Your parents have protected you from visitors because you were so sick, but Sister said that you were ever so much better.

I hardly recognized you, my darling. I said to Sister that's not Lorcan Flynn and she said yes it is, dear. He's been dreadfully ill.

You really scared us with your fever. I prayed and prayed and prayed. It was partly my fault. I should have noticed you were burning with heat. When I hugged you after you hit the home run I thought you were terribly warm even for a hot day.

I should have said something, especially since your parents and your uncles were so worried by the terrible accident. I was worried too. They were my family that was killed—the only family I've ever known. If I hadn't taken my long walk all the way to New Buffalo, I would have been blown up too. I still wake up at night seeing that flame against the sky and wondering who was hurt.

The next days were horrible. I couldn't believe what was happening. My family had been killed. You were dying. There was no one to talk to. People blamed me—as if it were my fault they had died and I had survived. There wasn't even any place for me to stay that night. Anne Hanlon had been very nice to me during the summer. I asked her if I could sleep at her house. Otherwise I would have had to sleep on the beach. I'm not complaining, Lorcan. I'm saying how lucky I was to have a friend like Anne whose parents would let me stay with her. The day of the funeral, I sobbed in Mrs. Hanlon's arms.

She insisted that I come with them to New York. I stayed with Anne's aunt in Beverly for a couple of days and then came down here on the train. It's a big change from Chicago. I don't know how long I'll stay. They want me to start school at Hunter College, but I don't have enough money for that and I don't want to impose on them. Maybe I'll try to find a job as a waitress somewhere and rent an apartment of my own.

I love you, Lorcan. I love you more than anything else in the world. Write me as soon as you can and tell me that you love me.

All my love,
MAURA

Oyster Bay
September 18, 1954
Dearest Lorcan,

I tried to talk to you on the phone again today. Your mother was very firm. You were too weak to be bothered by phone calls. When you're better she'll tell you and you can phone me, if you want.

Anyway, I learned today that Uncle Joe left me some money—enough so I can finish college and buy some clothes and not be a burden on anyone. I'm not sure yet what I'll do. I guess I'm independent now and can make my own decisions. That scares me, although I'm confident that I can make it on my own.

It was a wonderful summer, wasn't it, Lorcan? We had so much fun—movies, long talks, walking on the beach, swimming at night, lying on our magic beach towels, playing softball. I was so happy when we won that game I thought my heart would break. Then, later, when you told me how much you loved me, I knew it was breaking. It was too bad what happened next, but I don't blame anyone.

I knew you weren't feeling well, because you seemed kind of incoherent some of the time.

And if there had not been the problem, I might have been in the house when it blew up.

No, I surely would have been in the house.

I guess God wants me to live. I wonder why. There's no one in the world that cares about me anymore—except you. I guess I'm supposed to do something important with my life. Well, I'll have to try. I'm pretty confused now.

I keep hoping that it wasn't the fever talking that night on the beach. I'm sure deep down it wasn't, because you'd been acting like you loved me all summer and telling me how much you loved me. It's just that it seemed very special that night before we were interrupted.

I have to talk to the Hanlons now about my future. God bless you, Lorcan, and make you well.

I love you very much. I always will.

All my love,
MAURA

Oyster Bay
September 25, 1954
Dear Lorcan,

Still no letter. I'm worried about you. Mrs. Hanlon talked to some people at Long Beach today and they say you're still in the hospital and out of danger but very weak. They told Mrs. Hanlon that it was possible you'll be released next week.

Maybe you'll be strong enough to write then. My heart breaks for you. That ugly war hurt you so badly. Then the conflicts in your family upset you—I could tell that even if you didn't say it. Now, when you are about to go off to school and begin your new life, you have this awful fever that almost kills you. I hope and pray that you recover completely and soon and that you can still make it to Notre Dame this semester and play basketball like you want to.

Sometimes my heart breaks for me too, just a little. I will survive and be all right, Lorcan. I always have.

I miss the touch of your fingers on my body and your lips pressed against mine. I'm sure we'll be together again somehow. I'll always love you, Lorcan. Always.

My deepest love,
MAURA

Oyster Bay
September 29, 1954
Dearest, dearest Lorcan,

Just a short note to tell you how much I love you and how much I miss you.

It's been decided. I will attend Hunter College. They have a wonderful graphics design program and as you remember that's what I really like. I'll live there in an apartment with three other students during the week and come out here to Oyster Bay on weekends. The Hanlons insist I won't be a bother to them and that it will be good for me to escape from Manhattan on weekends.

I'll also find myself a part-time job near school, maybe in a printer's or typesetter's place. That way I can stretch my inheritance a little further.

I'm kind of scared at beginning school. Hunter is so different from St. Xav's. I cover up pretty good—as you well know—so everyone marvels at how self-confident and poised I am. That's funny, isn't it?

I miss you most terribly and I love you with all my heart. Please write, Lorcan. PLEASE!!!
Love you,
MAURA

New York City
October 5, 1954

Hi Lorcan!

It's a little easier now than it was a couple of days ago. This place and this city scare me. Hunter College is part of the city system and is a women's college for bright kids. Many different kinds of girls are here—Negroes, Puerto Ricans, Jews, Chinese, even a few Irish. About half the school is Italian. Everyone talks all the time. There's not much listening and no peace and quiet.

I'm in an apartment with three other girls, one Jewish and two Italian. They're all dreadfully homesick. They talk and cry a lot so they won't feel so bad.

And Lorcan, none of them live more than forty-five minutes from here!

For some reason they think I'm their mother or something like that. Each of them pours her heart out to me. What am I supposed to say? It seems to be enough that I just listen. Good old Maura, the earth mother!

I miss you, Lorcan. When my apartment mates are asleep at night, I cry a little for you. I don't dare cry any other time, because that will shake their faith in me. So I cry at night, not much. I love you and will love you always.

When you find the time, please write.

I still love you.

Maura

October 21, 1954
Dear Lorcan,

This will be my last letter.

Although the Hanlons didn't want to tell me they finally admitted that you have been out of the hospital for almost a month. They said you are down at Notre Dame, even playing a little basketball. I'm happy to hear that you are healthy again.

I'm embarrassed by the silly letters I've written. I was a foolish adolescent girl who confused a summer romance with love. I ought to have known better and I'm sorry I was so presumptuous.

I won't bother you anymore. I don't imagine that we'll ever see each other again. That makes me sad, but it's probably wise that we don't.

I hope your life is blessed by God's grace and that you have all kinds of love.

Please remember every once in a while a second baseman who loved you a lot one magic summer that ended in tragedy.

God bless you and keep you, Lorcan.

Always,
MAURA

8

Motionless, like one of his own statues, Lorcan Flynn sat in the storeroom for hours. He lost track of time. In one hand he held the letters, in the other his face, as if to blot out the agony which jumped up from the pages of the letters. Occasionally he would reach for his tumbler of Irish whiskey. He continued to sip from it even after he had drunk the last drop. He was too stupefied to notice that the glass was empty and that a bottle was only a few inches away from it.

He was beyond anger, beyond pain, beyond sympathy for the poor, brave, lonely girl who had written such poignant words. All those emotions would come eventually. Now he was bewildered, overwhelmed.

Moire was wrong: they were not silly letters. The girl that wrote them was not silly. He would show them to her when she came for the wedding.

Would he? Perhaps. He would have to think about it.

Finally, as if still in a trance, he stood up and began to pack up his mother's cartons. Later he would burn them all, blotting the last trace of her from the face of the earth. Or, no, he wouldn't. What good would that do?

Let the dead bury their dead, as Moire had said.

Lorcan couldn't resist considering the what-ifs. What if he hadn't gotten ill? What if his mother hadn't intercepted Moire's letters? How different his life—and Moire's—might have been then. Suddenly Lorcan began to feel again.

The fury came like a summer storm, sudden, unannounced, and destructive. He looked for something to fling.

The whiskey bottle.

He snatched it up and flung it against the wall. The bottle smashed and the precious liquid drained down the concrete like a bloodstain.

"Goddamn them all!"

9

DENNIS ROONEY AND ASSOCIATES

From: D. Rooney
To: L. J. Flynn
Subject: Dinner Party at Meehans', Labor Day Sunday, 1954.

I have been able to talk to three people who were at the dinner party the evening before the explosion—Mrs. Norine McCarthy and Mr. and Mrs. Martin Kennedy. Their reports are in substantial agreement. I have the transcripts of my conversations with them if you wish to peruse them in detail.

Their recollections of the evening are vivid, not a surprise given what happened the next day.

Usually, when a tragedy follows a routine social engagement, the participants will tell you that everyone seemed perfectly normal a few hours earlier. Such is not the case in this instance. The three people I interviewed asserted there was tension in the air that evening and that they left the party with a sense of foreboding that something was about to happen, "something more than a terrible thunderstorm," remarks Mrs. McCarthy, "something just awful."

Like:

"Like a death."

Perhaps after the fact she is reading that back into her memories.

I pressed each of them on this premonition. They cannot describe it precisely. Rather they said it was a result of a combination of events which transpired. Your mother and father were bickering as they had all summer. To be more precise, your mother was complaining and snipping at your father and he tried to calm her down. Somehow the bickering seemed more intense and your father less responsive than he usually was. As Eve Kennedy said, "Poor Eileen hadn't been herself all summer. I suppose it was the strain of that boy coming home from the war and conflict between him and his father. Pat Flynn was a nice, happy-go-lucky man, life of the party. His son was a disrespectful boor. Always has been. Poor Eileen was caught between them."

Joe and Sally Meehan were extremely tense, a rare condition for them. They were usually enthusiastic. They enjoyed parlor games, practical jokes, and good times. They were tall, handsome, gregarious people who loved to celebrate, as Martin Kennedy put it, "the end of summer. Also the beginning and the middle of it."

Martin Kennedy said that they seemed to be listening for something—outside on the lake or the beach. They jumped at the slightest sound. They exchanged nervous glances. They were irritable with their daughters, to whom they paid almost no attention ordinarily. Sally did not try to calm down her friend Eileen Flynn as she usually did.

With Sally and Pat Flynn both paying little attention to her, Eileen Flynn drank herself into a rage. That attracted some attention but not much.

They all remember leaving the party early, about 11:30, and remarking as they walked or drove home that there was something unusual afoot. They also agree that there was a peculiar aroma in the air—"like a dead animal or something," says Mrs. Kennedy. They state that they blamed much of the tension on the Meehans' adopted daughter, who was "carrying on" with young Flynn, both of them a scandal to the community. She was a mysterious, sullen young woman whom no one liked or trusted. After the tragedy she inherited money from the Meehans, then disappeared, to California they believed. They could not understand why the police did not arrest her. She was the one who profited from the death of the Meehan family.

They report a brief and violent thundershower in the early morning hours—one or one-thirty; they disagree whether it cleaned away the terrible smell—Mrs. McCarthy saying that it did not. Then the night was quiet until the explosion at 4:30. It came during another storm, a much more violent one. They felt at first that a house had been struck by lightning. Eve Kennedy, who lived on the other side of the Meehans' from your family, added that she heard a noisy argument on the beach about 2:30. She assumed that it was drunken college boys fighting with one another.

I asked if there had been talk on the beach of unusual visitors the week prior to Labor Day. Mrs. McCarthy replied that she had a vague recollection that a few nervous older women reported that there were mysterious strangers walking the road or the beach at odd hours. However, she added these women were afraid of their shadows and frequently imagined things.

I interviewed the Kennedys separately from Mrs. McCarthy. There are, however, no glaring inconsistencies in their accounts: it was an odd night—hot, humid, tense, fetid. They agreed that Maura Meehan was suspicious and mysterious and that Lorcan Flynn probably ought to have seen a doctor—the wording was so similar in both interviews that I suspect they were repeating the conventional wisdom of their generation that summer.

Martin Kennedy added a word at the end about your father. "Pat Flynn was a clever, clever man. Still is, as far as I know. He kidded around a lot but he didn't miss much. He was kind to a wife who would have driven most men crazy, I'll give him that. I wouldn't have trusted him completely, though. That night there was something on his mind, too, something, well, I'll say a little devious. He was watching Joe Meehan like a hunter watches a duck. I didn't like it. I figured, though, that it was none of my business. Made me kind of wonder the next day."

None of them were interviewed by police after the disaster, nor by the federal agents your brother reports were present. The most rudimentary principles of police work would have demanded that questions be asked of those who had attended a dinner party with the victims a few hours before their deaths. It would appear that there was a frantic rush to the verdict of accidental death and that no one wanted any record that would interfere with the verdict.

What do we make of these memories?

I suggest the following:

1. There was a political cover-up of a murder or an accident that was embarrassing to many different important parties.

2. Joseph Meehan was involved in activity that was dangerous.

3. Your father either knew about the activity or had begun to suspect what it was.

4. Joe's brother Tim was an activist, as we say today, in Irish nationalist causes. Joe, for all his conservative political leanings, sympathized with violent nationalism in Ireland. (I gather that this is a family tradition. Their father, as a young man, had been a member of the *Clan n'a Gael,* a militant nationalist organization that was active in Chicago at the turn of the century.)

5. While the IRA was quiescent in the nineteen-fifties, plots and schemes were nonetheless hatched with some frequency. Arms were smuggled into Ireland by sympathizers in this country. These shipments were usually confiscated by the British or the Royal Ulster Constabulary, whose agents had been part of the plot from the beginning. The Irish have developed treason and betrayal of one another to a high art.

6. In conclusion, I suspect some kind of IRA involvement; I don't mean the present Lads in Ulster, who couldn't care less about what happened thirty-five years ago (they are more concerned about what happened three centuries ago or what happened yesterday). I mean rather the group that was active in this country in the years after the war—mostly exiled gunmen. They're not a pleasant lot (although many of them are daily communicants) and were and are quite capable of every kind of insanity. Very often they embarrass their successors.

I will make inquiries.

P.S. I am still pursuing the matter of Father Gregorio. It is very opaque—and very bent.

10

"You blame your father for intercepting mail from the young woman?"

"Yes, damn him."

Doctor Murphy had read the letters from Maura without comment. Lorcan had strained from his couch to hear a reaction. Once he thought he had heard a sigh. If she had sighed, no doubt it was deliberate.

"Would your mother have not been more likely to receive the mail at home or the hospital?"

"He told her to keep it from me."

"Pure speculation, Lorcan."

"Why would she do it?"

"You yourself have said that she didn't like the young woman—or any young woman you found attractive. They were rivals for her affection, Lorcan."

"Why didn't she throw them away?"

"I can't answer that," Doctor Murphy said slowly. "Perhaps she intended to show them to you someday. She might have persuaded herself that the letters offered all the evidence that was necessary to prove that Maura Anne Meehan was a conniving schemer. Perhaps she feared that you might find out about the girl's letters and demand them. Or perhaps she could not bring herself to destroy them. Maybe she simply forgot about them. In any case, Lorcan James Flynn, you're looking in the wrong place to find the guilty party."

"Where should I look?"

"In the mirror, where else?"

"I didn't intercept the letters!" he shouted. "They did."

"And when you regained consciousness and sanity you asked, did you ask, if Maura Anne Meehan had called or written to you?"

"No."

"When did you find out that she had moved to New York?"

"Someone told me at school, before Thanksgiving, I think."

"You *think?*" She was tapping her pen, a sign he understood now of acute impatience with him. "This is the great love of your life, a woman whom you adored, and you do not even inquire where she is and barely remember when you finally learn where she is? Do you seriously expect me to believe that?"

"I had been seriously ill."

"I marvel that the woman does not think you an insensitive boor."

"Something happened that night, Doctor Murphy. Something terrible."

"Something that blotted Maura Anne Meehan out of your life?"

"Yes."

"Are you sure you're not rationalizing your own fears of her?"

"That's not enough to explain what happened. There was something else."

"Will it stop you again?"

"My father took her away from me once. If he can, he'll take her away again."

Moire Meehan's letters are profoundly moving. My patient imagines she's mysterious, reserved, distant. Yet I cannot conceive of more candid self-revelation. Perhaps her kind of candor does create mystery. She is a brave, resilient, honest woman who can accept the pains of life without complaint and face the certainty of future pain without flinching.

Which choice will my patient make?

What he should do is evident. Humans often don't do what they should do. Hence when the right choice is evident they blur it with monumental rationalizations.

*Being an exceptionally intelligent man, my
patient is most adroit at rationalizations.*

*What am I to make of his notion that in addition
to his fears of her, there was another barrier which
was set up that night on the beach?*

*Perhaps his fears were powerfully reenforced.
Something that was done or said on the beach
towels.*

11

Betty Keeley Allen smiled graciously at Lorcan Flynn.
In fact, she smiled at him nine times—the same smile
in each of the nine pictures on his desk.

Maura's smile.

The pictures covered forty years of Betty's life—Betty
O'Leary, Betty Riordan, and now Betty Keeley Allen. No
pictures of Betty Lyndon, the daughter of a streetcar motor-
man from Visitation Parish who had married, at the age of
nineteen, James Patrick O'Leary, a railroad vice president—
thirty years her senior.

Betty at the World's Fair; Marshal Italo Balbo, who had
led a flight of seaplanes from Italy to the United States for
the fair, kissing Betty's hand; Betty at the races; Betty at the
World Series; Betty in a Red Cross uniform during the war;
Betty coming home on the *Queen Elizabeth* after a three-
month honeymoon with her new husband, Robert Riordan,
the banker; Betty displaying her home on North Dearborn
Parkway; Betty at a benefit dance at Geneva Lake. . . .

In all the pictures the same smile—natural perhaps at
first, practiced and automatic later. It was eternally dazzling, even in the most recent picture of Betty at seventy-
three, a handsome, durable, regal woman.

Maura's mother?

How would he find out save by asking her?

Dad knew, perhaps, but he would never tell. Rory might know, but then again he might not. If he did know he would be afraid to tell. Father Frank would have known, but he was dead. Hank probably did not know, but he was not to be trusted anyway.

Lorcan had made a promise to Ed. He could not talk to anyone about his suspicion. Perhaps, someday, if it were absolutely necessary, he would walk down to Betty's luxury apartment, a block and a half from his house, and lay out pictures of Moire at the same time in her life. What would she say?

What could she say?

He knew Betty Allen reasonably well. Charm was part of her arsenal of weapons. She had been friendly to him, unusually so he had often thought. Or maybe she could flatter every man into thinking that he was special.

In style and personality she was not at all like Maura. Moire. Whatever.

Yet the physical similarity was striking. Lorcan had invariably felt after his few cheery words from Betty Allen that he had seen her before someplace.

Despite her divorce from Bobby Riordan—a marriage later annulled by the Church on the grounds, whispers had it, of impotence—Betty was now a pillar of Catholicism, a friend of whoever happened to be Cardinal, a member of the Board of Catholic Charities, a daily Mass-attender. Or, rather, Eucharist-celebrator.

Whispers said that she had been a wild one when she was young and that her first two marriages had not ended the wildness. It was even muttered sotto voce that her son, Ken, had been conceived out of wedlock to push old Jim Allen to the altar.

Well, Ken was a promising young man, smarter than the rest of the family, and Jim looked happy enough.

All's well that ends well.

Except for an illegitimate daughter you might have left behind.

Lorcan pushed that notion aside and began to read *The Wall Street Journal*. He was back on schedule now that

Cindi Horton had drifted out of his life, he had to admit to his relief.

He had finished the clay work the other night before the Ten O'clock News. She had pecked him on the cheek and said she had to run. He would call her when he did the casting, wouldn't he?

So that was how relationships ended these days.

He put aside the *Journal* and took out a legal-size pad from the credenza behind his desk. He decided to try to put together a chronology for that fateful period around Labor Day. *August/September—1954* he wrote across the long side.

Late August: Strangers appear at Long Beach, perhaps foreigners. They ask odd questions. Rumors fly about them. Sensible people discount rumors.

Sunday of Labor Day Weekend, noontime: We beat Grand Beach for the softball championship. Maura scores on my home run, according to her version. She hugs me. Later realizes I'm already on fire with fever. We rush to the lake for a swim.

Late afternoon: Humidity thick, putrid smell in the air, rainclouds threaten, cocktail parties begin. Did we have one at our house? Probably. Where are Maura and I? On the beach, perhaps reading. We are, without realizing it, already a scandal to the older generation, which gives us credit for more sexual experimentation than we deserve.

Early evening, 7:30: Dinner at the Meehans'. Mom is irritable and drinks too much. The Meehans are preoccupied, nervous, listening for something. Dad seems to know or suspect what's happening.

Party ends, 11:00: Maura is presumably not around. On the beach with me still? Where else? My fever is already soaring over a hundred.

Monday morning, 1:00: The storm we'd been expecting all day finally hits. It is furious and brief. Where are we? Probably necking in the boathouse.

Circa 2:00: Disturbance on our section of the beach, fight or argument. College drunks perhaps. I am there. Maura too, no doubt. The something that happened to which she referred in her later letter. She leaves to walk down the beach.

I assume that we had been embracing on the beach towels.

4:00: Another storm, much worse, rolls in off the lake, thunder, lightning, a deluge of rain.

4:30: Explosion. Maura sees the light of the fire from the distance. I recall searing light. Dad reports gas smell. Police and fire departments appear.

Noon: I'm driven by ambulance to St. Anthony's, unconscious, delirious, near death. Cover-up already under way.

How do I know by ambulance? Do I remember or was I told later?

Why does it matter?

Later that week: Meehans are buried. Death declared accidental. FBI agents allegedly appear. Talk to Dad, who seems pleased with himself. Maura leaves for New York. I'm still in the hospital.

He paused and turned over the paper.

Still later: Rory shows up in New York with money for Maura. From Betty . . .? Her name is Allen now and she has lots of money. I'm still in the hospital.

First week in October: I leave the hospital and go right to Notre Dame, without returning to River Forest. I've forgotten about Maura. She writes her last letter to me.

He looked over the synopsis.

It covered all the pertinent details. It did not reveal who blew up the house. In all probability he was not responsible, yet he could not be certain even about that. Would he invest in the market on something as problematic as his own innocence?

Not very likely.

There were two mysteries, perhaps unrelated. He wrote them on his pad:

1. What was the fight on the beach about?
2. Who blew up the house?

Maura could answer the first question. He must work up his courage and ask her.

Wait a minute. They were related questions in a certain odd way. Whatever happened on the beach saved Maura's life. If she hadn't walked for two hours, more or less, she would have been in the house when it went up in fire and smoke.

"Paddy on the phone," Mary buzzed him. "Sounds terribly upset."

"Lorcan Flynn."

"Terrible car accident, Dad. They're all alive, thank God." Patrick Michael Flynn was weeping. "Maeve and kids, they're fine. Scared and shook up, still they're alive. . . . Dad?"

"I'm OK, Pat. I'll be right over."

12

"Mr. Eammon Rafferty?"

"It is."

"Lorcan Flynn here."

"I beg your pardon, Mr. Flynn." The voice at the other end of the line was anxious. "I believe you have the wrong number."

"No, I don't, Rafferty. How does it feel to know that you're dead?"

Lorcan was in a public phone booth on Wells Street, around the corner from North Avenue; a two-way radio rested on the shelf under the phone. It was middle afternoon, the week before Holy Week. Bright sunlight stung Lorcan's eyes.

"I've never spoken to you in me life." The thick Cork brogue had returned. It was the voice of the threatening phone call. Rafferty was scared.

"You're not about to be dead this minute. You'll live to see your kids crippled and your wife disfigured. Then you'll die."

"For the love of God, man, who are you?"

"You know who I am well enough. You think you're hot shit, don't you, Rafferty? A long time ago you shot a couple of people in the back and that made you tough. Well, that was a very long time ago. I have a lot more resources. I intend to send you to hell and teach you and those like you a few lessons in the process."

"I don't know what the hell you're talking about!"

It was not all that difficult. Sound tough, use foul words, talk about death, you can scare anyone—particularly an aging gunman with kids.

"You tried to kill my family, you fucking bastard, and you blew it. Now I'm going to kill your family—and I'm not about to blow it."

"It was all a mistake. We wanted to send a message. We didn't intend to hurt anyone."

All right. Lorcan smiled. *That's a confession. Now we can go ahead.*

He had found Paddy and Maeve and the two wee punks in the emergency room at Lutheran General's Lincoln Park branch. Derm and Con were running around like they were in a play yard. Maeve was confused and unnaturally quiet. Paddy had displayed a large bandage above his right eye.

"They're looking at the X rays," Paddy had said lightly, "to see if the woman has a concussion. They said she might act strange for a few days. I asked them how I could tell the difference."

Maeve had struggled to regain her form. "If I were driving I would have destroyed them bastards altogether. Really, Lorcan, I would."

"I bet you would. Derm, Con, come here!"

"Yes, GrandDa!" They had rushed over to him, one hugging each leg. His son's kids had no difficulty displaying affection, that was for sure.

"I suppose you expect chocolate bars?"

"Yes, GrandDa," said Derm, the younger of the two.

"Only if we ask Ma first." Con understood the game better.

"Ma!" pleaded Derm.

"You'll spoil the brats rotten, Da," she had said with a sigh. "No good will come from it!"

"Yippie!" the lads had screamed in unison, understanding well their mother's code words for approval.

"You'll sit down and eat them quietly because of your mother's headache, won't you now?"

"Yes, GrandDa!" they had agreed solemnly, which meant perhaps three or four minutes of relative peace.

"It's all a game to them," Paddy had beamed proudly. "Old-country genes, no doubt."

"What happened?" Lorcan had sat down on the stiff, Protestant couch which the Lutherans provided for their emergency room lounge.

"It was a near thing," Paddy had admitted, his upper lip quivering slightly. "We were pulling out of the parking lot at Lincoln and Fullerton—"

"Minding our own friggin business," his wife had added.

"This old Chevy that had been in the parking lot behind us suddenly seemed to be in an enormous rush to get out. It sideswiped us and knocked us into a big lamppost. They shot off down Lincoln like they were trying to go into orbit. We didn't get a license number. Neither did any of the witnesses."

"Focking drug pushers," Maeve had murmured. "I'd smash into *their* carful of kids if I could."

That gave Lorcan an idea, a vicious, delightful idea. Eammon Rafferty was about to be taken out of play.

He called Dinny from a public phone booth in the hospital, told him what happened, and outlined his plan.

"They were sending a message, Lorcan, a clumsy message. I don't believe they intended to kill or maim anyone."

"So what? I want to send a message back. Will it work?"

"Like I said, Rafferty is a has-been. He won't have a clue how to react when someone intimidates back. It's been a long time since he crawled around the bogs of Kerry, like a fucking swamp rat, with a Lee-Enfield in his arms."

"Then you'll help."

"No law violation on my side as far as I can see, Lorcan. You're probably going to break a few. No one is likely to drag you into court for it."

"Great!"

"Are you sure you want to do it?" Rooney had sounded dubious.

"Why not? I have to protect my family, don't I?"

"Maybe the difference between you and Rafferty is that he's over the hill and you aren't."

"Fine."

"And never will be. . . . You're what the South Side Irish would call a terrible man, Lorcan James Flynn."

"That's better than being a grand fella?"

With heart thumping, head pounding, Lorcan Flynn was now sending a message back to Eammon Rafferty.

"Look," he snarled into the phone, "you're not toting a Lee-Enfield around a Kerry bog anymore. You're fighting with someone who has killed more men than you ever dreamed of killing. I like it. And I'm gonna kill you, slowly. But first, you can expect the same for your family: your wife, your kids."

Lorcan had not killed anyone, as far as he knew, even in Korea. He was sure he wouldn't like killing. However, he was enjoying every minute of the drama that he had created.

"You're talking, just talking," Rafferty blubbered. "You wouldn't be after doing that."

"Well, we'll just have to see about that, won't we, Eammon, me boy. Why don't you look at the car that's parked across the street from your house? The black one. Listen for them to honk their horn."

He put his hand over the phone and whispered into his transceiver, "Now."

"Glory be to God!" exclaimed Eammon. "You're out there!"

"I'm not such a fool as all that, idiot. I won't drive a killer's car like you did."

"We intended no harm!" Rafferty pleaded. "Maybe I was in too much of a hurry."

"Well, I intend harm. Now let me tell you what's gonna happen first. Your daughter Mary Alice will be walking home from school in a few moments. She'll come up the steps of your bungalow. Don't try to stop us or we'll kill her. When she reaches the top of the steps she's gonna take a rifle bullet in her left leg, mind you Eammon, me bucko, the left leg. That shows how good my men are. They'll not try to blow it off her, but I'm making no promises about that."

"Dear God, no!"

"That will be the first one. By the way, don't try to hang up. As soon as you do, the line will go dead on you. My men are good shots though they have unsteady nerves, if you take my meaning. I wouldn't want the bullet to go in her back as yours did when you killed Tim Meehan."

"I didn't kill him," Rafferty moaned. "That was just talk."

"Well, you're about to learn that I'm more than just talk. I hear the kid is pretty good at Irish dancing. Too bad, I guess she'll have to do it from now on with an extra hop or two."

"Sweet Mother of God," the other man slobbered. "Please don't!"

The transceiver light flicked on. Lorcan put his hand over the phone and picked it up.

"The kid's coming down the street," said Rooney. "You'll have to work quickly. How's it coming?"

"Loads of fun!"

Lorcan returned to the phone.

"She's coming down the street now, isn't she, Eammon, me grand fellow? Get a good look at her walking naturally. It's the last time she'll do that the rest of her life."

"No! No! *No!*" Rafferty wailed. "We'll never do it again. Dear God, don't do it. We'll pay. We'll answer all your questions!"

"I don't believe you."

"Jesus, Mary, and Joseph, I swear it. Give us another chance."

"If you're lying to me, we'll do a lot worse to them. I'll force you to watch as we carve patriotic slogans on your wife's tits and belly. Then we'll cut off the tits and make you eat them. Understand?"

"I promise. I'll do anything! Anything!"

"You want to deny me my fun, Eammon? I'm not sure I want to give it up."

"I beg of you, have mercy on us." The man had broken down. "Don't do it!"

"The slightest false move, Rafferty, and there'll be no phone calls. No warning. You see how easy it is to do it when you have the guts and the money."

"Sweet Jesus, I promise! I promise!"

The transceiver light blinked on. "The kid is coming up the steps."

"We could kneecap her this instant, Eammon, me brave lad, instead we're just going to beep the horn." He heard the horn, both on the transceiver and the phone. "Next time it'll be a shot. Do you take my meaning?"

Rafferty sobbed incoherently.

"Don't try a thing. We're watching every move you make. One of my lads will be in touch with you. You're gonna pay me a little visit, Rafferty, and you're going to spill everything, understand, or we'll spill some things out of your wife's guts."

"I understand." The other man's voice cracked. *"Please* don't hurt them."

Lorcan, exultant, hung up.

Later he would agonize with Mary Kathleen Ryan Murphy, M.D., about his exultation.

"I feel guilty," he confessed.

"Naturally, Lorcan. If you didn't feel guilty much of the time you wouldn't be on that couch."

"I loved the fight. I'm as much a war lover as Tim Meehan was. I enjoyed listening to him collapse."

"Hmn . . ."

"I could be dangerous. . . . I'm scared of myself."

"Hmn . . ."

"Stop saying hmn!"

"Why?"

"I want to know what you think about my story."

"Is it necessary that I think anything?"

"Isn't that what shrinks are for?"

She sighed, more loudly than even the Maeve. "Very well. . . . What was the term—the one the police officer used?"

"A terrible man?"

"And the opposite, the one he used for the war lover, and you applied to your father?"

"A grand fella?"

"Which would you rather be, Lorcan James Flynn? A grand fella or a terrible man?"

"It's not hard to answer if that's my choice."

"It is."

"I'll have to settle for being a terrible man."

"Very well. That settles that."

"Wait a minute . . ."

"You will find neither approbation nor absolution in this office, Lorcan."

"Doesn't this incident prove that I'm dangerous?"

"Did you need that incident to prove it to you? If you did you have been singularly unperceptive all your life . . . and you have learned nothing in this office."

"I don't like being dangerous," he said miserably.

"Too bad."

"I really don't."

"The hell you don't."

13

"We meant no harm to the children," Eammon Rafferty protested. "Nothing happened to them, did it?"

"That was not your fault."

"Ah." Rafferty smiled genially. "That's the whole point. We could have killed them if we were of such a mind. We're not killers, Mr. Flynn. Not at all. Our mutual friend, Commissioner Rooney here, suggested that you had received our message and that now we should have a friendly little talk. You want to find out what happened when Joe Meehan blew himself up. Fair enough, we'll tell you what we know. Then you'll let the matter drop, won't you now?"

Eammon Rafferty, a short man with a salt-and-pepper widow's peak, a neatly trimmed brown mustache, and uneasy gray eyes, used brave words—words that assumed that his blubbering on the telephone had never happened and that no threats were hanging over his head. However, his voice was unsteady and the motion of his hands as he rubbed them rapidly against one another was frantic.

He was still scared. Lorcan was determined to keep him that way.

"Anytime you crash one car into another, Rafferty, you endanger the lives of the passengers. We could easily charge you with attempted murder, isn't that right, Commissioner?"

"It is," Dinny Rooney said flatly, adjusting his tie clasp for emphasis.

"Mind you, I have other means of dealing with men like you, Rafferty, which I enjoy much more than slow and tiresome appeals to the law. Don't try to deceive me."

"Ah, no," the IRA man begged. "We're willing to cooperate completely. We'll tell you everything we know. I swear it."

"Fine. . . . The Commissioner will ask the questions. We are recording the answers. We will transcribe them and ask you to sign them. We'll only use the statement if we have to."

"We've done nothing wrong," Rafferty pleaded. "Nothing at all."

Dinny began the interrogation. "You murdered Tim Meehan, an American war hero."

"I never did, I never did," he insisted.

"You've bragged about how you shot him in the back."

"That was just talk. Nothing more. No one knows who

shot Tim. Some people thought that our detachment had done it. We were trying to build up our reputation as patriots in those days so we let them think we did it. Sure, everyone was saying that Tim had sold out to the Brits, so we didn't see any harm in them giving us credit, if you take me meaning."

"And you blew up his brother's house in the Dunes?"

"We didn't do that either. What would be the point of blowing up our weapons? We thought Joe Meehan was a patriot. He said he'd get the guns for us and the ammunition and the explosives—"

"In exchange for information about his brother."

"Well, we told him that we'd find out everything we could. Poor man believed Timmy was still alive. Couldn't accept his death."

"Arms for information?"

"And for a hell of a lot of money, Commissioner, a hell of a lot."

"Where did he steal the guns?"

Eammon Rafferty shrugged his shoulders and winked. "We didn't ask and he didn't say. Military black market, I suspect. Your Browning Automatic Rifles were a lot harder to find in those days than your Uzis are today."

"A master sergeant somewhere made a deal with a congressman," Lorcan suggested. "Exchange of favors."

"He held out on the ammunition, did he now?" Rooney cocked a fierce eyebrow. "And so you blew him up."

"Sweet Mother of God, how did you know that he held out on the ammunition? We never told a soul!"

"Never mind that." Dinny spoke harshly and then jabbed a finger at Rafferty. "He held out and then you killed him."

"He did and we didn't," Rafferty whined. "He wanted more money, needed it he said for his congressional race. We could view it as a contribution to his campaign that autumn—keeping an Irish patriot in Congress. Like I say, Commissioner, why would we blow up our weapons? Wouldn't it be better for us to be after taking the guns and the explosives and maybe the ammo too if we'd been able to dig up the funds from Irish patriots in Chicago? After that we might have killed him. He was a traitor same as his brother. The Organization, however, never guns down women and children, much less blows them up."

"It is content with smashing their cars," Lorcan cut in.

"Wasn't I admitting just now that was a terrible mistake altogether? Sure, there was no one in the world more disappointed than we were when we heard the explosion and saw the fire against the night sky. One of the Lads said, 'Well, there goes our guns.' And another said, 'And like as not the Meehans, too.' "

"You expect us to believe that?" Rooney exclaimed derisively.

"We wouldn't have destroyed our own weapons, would we now? And most likely we wouldn't have killed Joe. He had good contacts with the military, and he was the only patriotic Irish voice in Congress at the time."

Lorcan trusted Eammon Rafferty no more than he would any other psychopath. On the other hand his argument was plausible.

"And after the explosion?" Lorcan asked.

"We got the hell out of there, that's what we did. We were not after taking the blame for something the Brits did."

"You're suggesting the British government was responsible for the explosion?"

"Who else?" Rafferty extended his hands in a plea for belief, one reasonable man talking to another. "These days thirty assault weapons wouldn't make much difference in our military operations. In those days we could have wiped out half the Royal Ulster Constabulary with them. The Brits killed two birds with one stone. They destroyed our equipment and rid themselves of an enemy in the American Congress."

Dinny continued to stare at Rafferty, a hard skeptical look which made the man twist in his chair.

"I suppose you're wondering," Rafferty continued, "why we didn't like your investigation."

"That question had occurred to us," Lorcan said dryly.

"Look at it from our point of view," Rafferty wheezed anxiously. "We had hightailed it out of there because we were sure that everyone would be looking for a scapegoat and it would be us. If we had been seen, there'd have been a big investigation and some of our people might have been deported or, worse, turned over to the Brits. Well, there's no statute of limitations on murder. The other two Lads are still alive and living peaceful lives in Chicago. If you continued to snoop around, you'd find out about us, like you did. We'd be in trouble again—and so would the Organization. The Brits would have a grand time with the news."

"Yeah," Dinny Rooney said cautiously. "Chicagoans would get the crazy idea that the Noraid fund-raisers here are the same folks who sent a congressman and his family on a quick trip to eternity a long time ago."

"Now we can tell them"—Lorcan took up the cudgels—"that the Organization is still trying to kill innocent women and children."

"Yeah!" Rooney jabbed his finger. "We have witnesses who saw the car and other witnesses who saw you steal it. And we know your history. Maybe we wouldn't win a conviction. But we'd sure destroy you and your business and your collections."

"We're patriotic Irishmen." He drew himself up to his full height and still seemed pathetic. "Fighting any way we can to defeat the British oppressors and those bastards in the puppet Free State government in Dublin."

"The Republic would be mighty happy to get their hands on you too, wouldn't they?"

"Now you begin to understand . . . Sure, Mr. Flynn, we didn't mean any harm to your family. We wanted to warn you off, that's all."

"Now you think you expect me to believe that?"

" 'Tis the God's honest truth. Haven't I told you enough so you could be after putting all of us in jail?"

"Why are you doing that?" Lorcan frowned ominously.

"Because I want you to believe that I'm telling the God's honest truth, that's why."

Sweat was pouring down his face. He was close to tears—the young rebel gunman turned troubled and aging father. Suddenly Lorcan felt sorry for him.

Eammon Rafferty was telling the truth, not the whole truth perhaps, but a lot of the truth. Lorcan was not quite ready, however, to let the pitiful little ex-gunman off the hook.

"You stand by that story, do you?" he asked in a tone of voice that he hoped might be appropriate for a man who was about to throw the switch for the electric chair.

"I do." Rafferty straightened his shoulders, the IRA volunteer of long ago. "So help me God, and Mary the sweet Mother of God."

"We'll see, Eammon Rafferty, we'll see. The Commissioner and I have our ways of checking up on you. If we find you're lying, there won't be any warning phone call. The Mother of God will have her work cut out for her if she intends to keep you alive, which in my opinion would be a waste of her time."

Rafferty shivered. So, Lorcan thought, did Dinny Rooney.

After Rafferty had left the office, Lorcan noted that Rooney was gazing at him with a mixture of respect and uncertainty.

"What's the matter, Dinny, I offend your educated-cop conscience?"

"I'm telling myself that I'm glad you didn't decide to become a crook instead of a professional gambler."

"And sometimes you're not all that sure there's a difference, huh? Anyway, what did you think of him?"

"He's probably telling the truth, or a substantial part of the truth anyway. They had no good reason to kill the Meehans, and several good reasons to keep them alive. They had excellent grounds to fear us. Now they have excellent grounds for telling us the truth and hoping that it doesn't suit our purposes to reveal all of the past."

"His account would be grist for Larry Whealan's mill if Donny tries to pin a murder rap on me, wouldn't it?"

"Larry's a better lawyer than I am, God knows. I suspect, however, that you're right. It would blow any case the LaPorte prosecutors might have out of the water."

"You think the Brits were involved?"

"I'd sure as hell would like to know. The more the merrier from our point of view."

"Would they dare assassinate an American congressman?"

"And blame it on the Lads? They've done worse. Do you have any decent contacts at the British Embassy?"

"Yeah." Lorcan reached for the phone. "There's a guy there that owes me a big favor—not that they believe in honoring favors. He'll honor this one, though, when I tell him that I could break a story about British agents assassinating an American congressman."

As he punched in the number from his Sidekick phone directory, Lorcan noted Dinny Rooney's eyes narrowing.

I scare him, all right.

Hell, I scare me too.

14

"The Order of Saint Justin the Martyr," Dinny Rooney said, opening a dark brown folder, "was founded in the late eighteenth century by Saint Charles de Lorenzo in Perugia to promote Catholic education by fighting the errors of the time—Voltaire and that bunch."

"I think my brother told me that."

Larry Whealan had called him earlier in the morning and told him to use a public phone to call back. Donny and Maynard were having trouble with the LaPorte County Prosecutor, who didn't like the smell of the case, but nothing would happen till after Easter.

Just about the time of Marie's wedding, Lorcan thought as he watched a cold March rain beat against the windows of his office.

"Yeah," Dinny continued, "so naturally the Justines went into the business of running schools. San Carlo, as he has always been called since Pius the Twelfth canonized him in 1943, was a pretty tough customer. He wanted his men to be contemplatives as well as teachers. So they had to sing the Divine Office in Common as well as teach eight hours a day. He figured they could get along on four, maybe five hours of sleep a night."

"That isn't true anymore."

"Carlo was a man of great virtue. According to his biographer, he fasted every day of the week for the last ten years of his life. His 'custody of the eyes' was so powerful that he never looked directly at a woman after he was ten years old, not even his mother and his sisters."

"He missed a lot."

Dinny chuckled but did not comment. "And they fasted three days a week. . . . Carlo was hard on himself. His lungs were weak but he traveled all over Italy, founding schools and preaching. Seems he took a vow always to do the more perfect thing—ever hear of that?—and so he traveled on foot. No wonder he died at forty-four."

"Is this history necessary, Dinny?"

"Yeah, it is. You've got to get the flavor of the thing to understand all that's happened. The Vatican was running most of Italy in those days, and like most baroque courts was into art and music and parties, but not into piety. So they were not much impressed by Carlo and his band of uneducated peasants who fasted and prayed and ran schools that were long on doctrine and short on culture. They were about to suppress the whole outfit when a pope died, and then San Carlo, though he wasn't officially a saint yet, died right after."

"Napoleon suppressed them, didn't he?"

"I'm getting to that. The point is that they didn't have any money, not after they'd gone through Carlo's personal fortune. So they had to raise funds the hard way—preaching, begging, small gifts at the shrine at Carlo's tomb, an occasional larger gift from someone who thought there had been a miracle at the tomb, you get it?"

"Most religious orders had to do that."

"And still do, as far as that goes, Lorcan. They're always scraping together money to keep going. In those days the Vatican needed money to pay its army. Today it doesn't have enough money to pay its own bills. The orders have to grub. We take the Sunday appeals and the mailings and raffle books and two-bit carnivals and the slick fund-raisers for granted because that's all we've ever known in the Church. We might make a contribution because we feel generous or guilty or to get them off our backs. For them it's survival."

"I understand."

"Well, after they're restored in 1820 and can come up out of the cellars, they grow pretty fast, build a lot of schools, and found an Irish province and eventually an American one, and begin missionary work, first in Africa and later in China. This means they have to grub for more money, always chasing the buck or the lira or the pound or whatever."

"Otherwise their important work cannot go on."

"You got it. And their work costs money. Figure a steelworker back in the thirties or early forties is sending a kid to St. Justin's. He shells out fifteen, maybe twenty dollars a month tuition for what turns out to be quality private education and thinks they're demanding a lot from him and bitches like hell when the first raffle book comes home. He doesn't comprehend that it's costing at least three times as much to run the school, plus the cost of educating the teachers and the missions and the old guys who are too sick to teach and medical bills. So they're still grubbing for dough."

"They gave us something for next to nothing." Lorcan nodded. "And we complained when they asked for a little more."

"Yeah. They're always chasing the buck, and there aren't any big endowments like some of the Protestants have and only a few wealthy benefactors because there aren't that many wealthy American Catholics. In the meantime they're building new schools like crazy and sending more guys off to the missions. Where's the money coming from? From the ordinary Catholic who sends them a couple of bucks a year, from mailing lists and Novenas and Masses and miracles and holy cards and stuff like that."

"Pretty degrading."

"Hell, they were poor and so were we. But—you get it—they were always chasing the buck because they had to. Otherwise the old Order would collapse."

"So enter Father Gregorio."

"He was just plain Gregory when he was growing up in

Jersey, the son of a guy who owned a meat market. Somehow that gets translated into him being a financial wizard because he's the son of a businessman."

"He becomes treasurer of the Order?"

"Only of the Chicago Province, which is the biggest in the world. He's a big, handsome, fast-talking Clark Gable kind of guy with a great smile—the affluent widows love him—and lots of energy. He's a big success as a high school principal in Detroit so they make him treasurer. He reads the papers, even *The Wall Street Journal,* and figures after the war—World War Two—that maybe it's time to put some of the money in real estate and stocks. Maybe some of the real estate is connected to the Outfit. What the hell, they're good Catholics, too, aren't they?"

"He makes a lot of money?"

"A whole hell of a lot of money. He gets into commodities and maybe racehorses. He becomes a big spender, joins Olympia Fields, and moves into an apartment of his own. The Order doesn't mind because he's bringing in so much cash."

"Then the bubble bursts."

"Not all at once. He has a few setbacks. He covers with contributions. He doesn't distinguish between his own account—which, since he's got this vow of poverty, he's not supposed to have—and the Order's account. Then, when his back is up against the wall, he gets a loan from the Outfit. A lot of loans. The Order doesn't notice because it still thinks he's magic and because no one is minding the store."

"Loan sharks?"

"Nah. That's penny ante stuff. He's dealing with the real high rollers. He gets straightened out, makes a couple of more plunges, and first thing he knows, he's into his friends on the West Side for a couple of million. He scrapes enough together to pay off some of it, but he's still up shit creek with no visible means of transportation. Then his friends get ugly and make a few blunt threats, know what I mean?"

"And he still doesn't pay and gets himself garroted?"

"You figure the time wrong. That's later on. No, he finds the money and pays his friends off."

"Where does he find the money?"

"Funny thing. A guy dies and leaves him all the money."

"Joe Meehan!"

"The very same. And some of the young guys in the organized crime crowd in the Chicago Police Department say isn't it a funny thing that Padre Gregorio—whom they're watching real close—gets the money just when he needs it. Especially since he's hanging around Grand Beach with some lay benefactors just when it goes down at the Meehan place. Got it?"

"Dear God!"

"Yeah—well, he probably wasn't consulted. Anyway, these young Chicago cops, one of whom tells me all this thirty-five years later, want to poke their nose into this funny circumstance, but they get orders from higher up to leave Father Sabatini alone. They figure the fix is in, so they shrug their shoulders. They figure Greg baby will overreach again and it'll be the big one for him. Sure enough, he does six years later and they find his body with a piece of chicken wire around his neck. Lucky thing a contract isn't put out on the whole Order."

"Which believes he died a martyr's death."

"Some of them know better, especially the poor guys who have to straighten out the books when they take over. The others, well"—Dinny shrugged his shoulders—"it's not hard to be innocent when you don't have to look at what you don't want to see."

"Nothing more to link Gregorio with the explosion?"

"Not a thing, but, hell, he wouldn't have done it himself. Maybe he was hanging around the neighborhood just to make sure it went down. My guys tell me that they later learned he had only a few weeks to live if he didn't come up with a cool million."

"All of the Meehan money went to the Mob?"

"All but small change. Which may not be totally unfair because Joe got a lot of his cash from them."

"That's the story?"

"Pretty much. The Order falls apart in the sixties and the seventies, like a lot of orders. This Polish Pope takes it over and puts in a bunch of conservative guys who try to put the lid on what's left. It's a toss-up whether they'll survive."

"Guys like my brother?"

"You got it. They say he's the best fund-raiser since Gregorio, God be good to him."

Lorcan paused to ponder the history of the rise and fall of the Justines, a history, he suspected, that was not much different from the story of a lot of other orders except for the Outfit link.

Dinny resumed the conversation. "What do you make of it, Lorcan?"

"I think I'm going to have to pay a quick trip to Rome and have a long talk with my dear brother."

15

"I have to go to Rome for a few days, Moire."

"Oh?" She sounded breathless, like she had run to answer the phone. Or perhaps had been exercising. "I hope you'll be back for the wedding."

"I'll be there for no more than a week."

His decision to phone her had been impulsive. Then he'd realized that he didn't have her number. Maeve had provided it, with only a mildly suggestive lilt in her voice.

"That's nice." Moire was trying to figure out the reason for his call.

So was he. His nerve had diminished sharply since he heard her voice on the other end of the line.

"I was wondering"—he took the big leap—"if you'd like to come with me."

"Come to Rome with you?" She sounded surprised, but perhaps not unpleasantly so.

"I'm leaving Kennedy tomorrow afternoon on Alitalia 811. I'll be staying at the Hassler in Rome."

He had decided to fly to New York in the morning and have lunch with a couple of his Wall Street contacts, then take the evening plane to Rome instead of doing the Chicago-Milan-Rome trip. Then it had occurred to him that he might have a drink with Moire at the airport. Then he wondered if she might come with him.

"Why?" she asked.

"Have you ever been to Rome?"

"No . . ." She hesitated. "I can get airline passes because of Tom. But I resolved I wouldn't go on any long trips till both the kids were out of college."

"It's spring there now. I thought it might be fun to see Rome together. I could be your guide."

"I bet you could." She laughed, recklessly he thought.

Well, that made the implications of his invitation clear.

Maynard Lealand had phoned him earlier and warned him that it "would look bad" if he left the jurisdiction while he was a "target." Lorcan had replied with an expletive and said he was going ahead. Mary Murray had rescheduled his appointments. Doctor Murphy had given him a week off. Dennis Rooney had given the name of an important "source" in Rome.

"It's up to you," he said, but then decided that wasn't enough. "I'd love to show you the city," he added. "It would be my pleasure."

"I'd really love to . . ." Moire began. Lorcan could hear the "but" coming. Instead of encouraging her—one little push and he knew he could convince her—he backed off.

His loss of nerve infected her. "I have important staff meetings all next week," she said.

Lorcan couldn't believe what an idiot he was being. He'd let her go once. How could he let her slip away now? He knew he could persuade her even now, if only he tried. Instead he heard himself say, "Maybe some other time."

"Definitely . . . give me a little bit more advance notice."

"I'm sorry it was such short notice this time. But I made the decision to go only yesterday."

"Well, I'll certainly see you in Chicago in a couple of weeks."

"You bet."

He almost said "I love you" before they hung up. But he didn't. He'd lost his nerve for a second time in the space of a few minutes. *Call her back,* a voice told him. He could persuade her, he knew. She wanted to go. He wanted her to go with him. In a few days they could be together in Rome. All it would take was a phone call. His hand was still on the receiver. He picked it up and began dialing her number. In the past few weeks Moire had become his chief source of motivation for everything from fighting Donny Roscoe to delving into his past with Doctor Murphy. Yet somehow he could not bring himself to finish punching in Moire's number. Instead he hung up the phone.

16

E dward savored the seventy-five-dollar Frascati. "Excellent wine, Lorcan. It doesn't travel very well, as I'm sure you know. But here in the Eternal City it's fabulous."

They were eating lunch in the Ristorante Tre Scalini on the Piazza Navona. Good food, even if it was a tourist trap. Edward probably brought all his rich benefactors here. They'd feel right at home. There were more Americans in the restaurant than there were Italians.

"I'm terribly upset to hear what Henry has done to you." Edward sipped the wine again. "I always did think him a bit of a sociopath, you know. Like Uncle Rory."

Edward was wearing a gray suit and a black tie, accepted garb in Rome, even for presidents of religious orders. In the Tre Scalini it said "priest" every bit as much as a Roman collar would in the States.

The maître d' had called him "padre" and the wine steward "monsignor." Edward was clearly an important man in the Rome of John Paul II.

"I think the reform is a success, Lorcan," he had said over their Campari and soda at the beginning of the meal. "The present Pope is a providential man. He's restoring a sense of order and discipline to the Church. You have no idea how much chaos we've had to live through during the years of Paul the Sixth. He was a fundamentally weak man, you know."

Fifteen years ago my little brother was an enthusiastic supporter of Paul VI and the changes of the Vatican Council. He's a bit of the Vicar of Bray, shifts with the changing winds. Maybe you have to do that if you want to be a cardinal.

"The lay people are confused, you see," Edward had droned on, as if repeating an oft-spoken homily. "Some of the crazy theologians who wander about the world as media celebrities have deceived them about what Catholics believe. Fortunately John Paul has no doubts on that matter. He is appointing bishops who will make it very clear what the Catholic teaching is. Then the lay people will return to orthodox belief and practice."

"On birth control?"

"Certainly. Of course we must be sensitive pastorally to the problems people experience in marriage."

Same old shit, Lorcan had thought.

"It is my impression, Ed, that the laity have turned off the Holy See and their own bishops when the subject is sex."

"Perhaps in America," Edward had agreed complacently, glancing at his empty Campari and soda glass, "but the future of the Church is in the Second and the Third World. Catholics are still loyal in those countries."

"But the money still comes from the West, does it not?" He had signaled the waiter for another drink for Ed but had declined one himself.

"Oh yes, mostly from Germany and the United States."

Lorcan had wondered whether he liked his brother. Ed was too smooth, too well dressed, too confident in his knowledge of people and the world, too complacent in a papal strategy which had alienated most American Catholics. Like some other important and articulate priests that Lorcan knew, Ed thought he understood everything and actually understood nothing.

Was this the kind of man that John Paul had gathered around him? Hell, Edward wouldn't survive in a middle-level job in a small American corporation.

"Let me propose a case for you, Ed. There's a couple at the Hassler, a little younger perhaps than I am. They're not married to each other and probably at the moment to anyone else. Attractive people. They're obviously lovers. Very happy with one another. Probably spend much of the night in love play. Would you say they were sinning? Didn't one of your moral theologians back in the eighteenth century teach that fornication was only a venial sin?"

"Father Barone." Ed had colored, apparently embarrassed by the question. "Actually the book was withdrawn long ago. He was a devout man but not very sound theologically. His position was that passion usually eliminated full responsibility. Perhaps that's true enough but we can't trust the laity with that kind of knowledge, can we?"

"I suppose not."

"In the case of your couple, I'm not sure how appropriate the argument would be, even granted its validity. At their age passion can hardly be so strong as to deprive them of their senses."

Lorcan smiled. "What if they were big contributors of yours and you were showing them around Rome?"

Ed waved his finely manicured hand dismissively. "I would not make any judgment about their moral state. It would not be my affair."

Lorcan had decided to ignore the unintended pun.

"If you had a drink with them in their suite and they were clearly sharing it and were clearly lovers?"

"I think I would discreetly ignore the situation."

"If they asked you whether what they were doing was wrong?"

Ed remained serenely untroubled by the catechism. "I would tell them that as a priest I could not approve, but that as a friend I could sympathize with their predicament. I might quietly suggest marriage as soon as possible."

"And continue to take their money?"

"Certainly. Their generosity would not be tainted by their, ah, relationship."

Lorcan decided to get to the real subject he wanted to talk to Ed about. He told his brother about the possible murder charge against him.

"You say you have evidence that the charge cannot be true?" Edward was as complacent as when he was dismissing the fictive lovers at the Hassler.

"Pretty good evidence. How much do you remember of that day?"

"I can understand now why you were so interested in the subject when we met at the Daley party." Ed nodded as Lorcan refilled his wineglass. "Let me see. . . . I was very young then, you remember. I can certainly confirm that you were desperately ill. Indeed, I distinctly remember seeing you through the doorway of your room at St. Anthony's Hospital and hearing the doctor say that you might not live till morning. I believe I went to the chapel to pray for you. So in this respect, as in so many others, it is morally certain that Henry is lying."

"You would be willing to testify in court to this effect, if it came to it?"

"Oh, my, no." He wiped his lips daintily with a napkin. "As a major superior of a religious order it would be quite inappropriate for me to appear on a witness stand in a case like this, especially since I would seem to be choosing one brother over another. . . . I could of course give private assurances to those in authority."

Lorcan had not expected any other answer, but he was angered by how untroubled Edward was. Perhaps by the standards of the whole Catholic world as viewed from the perspective of the Vatican, a murder trial, even of one's own brother, was unimportant.

"I see."

"But you have the good nun's statement, don't you? That should be sufficient."

"I suppose so. . . . Now, what can you tell me about Gregory Sabatini's involvement in the death of the Meehans?"

A look of sheer terror flashed across Ed's normally bland face. It vanished quickly, but even so its significance was not lost on Lorcan. The Father Greg connection could destroy his career and perhaps the remnants of the Order of St. Justin.

"I don't know what you mean," he said tensely.

"I mean, Ed, that if it hadn't been for the death of the Meehans, the Mob would have put down Father Greg six years before they actually did. I mean that he was into them for at least a million dollars. I mean he was over in Grand Beach the day of the explosion. I mean that every cent of their estate went to him. I mean he turned almost all of it over to his friends on the West Side. I mean he was the prime beneficiary of the murder of four human beings. I mean that I am perfectly prepared to bring out this information if there is a trial—or even before the trial if necessary to avert it."

"Surely you wouldn't do that!" Ed turned the color of the napkin with which he once again patted his lips. "It would do great harm to the Church."

"A murder conviction would do great harm to me."

"But that's not likely, is it?"

"With juries, you can never tell."

"I can't believe that you have proof for all those reckless accusations."

"I have all the proof I need to go to the media with the story."

That was not quite true. And he was not about to go to the media with it yet.

"That would be dreadful." Edward's eyes were darting nervously. "Simply dreadful."

"I'm fighting for myself and my family, Edward. If you can give me evidence about Gregorio that I can show to the prosecutors, they might back off. They're not likely to want to take on the Catholic Church, not in Chicago."

"That would be out of the question!"

"I know the whole story, Ed. He was your hero, the man whom you followed into the priesthood. . . ."

"He was so kind and gentle with Mom. . . ."

A love affair there? Not likely. Still, anything might be likely in this twisted story.

"He was a hardworking and dedicated man, as well as attractive and charismatic. He began with nothing more than the good of the Church, to use your words, and of the Order as his goals. But he became corrupt, Ed. I don't know how corrupt, but corrupt enough. The Meehans' death saved him the first time. Nothing saved him the second time."

"None of this is true!"

"It is and you know it is."

"Greg was not a killer."

"I don't think he actually killed them. He was not a bomb thrower. He merely had to tell his friends on the West Side where the money was. They would have done it for him and he might even have kept a clear conscience."

"I know nothing about any of that."

"You do too, Ed. You doubtless hear rumors from others in the Order. When you became Provincial and President, you checked the rumors out. Most of the records have been destroyed, but you and your predecessors kept a few of them just in case you ever needed them."

"That is not true." Ed averted his face. "None of it is true. I can't imagine, Lorcan, why you are doing this to me."

"I can't ask and I don't expect you to go on the witness stand to testify against Gregorio. I merely want the evidence you have to raise a solid probability in the mind of the prosecutors in Chicago and in LaPorte that there is a can of worms in this case that they do not want to risk opening."

"That is quite impossible." Edward's face tightened into a mask.

"You do not have the evidence or you will not share it with me?"

"I do not know what you are talking about! I would help you if I could, Lorcan," Edward begged. "But in this matter I can be no help at all. I am . . . I am bound by obligations of secrecy that are reserved to the Pope himself."

"I understand, Ed. I understand completely."

What he also understood was that money and power were necessary for religious institutions but that they were also dangerous and corrupting.

Back at the Hassler, he decided to give Moire a call. The next best thing to being there, he thought ruefully, but still a very poor second.

"Lorcan! How nice of you to call!"

"I don't want to disturb you . . ."

"You're not disturbing me at all. It's nice to hear your voice."

"I've been thinking about you," he told her. "And missing you."

"You're sweet, Lorcan," she said tenderly. "You were always sweet."

"Crazy and sweet."

"And a lot of other things."

Lorcan hadn't felt so good in months. How could he have let her stay in New York? One thing was certain: he wasn't going to let the opportunity to be with Moire slip by the next time it was presented.

17

"I have heard the rumors, of course." The reporter, who had spent the last thirty years in Rome, spoke with a faint South County Dublin brogue. "You hear many such scandalous rumors here in Rome. Most of them are pure gossip. However, since there is no way to learn what is true, there is also no way to learn what is false."

"Secrecy defeats itself?"

"Especially in a world dominated by the mass media. Your men up there"—he nodded his head in the direction of Vatican City—"haven't learned that yet."

They were sitting at a small sidewalk table in front of the Columbus Hotel, halfway up the Via Conciliazione, a place where the journalist assured Lorcan it was possible to get a drink of Irish whiskey. The dome of San Pietro's shimmered against a pastel blue sky. Vatican bureaucrats scurried back and forth on the street, looking dour and important.

"You've got to understand," the reporter continued, "that there are thousands of separate and independent entities in the Catholic Church—religious orders, schools, hospitals, institutes, and of course the dioceses. The Church doesn't have a consolidated budget. Neither do the various institutions. So there's almost no supervision of how the money is raised or spent. Some corruption is possible under such circumstances."

"On the other hand, a centralized accounting system would destroy local initiative and ingenuity," Lorcan observed.

"You make your choice," the reporter replied, sipping his Bushmill's as though it were the most precious fluid in the world. "Personally I feel that a little corruption is a small price to pay for freedom. But around here it seems that there is more corruption than is tolerable."

"But no one does anything about it."

The Irishman sighed. "They'll tell you that the Church has been around a long time and can afford to move slowly."

Lorcan nodded. "And besides, it's broke."

"You can believe that, Mr. Flynn. Incompetent, broke, and corrupt. I don't mean the fellas up there"—again he nodded toward the dingy brown buildings of Vatican City—"are personally corrupt. I mean they have no way of dealing with the corruption that can occur somewhere beneath them."

"They wouldn't be broke if they could control the corruption?"

"It's a drop in the bucket, Mr. Flynn. Eliminate every bit of corruption and they'd still be operating at a deficit."

"Please call me Lorcan."

The reporter smiled. "And I'm Brendan. You have to realize that in the scheme of things here, the murder of a major superior of a religious order in Chicago doesn't rank high on anyone's agenda," Brendan continued. "Some *minutante*—clerk—over at the Congregation of Religious might make an inquiry of a counterpart at the Generalate of the Order. All he wants is that they reassure him, and they do, and that's that."

"I see."

"The Justines are kind of a special case. There were rumors all through the fifties that the Order was falling apart because of lax supervision from here and control by tight little cliques out in the provinces. They certainly fell apart quickly enough in the years after the Council. Your brother has barely held them together. He's a good man by the standards they use here—an effective and subtle ecclesiastical politician who knows where all the bodies are buried."

"Edward"—Lorcan drained his glass and decided he needed another—"couldn't deliver a single precinct in Chicago."

"But this isn't Chicago, Lorcan."

"You're right, Brendan, it sure isn't."

"If I may repeat some Roman gossip about him . . ."

"Please do."

"There's kind of an impression around here that he was elected general because he knew too much about certain things not to elect him general. Sure, he was the Pope's man and sure he had ability. But he seems to have known where some very special bodies are buried."

"Like the Provincial who was strangled in Chicago."

"And some of the important people who were making investments through your man."

"It was a long time ago—thirty years."

"Romans have long memories."

"So I'm told."

"The thing is"—the Irishman smiled as the third drink appeared on their table—"I can't provide all the details for you, much less give you any kind of proof."

"That's too bad."

But strict proof wasn't necessary for Lorcan's purpose. If Larry Whealan could talk knowingly about the Justine scandal, and if contacts at the Chicago Chancery could vaguely confirm that there was such a scandal, Donny Roscoe would be thoroughly intimidated.

"But I do know someone who can tell you more of the details."

"You do?"

"A certain retired American cardinal who lives up in the Città Leonina, around the corner from the Vatican, and who loves to tell tales, especially to someone who is willing to make a modest gift to his personal charities, as they call it. He was a bureaucrat in the Congregation of Religious at that time. If there was anything more to it than a routine Mafia murder, he'd know the details. You'd have to listen to a lot of bullshit, and your information would be mostly in the form of allusions, but you might be able to sort out most of the truth."

"Can you set up an appointment with him?"

"Do you want me to?"

"As soon as possible."

18

"So you know about that story, do you?" The Cardinal toasted him with a large glass of cognac. "From your brother, I presume?"

The Cardinal was old and maybe fifty pounds overweight and his conversation wandered through five papacies without any guidelines to time. But he was no fool.

"Come now, Eminenza, you must know that Eduardo is too smart to discuss such matters even with a brother."

"True, true! Well, anyway, here's to your continued good health and to the good health of all you love! May God bless them all."

He was sufficiently important to be invited to supper at the Cardinal's apartment, a spacious and crowded set of rooms only a stone's throw from the Bernini columns in front of San Pietro. The Cardinal and a long-suffering young priest who was his assistant had welcomed Lorcan with expansive courtesy and treated him to a superlative dinner and excellent drinks.

Lorcan's head was spinning from the aperitifs, the red wine, the white wine, and now the cognac. The Cardinal's head, he assumed, was a lot clearer than his at the moment.

Over much food and liquor, the conversation rambled through recent years of Catholic history, with the recurring theme that if the various popes had listened to the Cardinal, the Church would have very few problems at the present time.

Following the strategy Brendan prescribed, Lorcan approached the subject that concerned him indirectly. He paid the Cardinal compliments along the way.

"If they had followed your advice, Eminenza, there would not have been the grave financial scandals in so many religious communities in America."

The old man rose immediately to the bait and rambled on for perhaps a quarter of an hour about such scandals.

"I am not unfamiliar with one such, Eminenza. I knew personally the unfortunate Father Gregorio Sabatini."

"That was a humdinger of a problem, let me tell you. . . . I don't mean the second time. I mean the first time." The Cardinal's eyes twinkled.

"Was there a previous threat to his life? I mean before they killed him?"

"They?" The Cardinal looked at him shrewdly.

"The Outfit, as we call it in Chicago."

"Aha, you know that too. Well, from the point of view of the Church, that was not the more serious problem. Poor man, God be good to him, he was living dangerously, much too dangerously. As a matter of fact, we wanted to replace him after the first event, but his superiors thought such a démarche would be imprudent. Good old Greg knew a bit too much to be locked up in a monastery." The Cardinal threw back his head and laughed heartily.

"It was the murder in the early fifties that caused the first problem, wasn't it?"

The Cardinal laughed again. "You surely are well informed, young man. You could probably tell me some things about that case that I don't know."

"I doubt it, Eminenza."

Did the Cardinal know that Lorcan was searching for specific information and was willing to pay for it? Was the whole conversation a charade to get to the point where it was now? How much had Brendan told him?

"Well, what *do* you know?" the Cardinal asked.

"I know that Father Gregory was deeply in debt, and that if it hadn't been for a fortunate bequest, he might have died then."

"*Very* fortunate, Lorcan, very fortunate indeed. A whole family died violently. An important family, I might add. Public official."

"So I understand."

"Two members of his community," the Cardinal said, nodding to his secretary to replenish the cognac glasses, "two brave members of the community, wrote to the Pope himself to tell him of the coincidence of this fortunate death and Father's need for money. Pius the Twelfth was Pope then, and his housekeeper, Madre Pasqualina, was running the Church, particularly the religious orders. She sent the letter down to our Congregation and it ended up on my desk. If I may say so, I was horrified by the implications."

"I can well imagine."

"We thought of removing this priest to Rome immediately. I persuaded my superiors to permit me to make certain very informal inquiries of certain highly placed friends in American law-enforcement agencies, classmates of mine in school, if I may say so." He shook his head slowly in astonishment. "I must say that even today I find their reaction quite surprising, to say the least."

"They suggested he might be guilty."

"Quite the contrary." The Cardinal frowned. "They replied that he was certainly *not* guilty. Moreover, they begged me that for the good of the United States of America and of the Catholic Church we take no action which would call the slightest attention to the matter. It was, they insisted, absolutely essential that the entire affair be withdrawn completely from public view."

"Remarkable!"

The cover-up again.

"Oh, yes, very remarkable. I was able to satisfy myself and, with some effort, my superiors, that Father had not caused the incident which had redounded to his good fortune and that was that. I will admit that to this day I have wondered what really happened."

"I can well imagine."

"Indeed . . ." The Cardinal seemed to doze off.

Then his eyes opened wide. "That information would not be in your possession, would it?"

"No, Eminenza," Lorcan replied honestly. "I have heard that there was a cover-up, but no one seems to know who was behind it or why."

"I didn't think you would know." The Cardinal's eyes closed. "I can say, however, that it was sanctioned by the highest levels of the American government."

After he had slipped an envelope into the hands of the Cardinal's secretary at the door of the apartment, Lorcan, not sure he was walking a straight line, strolled across the Piazza della Città Leonina and into the great circle in front of San Pietro.

He stood in the center of the piazza and stared at the vast dome, a ghostly black shape blotting out the stars. The Church was made up of flawed human beings, that was for sure.

Father Gregory had been a fool and perhaps a knave. Perhaps he had started with the best of intentions and became trapped in his own shallow cleverness. But apparently he was not a murderer.

Lorcan had learned enough to use against Donny Roscoe if he had to intimidate with Catholic scandal. He would, however, do that only as a last resort. Flawed and imperfect, it was still his Church.

But why was the American government so eager to cover up what had happened that fateful Labor Day back in '54?

19

"You'll never believe it!" Liz cried.

"Never believe what?" Her father looked up from his blue and white computer screen, which was linking him at the moment with Singapore.

"Mom's getting married!" Liz paced up and down in his office like a filly about to jump out of the paddock and race back into the wild. "She's trying to ruin Marie's wedding."

"I won't let her spoil my wedding!" Marie Flynn declared grimly. "No matter what she tries. No way."

His two daughters had invaded the home on Astor Street at the beginning of the week, converting it from a quiet museum to a noisy sorority house. Lorcan did not particularly enjoy rock music. He was, as he often tried to explain to his children, a product of the jazz age. Nonetheless, his home reverberated all day and much of the night with two different rock systems, one in each of the young women's rooms. Liz, he gathered, was "into" something called Heavy Metal while Marie preferred "classic" rock, which her sister proclaimed to be rock for old folks like Dad.

When Lorcan was not at his office, struggling with his potential Japanese partners in the chip deal, he would retreat to the relative serenity of his attic studio. There he felt but did not hear the rhythms of, as he thought, the heavy metal.

"I'm confident that your mother didn't have the wedding in mind when she made a decision to marry again," he said uneasily.

"Sure she did," Liz fumed. "That creep Mark will sit on one side of her and you on the other and she'll beam proudly, not about Marie but about how she's snared two men. Can't you see it! Gross!"

"Mark?"

"Mark Reed." Liz continued to fume. "He's some kind of lawyer. He was over there tonight, completely in charge. I think he's kind of moved in with her. Can you imagine that, Dad, our mother has a live-in lover? Isn't that the most gross thing you ever heard?"

"It is a bit of a surprise."

"Wait till the Maeve hears about it." Marie shook her head, still not quite believing her mother's folly. "She'll hit the ceiling."

"He's a nerd." Liz bounded off the couch. "A creep, a dork . . ."

"Liz, that's uncharitable. We all should be happy that your mother need not be lonely any longer."

"Stop defending her, Dad," Liz fired back. "She's doing it to get back at you even more than at Marie. She wants to humiliate you at the wedding. You'll have to sit with the two of them."

"She'll humiliate me only if I let her. . . . I happen to know Mr. Reed. He's a pleasant, quiet man, works for Overton, McCoy, Randal, and Smith—one of the most prestigious law firms in the city. He's an able estate-planning attorney. There is no harm in him at all. His wife died a couple of years ago. I'm sure he and your mother will be happy together."

Lorcan knew Reed really was a creep, albeit a harmless one.

"She wants us to call him 'Father.'" Marie made a wretched face. "Can you imagine that? No *way*. Liz calls him 'Reedy,' which Mom doesn't like a bit."

"The Lord made them and the devil matched them, that's what I think." Liz's anger was winding down. "They deserve one another . . . and it'll cure Dad of his crazy idea that Mom is still his wife."

Doctor Murphy could not have put it more bluntly.

"It will surely do that," Lorcan muttered.

"There was a note for you shoved under the front door." Marie stood up. "It must have come while we were out."

With that, his two daughters went back to their rooms and no doubt their respective styles of music.

By the time he had opened the note from Dennis Rooney, the house was pulsating with mind-numbing rhythms.

"Lorcan," Dinny had written, "your clout with the Brits is heavy. They're sending an intelligence officer, a 'senior' one, to use their word, out here next week. They want us to meet him at the consulate. I'm not sure I'd trust him any more than your friend Eammon Rafferty. Maybe less. No harm in listening to what he has to say. If you ask me, everyone is too willing to talk to us."

Lorcan folded the note thoughtfully. He could not banish the notion from his head that the body in the car in Ireland was not Tim Meehan's. Joe Meehan apparently had had his doubts. Eammon Rafferty had been vague on the subject. What had really happened to the war lover?

Might he have been Moire's father? Might he still be on the loose somewhere in the world, retired now from whatever he'd been doing, but still a little daft?

At the moment, Lorcan seemed to be entertaining far more questions than answers.

20

On Holy Thursday Lorcan Flynn returned to Long Beach for the first time in thirty-five years.

He made the decision to drive down to the Dunes impulsively after he had left Doctor Murphy's office. It was a lovely day, the Japanese were conferring among themselves, and he was even again with his schedule. He might as well take a drive in the country and see if the beach itself could bring back to the surface his suppressed memories.

Doctor Murphy was not surprised by the news of Dorothy's remarriage—almost as though she had expected it: "So perhaps at last you will begin to view yourself as a single man. You will finally be able to feel free to seek out an appropriate companion for yourself should you choose."

"You mean Moire?"

"I didn't say that."

Nevertheless, that's what Lorcan felt she meant. And, for his part, he still hoped Moire would be in his not-too-distant future.

"No bet."

His impulsive decision to drive to the Dunes was perhaps related to his new obligation now to start his life anew. Or so he thought as he turned the Mustang off Lake Shore Drive into the I-55 connection with Dan Ryan.

He left the Ryan for the Chicago Skyway and stayed on I-90 to Exit 20. He paid his toll and then switched to I-94, on which he would drive to the Michigan City Exit 32.

It was much easier to drive to the Dunes now than it used to be when there was no Interstate system. Easier to drive to Notre Dame football games too.

He had not returned to the house in Long Beach the summer after his illness, despite entreaties from his mother and nasty criticism from his father. He pleaded summer school and basketball obligations at Notre Dame. The school had become his home. His family's bickering and complaining had made life with them intolerable.

"You're not a part of the family anymore," Mom had said tearfully.

"That's all right, Eileen," Dad had sneered. "We're better off without him."

The following year Dad had sold the house on the Dunes and bought a smaller but more elegant home on Green Lake, north of Lake Geneva in Wisconsin. Lorcan had gone there once or twice. The family environment continued to be stifling, so he never returned after that. The others drifted away too, Hank to his own marriage, Edward to the Justines, and little Eileen to Seattle and her new husband. Dad eventually sold that house too—his lifelong dreams of a "summer place of our own" shattered permanently.

As he drove through Michigan City, around the band shell in Washington Park and through Sheridan Beach, the memories of the summer of his first love flooded back. He stopped the car at the turn from Sheridan Beach into Lake

Drive. *It was right here,* he reflected, *that she took my hand in hers for the first time.*

He started the car again and drove slowly along the Drive. He'd forgotten how beautiful the dunes were on a day with clear sky and bright sunlight. Maybe he'd never recognized their beauty in the first place.

Lots of homes were for sale. Perhaps he should buy one—Paddy and Maeve and the kids would love it. Maybe the old dreams could finally come true, a dream which might include Moire.

On a sunny Holy Thursday, with Easter around the corner, that dream seemed both plausible and desirable. *Why the hell not?*

The blue Lake, the quaint homes, the broad beach, and the high dunes made a picture postcard combination of land and water. How could he have forgotten! It may not have been the Amalfi Drive or the Corniche or the Costa Brava, yet for Middlewestern America it was a pretty damn good imitation of those other beauty spots.

He drove by their old home without recognizing it. He realized that he had gone too far, backed up into a driveway, turned around, and drove west much more slowly.

Finally he saw it: a big, handsome Dutch colonial with a green roof. An owner after them had applied aluminum siding to the walls and thus eliminated the need to paint it every year. It was less authentic with its new walls but more attractive.

On the land where the Meehan house had once stood there was now a home that was a mix of New England and modern styles—brown clapboard or more likely an imitation—and Frank Lloyd Wright shapes. Lorcan wondered when it was built. Probably many years later, after the memory of the Labor Day tragedy had faded.

Lorcan climbed carefully down the battered wooden stairs in front of what once had been the Flynn house. On the beach he stood on the exact spot where, as best as he could remember, he and Maura had spread their beach towels.

He walked slowly along the beach, zipping up his windbreaker. Despite the warm weather, it was still March, a passing day of grace and a promise for the coming summer. He walked a long way, probing his memory. But nothing turned up.

He turned at the creek which separated Michiana from Grand Beach and hiked disconsolately back toward his old home.

The sun was sinking rapidly. Lorcan thought about grabbing a bite at a restaurant in Michigan City and attending the Holy Thursday services at one of the many churches in the town. He could call the kids and tell them to go to the Cathedral without him, ask them to make his apologies to Bishop Blackie.

Again he paused in front of his old home. Again he stood on the spot he'd once placed those beach towels. He searched for vibrations but found few. Nothing definite or precise. Something terrible had happened to him on that spot. Yet he could not remember what.

"Are you all right, sir?" asked a friendly voice.

Startled, Lorcan shook himself out of his reverie.

"Sorry," he muttered. "Trying to recall some memories."

"That's what a spring day is for, isn't it?" The tall man with white hair still tinged with traces of red extended his hand. "My name is Jim Quaid. I live in the house up there." He nodded toward the home on the site of the old Meehan place. "I was just going out for my afternoon walk."

"Long ago I lived in the house next door—the Dutch colonial."

"That used to be the Slattery place."

"Before them."

"Crowley?"

"Thirty-five years ago."

"Brady?" The man laughed easily. "You have to own a house here, in a manner of speaking, for at least a decade before the folks identify it with your name."

"My name is Lorcan Flynn. Sorry I forgot my manners."

The other man was slender, good-looking, relaxed, and roughly ten or fifteen years older than Lorcan. His baritone voice was rich, his laughter strong, his handshake firm. He was wearing old chinos and a thick gray wool sweater. He could have been a retired actor or college professor.

"Have you been back often?" he inquired politely.

"In thirty-five years, not once, Mr. Quaid."

"Jim, please, Lorcan. . . . How do you find the place?" He waved his arm in a sweeping gesture, embracing the whole area.

"Attractive, one of the most beautiful spots in the world. I have a crazy notion of buying a house here. I suppose I'll forget it when I drive back to town."

"I agree about the beauty." Jim Quaid chuckled. "I was in government service. My wife and I have been everywhere in the world. We came out here once when we were at a conference in Chicago. We were astonished, and, in a manner of speaking, made up our minds on the spot to retire here. We've never regretted it, although it does get kind of bleak in the winter—bleak and peaceful."

"I could learn to like that."

"Look." Quaid laughed. "I hate to admit this and I didn't come down here looking for business. *However,* I supplement my retirement income by doing a little real estate. I won't bother you and I won't do a hard sell. If you're interested"—he handed him a business card—"you might want to call me."

Lorcan glanced at the card and put it in the pocket of his windbreaker. "If things work out in my life, I might just give you a ring. . . . A place up here would be great for kids."

"It makes my wife and me regret all the more that we didn't have any. We were on the go so much we never got around to adoption. Well, as my mother used to say, God shapes the back to fit the burden. We're marvelously happy with one another."

"You're a fortunate man," Lorcan said, "and you sound like you know it."

"Do I ever!"

Lorcan abruptly changed the subject. "Do you know anything about the history of the land on which your house is built?"

"In a manner of speaking, I do. A couple of years after we bought it one of the summer residents said something about an explosion in the previous house in which a whole family died. We didn't want to learn any of the details, as you may imagine. There aren't any haunts around as far as we can say. . . . Were you here by any chance when the accident occurred?"

"Yes, though I was sick with a high fever and don't remember the details. . . . I was dating a girl who lived there."

Jim Quaid raised a sympathetic eye. "I hope she survived?"

"As a matter of fact she did."

"Astonishing how time dulls the memory of tragedy, isn't it?" Jim Quaid looked off over the lake. "For those who survive."

"It certainly is," Lorcan replied, observing to himself that his new acquaintance was a sensitive and intelligent man. "Except in the dreams."

"Right," the other agreed. "Except in the dreams."

"I won't hold you up any longer," Lorcan said. "And I'll keep your number in mind if I do decide to buy."

"I'll be much obliged to you." Jim Quaid bowed rather formally and strolled down the beach. As Lorcan was starting the car, a woman emerged from Quaid's house with a hoe and rake in her hand. He walked the beach and she worked in the garden for their Holy Thursday exercise. She was a handsome woman in her middle forties with a nice figure. She waved at Lorcan. He waved back as he drove by her.

A happy and satisfied man, Jim Quaid. And a lucky man. He'd be a good man to have as a neighbor.

Lorcan did attend the Holy Thursday service in Michigan City. It was disappointing, not much like the liturgy at the Cathedral.

What did I drive up here for? he asked himself when the service was over and he was walking back to his car. *What did I expect to find? Ghosts?*

There weren't any to be found.

All the ghosts were dead.

21

On Good Friday Lorcan Flynn talked to his Uncle Rory about his brother Henry. It was the perfect day, he reflected, to discuss his own personal Judas Iscariot.

Rory tugged at his vest and looked around the office nervously. "I'm glad you found time to fit me in your schedule, Lorcan."

"When have I not had time to talk with you, Rory?"

"I realize how busy you are."

"Never too busy for family."

"It's about family I've come." Rory lowered his voice to his usual conspiratorial level. "I have personal subjects to discuss."

Rory's whisper constrained Lorcan to reassure him. "It's safe for us to talk here, Rory. The FBI bugs are on the phone line. If there's a tape recorder going it's mine."

"Your girl?" He jerked his head toward the outer office.

"My assistant is absolutely trustworthy."

"Yeah . . . I hope so. The family has never been confident about your taste in people, as I'm sure you understand."

Lorcan let that comment sail by him. It was his father and Hank talking and he would be a fool to try to argue with them.

"It's up to you, Rory. If you don't want to talk here, then don't."

"Well . . . all right; it's your funeral."

"I'll take that chance," Lorcan said wearily. "What's on your mind?"

"In the first place." Rory ticked off the agenda on the fingers of his left hand, starting with the little finger. "Your brother Henry is upset with you."

"So what else is new?"

"I think he has a point, candidly I do."

"Perhaps he does. Why don't you tell me what bothers Hank this time around?"

"You haven't said anything to him about the investigation he's undergoing. It's damn hard for Hank and his family."

"You'll have to tell me why it's hard." Lorcan struggled to maintain his patience. "Donny Roscoe has given him immunity, has he not?"

"Yeah—well, that's true."

"Moreover, he's given him immunity because Hank has perjured himself by accusing me of blowing up the Meehan house thirty-five years ago next summer. It seems to me that if the investigation is hard on anyone it's hard on me."

"Hank believes you ought to understand why he had to do it and be more sympathetic toward his position."

"Hank falsely accuses me of murder and I'm expected to be sympathetic with his position?"

"The FBI had him by the short hairs, Lorcan." Rory spread out his hands as if he had just uttered a total justification for perjury and betrayal.

"So he lied to them about me."

Rory lowered his eyes. "I am not persuaded that it was a lie."

"It may be that neither you nor Hank know who the killer was. I suspect that Dad does. Maybe you do too. You all know, however, that it wasn't me. I was too sick to move at the time the Meehans went up in smoke. Don't tell me that I wasn't."

Lorcan had stabbed in the dark, hoping to trick his uncle into admitting his innocence.

"Be that as it may, Lorcan"—Rory stumbled, knowing that he was in deep water and had to say something— "Hank insists that all you have to do is snitch on the Allens and you're out of danger. That doesn't seem to any of us too much to ask of a brother."

"Perjure myself to condemn innocent people?"

"You don't know that they're innocent, Lorcan," Rory said sharply. "You don't know that as a fact at all."

"I suspect that they are. I certainly have no proof that

they have done anything wrong. You're asking me to help put innocent people behind bars so that my brother, who presumably is guilty, goes free?"

"He's your brother, Lorcan."

"A brother who has falsely charged me with murder."

"He says that you can escape the charge if it comes to trial. You have good lawyers."

"Yeah, I have good lawyers. Yet if there's a trial the jury will be small town and likely hostile to a financier from Chicago. It'll cost me a lot of time and money and plenty of heartache for my family."

"You got the money, Lorcan, and so does your family. Henry's family has to depend on him."

"So because I have money and Henry doesn't, I'm to take the rap for his crime? I must either risk a murder indictment or perjure myself against men who, for all I know, are innocent victims of a publicity-hungry United States Attorney?"

"We thought you would see it this way." Rory shook his little head sadly. "You always did resent Henry."

"Resentment has nothing to with it, Rory," Lorcan said evenly, patiently. "He's lied about me. Let's suppose the murder charge comes to trial. A favorable verdict will depend upon my lawyers proving that my brother has lied about me. We will be able to do that. Are you suggesting that I should risk a prison term or arguably even a death sentence to protect the lying son of a bitch who put me in the dock?"

Rory sighed in disappointment at Lorcan's inability to comprehend the real issues. "He's *family,* Lorcan. You don't seem to grasp that fact: he's family."

"That I'm family doesn't stop him from falsely accusing me."

"How many times do I have to tell you?" Rory snapped. "Can't you understand? He had to do that."

"This is pointless conversation, Rory. My brother is a miserable, lying bastard. I'm not about to waste my time swatting him unless Donny Roscoe goes public with Hank's perjury. If that happens, I promise you and Hank and Dad, Hank is a gone goose. He'll never work in Chicago again. And it will be his fault, not mine."

"Yeah, well, we thought you'd take that attitude. But, frankly, Lorcan, I'm disappointed in you."

"That's your privilege, Rory."

Lorcan's uncle stood up slowly, a weary and disappointed old man. "I don't like to have to say this to you, Lorcan, but your father gave me his orders. If you're not willing to stand up for your brother, then he doesn't want to have to put up with you at any more of those Saturday lunches that are such a burden to him."

For a few moments Lorcan was speechless. One retort after another sprang to his lips. He suppressed them all and finally said, "That's his right, Rory."

Rory nodded his head sadly. "Yeah. Well, I told him you'd say that."

"Just a minute, Uncle Rory," Lorcan said as his uncle turned to leave the office. "Where did you get the money you gave Maura Anne Meehan in New York in September of 1954?"

"I never gave her any money."

"Yes, you did. I know the date and the amount. . . ."

He didn't exactly but he would find out in a few days.

"It was from Joe Meehan's will."

"You're lying, Rory. The will could not have been probated that quickly. Moreover, Joe Meehan's will left nothing to Maura. Where did you get the money? From Father Gregorio?"

"I don't have to answer that question."

"Yes, you do, Rory. Either now or under oath at a trial. Suit yourself."

"You wouldn't do that to an old man."

"Try me."

Rory shook his head, more sadly even than the first time. "You really don't give a damn about family, do you?"

"I give a big damn about my kids. That's why I'm not about to let you and Hank and Dad railroad me into prison. Answer me now or face a subpoena on Monday."

"Your father gave it to me."

"Dad?" Lorcan could hardly believe his ears. The response was so impossible that it must be true.

"Yeah. He told me to take it to her and not ask any questions. Unlike you, family means something to me."

"Where did he get the money? Why did he send it to her?"

"I don't know! I tell you I don't know!"

Lorcan had found out all he needed for the moment. To Rory all he said was, "Yes, you do, Rory Flynn. And you're going to tell me before this is over or you'll never practice law in Chicago again. Now get out."

Uncle Rory had the last word, "You'd be a big disappointment to your mother, Lorcan. I hope God protects her from knowing how selfish you are."

Lorcan leaned back in his chair exhausted.

"What a vile old man." Mary Murray came into the office and handed him a tape. "Every Irish family has someone like him: my Uncle Tom is the same way. You did warn him about the tape, didn't you?"

"In such a way that he heard the warning but didn't grasp it. So I didn't break the law." Lorcan sighed. "Which doesn't make me feel any less miserable."

"You want me to make another copy and put it in the box over at the First Chicago?"

"No, don't bother."

"Lorcan!"

"Yeah, you're right. Put a copy in the bank and when you get a chance next week transcribe it for me."

"You'd better hurry. You'll be late for your appointment."

"What appointment?"

"You've forgotten about your friend Doctor Murphy?"

"Oh, my God! I'll be in awful trouble if I'm late. We'll spend the whole session discussing why I resent her."

He was on time. Mary Kathleen listened attentively to his story about the conversation with Rory.

"What do you think, Doctor Murphy?"

"The pertinent question is how you feel about it."

"Confused. It's sick and twisted. Whatever I do, whatever I say, they contort to fit this sick image they have constructed of me."

"You've just discovered that?"

"I've just recognized it for the first time. Why? What did I do?"

"You have done, Lorcan James Flynn"—she was tapping her pen—"that which is most intolerable about you, what you have done again today, what you can't help doing and what you will continue to do in the competition with your brother and your father and, I presume, your pathetic uncle."

"I've won?"

"See, you did know, didn't you?"

"That's what it's all about? How silly!"

"To the winner, not to the losers. I presume that you were your mother's boy and Henry was your father's boy—as far back as you can remember."

"How did you know that?"

"The competition was not merely between you and your father and your brother, it was also, and primarily, I think, between your mother and your father. You two were enlisted early in life to be surrogates in that battle."

"Why would Dad want to compete with Mom?"

"I suspect that it was rather the reverse."

"Mom competing with Dad? Like Dorothy with me?"

"The difference being that Dorothy was unable or perhaps unwilling to enlist Paddy, uh, Patrick, as an ally. . . . And how do you feel about your banishment from the Saturday lunches?"

"God help me, I feel elated."

"It's been a good Holy Week, Lorcan James. You've been liberated from two neurotic systems."

"My wife and my family."

"What do you think you could have done differently?"

"I don't know."

"I'll give you a hint, Lorcan. Your wife, your father, your brother, your uncle would have all forgiven you if you could have done the one thing that it would be impossible for you to do. And that is?"

"Not win?"

"Precisely. Lorcan as a loser they could endure, even love. Lorcan the perpetual winner in the competition they never could and never will accept."

*After all these years patients continue to surprise
me. I would not have imagined that Lorcan James
Frances Flynn could have so readily accepted the
premise that his mother, poor woman, engineered
the rivalry between the men in her family. Yet he
now seems ready to accept it as self-evident truth
and to leave my office on this day of grief elated and
cheerful. For him Easter came early.*

*There is much evil in the collective neuroses from
which he is escaping, though perhaps not the only
evil and possibly not the most serious evil that
threatens him.*

22

Early Holy Saturday morning Lorcan went straight to
his pool, stripped off his clothes, and dived in. He had
swum only one lap when the phone rang.

"Lorcan Flynn."

"I have no time for frivolous talk," the Maeve began
sternly. "There's too much to be done with this friggin
wedding of yours."

"Is it my daughter's wedding you mean?"

"The schedule is already focked up and it's still a week to
the wedding. I don't know why I ever got meself messed up
with this disorganized family."

"Liz is coming home later today, Marie is moving back
on Wednesday. Where's the problem?" He leaned against
the side of the pool, enjoying the verbal game.

" 'Tis the woman!"

"Which woman is that now, Maeveen?"

"Isn't she coming in tomorrow morning instead of Monday?"

"Ah, is it *that* woman?"

"What other one?"

"Well, can't we reserve her a room at the Four Seasons?"

"You wouldn't be after doing that, would you? I mean one more day in your home isn't going to put your immortal soul in danger, now is it?"

"Not unless she swims naked in me pool, woman. Then I can make no promises at all, at all."

"Jaysus, Da, you're in a vulgar mood and this being Holy Saturday!"

"You wouldn't be objecting to my fantasies about the woman in my pool, would you, now?"

"You're trying to distract me with your obscene imagination." Her face was probably burning and she was grinning wickedly. "You wouldn't be after objecting to her spending one more night there? Liz will be in the same house, won't she now?"

"I suppose I can risk it. . . . You'll be warning the woman to wear her swimsuit in the pool, won't you now?"

"Dragonfly shite, Lorcan James Flynn."

"Dragonflies don't shite, Maeveen. They don't eat either. They're born with all the protein they need already in—"

"Sure, wouldn't I be after knowing that and meself a doctor?"

"Can't tell how much you remembered from your undergraduate days."

"You're after distracting me again." She struggled to recapture her stern voice. "Will you let the woman in your house tomorrow night?"

"Late at night?"

"Isn't she coming in on the ten o'clock shuttle?"

"Is she now?"

"Isn't that what I said?"

"Is it ten in the evening you'd be meaning?"

"Holy saints preserve us, would you ever stop focking around! Are there shuttles at that hour?"

"Don't you have a point now?"

"Will you let her in the house?"

"Doesn't ten in the morning give us a lot of time to work on my swimming pool fantasies?"

"Ah, sure, I knew you would . . . and I have another idea, too."

"That is?"

"Well, instead of picking her up in one of your solemn old limousines, couldn't you be after using that green thing you have stored away in its focking garage?"

"Me frigging 1955 T-Bird?" He tried to sound horrified.

"Isn't it perfect weather for it?"

" 'Tis." He sighed. "And would it be after surprising you, Maeveen, old gal, if I told you I had already thought of it?"

"You never did," she protested.

"I did so, woman. . . . Now would you mind if I return to me swimming and me images of herself naked in the pool with me?"

"You should go back to the Cathedral"—she giggled—"and tell the priest that you had them terrible dirty thoughts, that's what you should do!"

"He'd say that God understands."

Lorcan disconnected the line, quite pleased with himself. Reconciled or not, he was winning more of his encounters with Mad Maeve than he was losing. He had stopped her cold that time.

He must remember to ask Patrick whether he resented the quasi-flirtation between him and Maeve. He had worried about the possibility, but had never found an opportunity to raise the question with his son.

He had not thought of the T-Bird. Nor had he fantasized about a naked Moire in the pool with him.

Now he could think of little else.

In his imagination she stood on the edge of the pool, hands on her hips, breasts thrust out, head thrown back, as she had stood on second base the day they won the softball championship. Now she would be naked in reality as well as in his imagination.

He had repeatedly insisted to himself that his old love's durable good looks were, if not exactly unimportant, a secondary matter. It was the woman herself that counted, not her body.

That body, however, would cloud his judgment, ignite his passions, dim his common sense. He would have to be cautious—not leap into a dangerous new intimacy merely because he desired the woman.

Such careful thoughts did not make the desire disappear.

That was the reconciliation that counted, wasn't it? Not the impossible one with his family, but the difficult and intricate reconciliation with his lost love. Would that it were as easy as delightfully obscene fantasies.

At the Easter Vigil service, presided over by Cardinal Cronin, Bishop Blackie preached about light shattering the darkness and water quenching thirst. The light was Christ, the water was the Church. The lighted candle represented the male, the water the female. When the candle was plunged into the water, it represented the consummation of the passionate love between Jesus and his people at the moment of the resurrection. Those who were baptized with the water were the first fruits of this passionate union.

"That sexual passion is a hint of God's passion," the little priest insisted, "will shock only prudes and those who know nothing of either the Scriptures or the history of Christian symbolism. The metaphor errs only by defect. Easter reveals that God is far more passionate than the most aroused of human lovers—and of course that he understands and loves human lovers."

The Maeve, from her usual position next to him, buried her elbow in his side—standard behavior when she wanted to insist that the homilist's message was aimed right at him.

Lorcan ignored her. The whole world was conspiring to push him and Moire together, including the Bishop and God. Well, he wouldn't be pushed. He would proceed slowly and carefully. He'd made enough mistakes in his intimate relationships already in his life. He didn't need one more.

No more swimming pool fantasies.

Not in the Cathedral during Mass anyway.

After Mass—no, the Eucharist—was finished, he wished the Cardinal, who was milling around among the people like a young associate pastor, happy Easter and asked him about Blackie Ryan's orthodoxy.

"We'll probably be denounced to Rome again." The hoods flew back on Sean Cronin's wild Gaelic eyes and the light of battle shone in them for a moment. "They won't be able to do anything about it, as much as they would like to. Blackie is utterly orthodox in his doctrine if a mite unorthodox in the way he presents it."

"Human passion is, then, a hint of divine passion?"

"Although it would embarrass the Romans to admit it, the metaphor is all over the Bible. . . . Listen to Blackwood, Lorcan, he's almost always right."

"Oh?"

"Almost never in error." The Cardinal grinned wickedly. "And absolutely never in doubt!"

Lorcan's family was scattered about in the crowd of those exchanging Easter greetings. He cornered his son. It was time, while the reconciliation mood was upon him, to resolve a worry.

"Paddy, could I ask you a personal question?"

"Sure, Da." The young man smiled behind his black beard.

"Are you upset about my relationship with Maeve?"

"What . . . ?" Paddy looked as astonished as if his father had proposed blowing up Holy Name Cathedral.

"Uh, well, I mean we enjoy kidding one another. I didn't want—"

"The Holy Saints preserve us, as herself would say! Is it that Mary Kathleen Ryan Murphy that's putting such ideas in your head?"

"Not exactly."

"It is, too. . . . To be serious for a moment, it's also a fair question. Let me think about how to answer it so that it will satisfy you and the good doctor. . . . Ah, let's put it this way. My overriding and dominant reaction is happiness that my father and my wife like one another. A secondary reaction is also happiness that you have to put up with some of her enthusiasms so you know how much I suffer. Can you remember that now?"

"I think the good Doctor Murphy will be satisfied with the first response . . . as the Greeks say, Paddy, Christ is risen!"

"He is risen indeed! . . . Should I take seriously this plot that herself seems to be hatching about you and Mrs. Halinan?"

You redefine your relationship with your son so there's more candor in it and you find yourself being asked a candid question. Better give a candid answer—a reasonably candid one anyway.

"The possibility intrigues me, Patrick. That I must admit. I intend to be careful. I've made enough mistakes in life. I won't be irrationally careful."

"That sounds wise." His son nodded in agreement. "She is an impressive woman—no matter how you look at it."

"We'll see what happens."

Everyone, Lorcan observed to himself, *wants to fix up poor old Dad with a presentable woman.*

So they won't have to worry about him anymore.

BOOK IV

BOOK IV

1

On Easter Sunday, Lorcan Flynn met his first love at O'Hare International Airport. She was so lovely when she walked off the United shuttle flight from New York that his heart almost broke.

She was wearing a large white hat and a pale aquamarine spring dress, with a thick white belt that emphasized her trim and curving body.

"Moire!"

"Lorcan! You didn't have to come up here on Easter morning!"

"You're dazzling!"

She laughed. "An impression, I fear, that I hoped to create."

His plans to be cautious collapsed immediately.

"Welcome to Chicago!"

"I really could have taken care of myself."

"I doubt it."

She was carrying a large flight bag in one hand and a garment bag in the other. Hence she was unable to ward off Lorcan's kiss. It began as a gentle touching of lips. On its own it became a passionate invasion of her whole being. She accepted the kiss. Then, as it became more wanton and demanding, she sagged against his hands, which were holding her face in place.

He wanted it never to end.

Finally he stopped.

"Well," she said, slightly breathless, "is that a preview of the week to come?"

"If you continue to look as beautiful as you do now, I can't promise that it won't be."

Moire smiled. "I'll have to be on my guard . . . and thank you for the compliment."

"You're quite welcome. Now give me those bags."

"I can carry them myself." She frowned, not sure that her independence was secure.

"That," he said, prying them loose from her fingers, "is not the issue. If I want to be gallant, you should let me be gallant."

She tilted her head to one side, lifted up her chin, and considered him thoughtfully—a gesture he had seen before and of which he was growing fond. It meant that she was making up her mind about something or someone she rather liked though she was not about to rush into a hasty, adolescent response.

He led her through the towering corridors of the new Helmut Jahn terminal, a wild and vigorous allusion to the old railroad terminals.

"My, it is quite powerful, isn't it? It certainly beats La Guardia. Do people in Chicago like it?"

"Definitely. . . . My argument in favor of it is that all other terminals in the world look alike. This one is not only different, it is strikingly different."

She nodded. "I quite agree. I haven't lived here for thirty years, yet somehow it is still my city."

"Thirty-five."

She glanced at him, startled. "That long? Oh my, you're right. Thirty-five years this summer."

"And people still stare at you when you walk through the airport."

"Nonsense." She blushed for the second time. "They're wondering who that old woman is with the celebrity Lorcan Flynn."

"Elderly celebrity."

"You distracted me so completely"—she looked mildly vexed—"that I forgot to explain that I had to come this morning because all the flights tomorrow are already booked. Josie will fly in from Boston after her class on Tuesday morning."

"The Maeve makes the logistical decisions, Moire. I do what I'm told with a modicum of questions being asked—

and then because she would be disappointed if I didn't give her some argument."

"She is quite a blessing to your family, isn't she?"

"Pure delight."

"Oh, yes." Moire frowned; he was missing something. "In addition to that, however, she's playing the mother role at this wedding, a help which poor Marie desperately needs."

Lorcan suddenly felt guilty for his own failure to be both a mother and a father and then felt guilty for not being sufficiently grateful to Maeve the Mad.

"She's playing that role with so much discretion that one notices what she's doing only on reflection."

Moire nodded.

"Your wife is remarrying, I'm told." They were riding down the elevator to the baggage section.

"A week after Marie's wedding. Marie is taking it well. Liz, however, is quite furious. As far as I'm concerned, the major issue seems to be whether I should sit in the same pew with Dorothy and Mark or in a pew by myself."

"Oh?"

"What do you think?"

"What does it matter what I think?"

Lorcan feared she was beginning to sound like Doctor Murphy.

"You're the mother of the groom."

"That shouldn't give me any rights to offer advice about what happens on the other side of the aisle."

"I suppose not."

"It really ought to be Marie's decision, shouldn't it?"

"I guess so."

"You guess so?"

"Marie says that Mark isn't her father or yet her stepfather."

"Which settles the question, doesn't it?"

"I don't want to hurt Dorothy."

"She'll only hurt herself."

As they waited for her baggage, she lost no time in approaching more serious subjects.

"You found my letters, I presume."

"Why do you presume?"

"You made up your mind that you would find them. When Lorcan Flynn makes up his mind, he gets what he wants."

"Not always. . . . This time I did. Do you want to see them?"

"I'm not sure." She hesitated. "Should I?"

"I'm inclined to think so. The author is something more than an adolescent girl with a crush."

"You like her?"

"More now than then."

Moire smiled a second time. Was it Lorcan's imagination or was her smile coming more easily than it had been?

"Maybe I'd better read them."

He put down her bags and withdrew the letters from his inside jacket pocket. Silently he handed the small, almost pathetic packet over to her.

Standing at the foot of the escalator in the United Terminal, she read them slowly and carefully, her jaw tightening as she read. She finished them, swallowed once, and handed the packet back to him.

"I was too harsh on her."

Lorcan nodded.

They collected the two bags once they appeared. Moire insisted on taking back the carry-ons while Lorcan managed the larger luggage.

It was a long walk on a hot day to the elevator which carried them to the top level of the O'Hare lot. They were panting by the time they turned down the row of cars where Lorcan had parked the T-Bird.

"Good heavens, Lorcan! No! That isn't it! A '55 T-Bird convertible! Did you rent it for today?"

"I gotta admit, I own her. Normally she sleeps in a heated garage next to my pool. Today seemed to be the day to take her out for a spin. I note she matches your dress."

"T-Bird green! You *own* her?"

"I had a fantasy long ago of driving you around in such a car. Now the fantasy comes true," he said as he opened the trunk and piled her luggage in.

Moire's face glowed with high color. They were both young again. Lorcan put his arms around her, drew her close, and kissed her. This time she responded in kind, her eager, demanding lips tasting of mint and, faintly, of tea. Her lips and agile tongue probed into the center of his personality, challenging him to the depths of his selfhood.

It was her turn to end the embrace. They were both shaken.

"What would people say if they see us?"

"Still some South Side Irish in you, Moire? They'd probably say how come that old man has such a beautiful car and such a beautiful broad in it?"

"Silly." She tapped his arm lightly.

He started the car and drove it carefully down the ramp, paid his charge, and then headed out onto the John F. Kennedy Expressway.

"Glorious!" exclaimed Moire.

"I hope I'm not messing your hair."

"Who cares! I own a comb! What a beautiful city!"

This time I will not lose you, Lorcan vowed.

She returned to the subject. "How do you feel about the letters?"

"Sad for the pain on both sides. . . ." He pondered carefully. "Doctor Murphy says I would have lost you anyway, that I am afraid of strong women like you. . . ."

"Nonsense."

"I certainly didn't marry a strong one. Anyway, I'm glad we have a chance to straighten it out."

He pressed the tape deck—which was not, strictly speaking, allowable in a '55 T-Bird—not by the standards of the purists. The music of *Pajama Game,* the hit musical of 1954, began.

"Lorcan! You've thought of everything. Is a drive-in next?"

"No! An Easter parade, if you don't mind." Lorcan smiled. "I realize that you're the one who says the pious things these days, Moire. Yet I want to say this: it's a grace for us to know each other again."

"And good kissing too!"

"Right!"

Then, almost without reflection, he asked the most crucial question of all.

"What happened on the beach towels that night?"

"Pardon?"

He glanced at her out of the corner of his eye. She was looking at him curiously.

"Before the explosion. Something frightful happened. My fever seems to have blotted it out completely. It might help my sessions with Doctor Murphy if I could figure out what it was."

"It wasn't all that awful, Lorcan. It was unpleasant. I cried a lot, once I ran away from our beach towels—toward New Buffalo. It was not really traumatic."

"I don't remember any of it."

"Well, you and I were lying on the towels as we so often did. We were both feeling amorous—victorious in the championship, it was the end of summer, a romantic time. We both are romantics, as you well recognize."

"That's what Doctor Murphy says."

"How perceptive of her. . . . As I said, you were particularly amorous. I suppose it was the fever. I won't pretend I didn't like it. Especially in the boathouse, where we huddled during the storm."

"Did I . . . did I try—"

"To rape me? . . . Good heavens, Lorcan, it was 1954! Certainly not! You could have done anything you wanted to me, I loved you so much. Yet my integrity was hardly under assault."

"Then what . . . ?"

"You really don't remember? Your mother and father found us in an embrace which probably was less passionate than the kiss back at O'Hare. She was drunk, I think, poor woman. She screamed horrible things at me. Your father pulled me away from you and slapped my face. Hard. Twice. He called me names, too. I ran off crying. That's all."

Lorcan eased the car to the right as the Kennedy merged with Edens Expressway and they entered the final lap of the dash to the Loop.

Moire's hair was blowing across her face. She looked young and vibrant and playful and immensely lovable.

"What was I doing during all this?"

"The whole moment lasted less time than I just took to

describe it, Lorcan. You were shocked and, as I understand now, dreadfully sick. Maybe you pushed your father and cursed him. I'm not even sure of that. I ran off into the night."

Lorcan tried to concentrate on the flow of Easter traffic on the expressway as they neared the Ohio Street off-ramp.

"Nothing else?"

"Nothing. I was scared. The Meehans never fought with one another. I wasn't accustomed to such outbursts of anger. I calmed down when I had walked beyond Grand Beach almost to New Buffalo. I dove into the Lake and swam for fifteen minutes or so and then turned and walked back, more slowly than I had rushed away. I was caught in the rainstorm but I didn't mind that. I like walking in the rain and watching thunder and lightning, as you may remember. . . . Silly kid, taking that kind of chance. . . . Then I heard the explosion. I thought it was thunder at first. Then I saw the flames in the sky. . . ."

Somehow it wasn't everything. Moire was telling what she remembered, but something else had happened that night.

"An appalling experience."

"I survived, Lorcan . . . and I wouldn't have survived if it hadn't been for your parents' attack on me. I would have been in the house when it blew up. I'll never forget that."

Automatically, he turned off Ohio to La Salle; in his mind's eye he saw not the blue sky, the tall buildings to the east, and the young people on the street in their Easter finery, but the moonless night sky over Long Beach thirty-five years ago.

He could recall nothing more than the sky. Moire's description of what had happened stirred no recollections of his own.

"It was a long time ago, Lorcan," she said tentatively as he turned into the driveway of his home. "We both have had good lives since then, not perfect perhaps, yet better than most."

"That's true." The garage door opened at the touch of his control button—also a violation of the purism of a T-Bird restoration. "I'm sorry for my preoccupation. . . . We'll leave her here and go over to the parade in a limo. I wouldn't want to trust her on a Chicago street."

"A sister sacristan could not have been more careful with a chalice in the old days."

"Fair comparison," he agreed ruefully as he lifted her luggage out of the trunk and put it inside the house. "All right if we leave it here in the pool until we come back?"

"Fine. . . . I should rescue my hat, though. It's de rigueur for an Easter parade."

He wanted to kiss her again. The dark and turbulent images of the Sunday night on the beach, however, intervened and dampened his passion.

They walked up the stairs from the basement and toward the front door.

"Thank God," he said finally, "that you didn't die in that blast. . . . Those letters break my heart."

"They make me want to cry," she admitted, "and I don't cry much."

"I'm sorry."

"I've loved two men in my life, Lorcan." She turned and faced him. "Let me finish what I want to say before we go outside. . . . I've loved two men and I've lost both of them. Now I find that there is perhaps an opportunity of loving one of them again. I appreciate the possibility. I'm not completely sure I want that."

Lorcan looked crestfallen.

"But if I do decide I want you, Lorcan," she continued calmly, "I won't give up easily."

Lorcan knew he'd better say something.

"I've always loved you, Moire. You're more appealing now than ever. It's not merely your physical beauty— though that quite overwhelms me. Even if you weren't so attractive, I'd still want you because of who you are."

He rested his hands on her shoulders.

"We've made our positions clear enough. . . . This should be a lively week for both of us. Now you said something about an Easter parade, didn't you?"

Deftly she slipped away from him. The erotic spell which had engulfed the two of them abruptly lost its magic.

The street in front of Old St. Patrick's Church was

swarming with men and women of all ages in their Easter apparel. The street looked like a setting for a musical comedy. Horsedrawn carriages came and went, disgorging and picking up passengers. A quartet was playing Mozart. Teenagers were serving lemonade under a red and white awning. The ushers in front of the church wore morning suits. Some of the young women were wearing bonnets. The trees in front of the church were decorated with Easter eggs. One expected a chorus line to form and a larger orchestra to break into the music of "Easter Parade."

Aquamarine was the color of the day for women of every age, so Moire fit right in—and continued to turn heads.

The quartet switched from Mozart to Irving Berlin. The crowd joined in with the lyrics of "Easter Parade."

Lorcan took his date's arm and escorted her into the crowd. They sang the Irving Berlin song together. She sang, naturally, right on key.

Lorcan spotted his two grandsons in the distance, one in a light gray suit and the other in a light blue one. The Maeve would be hard put to keep either clean for more than a couple of hours.

"A marvelous celebration of the new life we put on in baptism, isn't it, Lorcan? . . . As chairman of our parish liturgy committee, I suppose I should say our Christian initiation."

"You're one of those?"

"Don't hold it against me." She smiled.

He took her arm, suddenly confident of himself. "I'll try not to. . . . Let me introduce you to my two grandsons. Con, Derm," he called out. The two boys instantly ran to their GrandDa.

"No candy bars today unless your ma says yes and we all know, guys, she won't say yes as long as you have your good suits on."

"Yes, GrandDa," they agreed sadly.

"Guys, this is Robbie's mother. Her name is Moire."

Moire crouched down so her eyes were on the same level as the kids'. "How do you do, Diarmuid and Conghor? Do you think you have a hug and a kiss for Robbie's Mom?"

Did they ever!

"What adorable little boys." She accepted Lorcan's hand to help stand up again. "They both look like you."

Just then Maeve appeared.

"Holy Mother of God, Lorcan! Where have you been? Aren't we perishing with the heat and the hunger and isn't our reservation at Jerome's after expiring? And aren't my brats in a dither because I won't let you give them chocolate? . . . Glory be to God, woman"—vast hug for Moire—"aren't you the hit of the Easter parade? And aren't my brats telling me how beautiful Robbie's ma is?"

They were swept off to an outdoor café on North Clark where a midafternoon brunch was being served. Liz, Marie, and Rob joined them. The little punks messed up their suits. Lorcan drank too much California Chenin Blanc, as if he were not already sufficiently intoxicated by his old love returned.

Liz and Moire hit it off in the first five minutes.

Moire lost her solemn dignity and laughed as hard as anyone, particularly when Maeve did her imitation of "the Old Fella negotiating with your frigging Japanese."

She played all the roles—the Old Fella and the three Japanese with whom he was negotiating.

The Old Fella won the negotiation. He outlasted "your frigging Japanese."

The sky was darkening when the limo picked them up for the return to Astor Street. Lorcan was exhausted but Moire looked as fresh as when she had emerged from the Boeing 727.

"You devour me, Lorcan," she said when they were seated in the car. "With your eyes. Hard and implacable. I feel . . . feel like you're undressing me every time you look at me."

"I'm sorry. I'll try to stop."

"I didn't say I wanted you to stop. I'm embarrassed and flattered—and just a little afraid of you."

"I don't want to scare you."

"It's a not unpleasant fear."

Together they walked into his house. "I'm glad Rob is marrying into such a vivacious family."

"Noisy, pushy, contentious, and they drink too much."

"Lorcan"—she slapped his arm lightly—"you don't mean that."

"I'm intoxicated, woman."

"You didn't drink that much."

"Intoxicated with the vitality of life," he said.

"That's what Easter is supposed to be about—the triumph of vitality over morbidity."

"This is the main guest suite. I hope you find it cozy."

"Good heavens! You could have the wedding reception here instead of at the Drake!"

"Fees are higher here. . . . There's a fridge in the bathroom, amply stuffed with snacks and even the stuff for breakfast. There's plenty more down in the kitchen. If you want to go out for supper—"

"I've already had more than enough for two days. I'll head for your pool if you don't mind. Then I plan to get a good night's sleep. I'll need my rest if you expect me to keep up with your madcap family."

"I must do a few calculations on my computer for my Japanese partners tomorrow. . . ."

"Will you join me in the pool?" She opened the top button of her dress, a gesture which sent his heart rate soaring.

"I've been virtuous again today—did my exercise this morning."

"I hate that sort of virtue. . . . See you tomorrow, then?"

"I guess." Lorcan, now thoroughly terrified, was searching for a path of quick retreat.

"Just a minute, Lorcan." She pursued him to the door of her suite; somehow two buttons were now undone, revealing a lacy white bra.

She captured his face in her hands and kissed him. It was not quite so vehement an assault as his earlier one on her. Rather it was playful, affectionate, provoking—and quite devastating.

She examined his face, satisfied that she had disconcerted and unnerved him. Her brown eyes glittered with amusement. "That was fun," she said. "Lots of fun. I think I'll do it again."

This time she leaned against him, her breasts against his

chest. Her kiss was yet more playful, her lips flirting with his like coquettes that were both innocent and knowing. Her mouth tasted of mint, her hair smelled of citrus.

"It was a wonderful day, Lorcan," she said. "Thank you for making me feel like I had the vitality of a teenager once more."

Then she was back in her room and the door was closed.

Bemused and content, Lorcan wandered down to his office, turned on his Compaq 386/20, and stared at the blue screen like a fifteen-year-old who had been kissed by his first girlfriend.

He heard the elevator chug to a stop on the second floor and then down to the pool. Liz would be out late with the engaged couple and their friends. Moire and he were alone in the house. She would surely not fight him off.

Lorcan considered the screen thoughtfully and called up the data base on which he wanted to work. The Japanese wanted to deal. They also wanted to wear him down. His response would be to inundate them with facts and hint broadly about the West German firm with whom he was negotiating. The Germans were brutes and not so subtle as the Japanese. If the latter thought he was bluffing, they would soon find out that they had underestimated him.

He could at least join her in the pool. That wouldn't do any harm, would it?

He reflected on that possibility and then began his calculations.

He was still tempted by thoughts of Moire in the pool, but decided not to pursue her—for the moment.

Moire was tired; she needed a rest. So did he. Tomorrow was another day.

2

On Monday of Easter Week, Lorcan Flynn met with a British officer and discovered that he was in his heart of hearts an Irish nationalist.

"Nicholson," said the British officer by way of introduction. "Radford Nicholson."

"Colonel Nicholson?"

The Brit laughed. "That will suffice."

The call arranging this meeting had come from the British consulate. Would it be at all convenient for Lorcan to stop by at ten A.M.? They would be most grateful. By himself if he didn't mind.

He had taken the call at the breakfast table. Moire had insisted on cooking breakfast for him and Liz after their swim in the pool. Sleepy-eyed Liz, who could barely function at that hour of the day, voted that they hire Moire as a permanent cook.

Moire had appeared in the pool area some ten minutes after Lorcan arrived.

"Morning," she said.

"Good morning," Lorcan replied. He was wondering just what—if anything—she was wearing beneath her terry robe. In the next moment his question was answered. Moire slipped off the robe to reveal a one-piece swimsuit that clung to her shapely body like a second skin.

She dove into the pool and did two lengths under water.

Lorcan dove in after her. He stood up in the shallow end by her side. Without another word, he took her in his arms and began kissing her, not one long kiss but many quick ones on her face and her throat and chest.

Moire struggled briefly but quickly relaxed, giving herself over to his amusements.

"What if your daughter should come in?" she asked when he paused to catch his breath.

"Liz is never out of bed this early. But even if she was, I suspect she'd be delighted to find us this way."

Moire smiled.

Lorcan drew her to him again.

With such delightful pursuits only an hour or two behind him, Lorcan was hardly in a mood for a walk to the British consulate general. But Nicholson was already before him and he had questions for the man after all.

"I understand you were in the Korean dust-up," Nicholson began. "D.F.C. Two of them in fact."

The British officer was a man of medium height, solid shoulders, high hairline, upper-class accent, about forty years old. Sandhurst graduate probably. Looked and acted like one of the officers on Alec Guinness's staff in *Bridge on the River Kwai.*

"Doesn't mean quite what it means for you folks."

"I'm not so sure of that. You'd probably be a lieutenant colonel yourself."

He pronounced it "leftenant"—silly British affectation.

"It was a long time ago."

"About as long ago as the matter which interests you."

"That's true."

"Well, then." The officer rubbed his hands briskly. "Shall we get down to business? . . . Oh—thank you very much, Jane."

An assistant had brought in a coffeepot and two cups.

"How do you take yours, sir?" she asked Lorcan.

"Black, Jane." He swung at an outside pitch. "You'll be recording our conversation, will you not, Jane? I'd like a copy of the tape, please."

Jane almost dropped the coffeepot. "Sir!"

Nicholson was not amused, but he tried to put the best possible face on the situation.

"I rather think Lieutenant Colonel Flynn's talents were wasted in the Air Force, Jane. He should have been in Intelligence."

"Yes, sir," the woman's face was red.

"Not Special Air Services," Lorcan continued.

"That's not my outfit, Mr. Flynn," the Englishman said huffily. "Thank God."

"Do I get a copy of the tape?"

Nicholson took a deep breath. "Of course. Jane will have a copy for you when you leave."

"Thank you."

The Colonel sipped his coffee, frowned his disapproval, put the cup back on the saucer, rubbed his hands once more, and began. "Let me say first of all, Mr. Flynn, that I was not involved in the project we are discussing. As a point of fact I was only seven years old at the time. I knew nothing about it till your request for information was called to my attention. Neither I nor any of my, er, colleagues approve of what was done."

"I understand."

"I might add that discussion went on at the highest levels as to whether we ought to speak of this matter with you."

"I'm not surprised."

"A very senior person, presented with the astonishing amount of intelligence you have already gathered, made the decision that our interests would be better protected if you had all the information we could make available to you. This person insisted that you were a responsible participant in international meetings with no evident desire to embarrass Her Majesty's Government or to help the Irish Republican Army."

"That's true. I have no more sympathy for the Lads than I do for SAS."

"Quite. Therefore I am authorized to relate to you, to the best of our understanding, the entire matter of the Meehans and their attempt to supply automatic weapons to the IRA in the middle nineteen-fifties."

"I am happy to hear that."

The Colonel pulled out a pair of half-glasses and opened a manila folder. "We were aware from our usual sources that Congressman Meehan was sympathetic to the Irish revolutionaries. You understand, I am sure, that the issue was less serious then than it is now. However, at that time there were a number of raids, involving heavy casualties, on police stations in Northern Ireland."

"I remember."

"We were shocked," he continued to read from the report, doubtless fashioned for Lorcan's consumption, "to learn from our sources within the IRA that the Congressman was willing to turn stolen American automatic rifles over to the revolutionaries. The Browning, as you may or may not know, is a heavy, cumbersome, and not particularly effective weapon in combat. However, in the hands of men in an ambush on a dark country road or in an attack late at night on a police station it could accomplish devastating effects. In those days, you understand, we were dealing with men who at the most had old Lee-Enfields and a few forty-five-caliber pistols. Thirty automatic rifles, even primitive ones, would have given them enormous power. We could have anticipated hundreds of constabulary casualties, indeed the possible destruction of the Royal Irish Constabulary."

"Oh?"

"Imagine, if you will, that on a given night, one or two gunmen would lie in wait outside of thirty police barracks in rural Ulster. At an agreed-upon time, a small explosion would disturb the police. Guns in hand, they would rush out of their barracks. They would be met by a withering fire. The death and destruction would be horrific. We would have no choice but to send in regular Army troops—a decision fraught with difficult consequences, as subsequent history has demonstrated."

The Colonel looked up to check Lorcan's reaction.

"Indeed."

"I might add that the police in Eire, as it was then called, would have been at similar risk. The IRA, then as now, view them as enemies too."

"So I understand."

"We—I mean, naturally, my predecessors—understood that the Congressman had certain debts he felt required to liquidate, campaign expenses and gambling losses which involved, ah, underworld figures in Chicago."

"The Outfit?"

"Yes, I believe that is what they are called locally."

The Colonel adjusted his glasses and returned to the report.

"He was also genuinely interested in and sympathetic towards the revolutionaries, as is typical of many Irish-Americans uninformed about the issues."

His eyes flicked up over the glasses to study Lorcan's reaction.

"I'm sure, Brigadier, that you do not judge ten million Irish-Catholic Americans by those who contribute to Noraid in bars run by the likes of Eammon Rafferty."

Nicholson watched him intently for a moment and said, "Quite right. . . . Incidentally, no further promotions will be necessary. You have the right rank this time."

"Yes, sir."

"To continue: A decision was made at a senior level to interdict the transfer of weapons. We felt that it would be far simpler to seize them in Indiana rather than try to intercept a ship on the high seas or as it approached an Irish port. We were able to learn where the weapons were stolen and, within some limits, when they were to be shipped to, ah"—he examined the report carefully—"Long Beach. We hoped to confiscate them on the highway. Unfortunately this was impossible for reasons that are not clear at the present time. The weapons arrived at the Congressman's house late one night the week before the explosion. They were quickly unloaded. Our information is that the wife of the Congressman was fully informed and that the three young women in the house were unaware of the delivery. They are all dead now, so it is impossible to be certain."

"One of the young women is still alive."

"How fortunate for her." The Englishman was not much interested. "As you discovered, we had men watching matters quite closely that week."

"American Intelligence?"

"We did not wish to alert the Federal Bureau of Investigation, as you may imagine. They would have stumbled in, perhaps alerted our quarry, and used the affair to win public notice for themselves and Mr. Hoover. We felt the matter had to be handled with the utmost discretion."

"They came around afterwards."

"Oh yes, and with orders from the highest authority to end the entire matter as quickly as possible. The Eisenhower Administration had no desire to reveal that an American congressman, even one from the other party, had been stealing weapons from American military arsenals and trading them to a foreign power."

"I can believe that," Lorcan said, although on the South Side of Chicago, they would not consider the IRA a foreign power.

"We did notify our counterparts in other agencies and inform them of what we proposed. They presented no serious objection so long as we undertook to promise that there would be no public notice."

"There was considerable public notice."

"Through no fault of ours, I can assure you. . . . Our plan was quite simple. We knew that those who would receive the weapons had a small yacht at their disposal. We were able to trace them and to lie offshore quite close to them. As soon as they had loaded the weapons on their boat and proceeded some distance offshore, we would have boarded the boat, disarmed them, and disposed of the weapons by consigning them to the Lake."

"Wouldn't it have been easier simply to have sunk the boat with all hands?"

"My predecessors had guaranteed their American counterparts that no such event would occur."

Lorcan doubted that, but he wanted the Brigadier to go on with his story, so he didn't express that doubt.

"There's not much more to tell." The Brigadier removed his glasses, folded them, and closed his file. "Our agents saw the explosion, knew what it meant, and promptly withdrew. Their seniors in Washington informed your counterpart agencies. The American government undertook to arrange matters as expeditiously as possible. That's all we can tell you."

"You didn't blow up Congressman Meehan's house?"

"Dear God, no! That would have been unconscionable folly on our part."

"Who did it, then?"

"Our field agents assumed that it was no accident. The IRA is savage enough to contemplate any barbarism. Hence we did not rule out the possibility that they were exacting some vengeance of their own. Frankly we were no longer interested."

"So your informer in the IRA Chicago group was spared?"

"Yes, quite."

The field officer in charge probably had not been told of the informer. He would have died with the rest. However, after the explosion, the British leader made a conservative decision: retreat while you could.

Lorcan pondered. "The only question I have is about Tim Meehan."

"Who is he, Mr. Flynn?"

"The Congressman's brother, who apparently died in Ireland four years before—shot in the back, it is alleged, and then tossed into a lake."

"One moment, please." He replaced his glasses on his forehead and skimmed through the report again. Then he removed his glasses and returned them to his jacket.

"I'm sorry, Mr. Flynn, there is no mention of him in my data."

"The name means nothing to you?"

"No, sir."

"One reason, so I understand, for the Congressman's willingness to deal with the IRA was his suspicion that his brother was still alive."

"I have no information on that, sir."

"Thank you very much, Brigadier." Lorcan rose. "You've been very helpful. We will guard this information carefully."

"I certainly hope so, Mr. Flynn."

He and Lorcan shook hands.

Lorcan wasn't sure how much he believed of the Englishman's story. In general outline it was probably true. The details might have been changed to fit their purposes, then or now or both.

He was lying about Tim Meehan, of that Lorcan was certain.

After thirty-five years the story would embarrass almost no one. However, intelligence agencies wanted to keep all secrets secret.

Or perhaps they wanted to protect someone who was still alive.

"If I may say so, Mr. Flynn," the officer said as he accompanied Lorcan to the door, "I am one of those Englishmen who fervently hopes that we will be able to disengage from our Irish responsibilities as soon as possible. We remain there now only to avoid the bloodbath that would surely occur if we should leave."

Lorcan extended a hand into which Jane, her face as hard as stone, dropped a tape.

"Funny thing, Brigadier." He smiled at Jane and bowed at the officer. "That's what we said about Vietnam."

Lorcan looked at his watch. There was just enough time to drop the tape at Dinny's and still arrive punctually for his session with Doctor Murphy.

No doubt Doctor Murphy would be eager for an update on how he was getting along with his houseguest.

3

"**W**hat do you want me to say, Lorcan? Do you expect praise for finally acting like someone approaching an adult in your relationship with the woman?"

"No, not exactly."

"You obviously have a decision to make with regard to her."

"And vice versa?"

"Naturally."

"What do you think, Doctor Murphy?"

"What do I think? How could that matter?"

"I don't want to make another mistake."

"If I told you not to bed her and/or not to marry her, Lorcan James Flynn, would that stop you?"

"Not if I had already made up my mind . . ."

"So why ask?"

". . . unless you warned me very solemnly not to."

"I may have issued similar warnings in some cases. Not, however, in this one."

Dinny had praised him for his ingenuity in obtaining the tape from the British officer. He should not have expected praise from Mary Kathleen Murphy.

He and Dinny had listened to the tape together in the latter's office.

"Bloody smooth lying Brit bastard. Lorcan, has it occurred to you that everyone is eager to provide us with information about that weekend?"

"It sure has. The facts have been covered up for thirty-five years. Now we have almost more than we know what to do with."

"Yeah. . . . This tape"—he had held up a copy he had made of the one Lorcan had brought him—"all by itself will scuttle Donny Roscoe's game if he ever tries to go public with it."

"I wouldn't be surprised that if we pushed hard enough, someone from the Bureau or Langley would come running out here to explain their version of the story."

"Most of which"—Rooney had closed his eyes to think—"would bear a reasonable resemblance to the truth."

"The American government was not unhappy to see poor Joe Meehan buried as quietly as possible in Holy Sepulchre Cemetery. They didn't want to confess to the world that an American congressman was selling stolen weapons to a foreign organization. They wanted a cover-up as bad as did the Brits and the IRA. So they devoted their energies to hiding the potential scandal, not to finding out what really happened, much less to arresting the killer."

"We don't know for sure who the killer was." Rooney opened his eyes. "Who do you think it was, Lorcan?"

"Tim Meehan."

"He was dead."

"Was he? How do we know that? An old newspaper clipping? A body buried in a sealed casket? Joe Meehan, poor man, didn't accept that explanation. Why should we?"

"The Brits know about Tim?"

"That guy does." He had gestured at the tape. "Maybe Tim turned informer for them. Maybe the reason for all the candor this morning is to cover up for him."

"Why wipe out his brother's family?"

Lorcan had slumped into his chair. "I admit it doesn't make sense right now. We don't have sufficient data yet."

"I'll be honest, Lorcan. We're not likely to find any more data. We might pry something out of the Bureau or Langley. However, it wouldn't add much. If Tim Meehan is the killer, and if he's still alive—and the latter is a bigger 'if' than the former—how will we ever find him?"

"I can't argue, Dinny. Let's keep looking."

"As long as you say so, Lorcan. We might turn up more to use against Donny. That wouldn't hurt."

Lorcan told Doctor Murphy what he had learned from Moire about that Labor Day night.

"Are you satisfied with Moire's description of the events that evening?" Doctor Murphy asked.

"I'm satisfied that she is telling the truth."

"But you are not satisfied that your problem is solved?"

"Something else happened that night."

"After she left?"

"Almost certainly."

"On the beach towels?"

"I guess."

"Is she free from your suspicions?"

"Mostly."

"You won't use the events you've repressed as an excuse to dodge your response to her present challenge?"

"She's far too attractive for me to do that."

"Hmn . . ."

"Honest."

"There are two problems, Lorcan. The murder and what happened earlier. They may or may not be the same problem."

"Do you want to hear about our investigation? I haven't told you the details."

There was a long pause.

"Perhaps I ought to know. Not, however, from the couch."

"I've begun to like it here."

He moved to the chair across from her desk and filled her in as succinctly yet specifically as possible. When he had finished, she remained silent for several moments.

"As you are aware, I'll be away for two weeks after your daughter's wedding. It's unlikely that you would need psychological support on an emergency basis."

"Probably not."

"Candidly, some of your difficulties are not in your head."

"I'm delighted to hear that."

She grinned, a most attractive, impish grin. "There are family relationship problems that we must still sort out. They impinge on your love for the woman and on the events of that evening in ways we don't understand. The real-world events, however, are distinct from your psychological problems."

"It's hard for me to remember that."

"What I am about to say is no reflection on your abilities or Mr. Rooney's. Certain cans of worms require a special kind of mentality to pry open, the kind of mind which sees the world differently."

"Oh?"

"I'm writing down a name on a card." She picked up her pen and began to write. "I'll seal this card in an envelope. If the real-world situation, as opposed to the psychological one, should become difficult, you might open this envelope and call the person whose name I have written."

"He is good, I take it?"

"The best." She sealed the envelope. "If he is on your side, your enemies are in deep, deep trouble. Do not judge by appearances."

"I'll take your word for it." He put the envelope in his pocket. "Thank you." Lorcan left her office pleased with his session. He somehow felt better for the card Doctor Murphy had given him, yet he wondered what she meant by warning that he should not judge by appearances.

I daresay that if the patient opens my mysterious sealed envelope and finds the name of his innocuous and befuddled pastor, presumably the priest who will preside over his daughter's nuptials this weekend, he will be disappointed. Fine. If the situation is sufficiently serious he will seek help nonetheless. If it is not serious enough, he will merely think that I've lost my mind and no harm will be done.

I almost hate to turn the Punk, the ineffable John Blackwood Ryan, S.T.L., Ph.D., D.D. (honoris causa), loose on such a case. He will enjoy it too much.

The woman is trying to seduce my patient. Unlike the others who have engaged in the same behavior—his mother included—she is honest with both herself and with him. I'm sure she has many uncertainties, perhaps more than he has. It will not automatically work out well.

Life rarely does.

4

Lorcan's family was not finished with him.

On Tuesday afternoon, after a long and exhausting session with the Japanese at the Nikko Hotel, he returned to his office disheartened and weary. They would hammer out an agreement eventually.

Preparations for the upcoming wedding were reaching a fever pitch. Moire's daughter, Josie, would be moving into his house the following day. And with her addition, Lorcan would no doubt find fewer opportunities for amorous encounters with Moire such as he had enjoyed early Monday morning. The way Lorcan was feeling, it was almost just as well. He really wanted to get to the bottom of the Labor Day explosion. It was very much on his mind. For the moment, however, he had business to attend to. He was just beginning to go over some financial statements when Mary Murray buzzed him.

"Your brother Henry is on the phone, Mr. Flynn," she announced over the intercom. "He's been trying to reach you all afternoon."

"Lorcan Flynn."

"I've been trying to reach you all day," Henry whined. "Aren't you ever in your office?"

"I've been busy with the Japanese."

"Still making money?" Hank sneered.

"What is it you want, Henry?"

"Gee, sorry I'm interrupting your busy schedule."

Lorcan waited patiently.

"Well," Hank began, "the family decided to give you one more chance about this wedding."

"I gather you and Joanne have not replied to the invitation."

Although Marie couldn't have cared less whether her aunt and uncle came, she was disappointed that her cousins would not be there.

"Certainly not. Hasn't the family made it clear to you that we don't approve?"

"I received that message, Hank."

Uncle Rory had not replied to his invitation either; Marie would not miss him.

"We decided that we'd give you another chance to intervene and stop the marriage."

"Today is Tuesday, Hank. The wedding is Saturday. I'm supposed to stop it now?"

"We think it's a serious mistake."

"You've made that point before."

"Well, we're urging you again to prevent the marriage."

"Why, Hank?"

"Because your family thinks it's a mistake. Haven't we made that clear already?"

"I should try to stop my daughter's wedding because you and Dad and Rory don't approve?"

"No one approves."

"I understand. . . . Would it be too much to ask why you don't approve?"

"How many times do we have to go over it?" Henry asked impatiently. "Dad thinks it's a serious mistake. Isn't that enough?"

"So what?" He shifted the phone from one hand to the other.

"So what? Don't you have any regard for the family?"

"I have a great deal of regard for my family, Hank. I do not believe, however, that Dad's opposition to the marriage of one of my children should be taken seriously."

"He says that the boy's family is trash."

"I don't happen to see it that way, Hank."

"You're making a terrible mistake, Lorcan."

"I have been duly warned."

Lorcan's hands were sweaty and his stomach tense when he had hung up on Henry. They were stark raving mad. Rory and Hank were so dependent on his father's approval that they were willing to accept his senile perceptions as valid, judicious opinions.

He'd been a fool to sit through as many Saturday luncheons as he had. In the future he would make it a point to steer clear of all three of them—Hank, Uncle Rory, his father—for fear of becoming as crazy as they were.

If he wasn't that crazy already.

5

On Tuesday night, Moire, in jeans and a jacket, came to the door of Lorcan's office as he was preparing his Sidekick program to spit out the schedule for the next day.

"Is it safe to walk on Oak Street Beach at this hour of the night?"

He looked up from the computer screen. Even in the most casual clothes, she was striking.

"Lots of people out there on a moonlit night: joggers, lovers, walkers, moon gazers."

"I need some fresh air," she said. "Too much wedding enthusiasm today."

Josie had arrived earlier. She was a tall, slender girl with a quick laugh and Moire's gentle brown eyes. She was far more gregarious than her mother and her brother and instantly joined the sorority gang that was occupying his house and shaking it with rock music. Their enthusiasm depressed Lorcan.

Lorcan had become increasingly absorbed with the notion Doctor Murphy had suggested to him that he had been a pawn in a rivalry between his mother and father. He still had so much to resolve, so much to straighten out in his own mind, before he could hope to begin a successful relationship. He would wait, he decided. He could always fly to New York later, once the wedding was over, perhaps after the Long Beach mystery was cleared up. Or so had his thinking run until Moire had arrived on his doorstep with thoughts of a walk on the beach during the week of the first full moon after the beginning of spring.

He wanted to say to her that it would be perfectly safe on Lake Shore Drive. Instead he said, "Let me get a jacket and I'll walk with you."

"I don't mean to disturb you when you're working," she protested.

"I need some spring air too." He turned off his computer. "It won't last much longer."

She didn't argue. Obviously she wanted to talk.

Yet they walked up to North Avenue and through the underpass to the beach in silence.

"North or south?" he asked as they emerged from the underpass.

"South," she said. "Toward the skyscrapers."

The moon had turned the calm lake silver. The Hancock Center and its coterie of lesser buildings were hulking deep purple giants against a glowing sky.

"Beautiful." She took his hand in hers just as she had on a beach three and a half decades earlier.

Lorcan wasn't sure he was prepared to have a serious talk with Moire. But if she had a mind to speak with him, he knew he wouldn't put her off.

"I'm not as tough as I act, Lorcan," she began.

Lorcan nodded, more by way of encouragement than agreement.

"I am reasonably in touch with my emotions. I'm not frail, but I'm not quite as courageous as I might seem."

"Hmn . . ." Lorcan tried to imitate Doctor Murphy's noncommittal response.

"I realize that I often seem distant, reserved, maybe even cold. . . . I worry about the children. They seem all right, but what happens to kids when their mother's self-restraint makes her seem remote?"

"I prefer the words 'challenging' and 'mysterious.' "

"In my defense I would say I've had to be reasonably tough and create the illusion of greater toughness."

"Hmn . . ."

"I've worked my way through four families."

"Four!"

"My real parents—whoever they were; the couple that adopted me and died in California; the Meehans; and now my own family—Tom dead, the kids gone or going."

"Dear God!"

"I hope I don't sound like I'm pitying myself? I hate self-pity."

"You sound like someone who is in touch with her own grief."

"I feel the grief. It's hard to express it. I confuse grief with self-pity."

He freed his hand from hers and extended his arm around her waist.

"Thank you, Lorcan. That feels nice."

"The couple that was killed in an accident were not your parents?"

"Congressman Meehan told me that shortly before the explosion. I wanted to find out more about them. He tried to be gentle. I didn't cry, though I wanted to. I did love the Meehans, Lorcan, I still pray for them every night."

"I see." Physical contact with her set his heart racing.

"Who were they?"

"I tried to find out when Tom and I were preparing for marriage. You see, all the records were fake, even my baptismal records. I could find no evidence of who they were or who I was or even whether I had been baptized. The priest at the parish baptized me again and told me I would have to do my first confession and receive confirmation again. That's when I decided to spell my name the Irish way."

"What! He baptized you again?"

"He said that none of the sins I had confessed had ever been forgiven because I hadn't been a Christian."

"Disgraceful!"

"Don't worry. I didn't pay any attention to him. I knew enough theology to realize that if I had not been baptized, the new ceremony took care of all my sins. I asked my present priest about it; he was almost as furious as you are."

"It's a wonder anyone stays in the Church."

"We mustn't blame God for what priests do. . . . Anyway, I've made peace with being an orphan three times over. I tell myself I'm not really angry at my parents for abandoning me or at God for taking my other families away from me. Usually I'm not. . . . The point in this, Lorcan, is that I am wary of being too close to anyone. Can you understand that?"

"Surely."

"The life of a celibate widow is not easy. I find it easier, however, than trusting myself to another person I might lose eventually."

"I understand that."

She paused, choosing her next words.

"As I told you Sunday, you scare me, Lorcan," she said at last. "You scare the living daylights out of me."

"I'm sorry."

"Don't be sorry." She leaned against him briefly. "It's not your fault. It's mine—that's what I'm trying to explain."

"Oh?"

"I've never encountered a man like you . . . not since I met you at the Lake. One could not live with you in some kind of quiet harmony. I'm used to that sort of relationship. I could do nicely in it. You want more."

"I do?"

"You look at a woman and you want everything—body and soul. You want to strip away her clothes and her secrets and her mysteries and possess her completely like you possess that statue you showed me the last time I was here."

"I understand that a woman is more than a statue."

"I realize that. You don't want to make a woman a thing. You treat her with respect and affection. She would not be a treasure but a treasured person. All the time."

"Would that be bad?"

"It would be exhausting. Lorcan, I melt when I hear your voice. My legs become wobbly and I'm afraid that I'll collapse. I have to restrain myself so that I don't become a giddy fifteen-year-old. I don't look forward to these responses. I find them dangerous. Yet when they capture me, I delight in them."

"Pleasant or unpleasant exhausting?"

"Oh—pleasant." She seemed surprised by the question.

"You wouldn't have to compete with me, Moire."

"Who's talking about competing?" she said impatiently.

"That's how other women would define it."

"I'm not other women, Lorcan." She rested her head on his shoulder. "I'm me."

"No doubt about that, Moire."

"I can keep up with you. I'd even enjoy that. I'd have to give up all my defenses and my secret hiding places: that's what's frightening."

"I'd have to give up the same defenses."

"You did that, poor dear boy, thirty-five years ago. That's what makes you all the more appealing."

"There's no rush, Moire."

"There is, Lorcan. We've wasted too many years."

"If I said that, I'd be bawled out."

"You would indeed. . . . And I don't mean it that way. I was happy with Tom. We loved each other. I wanted to die when he died. I'll never forget the last time he waved good-bye to me as he drove over to La Guardia. You're a different proposition altogether."

"We don't have to decide tonight. Or even this week."

"I understand, Lorcan. I wanted to give you a progress report."

"I appreciate that, Moire." Lorcan wondered how she could believe that a man who was so timid in his responses to her at that moment was powerful. "I'm not completely unafraid myself," he said, reviewing the conversation as they turned at Oak Street, hand in hand again, to walk back to North Avenue.

"That's all right." She dismissed his fears as though they were a minor problem.

For all of his prior diffidence, all he knew at that moment was that he wanted her, that was all, now and forever.

He took her in his arms, dug his hands into her hips, and pulled her close. He smiled down at her upturned face, kissed the tip of her nose, then her lips.

She went limp in his arms. He held the kiss for a long time.

When he stopped at last, she continued to lean against him.

"Well." She sighed weakly. "The teenager in me surfaces again."

"That's what men and women of every age do under a spring moon on a beach."

"I'm not complaining."

He understood clearly then that, however much she might

be afraid of the demands of the common life with him, he could overcome those fears with sheer raw physical affection. Moire Anne Meehan Halinan was his for the taking, as she had been at Long Beach. Her head might debate; her body would overrule her head. The responsibility from now on was completely his.

On North State Parkway they encountered an older couple walking in the opposite direction.

"Is that you, Flynn?" an elderly man's voice, firm and confident, asked.

"Yes, it is."

"Keeley Allen." The man extended his hand. "I believe you know my wife, Betty?"

"Surely. Betty, may I present Moire Halinan. Her son is marrying my daughter this weekend."

In the gloom of the streetlight's pale rectangle the two women spoke cordially to one another, Betty Allen expressing good wishes, Moire thanking her for them.

Lorcan was conscious of the high drama. If Betty was Moire's mother, she would realize who the younger woman was.

Perhaps the mixture of pallid, almost ghostly light and Lorcan's imagination created the illusion that he wanted: the two handsome women looked strikingly alike.

"I am told I have you to thank for resisting a blandishment from that toad at the United States Attorney's office. I am deeply grateful."

"Honest men must stand together against corruption, sir."

"I quite agree. . . . I'm sure that we're both Chicagoan enough for you to understand what I mean when I say that I owe you one."

Lorcan chuckled. "I'll remember that, sir."

"Nice woman," Moire commented when the two couples had parted. "Charming."

"She's had a fascinating life." Lorcan reviewed the story of Betty Lyndon, putting her in as favorable light as he could.

"She must have enormous resiliency to bounce back the way she has."

"She's a survivor."

"That and more. . . . What was her husband talking about?"

"Minor problem with the government. They leaned on me to accuse him. I wouldn't do it. No big deal."

Moire accepted that explanation. If they did come together again, there would be no such easy escapes. She would insist on all the news, good and bad.

She would demand the right to worry with him. He was not sure he liked that.

"Do you mind if I propose something kind of hokey?" she said as they turned down Astor at North Avenue.

"If you say it, it won't be hokey."

"Could we say some of the rosary? For guidance, I mean?"

Hell, prayer couldn't hurt. . . .

"That's an excellent idea."

They finished two decades before they reached his house.

"A nightcap?" he asked her when they had entered the house on Astor Street—the sorority house, now abandoned for the moment by the sorority sisters.

"Tomorrow will be another busy one. I had better devote myself to a good night's sleep."

"I'm for the pool. Thanks for the walk."

"Thank you for the walk."

He resisted the impulse to kiss her again. He did not want to shock the sorority sisters—Marie, Liz, and now Josie—should any of them appear without warning.

Perhaps the waters of the pool would cool his passion.

6

Lorcan paused at the door to her room and swallowed. This was a turning point. Did he want to pass it?

He was not sure that he did. Yet affection and longing, loneliness and need, had combined into an irresistible force.

The waters of the pool had only inflamed his passion.

He went to his own room and agonized. The young people were out somewhere having a good time, probably at an Irish bar singing rebel songs with Maeveen (like many of her generation of Micks both a nationalist and a pacifist). Lorcan realized there was little chance of shocking them. In fact, there was probably a silent conspiracy to leave the two aging lovers by themselves.

He wanted Moire for the rest of his life. Yet he was afraid of the demands that such love would impose. Moire was not a one-night-stand woman. A night in bed with her would represent in her mind a symbol of long-term commitment—it was that commitment that Lorcan feared.

Tonight was not the night, he told himself, throwing off his terrycloth robe. Not tonight.

He found another robe, black silk, put it on, and applied strategic drops of cologne—an Irish cologne called Patrick of all things, produced in a place called Ballybrack, the whole while continuing to tell himself that tonight was not the night.

Nonetheless his feet carried him to the door of her room and his hand knocked on the door.

"Yes?"

"Lorcan."

"The door isn't locked, Lorcan." A calm, self-possessed voice. "Come in."

She was standing in the middle of the small parlor of her

suite, wearing champagne bra and brief and holding a hair-brush in her hand. She seemed neither surprised nor abashed.

"You look darling in that robe," she said calmly. "If I had been certain you were coming, I would have put on something more alluring."

Unnerved by her beauty, he struggled to find his voice. "It would be hard for any woman to be more alluring than you are at this moment, Moire."

"I suppose we both knew," she observed thoughtfully, "that this event would be inevitable once we agreed I was to stay in this house."

"It doesn't have to happen, Moire." It was uncanny; at every turn he was prepared to escape.

She smiled gently at him. "It really does, Lorcan. We've waited too long. Thirty years."

"Thirty-five."

They both laughed uneasily.

He moved toward her. Suddenly shy and diffident, she backed into the wall, eyes averted, hands and body pressed against it defensively.

"I want this, Lorcan." She choked on her words and struggled to recover herself. "I'm afraid I've made that obvious. I'm out of practice and nervous and scared I'll disappoint you."

Her fear that she would disappoint him melted Lorcan's heart and all his hesitations. He tilted her chin up so their eyes met. She tried to look away. He held her chin in place.

"You'll never disappoint me, Moire. Don't worry. There's no rush. Let's neck and pet like we used to so long ago."

He took the brush out of her hand, led her to the couch, sat her down, and folded her in his arms. She nestled close to him.

"Maybe we should turn on the TV"—she sighed—"and pretend we're at a drive-in."

"If you want."

"I do joke sometimes, darling—I'm not totally serious."

He soothed her and caressed her and kissed her. She basked in the warmth of his affection.

Much later, after a long period of gentle preparation, she said, "I'm ready now, darling."

Her fingers, trembling and uncertain, unhooked the front of her bra—a symbol of the gift she was about to offer.

He removed her undergarments and his robe. She opened up her body and gave it to him enthusiastically.

For the first time in his life Lorcan Flynn encountered a woman who was a full partner in love, someone who demanded as much as she gave and challenged as much as she yielded.

Their love ended, as all good love should, in laughter.

7

"Call me from a public phone," Larry Whealan said. "All right." Lorcan's stomach muscles tightened. The call could only mean that Donny Roscoe and Maynard Lealand were about to make their move—two days before his daughter's wedding.

A leak at the time of the wedding would give them an extra smidgen of publicity, and since publicity was what they were after, it was logical that was when they'd make their move.

He had enjoyed his love affair with Moire for thirty-six hours. Would a public scandal blight it? He could not bear losing her again.

Moire was depriving him of his sanity with her playful aggression, a phenomenon on which Doctor Murphy seemed to have no comment other than a tapping pen and an occasional "Hmn . . ."

The morning after their first tryst—and his eventual retreat to his own bedroom lest Moire's sorority sisters be shocked—he had dragged his pleasantly exhausted body to the swimming pool and started his fifteen minutes of crawl.

He had finished it and turned to the more relaxing back-stroke when the door opened and Moire entered, wearing the usual immense terry robe.

"Good morning," she said briskly. "Don't I know you from somewhere?" With that she tossed aside the robe and dove, stark naked, into the pool.

Her daring flabbergasted Lorcan. Before he could protest, she had swum to him and pulled off his trunks.

"You set me on fire, sir." She hugged him fiercely. "You're responsible for whatever happens."

"What if someone—"

"I locked the door." She was assaulting him with her lips. "And anyway, just now I don't care who knows."

"In the pool," he managed to say.

"Why not?"

"I'm not quite sure how it works in a pool."

"Me neither. Let's find out. I've wondered since the first time you showed me this place."

Later she stood at the edge of the pool, hands on her hips, staring down at him fondly, proud of herself and amused by him.

She was a classic, timeless nude, a body well-shaped to begin with and now well-disciplined: long, slender legs, subtly curved hips, thickly forested loins, narrow waist, high full breasts with rich brown nipples.

"You're driving me out of my mind."

"That is what I intend to do."

"You'll pay for this, woman, I promise you."

"We'll see about that."

Lorcan postponed his meeting with his potential Japanese partners. He and Moire collapsed into each other's arms the moment they were alone. Lorcan couldn't recall a time when he had known more passion in the middle of the day. The more time he spent with her, the more determined he became to keep her. This time he would never let her go.

After a brief respite his passion grew again. He put his arms around Moire and whispered the words he'd been afraid to say aloud: "I love you, Moire. I'll never let you go. Never again." Later he would regret those words.

•　•　•

An hour later Lorcan surprised the three visiting Japanese by his vigor in the negotiations that afternoon. They had promptly yielded to him on the last disputed points in their contract.

After the rehearsal dinner that night, marked by wild early spring Chicago thunderstorms and lightning which crackled over the embattled Lake, he had gone to his study, turned on the computer, and worked on some final calculations. Then he had accessed the exchange at Singapore to find out if anything exciting was happening at that wild place.

Moire, in the rose and ivory robe he had bought for her that day at Neiman-Marcus, had entered his office. "I thought I'd find you here. Don't tell me you're working?"

"Singapore."

"At this hour?"

"It's late afternoon over there."

She had bent over him and turned off the machine.

"I love you, Lorcan. I am sad for all the years we missed and happy for what we have now."

Her fingers teased him gently.

"Are you trying to make up in two days for those thirty-five years?" he had gasped.

"Yes," she had said, sliding off her robe. "Come, my darling, let me love you under our beach towel painting."

He could hardly have declined.

Naked herself, she had disrobed him completely, slowly and lovingly, kissing him and caressing him as she went about her work.

"Someday I'd like to return to the beach and love you on real beach towels."

"I'm thinking of buying a house down there," he managed to say.

"Forget about Singapore and everything else. I want you to think about how much I love you."

It had been an easy challenge to which to respond.

As they cradled one another in their arms, she whispered in his ear, "I hope I wasn't too outrageous. I never tried anything like that."

"You were outrageous, all right; you're the outrageous

lover about whom every man dreams. I'm the luckiest man in the world."

"I quite agree." She chuckled. "Can we sleep here for a little while?"

"What choice do we have?"

Later, glowing with satisfaction, she made him wake up, dress, and join a madcap conversation with the next generation in the parlor, where Maeve was filling up glasses of Bailey's like it was Diet Pepsi.

The younger people did not seem to notice any electricity between the mother of the groom and the father of the bride.

Now the United States Attorney for the Northern District of Illinois and the Agent-in-Charge of the Federal Bureau of Investigation were conspiring to take his happiness away from him.

"What's the bad word, Larry?" he asked from the public phone.

"You can guess it. Donny and Maynard are doing a press conference about you Monday afternoon. There'll be a press leak Monday morning. They wanted to run it tomorrow to accompany the news about your daughter's wedding."

"Bastards!"

"A young woman's happiness isn't worth anything to them if they can get an extra line in a column item. . . . They're giving you till noon today to agree to testify against Keeley Allen. They think they can plea-bargain him. A man of his age and infirmity, Maynard says, will not want to risk a trial. So no one goes to jail, no one even goes to trial."

"They underestimate the old guy."

"I told Maynard that. He just laughed me off. He was heavy-handed about it all, Lorcan. He must be confident that he has a good case against you. That idiot Henry has spun out an elaborate fiction about you and the gas line. They're threatening to put that in the news leak before the press conference. I hope they do."

"Why?"

"They will have played their ace and we'll trump it before Donny can have his press conference."

"Ah."

"Maynard said you had one more chance."

"What did I tell you to reply the last time?"

"It was an obscenity, as I remember."

"Do you want to have the pleasure of relaying that same message or should I?"

"It would be more appropriate coming from your lawyer."

"Great. . . . What do we do?"

"We find out on Sunday the wording of the column item. Then we call a press conference for ten on Monday morning. You appear at it—you're great on the camera—and release copies of the Captain O'Rourke and Sister Mathilda testimonies. You quote excerpts from Dinny's interview with those who were at the party. You hint at evidence we have about foreign terrorists and secret agents of a foreign power which you are presently withholding so as not to embarrass the United States or its allies. You answer questions. Then the ball is in Donny Roscoe's court. Some of the people on his staff tell him he's making a big mistake by trying this caper and that in the long run he'll lose. Right now he's listening to Maynard. After he receives a report of your conference, he'll listen to the other people and probably deny all allegations of a case against you."

"Probably?"

"Donny is an ambitious lawyer of modest intelligence whom the media bug has bitten. He turns a little insane at the prospect of seeing his face on TV. There's an outside chance that he'll charge ahead. Then maybe we file suit against him, libel among other charges. I'll warn them of that right after your conference."

"And LaPorte County?"

"Are you kidding? After they read Captain O'Rourke's testimony, they won't want to touch the case. Their county prosecutor, who was coming up here to appear at Donny's TV spectacular, will discover other and more important obligations."

"Sounds pretty good."

"No, Lorcan, it sounds shitty. It's what people who have become public figures have to do these days to protect themselves from a government whose legal and law enforcement arms are indistinguishable from those of Hitler's Germany or Stalin's Russia. Even the KGB wouldn't try what the Bureau is doing these days."

"Can we sue them regardless?"

"Not worth it, Lorcan. The media will turn against them eventually and then they're finished. Those who live by press leak eventually die by it."

"If you say so."

"And, Lorcan. . . . That bastard Hank won't be at the wedding to spoil the fun of the rest of us, will he?"

"No way."

"Do me a favor, huh? Comb him out of the rest of your life."

Lorcan hesitated.

"He's done that for us already."

8

"God was watching Her television set one day," Bishop Ryan said, beginning the homily of the wedding Mass, "and the angel Gabriel stopped by for a visit. It is not altogether accurate to say 'one day,' because there weren't any days yet, since it was still eternity, more or less."

Lorcan caught Maeve suppressing a giggle.

"Gabriel, who parked his horn outside because it made God nervous when Gabriel played with the horn, thought that God seemed bored. Now you must understand that God's TV is like none that we know: it's several galaxies wide and has hundreds, well, actually, millions of screens. Thus, when God is relaxing on Her easy chair, She can observe large numbers of stories which are occurring all over creation at the same time.

"God made creation because She loves stories. Why else?

"So Gabe said to God, 'Are there any good programs on these days, Boss?'

"And God said . . . do any of you kids know what God said? Conghor? Diarmuid? That's right! God said, 'It's all *boring!*'

" 'Too bad,' Gabriel agreed. Gabriel, you see, always agrees with God. That's because God is the *Boss!* Right? *Right!* Just like most mommies.

"Then God said, 'The trouble is, Gabriel, that they don't make good love stories anymore.'

" 'That is a shame,' Gabriel agreed. You see, gentle souls, God loves love stories better than any other kind of stories.

" 'So you know what I'm thinking of doing? I'm thinking of making our new project—let me see, what do we call them? Oh yes: *humankind*—I'm thinking of making them male and female. Then we'll have plenty of love stories all the time.'

" 'That may not be such a good idea, Boss,' Gabriel said in his most respectful tone.

" 'Why not?'

" 'They'll fight!'

" 'That's true,' said God. 'I hadn't thought about that. Well, of course I'd thought about it, because I'm God and I think of everything. So what? Let them fight. They'll make up and love each other even more. And the real payoff, Gabriel—and you have to be as smart as God to figure out something this subtle—will be that when they make up after their fights and love each other more passionately than ever, they'll have some hint of how much I love them.'

"So, gentlepersons, we are here today to celebrate this admirable chapter in the love story between Rob and Marie because God loves love stories—all love stories and each love story. You can count on it: God has the volume turned up high on His TV so He can hear the words of love between Rob and Marie today. He's probably clapping His hands right now because they realize, as do we, that there is a second trick in this wonderful love story—God loves Rob and Marie even more intensely than they love one another. And all the rest of us too. . . ."

Lorcan contemplated the metaphor while the ceremony

continued. What had happened to the love story between himself and his wife? Had God enjoyed that story? Why then did He permit it to turn sour? Why was Dorothy sitting behind him with Mark, tearfully upset at his decision to sit in a different pew?

Lorcan's Jesuit education had taught him that there were no good answers to such questions. Nor did the questions destroy Father Blackie's metaphor.

Did God enjoy the sudden and manic passion of the renewed love story between him and Moire? He hoped so. He also hoped that theirs would be a story to please Him in years to come.

There had been nothing in the morning papers about the possible charges against him. Roscoe and Lealand would not want the news to break on Sunday; they wouldn't want their headlines to compete with the many other sections of a Sunday paper.

Lorcan was suddenly angry at his brother and his father and his uncle. They had tried to ruin his life from the beginning and were still trying.

He looked at Moire across the aisle again and concluded that, all in all, he was a fortunate man.

There was no receiving line in the back of the Cathedral after Mass. Limos whisked the bridal party to the Drake for photographs. The parents, four of them because Dorothy had squeezed Mark Reed in, were to follow in their own limo.

The ride from the Cathedral to the Drake took no more than five minutes. It seemed to last an eternity.

"Dad wasn't there," Dorothy observed petulantly. "Why not?"

"His health." Lorcan snapped the words out more sharply than he intended.

"Nor Father Edward."

"He's in Tanzania; he sent a papal blessing."

"Of course Eileen wouldn't come."

"She hardly knows Marie."

"Well, Henry and Joanne and their children certainly know her."

"They were invited but they did not respond."

"Your family certainly is a strange one, Lorcan."

"I wouldn't deny that."

At the Drake, after Maeve and Marie had arranged the receiving line, Dorothy slipped Mark into the line next to her. Lorcan noticed the addition when he heard her introducing Mark to one of her cronies and announcing her own marriage the following week.

Come what may, Dorothy was determined to steal her daughter's thunder.

Marie was visibly disturbed. Lorcan hesitated. Dorothy's behavior was out of line and would be so judged by most of the guests. Should he ask Mark to leave the receiving line?

That would send Dorothy over the edge. Lorcan could envision the protests, tears, maybe even shouts of rage. Which would be more embarrassing to the bride?

The Maeve saved him from the need to make a decision.

"Mark." She had slipped around behind the receiving line. "Marie does not think it proper for you to stand in the line, since you're not her father nor yet her stepfather."

No West of Ireland brogue this time.

"How dare you!" Dorothy began to sob.

"I quite agree," Moire said firmly.

His former wife's tears unnerved Lorcan, as they had through all the days of their marriage.

"What business is it of yours?" Dorothy demanded hotly.

"It's my son's wedding." Moire's voice was controlled, reasonable.

"Mark," Lorcan said firmly, stepping in now that he saw his chance, "I really do believe it would be better if you weren't in the line."

Mark shrugged his shoulders and backed off. Dorothy departed for the women's room, her face ostentatiously covered by a tissue—presumably kept at hand for just such an emergency.

"Thanks, Dad." Marie was beaming happily. Her father had frustrated her mother's attempt to spoil her wedding. He was a hero, however reluctant and however much his courage came from Maeve and Moire.

A few minutes later, red-eyed but calm, Dorothy returned to the receiving line and greeted the guests as though nothing had happened. She mentioned her forthcoming marriage a couple of times, though not to everyone.

The Grand Ballroom of the Drake, an elegant old cream-colored baroque room with crystal chandeliers, gilt trim, and wide view of the Lake, renovated many times in its history, was still a classic place for a wedding banquet. It had been Marie's first unhesitating choice.

The Mark crisis overcome, the rest of the celebration was like all wedding celebrations: festive and exhausting. Lorcan danced with the bride and with her sister and naturally with Maeve (several times) and with Moire—more than protocol required but not enough to cause comment.

He hoped.

"You dance well, Lorcan," she said, leaning against him. "Another improvement over the past."

"Thank you. It's my dancing partner."

"I'm sorry for the scene with Dorothy."

"It's my fault," he said. "I should have laid down the law as soon as I heard about Mark and her upcoming marriage."

Lorcan was among the last to leave the Drake. Before leaving, he and Dennis Rooney and Larry Whealan rehearsed again their plans for the press conference on Monday morning.

When he finally arrived back at the house on Astor Street at three in the morning, all the lights were out. He assumed that Moire, who'd left the reception around eleven o'clock, would welcome a respite from passion.

He knew he would.

Then he heard water running in the bathroom and what sounded like the jets of his Whirlpool. When he went to investigate, he found Moire reclining in the tub, a glass of champagne in one hand, a bottle in the other, breasts floating in the water.

"I am not really tuned, Lorcan"—she giggled—"or maybe a little bit. I've wanted to do this since I've seen your Whirlpool. Do take off your clothes and join me."

"It's an offer, woman, that I can't refuse."

9

Lorcan Flynn woke on Sunday morning to discover that he was floating on a sea of peace and joy. He reached across the bed for his partner on the raft and discovered she was gone.

Probably making breakfast. I'll eat good breakfasts for the rest of my life, no doubt about that.

He stretched out and relaxed. It had been quite a night, a wedding night one could call it. Lorcan and his love had celebrated a permanent union on the same night their children had celebrated their union. The former had yet to be ratified by a solemn ceremony in the presence of the Cathedral rector. That would come soon. Lorcan smiled.

Then he remembered his confrontation with the media set for the morrow. He quickly dismissed it from his mind, a minor challenge to be overcome before he and his bride were permanently united.

He thought about his bride again and his smile turned into a grin. Inside the calm and solemn woman there was a playful imp, a female leprechaun, a person who, Moire herself had admitted, she had never been previously.

Good enough. He sighed as he rolled out of bed. *We'll have to play once more before she catches the shuttle back to New York—only a few more days and she'll be back here where she belongs. Permanently.*

Was he imagining it or had she dispensed both of them from exercise today?

Well, he told himself as he struggled into a sweatsuit, he was the head of this house and he was granting a dispensation.

There had been plenty of exercise the night before, anyway.

He found Moire, Josie, and Liz in the kitchen, all in pastel traveling robes, babbling away and demolishing vast piles of pancakes along with thick stacks of bacon.

"Good morning!" he said brightly. "I see that my sorority has become a harem."

"Daddy! Don't be *gross!"*

"Lorcan! Have you been drinking champagne this early in the morning?"

"Good morning," the three women chimed.

He reached for a slice of bacon.

"If you're going to eat breakfast with us"—Moire's voice was that of a stern mother, but her eyes twinkled like those of a lover—"sit down at the table like a civilized human being."

"Yes, ma'am."

Her color was high this morning, the kind of glow that no amount of makeup could produce. *You're mine now,* Lorcan thought. After last night there could be no more question about it. And he knew he was hers too.

The conversation returned to the subject for the day—the wedding: the people who were there, the funny things people said, the funny things that happened, and, finally, the very funny things that Lorcan had done and said.

It was open season on the man of the house. Josie, still shy, lagged behind her mother and her new friend, though not by much.

"Come on, Jos," Liz announced when they had tired of the subject. "We should be out of here if you're to meet the people I want you to meet before you have to go back to creepy old New York."

The two young women bounded out of the kitchen.

Lorcan went over to Moire and slipped his hand inside her robe, moved one strap of a bra off her shoulder and caressed her breast, firm, warm, comforting. He touched a nipple and felt it grow hard under his finger. His other hand slid up her thigh.

Moire did not move. She closed her eyes, her mouth widened, her jaw slackened.

"You have my number, Lorcan," she murmured. "I'm a pushover now."

He chuckled. "That makes two of us."

The phone rang. He ignored it and continued his explorations. Moire moaned softly.

"Daddy! It's Grandpa!"

Lorcan frowned. "Excuse me a minute. I'd better talk to that old reprobate."

"I won't be going anywhere."

In his office he picked up the phone. "Thanks, Liz."

He heard the click as she hung up. "Good morning, Dad."

The old man cackled fiendishly. "Did you screw the trash real good last night?"

"What do you mean, Dad?"

Same old silly game, except that it was rare for his father to play it over the phone. In fact, he rarely telephoned, period.

"I hope you had a great time with her."

"Is that what you called to say, Dad?"

"I called to say you're going to regret that you let that wedding happen yesterday for the rest of your life—if you have much of a life left when LaPorte County is finished with you."

"I'm not worried about LaPorte County."

"Well, you should be. They got it all. They're going to fry you, Mr. Smart Ass. You'll go to the chair knowing that your daughter will produce retarded kids. Big joke on you, dummy!"

"If you say so, Dad," he said wearily. Lorcan would never understand what he had done to inspire such vituperative bile in the old man.

"I say so, dummy. That's what happens when first cousins marry, isn't it?"

"First cousins? Are you crazy?"

"I guess you were too sick to remember what I told you that night on the beach. Worse luck for you."

The office swirled in circles. The painting of the beach towels seemed to leap off the wall and envelop Lorcan. He suddenly remembered what his father had said thirty-five years ago.

Now his father said it again. "That tart is your sister. I

screwed her mother and got her preggers. So you fucked your own sister."

10

Cindi waved to Lorcan, a friendly signal from an old friend. Friendly though she seemed, Lorcan knew that nothing that had happened between them would prevent her from asking a tough question. Bed was one thing, career was something else.

There had been bad news earlier in the morning. Radio broadcasts had reported that the LaPorte County Prosecutor was already in Chicago and had told associates that he looked forward to prosecuting Lorcan Flynn. Larry Whealan laid it out for Lorcan.

"They're saying over at the Dirksen Building that Donny has made up what passes for his mind to turn you over to LaPorte. Then it's up to them. He figures he'll get the credit today and escape the blame if LaPorte blows it."

"Is that certain?"

"With Donny nothing is certain. If we hit them hard now, he may unmake up his mind."

Lorcan glanced at his watch. Three minutes to the press conference. May Rosen, the able media consultant whom Whealan had brought in, insisted that they start promptly.

"We must be upbeat and confident," she insisted. "We're dispelling the mist and fog of doubt and innuendo, remember that."

Lorcan nodded. Maeve and Paddy had joined him. Paddy looked grim. Maeve looked positively murderous.

Paddy had called his father at six A.M.

"Dad, did you see *Dink* yet?"

"There's nothing to worry about, Paddy. It's a lie and we will expose it as a lie this morning."

"Listen," Paddy said. " 'U.S. Attorney Donny Roscoe and FBI boss Maynard Lealand may have solved a crime thirty-five years old. *Dink* has learned that commodity mogul Henry R. Flynn, under investigation for illegal trading, has confessed that his brother, mega-celeb Lorcan Flynn, blew up the home of next-door neighbors in Long Beach, Indiana, on Labor Day of 1954. Sources close to the investigation tell *Dink* that Henry Flynn claims that his brother confessed in detail to turning on a gas jet in the home of Congressman Joseph J. Meehan and later throwing a match in a window. Henry Flynn says the family covered up for the crime and spirited Lorcan Flynn away to a hospital under the pretext that he had a high fever. His brother, says Henry, was not sick, except in his head. LaPorte County prosecutors will attend Roscoe's press conference today to share in the glory of another blow against crime. Stay tuned for more on this cosmic scandal.' "

"I've seen it, Paddy. It's a pack of lies."

"You're having a press conference of your own?"

"Right. Ten o'clock. At Larry Whealan's offices."

"One-eighty North Wacker? We'll be there."

"That's not necessary."

"The hell it's not."

After Lorcan's father had called that awful Sunday morning, the rest of the day had been a nightmare. Lorcan had charged out of the house and jogged from Oak Street to North Avenue and back. He couldn't think or feel or speak. Even if he could speak, there was no one with whom to share such a horrendous revelation.

He had avoided Moire. She had looked into his office, where he was bent over the desk, head in hands, trying to think.

"Some lunch, Lorcan?"

"I'm not hungry, Moire."

"Is there something wrong?"

"I'm trying to prepare for a press conference tomorrow," he had snapped irritably. "It's no big deal, I just have to be sharp."

"Oh," she said softly and departed.

By the time she took the limo for the airport later in the

day, she must have realized that something had changed their relationship. Perhaps she had understood that it was all over. Lorcan racked his brain. How could he explain to her . . . to anyone?

They had exchanged restrained good-byes when she and Josie left the house. Liz was accompanying them to the airport. The two younger women were baffled by the change in their parents. Discreet for once in her life, Liz had said nothing about it.

Lorcan had returned to his study to await a call from Larry Whealan.

When the lawyer did call, he was exultant. "Typical of that damn fool Donny Roscoe. They've overreached. Why did Henry lie about your not being sick? Doesn't he know there were witnesses?"

"Maybe by now he believes that I wasn't sick."

"We'll kill them."

"I hope so."

Lorcan did not want to bother with the press conference. What difference did it make? What difference did anything make?

He could never tell Moire, never attempt an explanation of why their love had ended so abruptly a second time.

Why had Doctor Murphy gone on vacation just when he needed her?

Where was the envelope she had given him? Someone else to talk to if his problems got too bad. . . . He had put it in his coat pocket. Which coat had he been wearing that day?

There was no time to think about it now. He had to prepare for the press conference—not for himself, his life was as good as over—but for the children. Their lives ought not to be ruined too.

What about Rob and Marie? Tell them? How could he?

He'd have to find out from a doctor if first cousins reproducing was dangerous. The Church didn't forbid such unions, did it?

Just before he was to go on, May Rosen coached him one last time. "Remember: be relaxed, confident, and restrained. It's all right to be angry—just don't lose your temper."

He winked at her. For fifteen minutes he could be a happy warrior.

He stood before the camera. The red lights went on. He saw Cindi with a mike in her hand.

"There was an item this morning in the print media which made certain allegations about a crime committed almost thirty-five years ago in Long Beach, Indiana. My brother, according to the item, had confessed to Donald Bane Roscoe that I had committed the crime by throwing a match into a house after having flooded it with natural gas released by a stove's valve. My brother is also alleged to have said that the family covered up the crime by putting me in a hospital with a trumped-up fever.

"On the face of it, my brother's story, as reported in the column this morning, suffers from many implausibilities. This morning I intend to provide you evidence that proves his account is totally false.

"Two preliminary points: Several weeks ago, my attorney, Mr. Laurence Whealan, of the law firm of Whealan, Bishop, and James—in whose offices we are meeting—was approached by Mr. Maynard Lealand, Special-Agent-in-Charge of the Federal Bureau of Investigation Chicago office. Mr. Lealand told Mr. Whealan that my brother had recited this story of the alleged murder of Congressman Joseph Meehan on Labor Day 1954 in a search for immunity from prosecution in the current investigation of the Chicago commodities exchanges. I would note in passing that my brother is not privy to any of my investments, and hence could not provide the U.S. Attorney and the FBI with any information which would incriminate me in financial scandals."

He paused, as May Rosen had instructed him to pause, to let these facts sink in.

"Mr. Lealand indicated to Mr. Whealan that in exchange for my cooperation in an investigation of another Chicago business figure—a well-known man, I would add—they would consider whether they had sufficient evidence to turn over to prosecutors in LaPorte County, Indiana, where the tragedy occurred.

"I replied that I had no information to indicate that the

man they were investigating was anything but honorable and honest. I added that I would not yield to their blackmail. The news leak this morning and the press conference this afternoon is Messrs. Lealand's and Roscoe's response to my refusal to play their iniquitous game."

"Will Lealand and Roscoe deny this, Lorcan?" Cindi asked.

"Sure they will." He grinned broadly. "They have played this game so often and with so many people, who will believe their denials?

"Prior to learning of this conspiracy, I had on my own initiative begun an investigation of the Labor Day explosion, using the good offices of Dennis Rooney and Associates. Since my younger daughter was engaged to be married to the son of one of the survivors of the tragedy, it seemed an appropriate time to attempt to clear up the mystery.

"Mr. Rooney and his staff obtained some illuminating interviews, two of which we are prepared to release to you today. The first is with a nun who is now the administrator of Saint Anthony's Hospital in Michigan City and was at that time on the staff of the emergency room. She testifies that I was indeed very sick and had been delirious or near delirious for at least twenty-four hours by the time of the explosion. Thus I could not have calmly confessed a murder. Moreover, the claim that I faked the illness is clearly false.

"The second document is from a former chief of police from Michigan City, Indiana. He states that there was a massive cover-up of the crime and that it was not caused by a gas explosion as the coroner then and my brother now claim. Rather, the blast was caused by high explosives stored in the basement of that house along with thirty Browning Automatic Rifles."

A murmur broke out among the crowd of reporters.

"We do not know how these materials came to be in the late Congressman's house or for whom they were destined. We have testimony which suggests that there was foreign involvement. We do not believe, however, that there is a need for us to make this testimony public at the present time. Should there be any interest in further investigation by the appropriate agencies, we would be happy to cooperate with them.

"In conclusion, let me reiterate: I did not kill Congressman Meehan and his family. My brother does not tell the truth when he says that I did. My illness was not faked. According to Sister Mathilda, I almost died. I did not turn on a gas burner in the Meehan house. I did not throw a match into the house. I did not confess that I did such things—I was far too sick to do or say anything. Finally, the Congressman and his family did not die in a gas explosion but in a blast from military armaments in their basement."

A torrent of questions were put to him the instant he finished speaking.

"Are you saying that your brother lied?"

"Are you claiming a government plot to get you?"

"Who arranged the cover-up?"

"What foreign powers were involved?"

"Was it Irish revolutionary action?"

"Have you spoken to your brother?"

"Will you sue the government?"

"Was there ammunition as well as guns?"

"One at a time, please." Lorcan smiled. "As you can see, I'm not quite used to dealing with the press like this. Give me a chance. . . . First, I'm saying that if my brother was quoted accurately to Mr. Whealan by Maynard Lealand and by the item in this morning's papers, he was not telling the truth. . . . Yes, I am a victim of a government plot, like many other Chicagoans whose indictments provide headlines for Mr. Roscoe. . . . I may sue the government as well as Mr. Lealand and Mr. Roscoe personally. I certainly have grounds to seek relief. . . . The cover-up seems to have been arranged by Mr. Lealand's predecessors in the Bureau. . . . I see no point in discussing foreign involvement at the present time. It is unlikely that the foreign parties were responsible for the death of the Meehan family. . . . Yes, I have spoken to my brother since Mr. Lealand's threat, but not about his accusations against me."

"Have you forgiven him, Lorcan?"

"What's to forgive, Cindi? He did what he thought he had to do to protect himself and his family. I regret that to protect myself and my family I had to expose his charges as patently false."

"Do you expect the government to proceed with its case against you?"

"I suppose that the question means whether the United States Attorney will turn over materials against me to the LaPorte County Prosecutor and whether the latter will seek an indictment. I would not want to make predictions about the behavior of Mr. Roscoe."

"Do you think there will be an investigation of the cover-up that Captain O'Rourke alleges?"

"There will be talk of one till the media attention dies down."

"Lorcan"—Cindi again—"has your own investigation turned up any hint of who the killer was?"

Later Lorcan was to regret his honest and spontaneous answer. He had not been prepared for the question, however. Even if he had been prepared, his advisers would not have warned him against it.

At the time it seemed harmless.

"I'm afraid not, Cindi. We may never learn the answer to that question. My personal hunch is that the late Congressman's brother, Tim Meehan, might have been responsible. He was supposedly killed in Ireland in 1950 and buried later in Holy Sepulchre Cemetery out on 111th Street. The evidence of his death is not all that persuasive. He may have been an operative for an intelligence agency of some government, conceivably our own. Presumably he is dead by now."

When he finished that response, Lorcan realized that he was shivering.

11

After Lorcan returned to his office from the East Bank Club, he received two phone calls.

The first was from Cindi.

"Lorcan, I'm off the record. You'll hear this from your friend Whealan in a few minutes; I wanted to get it to you as soon as I heard it. Roscoe has canceled his press conference. His spokesperson says there is no evidence linking you to any crime. LaPorte County denies all knowledge of the allegations."

Inwardly he gave himself over to a massive sigh of relief.

"They're running?"

"As fast as they can. . . . It looks bad for your brother, doesn't it?"

"He's probably home free. They'll want to put as much distance between themselves and Hank as they can."

"He lucked out?"

"I don't begrudge him his luck."

"Is that on the record?"

"No."

"I understand. . . . Also off the record: do you think Washington has intervened to kill the investigation?"

"The old cover-up returned?"

"Right."

He considered the question. "Maybe, Cindi. They had no case against me. They've run so quickly, though, it makes you wonder whether someone high up told them to."

"We're going to suggest that. May I say you had no comment on the possibility?"

"Sure."

Later he would wonder if that was a mistake too.

"How's the statue coming?"

"We're casting this week."

"May I see it when you're finished?"

"Who has a better right to than you?"

A bit of the cloud had lifted. He had beaten Roscoe. His children were safe from the horror of months of media attention. That did not ameliorate his own internal horror.

He no longer cared who had killed the Meehans. It was utterly irrelevant. The crucial mystery of the beach towels had been solved. After his father and mother had found him and Moire in their passionate embrace and assaulted both of them, his mother had run off and his father had told him that Moire was his half-sister. No wonder he had repressed it during his fever.

"Lorcan, another call. He won't give his name."

Rafferty again, no doubt.

"Lorcan Flynn," he snapped.

"First thing: I am not associated with that fool Eammon Rafferty. Got it?"

The voice sounded faintly computerized, like it was being run through one of those scramblers used to preserve a subject's anonymity on television.

"If you say so."

"Second: If you value your life and the lives of those you love, you'll forget about what happened that night, got it?"

"I hear you."

"Third: We're going to teach you a lesson, in a manner of speaking. No one will be hurt, but you'll see how powerful we are. Got it?"

"I haven't hung up."

"Fourth: You think you're tough, and maybe you are against the Raffertys and the Roscoes of the world. But, in a manner of speaking, you're dead against us. Got it?"

"I still haven't hung up."

"Don't fuck with us, Lorcan. We're not vindictive and we don't want to hurt anyone. Just don't fuck with us."

Lorcan understood who was on the phone.

"Tim, I have nothing against you, either. I don't give a damn what happened that weekend and I don't give a damn about you."

He hung up. His stomach was knotted and his hands were cold.

He'd been talking to a professional killer.

12

S till feeling numb from the events of the past few days, Lorcan forced himself to attend the Daley victory party at the Hyatt Hotel, on the River, east of Michigan Avenue.

Larry Whealan had called him the previous day shortly after his conversation with Cindi. He confirmed that the heat was off and congratulated Lorcan on his victory.

Dennis Rooney was next on the phone, also with congratulations and the question of whether Lorcan wanted to continue the investigation.

"Let's forget it, Dinny. It doesn't matter anymore."

"I'm glad to hear you say that, Lorcan. It's a big mess."

"Right. Let the word out that I've lost interest."

"Can do."

He called Cindi back and added to his statement that he was discontinuing his own investigation.

She agreed that it was an important comment.

The next morning his family weighed in. Rory called him.

"Well, Lorcan, I suppose you're happy that you've broken your poor father's heart."

"Have I, Rory? Why don't you tell me how I've done that?"

"The terrible thing you did to Hank yesterday. You've destroyed his reputation, you know that, don't you?"

"It was his or mine, Rory."

"You have money and he doesn't."

"Too bad for him."

"His wife and kids are hysterical."

"I'm sorry for them."

"Couldn't you have stood by your own brother?"

"He was trying to put me in prison, Rory, maybe even in the gas chamber. I didn't owe him a thing."

"Your father said you'd react that way. I told him I hoped you had some trace of family loyalty left."

"You told him wrong, Rory."

Lorcan hung up.

Lorcan was in no mood for a noisy celebration of an Irish political restoration. Nonetheless he felt an obligation to attend. He'd been at the same hotel six years ago when Rich lost the primary. If you stand by someone in defeat, you should help them to celebrate their victory.

The Hyatt was as phony as a hundred-dollar bill with Washington's picture on it: a gimcracky mix of reflecting ponds, string orchestras, glitzy mirrors, suspended stairways, expensive shops, and milling crowds of people—the idea of an architect imported from Alice's Wonderland of what a cosmopolitan hotel should look like. No, scratch that: his idea of what dumb Chicagoans would think a cosmopolitan hotel should look like.

The Fairmont was much more attractive. However, there were sentimental reasons to return to the Catch a Rising Star Club, a phony café off the lobby where allegedly rising comics sometimes performed. Inside, in a mix of tables, spotlights, crystal ornaments, and lots of food and drink, the core of the candidate's supporters waited for the news of victory, the opportunity to shake the winner's hand, and the big celebration in the grand ballroom after the other side conceded—complete, it was reported, with a laser light show.

He vowed to make it an early evening. As soon as the polls had closed, all three networks announced that Rich had won with a 15 percentage point margin.

"Hey, Lorcan. It's been awhile."

Jeff Carey, the captain of the Long Beach softball team, now wearing a Grand Beachers for Daley button. Jeff was a commodity broker like so many other Grand Beachers.

He was gray and heavy and as gregarious and cheerful as he had been thirty-five years ago.

"You've gone over to the other side."

"I married into Grand Beach. . . . You ought to buy a home up there, Lorcan. Great place."

"I thought about it recently," he admitted. "And decided against it."

"Too bad. Put on the button anyway. . . . Say, I noticed in the paper the other day that your daughter married the son of a woman from New York named Maura Meehan Halinan? Is that the—"

"The second-base player? Indeed, yes."

"As gorgeous as ever?"

"More so."

"Well, all's well that ends well, isn't it?"

"Sure is."

The candidate appeared, made the circle of the room, shook hands vigorously with Lorcan, and said, "I'll be needing your help, Lorcan."

"I'll do what I can."

"We'll be in touch."

The laser show was spectacular and the acceptance speech confident and impressive. As soon as it was over, Lorcan headed home.

He watched a little news, then was heading up to bed when the phone rang. "Lorcan Flynn," he said, answering it.

"It's Josie, Mr. Flynn. Josie Halinan." The girl was sobbing. "Mom's had an accident. She's in the community hospital here. I don't know whether to call Rob down in Jamaica."

"What happened?"

"There was an explosion in her kitchen. She got hit in the head by a piece of falling plaster. The doctor says that maybe it's a concussion. She looks terrible and she's really out of it."

"We can wait till tomorrow to decide about the honeymooners, Josie. I'll be out on the first plane in the morning."

Lorcan hung up the phone and shook his head. Tim Meehan meant business.

13

"**D**id you win the election?" Moire tried to focus on him. "Lorcan, there are three of you."

"Three too many."

"Only two. . . . The election?" She put a hand on her forehead. "Did I ask you that? I meant to."

"You did and I didn't answer and yes we did."

"I'm glad. . . ." She closed her eyes like she wanted to fall back to sleep. "You didn't have to fly down here. I'm fine."

Black rings circled her eyes. Her hair was a mess. Her face had been bruised. She was still wearing a white hospital gown. Nonetheless she looked beautiful.

"I think we'd better let her sleep, Mr. Flynn," the black nurse said gently. "She'll be all right in a few more hours."

"Of course." Lorcan tiptoed out of the room.

"Thanks for coming," said Josie.

"She'll be fine in a few more hours, Josie. Nothing to worry about. We can leave the honeymooners undisturbed. Why don't you go home for a few hours and get some sleep? Mr. Rooney and I will stay here."

"Good idea," Josie agreed. "The construction people will come tomorrow to start fixing the kitchen."

"What did you find out?" He turned to Dinny Rooney as soon as the girl left the hospital's family lounge, a sunny porch overlooking the parking lot.

"Mike Casey had called the locals, so they were ready for me and cooperated. They don't like it a bit. Professional job. A bit of plastic in the kitchen—enough to smash a wall and a cabinet and knock over an ice box. She has electric heat, thank God, so there was no gas explosion."

"Timer?"

"Yeah. Set to go off when she would normally be at work.

She came home early with a bad headache and had just come in the door when the thing blew. If she'd been in the kitchen, she might have been killed."

"That bastard. I'll kill him."

"Easy, Lorcan. He's holding all the cards now. He knows where we are and we don't know where he is."

"I'll find him."

"It might be a lot better just to leave him alone. He's made his point. Obviously he didn't want to kill her."

"He might have!" Lorcan shouted—and then looked nervously around the room to see if anyone had heard him.

Fortunately he and Dinny were alone.

"By chance, if you leave him alone, he'll leave you alone. What's the point in getting into a pissing match?"

"You're right. . . . What do the locals think?"

"Union war. Mrs. Halinan's shop is union. The Teamsters are trying to muscle in. She has supported her workers' right to make their own choice. They think this was intended as a warning. They have a cop down there by her room."

"I thought she was an extra nurse."

"They'll keep a guard on her for a couple of weeks. Then they'll have to leave her on her own. In most cases like this the warning changes the mind of the businessperson and the Teamsters are welcome."

"We know it wasn't the union."

"We're not sure, Lorcan. We're not sure."

"There'll be a call from him before the day is out, mark my words."

"We'll keep a guard of our own on her, naturally. It'll be off-duty cops from here. They'll do a good job. . . . What will you tell Tim Meehan if he calls you?"

"I'll tell him he's won, naturally."

"And you'll mean that?"

"I'll mean it. . . . You're right, Dinny. As always. What else can I do?"

There were a lot of things Lorcan Flynn might yet do. An honest cop like Dinny Rooney would not want to know about them.

Later, after another brief talk with Moire and a conversation with a doctor who assured him that she was all right, Lorcan returned to the motel where he'd placed a reservation. He hadn't slept much the night before. He'd take a nap and return to the hospital to talk to Moire again. Perhaps he should tell her now what the problem was. He owed her honesty, didn't he?

It was not absolutely impossible that she had information which would prove the old man wrong.

Not likely, but not completely out of the question.

As he searched his pocket for a pen to use to check in, he discovered the envelope from Doctor Murphy.

Of course! It was the suit he'd worn that day.

He opened the envelope. Her card, M.K.R. MURPHY, M.A., M.D., and her phone number.

On the reverse side she had written in bold letters, *Bishop John B. Ryan, Ph.D., Holy Name Cathedral, 730 North Wabash* and then the phone number.

In his room, after he had pulled the blinds and was collapsing into bed, Lorcan wondered what the purpose of that recommendation could be. The little priest was her brother and she was fond of him. He was a smart man and a fine preacher. What earthly use could he be in the present circumstances?

He had barely fallen asleep when the phone rang.

"Flynn?"

"That's right."

"Got me?"

"It would appear so, Tim."

"Good. You gonna drop the investigation?"

"I told you I was."

"I wanted a confirmation, in a manner of speaking."

"I said I didn't give a damn and I don't."

"All right. If I hear you change your mind, I might have to give you another demonstration."

"You almost killed her."

"That was a mistake. She came home too early."

"Your mistake or hers?"

"I said it was a mistake. Now don't you make any. Got me?"

"Yeah, I got you."

"Good. I don't want to have to talk to you ever again. I don't enjoy this stuff."

"The hell you don't."

The line was dead. Lorcan hoped Meehan had heard him.

The voice had been disguised again, but Lorcan thought there was something oddly familiar about it. He rolled over and dozed again. In five minutes the phone rang again.

"Lorcan Flynn."

Whoever was on the other end was sobbing. "You goddamn miserable no-good bastard. I hope you're satisfied."

"Who is this?"

"You know goddamn well who it is."

"Henry?"

"I hope you're happy now. You've finally done it."

"Done what?"

"Killed Dad. Does that make you feel good? He's gone. You got rid of him. You're no better than a killer, you bastard."

"When did he die?"

"Mrs. Sweeney went out to shop. When she came home he was dead in his chair. You killed him."

"What do you mean, I killed him?"

"You broke his heart when you destroyed me the day before yesterday. He always hoped you'd be something more than a shit. Now he's dead. Gone forever. It's your fault."

14

There were more Justine priests in the sanctuary for Colonel Pat Flynn's funeral than there were mourners in the congregation.

Ed had flown back from Sri Lanka to say the Mass. More than fifty members of the Chicago Province of the Order, including the Provincial, had come to the Mass. Bishop

Ryan seemed out of place and unnecessary in the Cathedral sanctuary among the many visitors.

The congregation was pathetically small. His father had been a grand fella once. That was long ago. Now he was an old man, most of whose friends were already dead. Henry's family was not there. Joanne had called him that morning to say that her husband was too grief-stricken to come to the Mass.

Both nights of the wake Hank had sat in a corner, caressing his beloved mustache, sobbing. Occasionally he had murmured curses aimed at Lorcan. He had tried to smash an IBC camera when it was pointed at him and a reporter, mike in hand, had asked whether his father's death would lead to a reconciliation with Lorcan.

Lorcan had replied to the same question with the brisk comment that death was a private, family matter.

Joanne was embarrassed by her husband's behavior, and her children were sheepish about having missed the wedding.

"We're sorry about everything, Lorcan. We wanted to come. Henry was insistent."

"I understand." He had held her hand firmly. "I understand."

Poor woman. Poor kids. They have a long period of hell on earth ahead of them.

Rory had slumped, quietly and sadly drunk, in a remote office of Carroll's Funeral Home, near Holy Name Cathedral.

Eileen, astonishingly, had flown in from Seattle with her husband.

"I told myself I wanted to make sure the bastard was in the grave and stayed there," she had said to Lorcan as she wept in his arms. "Now I realize I loved him too. He was impossible, Lorcan. I could not live near him. Still, I guess I loved him almost as much as you did."

Blackie had presided over the wake service the second night, with Cardinal Cronin himself in grim attendance.

"We must picture Colonel Flynn not as the weary and worn man that we remember from a few weeks ago"—as usual when the priest began to preach, his befuddlement vanished—"but young once more, the jaunty aviator in his white scarf and leather Eighth Air Force jacket, home from the war, with his life ahead of him. Pat Flynn is now almost as young as the youthful God with whom he can celebrate for the rest of eternity as he once celebrated with his friends on Madison Street and Austin Boulevard in the West Side of Chicago."

Eileen and her husband were at the funeral Mass as were Paddy and Maeve, silent and subdued for once, and the two wee ones. Other than that, it was Mrs. Sweeney—Dad's housekeeper—a few old-timers from St. Ursula, the daughter of one of his partners in real estate, and a couple of strangers, perhaps Cathedral parishioners who came to all funerals for lack of something better to do. No one else.

There would soon be even less of Pat Flynn than there was of his wife. The hope and the love in that wedding picture—two tall, handsome people with their lives ahead of them—had been wiped from the face of the earth.

Was there anything else?

Lorcan wanted to believe that there was not, that everything had been wiped out. Yet he could not quite accept such a melancholy conclusion. Too much Jesuit education perhaps, too much Catholicism maybe, too many priests like Blackie Ryan.

"Do you believe in life after death, Bishop?"

"Most of the time. Not when it rains, however."

Lorcan grieved more than he had expected he would. He was less angry than he had anticipated he might be. His anger at the old man seemed to have disappeared—even his anger over his father's late revelation concerning Moire.

He had been calling Josie every day. Her mother was out of the hospital and felt a little unsteady. The house was already being repaired. She had defied the Teamsters, who had pleaded ignorance and innocence. The police kept a round-the-clock guard. Josie had been ordered to return to school and study for her finals and prepare for graduation. Naturally they understood why he had to return in such a hurry. They appreciated his interest and concern. They were happy that Lorcan liked the flowers. They were having Masses said, too.

Edward preached the homily. It was dry and academic, philosophical and didactic, the sort of sermon one might hear from the Pope. Yet both Maeveen and Eileen cried— the two of them had become friends—and so did Mrs. Sweeney and the woman from the West Side.

Ed insisted that Father Blackie perform the final services in the chapel of Queen of Heaven Cemetery—the Archdiocese having long since abandoned a ceremony at the gravesite itself.

"It is inappropriate," the little priest said, his purple stole hanging lopsided from one shoulder, "to sing 'Off we go, into the wild blue yonder,' in this chapel. Nonetheless, we can hum it in our minds as we bid this temporary farewell to our friend Patrick."

Maeve and Eileen both burst into tears again. Lorcan felt a sting in his eyes.

Eileen and Leo, her husband, promised that they would return to Chicago often.

"You have a wonderful son and daughter-in-law, Lorcan. I want to meet the others. I want my own kids to meet them. You did a fine job with them."

"I didn't have anything to do with the redhead."

"She's a darling. . . . I hope you find some happiness, Lorcan."

"I'll try."

"More likely happiness will have to find him." Bishop Blackie had materialized by their sides.

"May I have a word with you, Bishop?" Lorcan said impulsively.

The Bishop nodded.

"My psychiatrist suggested that I might want to talk to you." He handed the priest Doctor Murphy's card. "It's a long story."

"Ah." The priest peered at the card as if trying to decipher a mystery. "M.K.R. Murphy, M.D. Odd. I am familiar with a Doctor Joseph Murphy, who I believe is a psychiatrist. As a matter of fact, I believe that he is married to my sister. But I don't believe I am familiar with this Doctor Murphy."

"She is your sister, Bishop."

"My." Blackie examined both sides of the card, still trying to puzzle out the meaning of the mystery. "What an unusual coincidence."

"She's on vacation."

"Yes." The priest frowned. "I believe someone told me that, arguably her daughter, the vivacious Brigid."

"She said that if I encountered problems while she was away, I should talk to you."

"To *me?* My sister suggested that? Most unusual. I am not a psychiatrist. I'm only a priest."

"She didn't have psychiatric problems in mind, Bishop."

"No?"

"It has rather to do with evil."

"Indeed?" The priest's pale, vaguely blue eyes glowed. "That's another matter altogether. Shall we say seven-thirty at the Cathedral Rectory, 730 North Wabash?"

"That's what it says on the card."

"Remarkable."

BOOK V

1

"**O** edipus did not have an Oedipal complex," the Bishop said, peering over his Waterford glass, long since emptied of Jameson's Twelve Year Special Reserve. "No more than you lusted for your sister. His love turned out to be his mother, but he did not realize that. Nor did you understand that the valiant Moire was your sister. We can dispose thus quite readily of questions of guilt."

"I still love her." Lorcan removed his face from his hands in which he had buried it at the end of his story. "I still want her."

"Who wouldn't?" The priest sighed. "May I offer you another drop against the cold winter night?"

He looked around for the bottle. Sensing that the little priest, left to himself, would never find it, Lorcan retrieved the Jameson's from its place next to the massive easy chair on which Blackie reclined and poured them both a second—and stiff—drink.

The Bishop's study, surely a torment to the Cathedral housekeeper, looked like a caricature of a room in a Charles Dickens novel—papers, books, magazines were piled everywhere; dust seemed to float in the air; the furniture was old and decrepit; an ancient rolltop desk stood in the corner. A huge and battered ottoman rested in front of the vast easy chair, just beyond the reach of the priest's feet. The Bishop himself wore an Aran Island sweater that had seen much better days (and perhaps had never seen the inside of a cleaner's) over a clerical shirt from which the Roman collar was permanently missing.

The Dickens theme was violated by the sunburst paintings on the wall and posters of John Kennedy, John XXIII and John Unitas—and a medieval ivory Madonna.

"The sunbursts are by my cousin Catherine Curran, of whom you may have heard." Blackie had waved his hand vaguely. "The posters are the three Johns of my young adulthood, and the Madonna was a gift from my father, who said it looked like my mother when she was a young woman, God be good to both of them."

The Bishop had struggled to find room for Lorcan to sit, finally lifting a set of galleys from a chair.

"Your book, Bishop?"

"Alas, yes. A certain bestseller entitled most attractively, *Transcendental Empiricist: The Achievement of David Tracy.* The publisher is in an unconscionable rush to receive my proof corrections. Tomorrow I must remember to send the galleys to him with a note saying that I have found no mistakes. I will neglect to inform him that I have found none because I did not look for any."

Belying the inefficiency of the room, a Desk Pro 386/25 occupied a place of honor on the rolltop desk.

Blackie Ryan was not, Lorcan Flynn had decided, as simple a man as he appeared.

"I have a book coming out soon," he had said. "My first. I'll admit to excitement about it."

He had not admitted that excitement even to himself in previous weeks.

Lorcan settled back in his chair while the priest absently sipped on his drink, apparently having quite forgotten about the purpose of their meeting.

"There is, of course," he said finally with a sigh, "the unusual matter of your father's warning to you in the early summer of 1954, a warning about Moire's antecedents, that is."

"There was no such warning."

"At the risk of sounding like Sherlock Holmes, that was unusual. Consider: The relationship between you and your father had not deteriorated then like it has in recent years. The rivalry was at work, but not with its later force, because he was a success in life and you were not yet a success. Moreover, he endeavored at all times to protect your mother. If he saw that your relationship with the valiant Moire upset your mother, why did he not bring it to an end quickly with a brief word to you about her presumed origins? Why wait till that evil night on the beach?"

"I don't know."

"It is also curious, is it not, that you do not seem to have questioned since last Sunday whether your father was in fact telling you the truth?"

"Why would he lie?"

"Is not the answer to that question obvious? To defeat you. He was old. He was aware that he would die soon. He foresaw the likelihood of death without a final triumph over his son. Why not revive a charge made long years ago which had devastated you?"

"I think he believed it was true."

"Perhaps. It does not follow, however, that it was true."

"Moire may not be my sister?" That idea both excited Lorcan and frightened him.

"I merely assert that it is far from a proven fact. The mother of the woman must be consulted."

"Elizabeth Keeley Allen?"

"Who else? By your testimony she was sufficiently fond of her probable offspring to send her money at the time of her guardians' deaths—through an unusual messenger, I might add. She may and probably does feel affection for her daughter. Surely she would be disposed to speak the truth to you under the circumstances."

"I'm not sure I could ask her."

Blackie ignored his fear.

"There are, Lorcan Flynn, three questions." He ticked them off on his stubby fingers. "The first is, who are the parents of the valiant Moire? The second is, who tried to kill her? The third is, who did kill her guardians thirty-five years ago? You suspect that the answer to the second two questions is the not-so-late Timothy Meehan, sometime basketball star, sometime war hero, and sometime secret agent. Is it not possible that his name belongs in the first answer too?"

"I don't see the logic of it." Lorcan shook his head. "There's no necessity."

"Just an existential probability. One looks not for logic in these matters but symmetry. I believe I know the answers to all three questions, although they may not be answers you would like or even the ones symmetry demands. . . . There is also the possible fourth question of where Tim Meehan may be found today, which may be more difficult than the first three."

"You know the answers to the first three?"

"Oh, yes, Lorcan. They are not all that difficult questions. However, we must proceed systematically, as in all things. The first step is an interview with the virtuous—in her latter days at any rate—Elizabeth Keeley Allen."

"I really don't want to talk to her."

"Let me see." The priest struggled to his feet, searched for a place to put his Waterford tumbler, placed it on top of the stack of galleys, poked around the rolltop desk in search of a phone book, and finally pushed a button on his computer. The screen turned several different colors and produced a phone directory.

He pressed another key, apparently an automatic dialer. He picked up the receiver of a phone on his desk. "Elizabeth," he said cheerfully, "this is Father Ryan."

"I don't want to talk to her," Lorcan insisted.

"A mutual friend would like a few words with you on the morrow about a matter of joint interest . . . Lorcan Flynn . . . I thought as much . . . three-thirty? Excellent . . . He'll see you then."

2

"I t was not necessary to use Bishop Ryan as an intermediary. My husband and I owe you many favors for your courageous refusal to implicate him in criminal behavior." The elderly woman, still a beauty despite her years, offered Lorcan a seat.

"Surely you understand"—Lorcan attempted his most charming smile—"the Irish love of indirection."

"We loved it on the South Side even more than did you on the West Side."

The late-afternoon sun cast a gentle sheen on Lincoln Park, still brown and bare, and the Lake beyond it. The unobtrusive light of early spring seemed appropriate for the comfortable—and expensive—turn-of-the-century elegance of the Allen apartment.

"I have some photographs I would like to show you," Lorcan said tentatively, still not quite sure how he had been constrained into this visit.

"How interesting," she murmured cautiously.

Elizabeth Keeley Allen, born Betty Jane Lyndon, was an attractive woman, well aware of her attractions and their impact on men. She had practiced the various modes of womanly appeal all her life and understood which one to turn on with which man so well that her masks changed with effortless skill. For Lorcan she was a *grande dame,* a woman of elegance and intelligence who could easily be a colleague in the investment world—despite her loosely fitting dark gray tea gown, not designed for wear outside her drawing room and yet too formal to be considered lingerie.

Her daughter, if Moire was really her daughter, was far more direct.

He laid out on the coffee table between them eight sets of pictures, two women of the same age though in the fashions of different times.

Betty watched him without comment. When he had finally arranged the sets, she picked up the newspaper clipping of Moire in a swimsuit.

"I really think she has a better figure than mine," she said, comparing it to one of herself in a swimsuit at about the same age. "More exercise perhaps, though more to begin with too, don't you think? Better breasts, if you'll forgive my honesty. You can imagine," she said as she continued to examine the pictures, "how thrilling our encounter on the street the other night was for me. It was the first time I've ever spoken to her. She is an impressive woman, as I hardly need tell you."

"Indeed."

"Would you believe me that through all this half century I continue to love her?"

"I would not doubt it."

"She was a beautiful child. . . . It is said now that a mother should not even see the baby she's giving up for adoption, much less track her through life. I understand the wisdom behind that, and yet it seems much too abrupt. She was my first; carrying her and giving birth to her were exciting experiences. I wanted to know what happened to her. As it turned out, I was able to be some help when her first foster parents died in an accident and when the Meehans were killed in that tragic explosion. . . . Do you know all of this?"

"Most of it."

"You will tell her about me?" She looked at him with pathetic appeal in her eyes.

Lorcan wasn't sure if she wanted Moire to know. "I see no need of that. If you wish to talk to her, you know who and where she is."

"Of course." Veils descended over her eyes—Moire's vast brown eyes. "I make no excuses for my life, Lorcan. Much that I did was headstrong and heedless. I thought I had no choice. Now I realize that I was—and probably still am—skilled at deception, especially of myself."

"You carried her to term."

"Yes, I did that—and I'll admit I am proud of it and of her. . . . May I keep these pictures?"

"Certainly."

"I will leave it to your judgment." She gathered the photos and clippings together in a neat stack. "If you deem it wise to tell her, I"—she struggled with her emotions—"I would not be averse to meeting with her and trying to explain."

"Continued love, Mrs. Allen," he said carefully, "is much better than an explanation."

"Surely." She rose and walked to the floor-to-ceiling window which overlooked the park. She spoke softly, her back turned to him, so softly that he had to lean forward to hear her. "How often I wished . . . well, that's neither here nor there, is it?"

Presumably she did not expect a response.

She turned to face Lorcan. "Will you marry her and bring her to Chicago?"

The question sent a surge of hope racing through him.

"I cannot, Mrs. Allen."

"Whyever not, Lorcan?" She returned slowly to her chair. "Whyever not?"

"My father told me before he died that he was also her father."

She shook her head sadly.

"Pat ought to have known better than that." She sighed. "Perhaps age confused his memory. Or perhaps he was indulging in the taste for revenge which marred an otherwise admirable character. In any case let me set your mind at ease immediately. I was already pregnant with Moire, as she calls herself now, when I first made love with your father."

"I see."

"You should sound happier, Lorcan. She's yours now for the taking, is she not? It was obvious the other night that you were both deeply in love. . . . Pat was a sweet man, but occasionally mean-spirited, to his own self-destruction it seems to me now."

"I guess I am confused, and a little sad."

"There are many regrets about which to be sad, Lorcan. None of them, however, should be yours. . . . May I bore you with my story?"

"I'm sure you won't bore me."

"I repeat"—she sat in the overstuffed chair, now nostalgic and vulnerable—"that I will make no excuses. I was passionate and shameless. Whether I have been punished enough for my mistakes I must leave to God."

"I'm sure She understands."

"You sound like Father Blackie." She smiled sadly. "I hope he's right. . . ." She dabbed at her nose with a piece of tissue. "In any case I was just out of my teens when I found myself pregnant. The father was even younger than I was. He was my first love. . . ."

"Tim Meehan?"

"My, your research is quite comprehensive! Yes, Tim Meehan. Later he came to have a reputation as a braggart and a womanizer. Perhaps he was. I wept bitterly when I heard of his death. Just as he was my first man, I was his first woman. He was gentle and loving and kind. We both thought we were in heaven. Sin—a great preoccupation with Catholics—was the furthest thought from either of our minds. We were certain we were meant for each other from all eternity. If things had been different. . . . But they were not and could not have been. I found myself pregnant. I did not, could not tell him. We had no money; it was the Great Depression and we were poor.

"You will think me terrible. Remember that I was young, frightened, and desperate. Pat had been, ah, romancing me for some time. I permitted him to make love to me—fully aware that he was a married man with two children—and led him to believe that he was the father of my child. Do I shock you?"

"No."

"I fear that I do. Pat was a charming man in those days; one could not help but be fond of him. He was more experienced in matters of love than poor Tim, much more experienced, yet he was also kind and gentle and loving. I became fond of him too. Despite my better intentions, I admit that I fell in love with him. There was no future in it, needless to say. I had behaved like a silly child, not the last time in my life by any means. Your grandfather arranged matters nicely and our relationship ended."

"Tim's family had no money?"

"His father was an honest policeman. They had some money. It would not have been enough."

"I see."

"When Maura's foster parents died, I made arrangements through your grandfather with the Meehans to adopt her. Joseph was in the service and planned to run for Congress when the war was over. I had money by then. I undertook to promise a large contribution to his first campaign. I was a hopeless romantic, still am as you doubtless perceive. I thought that it would be pleasant for Tim to know the girl and her to know him, even if they did not realize the actual relationship between them."

"I see."

"Quite by accident your father bought a house next to the Meehans'. He perceived the similarity in appearance between the girl and me and accused me of deceiving him. I must say it was a good-spirited accusation. He was rather more amused than angry: I had played a good joke on him and his father, now deceased. I didn't quite admit his charges, which, after all, were based on a misinterpretation of why the girl was living with the Meehans. Yet he was quite certain they were valid. He often referred to her as Tim's daughter."

"When was this?"

"In the nineteen-fifties. We had continued our friendship . . . exchanged letters during the war with, I confess, one or two subsequent romantic encounters. By then I was convinced that I was damned and was leading a reckless, even dangerous, life. Pat Flynn, I repeat, was a charming, fun-loving, generous man. I have no idea what was missing in his relationship with your mother. Perhaps I presume too much when I suggest that anything was missing. He certainly cared for her and would never have left her. He was, I might add, extremely proud of you and your astonishing gifts. He spent much of our time together, the few times we were together, bragging about your accomplishments."

Lorcan wanted to hear it all.

"So when the Meehans were killed, it was natural for you to ask him to see that money was sent to Maura."

"The money was delivered indirectly. I spoke with him on the phone. I could afford substantial support for her then. I stood ready to provide more. She did well on her own. I thought it wise not to intervene. . . . Does she wonder about her origins?"

"Moire is a self-possessed woman, Mrs. Allen. It is not easy to determine what she wonders about. I'm sure she has no animosity toward her parents."

The sun had disappeared behind the high-rises west of Lincoln Park. The Lake had turned from blue to deep purple. Shadows now fell in the corners of the drawing room. Betty Allen was still seated in the light; a dark rectangle covered Lorcan and the couch on which he listened to her.

"So what do you think, Lorcan Flynn? I wish you seemed happier."

"I have much to digest, Mrs. Allen." He rose slowly. "I am deeply grateful for your candor."

"I'm not sure what happened to Pat, exactly." She rose with him. "The fire seemed to go out of him twenty or thirty years ago. That terrible brother of his was a debilitating influence, I fear. He was the kind of man who counted up resentments and whispered them into Pat's ear. I found the brother's relationship with your mother suspect too. He was an insufferable little pest. She seemed quite dependent on him."

"Rory or Father Frank?"

"Oh, Rory. Father Frank was a nice priest, not as nice as Father Blackie, but nice still. I have met your brother Henry once or twice and found him a distasteful little insect. Pat never spoke of him at all, much less with the affection and pride he felt for you."

"I see."

"So whatever he may have said to you before he died must be judged in the context of his past affection for you. He was old and tired and sick. . . . I almost went to the funeral Mass, you know. At the last minute I lost my nerve."

"Pray for him," Lorcan said, his voice husky.

"I will."

"And for all us living."

"I will do that too. Especially for you and Moire."

"I appreciate that."

3

"Why is it necessary that you hunt down the elusive Tim Meehan?" Blackie Ryan was wearing his Cubs windbreaker and trying to make midmorning tea on this First Sunday after Easter. "The valiant Moire is once more available to you. Is that not sufficient?"

"I am astonished about what Betty said concerning my father."

Lorcan deftly removed the teakettle from the priest's hands and poured the boiling water into a pot in which he had placed four Marshall Field's strawberry tea bags.

"None of us can be painted in simple colors, Lorcan Flynn."

"Regardless, the mystery remains unsolved and Tim Meehan continues to be a threat."

"Only if you seem to threaten him. Moreover, is not the mystery already solved?"

"Not completely. I still don't know what happened between the fight with my parents on the beach and the explosion, between three, let us say, and four."

"Why, you tossed and turned on a bed of fever, and the valiant Maura, as she was then, walked the beach, the rain beating down upon her, in anger and confusion."

"Right."

"Suppose that you did locate Tim Meehan, what then? If you've surmised correctly, that he is or was an agent for the United States government and is still powerfully connected. Hasn't he threatened to do further harm if you insist on pursuing him?"

"He underestimates me, Blackie. I've served on government commissions. I have powerful connections too. I can make certain threats that would neutralize his ability to do harm to us. First I need to have proof of where he is and a set of charges that I could cause to be made public if anything happens to me. . . . Langley is protective of old agents let out to pasture, but not at the risk of embarrassment and exposure of the folkways of the agencies."

"Indeed. . . . So Tim Meehan is up against a more dangerous foe than he realizes."

"He's old, Blackie, almost as old as my father was. He's not invulnerable."

"Whereas you are? . . . But you know, if I were to seek refuge from the demands of my Lord Cardinal and my bumptious staff of associates, I would hide myself in the place where they would first look for me, because they would never look there."

"I beg pardon?"

"It is always said that one hides in the place searchers would least suspect. However, if searchers have any imagination, they promptly go to the place they would least suspect and ignore the place they would most suspect. Thus, after suitable cosmetic change, I would obtain for myself employment, let us say, as a member of the janitorial staff here or perhaps as a salesperson at the McDonald's on Chicago Avenue or, more desirably, at the Chicago Ice Cream Studio. Who would ever think of looking for the elusive Blackie Ryan there?"

"Everyone who knows his fondness for chocolate ice cream."

"So, since they would think immediately that I might hide out in a junk food emporium or the best ice cream shop in Chicago, they would never look in those places."

Lorcan chuckled. "Excellent psychology—and worthy of Chesterton's Father Brown, but I don't see—" Then he remembered. It wasn't the voice.

"I know where he is, Blackie. Exactly where he is. I'm going to get him."

4

The cherry blossoms were past their prime, but the view outside of the Old Executive Office Building was still stunning, white and pink against a rain-dark sky.

"We did call off Maynard Lealand for you." The large man frowned at Lorcan. "Doesn't that count for something?"

"That favor was for yourselves, not for me."

"I don't see, to be candid about it, Lorcan"—the man was important enough to possess a corner office in the baroque building (long ago the State War Navy Building)—

"why you think we would want to do anything, always admitting, which I don't for a minute, that your suspicions are valid."

"Come on, Barney. It's me, Lorcan Flynn, remember. I'm not a dumb career bureaucrat."

"I would never claim that you were." The man coughed discreetly. "I realize that you are smart enough and ruthless enough to have been an excellent agent yourself."

"My game is more exciting and less dangerous." Lorcan leaned forward. "That, however, is irrelevant. I want this mystery resolved. If I have to denounce the President of the United States as an accessory after-the-fact to murder and attempted murder, I will not hesitate to do so."

"How could you possibly prove that?" The man slouched in his chair, his paunch resting on the desk in front of him, his shrewd, hard little eyes watching Lorcan carefully.

"George Bush was head of the CIA when they let Tim Meehan out to pasture. He authorized the protection and the payment, perhaps even the unit responsible for his protection."

"I'm not sure the event you hypothesize could have happened at that time."

"If I make the public accusation that it was, no one will believe a denial."

"I'm also certain that the DCI would not have been involved or even informed about such a decision."

"Which would prove what an inept—did I almost say wimp—director he was."

Barney played with a pen on his crowded desk.

"What exactly is it that you want, Lorcan?"

"Two things. First, I want the unit which is protecting him disbanded. Now. It's probably a rogue unit anyway. I want it effectively disbanded and I don't want Meehan to know about it. Presumably your people have a way of accomplishing those goals?"

Barney shrugged. "Naturally."

"Secondly, I want him brought in and questioned about the murder of his brother and his family. I want to know the how and the why of it."

"That's all?"

"That's all."

"You don't want him charged with murder?"

"Your people wouldn't tolerate an investigation and a trial. They would rather take care of it themselves—as you well know."

"I see. . . . You'll excuse me, Lorcan, while I make some calls?"

"Let me remind you once again so you can impress it on those with whom you talk that if anything should happen to me—"

"I quite understand, Lorcan. Your death would be charged against the occupant of the Oval Office."

"Absolutely."

Barney sighed and heaved his heavy bulk away from his desk. "I'll see what I can do."

It took him a half hour, during which Lorcan worked on a sonnet about cherry blossoms against a rain-drenched sky.

Barney returned, seated himself ponderously, and said, "Your arguments are extremely persuasive, Lorcan. We're prepared to give you most of what you want."

"Most may not do."

"The rogue unit is already, ah, terminated. You need fear nothing from them."

"Fine."

"My friends are prepared also to conduct an interrogation, with you present, of the Meehan murder."

"Fine."

"They are reluctant, however, to bring him in—internal morale, you understand."

"So?"

"They do not object if you bring him in. They will set up a center in the area for the interrogation."

Lorcan stared coldly at the man across the desk. "They—and you—are hoping that he may kill me in the process."

"Lorcan . . ."

"You'd better pray he doesn't. My evidence will be just as good whether I'm dead or alive, whether he kills me or your rogue unit does."

"Lorcan . . ."

"Don't worry about it." He rose from his chair. "Meehan said he could piss higher than I can. He's about to find out he can't. Tell your contact that I'll be at the Hay-Adams for the rest of the day."

"When this incident is over, are you sure you wouldn't consider an appointment in the Administration, extremely high level of course, much higher than mine?"

"I'm a Democrat."

5

The ambush had been carefully set.

The target crossed the creek on the tree branch which acted as a bridge and walked around the large concrete pier which separated Long Beach from Grand Beach.

Lorcan stepped out from his shelter next to the pier.

"Good afternoon, Tim."

The man who had called himself Jim Quaid stopped instantly.

"Lorcan Flynn." He stepped forward, his hand out. "What a nice surprise! Have you decided you want a house down here in Grand Beach?"

Lorcan backed up a pace to avoid the outstretched hand. Dennis Rooney appeared behind him, an AR-15 cradled in his hands.

"Good, Tim," Lorcan said, "but not good enough. You're old and you're slipping. There are guns pointed at your head from up there. Don't try anything or you're dead. I imagine you know what your former friends will do with your wife when they learn you're out of the picture."

From the dune, Rooney's colleagues emerged, weapons aimed at Tim Meehan.

The man hesitated. "I don't know what you're talking about."

He stood, carefully tense, parrying for time, considering the options left to him.

"We are arresting you for the attempted murder of Moire Halinan and the murder of your brother Joseph, his wife, and their two daughters."

"I didn't kill them," he said evenly.

"So you admit you are Tim Meehan, sometime basketball star and war hero and longtime CIA killer?"

"I wasn't a killer, in a manner of speaking."

"Your tradecraft is slipping, Tim." Lorcan watched him closely, knowing that the conversation was playing Tim's game, yet still savoring his triumph, despite and perhaps because of the danger. "That little speech mannerism betrayed you—in a manner of speaking."

Meehan reached for his calf with astonishing speed. Before he could use the knife which he had grabbed, Lorcan was upon him.

"Watch out!" Dennis Rooney yelled.

Meehan swung the knife down in a swift arc toward Lorcan's chest. Lorcan ducked under the man's arm, barely missing the descending blade. Meehan swung again. Lorcan brushed his arm away and buried his knee in the other man's groin. Meehan collapsed into the sand, Lorcan on top of him.

Gasping in pain, Meehan fought back. He shoved his shoulder toward Lorcan's stomach. The blow was a direct hit, but a weak one.

Lorcan pounded his fist into the man's face. He drew back, then hit him again.

Dennis Rooney calmly fastened the cuffs on Meehan's hands.

"Let him go, Lorcan," Dinny said. "We've secured him. He's no longer dangerous. He's an old man."

"He's a killer!" Lorcan shouted. "He would have killed us like he killed his own brother."

"I didn't kill them," Meehan sobbed, blood streaming from his mouth. "I didn't kill them. I was in Egypt. I didn't kill them."

"And you tried to kill your daughter." Lorcan's fist was poised for another savage blow into the man's face.

"I don't know what you're talking about."

"Yes, you do, bastard." Lorcan held back the blow. "Moire Halinan is your daughter. Betty Lyndon is her mother."

Tim Meehan collapsed completely. He slumped against the ground as though he wished he were already a corpse.

Lorcan brushed the sand off his clothes and permitted Dinny and Mike Casey to lead Tim Meehan away.

6

"It's up to you, Mr. Flynn." The operative was young, a crew-cut blond with the blank, emotionless blue eyes of a professional psychopath. "If you say so, we can terminate him and his wife. He broke the rules with that sloppy operation on Long Island. He understood the risks he was taking. Or we can let him go. He knows that one false move, even the hint of one, and we terminate them. We'll do whatever you want."

Lorcan considered his adversary, a battered old man, trussed up in a kitchen chair in the basement of a farmhouse outside of New Buffalo.

"Kill me but don't kill her," Meehan pleaded. "She hasn't done anything."

"You know the rules," the agent said. "You broke them. If you die, she dies."

"What a pathetic bastard you are," Lorcan snarled. "You learned to love killing during the war, a lot more fun than football and seducing virgins on Fifty-fifth Street. You sold out the IRA for the thrill of it, killed with impunity for years, and now expect a peaceful retirement with an occasional murder thrown in for extra kicks."

"I didn't want to kill her," Meehan said sadly. "She shouldn't have been in the house."

"Wrong, Timmy, the bomb shouldn't have been in the house."

"The IRA were crazy, too busy killing each other to fight the Brits. I was an agent, not a killer. I killed only when I had to. I didn't like it."

"You liked being a spy, loved every minute of it. The Brits recommended you to Donovan when he was starting the CIA, didn't they? Said you were reckless and bright and ruthless and would be a great asset to his new organization. Allen Dulles loved you. You were the kind of agent he wanted. Irish and Catholic and without a conscience."

"You think you know so goddamn much."

"You tried to kill your own daughter."

"I didn't realize she was my daughter," Meehan screamed. "Betty never told me."

"That wouldn't have stopped you. The game was fun, scare the innocent civilians, show that you're still a good spy."

"I didn't know . . ." he blubbered. "I wouldn't have done it. I would have loved her. . . ."

"Like you love your wife, whom you put in danger just so you could try to scare me."

"I didn't mean to do it. . . ."

"Sick, pathetic bastard!"

"Washington on the phone, Mr. Flynn," the agent said.

There were two other agents in the room and a half dozen outside. Dinny Rooney stood next to Lorcan, still cradling his automatic weapon, his face impassive. Outside, Mike Casey and a couple of his staff were watching the other agents.

Lorcan spoke into the field phone: "Yeah."

"Barney here, Lorcan. It's entirely your decision. He broke the rules and he has to face the, uh, consequences. However, our records show clearly that he was in Egypt at the time, working on the Suez fiasco, which wasn't his fault, by the way. The English and the French blew it by not winning the first day. He wasn't sufficiently senior then to organize a hit team on his own initiative, not without our finding out. As a matter of fact, it would appear that a serious effort was made at the time of the uh—"

"Cover-up?"

"—before the matter was closed to determine whether he was involved. If he had been, we would have terminated him at that time. One cannot afford to support agents who engage in their own vendettas."

"Uh-huh. . . . Who was the killer?"

"We were not interested in that issue. We wished to avoid public exposure of the events which transpired and about which you seem so well informed. We also wanted to make sure that Meehan was not a rogue. You can take it as certain that he was not involved in the killing."

"I'm skeptical."

"Why would we lie about it, Lorcan? We are not interested in protecting him anymore. He broke the rules. He is of no more use to us. It would be simpler for us to terminate him and his wife. He deserves to be sanctioned for the Huntington affair. On the other hand, we are not determined to do away with him; he's harmless now that his support unit has been broken up."

"So?"

"We will abide by your decision. . . . Those in authority are impressed with your intelligence and determination. Once again I have been authorized to tell you that we would like—"

"I said I was a Democrat, didn't I?"

He stared at Tim Meehan. *They want his blood on my hands.*

"Let him go." He waved at Meehan. "You hear that, Barney? I'm not God. I won't play God. I won't make your lousy decisions for you. Let the pathetic bastard go."

Dinny Rooney's frosty eyes twinkled in approval.

7

"You continue then to be invulnerable?"

Bishop Ryan handed the Jameson's bottle to Lorcan; their implicit division of labor had assigned him the task of keeping the Waterford tumblers filled—after he had washed them out.

"Very vulnerable, Blackie—to both death and to murderous fury. I might have killed the man."

"The point"—Blackie sniffed his drink as though he were not altogether sure it was authentic—"is that you didn't."

"I came close."

"It was not, I assume, a game of horseshoes of the sort I am told is currently played at Mr. Bush's White House."

"I savaged him."

"Come now, Lorcan, the man was trying to stick a knife into you. As soon as your associates secured him, you ceased hitting him."

"Once he knew we were not going to kill him, Tim Meehan's only interest was his daughter: he wanted to know everything about her, even asked if I would introduce her to him, not, mind you, as her father. He merely wanted the chance to talk to her."

"Remarkable."

"Later he even asked whether I still wanted to buy a house in Grand Beach—a total transformation of personality."

"Truly remarkable."

"You trust him?"

"Sure. No reason not to anymore, is there?"

"None that I can see."

"His cover is both blown and irrelevant. He can spend the rest of his life trying to catch up on what he left behind, as Jim Quaid, who is now the only person he can be."

"Perhaps a fortunate circumstance. . . ." The priest sipped at his drink. "You will introduce him to the valiant Moire?"

"I don't know. I'll have to think about it. I'm not sure she'll be in Chicago all that much."

"Ah?"

"We still have a lot to work out." Lorcan swallowed a gulp of his drink as he tried to evade the subject of the "valiant Moire."

"You have been in touch with her, I assume, since you have learned that she is not your sister?"

"Uh, no. . . . I have to solve the mystery; then I can try to work things out with her."

Blackie put his drink on a coaster on top of the coffee table and stared intently at Lorcan.

The latter expected him to challenge that evident fallacy.

Instead he said, "You have, however, solved the mystery, Lorcan James Flynn. You have suspected for some time a solution, one that was obvious to me when you first came into the hallowed precincts of the Cathedral Rectory." The priest's blue eyes bore into the depths of Lorcan's soul. "The relative exoneration of Tim Meehan leaves that the sole plausible solution."

"I haven't solved it," Lorcan argued hotly.

"You know who touched off the explosion." The priest's eyes continued to eat at him. "I invite you to know that you know."

Lorcan knew.

"Perhaps I do," he said.

"There is, in all probability, only one living person who also knows."

"Yes," Lorcan said dully.

"You must seek confirmation from that person."

"I don't want to."

"Regardless."

8

"I've warned you to expect neither praise nor approval in this office, Lorcan James Flynn."

Doctor Murphy had returned from her vacation suitably tanned. Her good color was all the more noticeable given the white spring dress she was wearing. Lorcan had spent half his allotted fifty minutes on the couch pouring out the story of the last two weeks. Doctor Murphy was now tapping her pen impatiently.

"Not even a little admiration?"

"I will acknowledge that you survived."

"That's not much."

"And that you have presented much material in your reactions to the events with which we may work."

"It will take a long time."

"Shall we begin?"

"Who was my father? Who was my mother? I know little more about them than Moire does about her parents."

"Like Tim Meehan and Elizabeth Lyndon, they were complex human beings, living in more difficult times than we can imagine, with conflicting emotions and motivations, problems and hopes. They both loved you in their own often mixed and imperfect ways, just as the woman's parents love her. Can you not accept that and be content with it?"

"Not much choice, huh?"

"Then we can turn to the identity of someone about whom we can learn more."

"Me?"

"Who else . . .? Tell me, does the beach-towel dream still recur?"

"Yes," he said. He'd not wanted to talk about it.

"It is still malign, although you have unraveled most of the mysteries surrounding it?"

"Now more than ever."

"There remain, you realize, still two issues in the world beyond this office that you must resolve as quickly as possible."

"Which ones?" he said irritably.

"The not unrelated questions of your relationship with the woman and the identity of the killer."

"I don't want to address them," he said, surprised at the childish pique.

Doctor Mary Kathleen Ryan Murphy's response was emphatic. "Regardless."

> The Punk disgusts me. He solved it all without ever stirring out of his damn easy chair. As my Brigie would say, "Uncle Punk is like totally awesome, really!"
>
> My patient's behavior was quite impressive too. Not only did he act with unerring instinct, he did so with remarkable self-awareness and restraint. We may make rapid progress once he faces the final problems of this interlude.
>
> It is altogether likely that he has lost the woman, an unfortunate occurrence. She made herself as vulnerable as a woman can and was rejected, or so it must seem to her. By the time he works up the courage to explain the reason for this rejection to her, she will have had time to reflect on the apparent folly of their passion. Moreover, his own passions have obviously diminished. He is not sure either.
>
> He is most reluctant to admit that he knows the explanation of the death of the Meehan family, though he admits quite freely that the Punk claims that he knows.
>
> The long-run prognosis for my patient is now excellent; the short-run prognosis is still guarded at best.
>
> Granted that men are stupid in their dealings with

*women, this man, if he loses the love of his life, will
be one of the stupidest I have ever known.*

9

"So what about Rob's mother?" Liz demanded as she and her father danced at the Rich Daley Inaugural Ball.

Spring was beginning to win its struggle to come to Chicago. Leaves were cautiously appearing on trees; the Lake had turned a gentle blue; light-pastel dresses were blossoming on Michigan Avenue. Rob and Marie had returned from Jamaica, brown and blissful.

The new Mayor had been inaugurated at Orchestra Hall in the morning. Saul Bellow had indulged in a vain and self-serving address in which he claimed to be the first literary figure to participate in an inauguration. He apparently did not consider Gwendolyn Brooks, the black poet who had participated in Mayor Washington's inaugural, to count.

Otherwise the event had been festive and splendid. The new Mayor had delivered an excellent speech, and his elder daughter wore a hat which was the envy of all young womenfolk in the city.

At night a five-hundred-dollar-a-couple reception and dance (proceeds to children's hospitals) took over the rotunda at the far end of Navy Pier, its crumbling walls disguised in festive decorations. White balloons hung like canopies over every table. People began to dance upon arrival, even before dinner. The Ramsey Lewis trio played during cocktails, and four orchestras performed at dinner—jazz, big band, classic rock, modern rock.

The lights of the Chicago skyline glittered in the distance; friendly stars reflected on a serene lake. From the other direction a full Passover moon had peeked over the rim of the sky and seemed to smile benignly on the celebrants.

Lorcan did not want to attend the ball but his daughter-in-law insisted that they all must go since her hospital would benefit. Liz was summoned home from Tufts to be his date. She congratulated the new First Lady and First Teenager on their gowns.

On the dance floor, after the Mayor's forty-seventh birthday cake had been produced, she had spoken of her mother's wedding. It was the first time Lorcan had heard of it.

"It was silly, Dad, really silly. She tried to act like she was twenty again. Mom was a good mother in lots of ways and I love her. Yet I have to be candid: she's a silly woman."

"Liz! What a terrible thing to say. . . . You ought to respect your mother."

"I *do* respect her. That doesn't mean I have to be dishonest about her, like you are."

Ouch!

"The world is more complicated than that, Liz."

"I *know,* and when I grow up I'll understand that. Consider it said. . . . So what about Rob's mother?"

"What about her, Liz?" he asked uneasily.

They were closing in on him.

"She's in love with you and you know it, Daddy," Liz replied impatiently. "I never would have believed that such a composed woman was capable of a teenage crush."

"You're exaggerating, Liz."

"I am *not.* . . ."

"Very well, then," Lorcan said. "I won't disagree."

"Well. . . ."

"Well, what?"

"Well—are you planning to marry her?"

"I'm not sure that's an issue."

"It sure is. . . . You're not being fair to her."

"You're on her side against your father?"

The music stopped. They stood on the floor, neither prepared to budge.

"You *bet!"*

"We'll see." He searched for a way to escape his daughter's angry eyes.

"You haven't decided definitely not to marry her, have you?"

He replied slowly and carefully. "Not yet."

"Well, *don't!*"

10

"I don't see any point in an explanation, Lorcan. We both regret what happened in Chicago. Can't we leave it at that?"

He had finally phoned Moire, two and a half weeks after the wedding; he proposed to fly to New York and explain everything to her. To his astonishment she was not eager to see him.

"It wasn't what you think, Moire. You have to give me a chance."

"I don't *have* to do anything, Lorcan."

"I didn't mean it that way."

"However you meant it, we ought to forget the matter completely."

"I don't agree."

"That is your privilege."

"I don't want to fight with you, Moire."

"Who's fighting?"

She could be a difficult woman.

"Only an hour?" he begged.

"I am extremely busy at work. Moreover, I must give a lecture at a meeting in Tucson in a couple of weeks. It is quite important to my career that I do it well. I cannot permit myself to be distracted from its preparation."

"I have a home in Tucson. Maybe—"

"*Absolutely not.*"

"That sounds definitive."

"It certainly is."

"Can I propose a compromise?"

"I'm listening."

"You'll have to change planes flying from Tucson to New York. I can meet the plane and we can talk for an hour at the United Red Carpet Club."

There was a long pause.

"I'll think about it."

11

"**C**ould you not have simply flown to New York, arranged for one of your limousines to bring you to Huntington, and insisted that she listen?"

"No."

"Why not?" Doctor Murphy demanded.

"She wouldn't let me."

"I see."

As I have reported in these notes before, like most men in their responses to women, the patient is a fool. More of a fool than the average. Notably above the standard deviation from the average.

12

"**D**id she start many fires?" Lorcan asked his Uncle Rory.

Rory carefully replaced his spoonful of raspberries. He tried to pretend that Lorcan had not startled him.

Rory had proposed lunch, as though nothing had happened since their past lunch. "Family problems," he had said.

The problem was that Hank was in the hospital for "a rest" and had no medical insurance. Moreover, the family was running short of money for "day-to-day expenses."

Lorcan did not need to ask whether he was in the psychiatric unit.

"I'll take care of it, Rory. Have them send me the bills from the hospital. I'll call Joanne. She won't mind, I trust?"

"No. . . . She can hardly afford to mind, can she?"

Still nasty.

Lorcan was determined not to ask the key question. Somehow, at the end of the meal, it slipped out.

"I don't understand," Rory stammered.

"Yes, you do, Rory. I want the truth. All of it. Now. At last."

"She was a great woman, Lorcan. A great, great woman. You never realized how great. I did. Poor Father Greg did, too. There was a family history of nervous exhaustion. You could have found that out."

"Nervous exhaustion." His parents' generation could not cope with even the words "mental illness." To admit that someone needed psychiatric help—even now in the case of Henry—was somehow to admit "bad blood."

What would people say?

"I know she was a great woman, Rory. I remember her before she was sick. I didn't know about the family problems. No one told me."

"You should have asked," Rory said sullenly.

"Damn it, Rory, I did ask. Now tell me the truth."

Rory pulled out a cigar. "May I?"

His voice wavered; the fingers holding the cigar trembled.

"Sure. Now answer my question: did she start a lot of fires?"

Carefully the old man—for now he looked extremely old—removed his cigar from its wrapper, clipped the end, put it in his mouth, and lighted it with loving care.

"Not often, Lorcan. A couple of times. When she was very sick. Normally we managed to put them out. Father

Greg was good at calming her down, even though your dad—God be good to him—never liked Greg much. She never meant to hurt anyone, not even that night. She didn't know that there were explosives in the basement. Pat—your father—knew, but he didn't expect her to start the fire. One could never be sure when these nervous incidents would occur."

"How did she start it?"

"A gasoline can from the fishing boat . . . only a half gallon. Not much. She never believed there was any connection between what she did and the explosion."

Or wouldn't, couldn't, admit it to herself, poor, poor woman.

"You and Dad and Henry and Father Frank cleared away the evidence before the fire and the police came?"

"Henry did not participate. He was too young to be trusted. Father Frank arrived after the police. He gave us prudent advice. We were fortunate that the police were under orders to get the incident out of the paper as quickly as possible, fortunately for us. Your illness was an added burden we did not need."

"Were these nervous incidents related to Dad's, ah, misbehavior?"

"I don't know what you're talking about, Lorcan."

"Come on, Rory, cut it out. You do too."

The old man laid his cigar on the saucer of his coffee cup.

"Your father wasn't worthy of her, Lorcan. Neither were you. She was more sensitive and loving than anyone I have ever met. Pat meant no harm, but he didn't understand how she suffered. I was often the only one who could cheer her up."

"I see."

"That night, however, it was your fault not his."

"My fault?"

"She had lost him to other women, trashy worthless women. Now she feared that she would lose you."

"She wanted to kill Maura Meehan?"

Uncle Rory seemed surprised. He picked up his cigar. "Of course. Why else set fire to their house?"

Why else indeed?

Lorcan's body went cold with horror. Yet he had to ask one more question.

"Did you or Dad or Father Frank or Father Gregorio try to obtain psychiatric help for her?"

"Psychiatric help?" Rory recoiled in dismay. Ash fell from his cigar to his vest. "Why would we ever do that, Lorcan? There was nothing wrong with your mother."

13

"The Holy Spirit," Blackie Ryan said, peering out over his vast red chasuble at the Cathedral congregation, "is like Tinker Bell."

Predictably the Maeve, still angry at Lorcan for his treatment of Moire, doubled up.

She had not been ready to forgive him even when he had informed her that they would meet briefly at O'Hare that Pentecost Sunday afternoon.

"You're a coward, Da," she had protested. "The woman scares you."

"And vice versa, Maeveen."

"That makes no difference at all, at all."

"You will remember Tinker Bell," the Bishop continued, "a playful, dancing spirit in the Walt Disney version of *Peter Pan,* who flits blithely about, sparking into life with her magic wand all matter of wonders and surprises and enchantments. So too with the Spirit of God. She spins about creation, calling forth and presiding over variety and diversity and uniqueness. She is especially responsible for that which makes each creature most particularly itself. Offer Her gratitude for the splendid, attractive, overwhelming diversity of God's creation.

"If one has the choice of accepting and rejoicing in the variety with which God's Spirit has filled the world and resisting Her variety, one would be wise to accept and enjoy her playfulness. It is a mistake to try to fight the Holy Spirit."

Just in case he missed the obvious application of the priest's words to his meeting with Moire, Maeve buried one of her sharp little elbows into his side.

Lorcan thought of the different women in his life—his mother, his sister, his wife, his great-aunt Marie, his daughters, his daughter-in-law, his mistress (if that's what Cindi was), his assistant, his psychiatrist. Diversity indeed. Most of them—no, all of them—loved him one way or another.

He'd left one woman out. What should he call her?

The love of his life?

Or, better, in Doctor Murphy's terms, the Woman.

He thought again about his mother. In the nineteen-fifties the researchers had already developed the first of the psychiatric drugs. Some of them might have worked. If his family had not feared the stigma attached to mental illness, she might have enjoyed a reasonably normal life. Of course it was all too late for second-guessing.

The plane from Tucson landed forty-five minutes late. They wouldn't have much time. Lorcan felt the small box in his jacket pocket. Yep, the ring was still there. He probably wouldn't offer it to her. If he did, she wouldn't take it. But still, it was wise to be prepared.

Moire, flying coach, naturally, was the last to leave the plane, regal in a peach suit with a matching hat. She seemed fitter than ever.

She permitted him to kiss her cheek. She was sorry to be late. The conference had gone well. The Arizona Inn was charming. Tucson was hot but nice. The reaction to her presentation seemed positive. She had driven by his house. It was quite nice. Josie still intended to come to Chicago at the end of the summer. The Teamsters had decided to leave them alone. She asked after Father Blackie.

"Father Blackie is a very dangerous man," Lorcan murmured.

"Of course."

In the Red Carpet Club on C Concourse, Moire ordered a Perrier with lime.

"I have some things I must explain, Moire," Lorcan told her.

"I told you several times on the phone, Lorcan, that I need and want no explanations and I will accept none."

"Damn it, woman, will you give me a chance to talk?"

She opened her mouth to say she didn't want to hear him talk, changed her mind, and said, "I'm listening."

"The morning after the wedding, when I was called away from our breakfast, my father told me a terrible lie. That may not be the right word. He may not have known it was a lie. Let us say he told me something that was not true."

"Oh?" She frowned, surprised, troubled, prepared to be shocked. "What was it?"

"He said you were my sister, half sister to be exact."

The color drained from her face. She put down her drink and closed her eyes.

"You said it was not true?"

"Yes."

She opened her eyes. "You're certain?"

"Absolutely."

She closed her eyes, shook her head, and picked up her drink. "Mind you, Lorcan, I think you'd make a wonderful brother. I couldn't ask for a better brother, but—"

"I understand."

"Would you understand if I asked for a stronger drink?"

"I think they have Jameson's here."

"By all means."

She was still tense and pale when he returned.

"Dear God, Lorcan." She touched his arm, her eyes round and gentle. "How horrible for you."

"It was at first."

"You found out who my father really was?"

"Yes." He had ordered a drink for himself and swallowed most of it in one gulp.

"And my mother?"

"Yes."

"When Lorcan Flynn makes up his mind, he succeeds."

"I had to find out, Moire."

"Oh, I understand that." She smiled thinly. "I didn't mean to question your intent."

"It's all over."

"You solved the mystery of the murders?"

"Yes. Do you want to know it?"

She drank from her glass. "Is it necessary?"

"I don't think so."

"Then I don't want to know."

Someday perhaps she might want to know. For now, the less he told her the better.

"That's all I wanted to say."

"Do you intend to tell me who my parents are?"

"Do you want me to?"

She stared at the brown liquid in her tumbler. "I'll have to think about that. . . . Should I know or would I be better off not knowing?"

"I'm not sure."

"Are they still alive?"

"Yes. . . . They're both flawed human beings, as we all are. They both love you, quite powerfully as a matter of fact. I don't think you need to know who they are, but you should remember that they do love you."

She bit her lip. "That's hard for me to believe."

"Moire." He took her hand. "You are the result of a young and innocent love, a romance in difficult and lonely times between two impoverished and impulsive young people. They meant no harm. Each, in their own way, has paid terribly for what happened. You talk about God's forgiveness. You should forgive them."

She nodded. "I'll try. I've tried all my life."

"Try isn't good enough anymore." He squeezed her hand.

She closed her eyes, bit her lip, and then nodded slowly. "They're probably more pleasing to God than I am. Certainly I forgive them."

"That's my Moire."

She removed her hand from his.

"I'll have to think about it all, Lorcan. You've quite taken my breath away."

"I agonized over how to tell you."

She patted his hand. "You could not have done it better."

"About us, Moire . . ."

"Lorcan." She glanced at her watch. "I have to catch the shuttle."

"Of course." He stood up. So did she.

"I can say what I want to say quickly." Then she began reciting what sounded to Lorcan like a memorized statement. "I have no regrets about what happened the week of the wedding. We both realize, don't we, that it would never work? We are strong-willed, tough-minded, independent people. Set in our ways, accustomed to our privacy, jealous of our freedom. The friction between us would be intolerable. Sex would heal some of it, but we would hate one another most of the time. . . ."

"I'm not sure that's necessarily true."

He had no answering arguments even though she was probably wrong or at least possibly wrong.

"It is true, Lorcan. You realize it as well as I do. I'll always admire your courage and determination. I'll always be grateful for your honesty today. I'll always sympathize with what you've suffered. . . ."

"I'll always love you, Moire."

Hesitation flickered in her eyes. "And I you, Lorcan. My plane is boarding. I'd better run. Thank you ever so much." She brushed his lips and rushed to the door of the jetway leading to a 727.

She turned at the door and lifted a hand. Was she weeping?

As Lorcan waved back, he wasn't sure.

He waited in the boarding lounge until the red, white, and blue nose of the 727 slipped away from the jetway and disappeared on the ramp. He hurried around to the other side to watch it inch out toward the runway.

It's over, he told himself with an enormous feeling of relief.

In the tunnel from C Concourse to B Concourse, he rode the moving walkway, tired, depressed, but free. He did not try to push his way around the bands of oblivious travelers who, despite the computerized voice requesting them not to block the four walkways, insisted on doing so anyway.

Lorcan's head was reeling with half-formed ideas, and his heart was aching with loneliness.

14

At the end of the first section of the walkway, Lorcan paused before stepping onto the second. The neon lights flashed above him. People pushed by him as though he were not there, a surrealistic film's metaphor for hell.

Tomorrow he would have to face Mary Kathleen Ryan Murphy, M.D., and report on this venture.

So the woman rejected you?

Yes.

Definitively?

Yes.

She would not have remained in Chicago with you if you had insisted?

She flew back to New York.

I see. You could not have stopped her?

Restrained her physically?

This is not a male fantasy story, Lorcan Flynn.

I understand that, Doctor Murphy. Are you asking me if I had put my arms around her and begged her not to fly back to New York, would she have agreed?

Precisely.

Well . . .

Well?

She might have.

I see. So you rejected her. Again.

I didn't say that.

And this time without the excuse of a high fever?

Well . . .

Do you imagine she wept all the way back to La Guardia Airport?

I suppose so.

And if you had pursued her on the next plane . . . ?

Are you trying to tell me that I rejected her because I didn't get on the next shuttle and chase her?

Rejected her again. You had an opportunity you chose to waste. It was your decision, not hers.

It's not fair to put the responsibility on me.

Lorcan Flynn, who's talking fair?

Lorcan was oblivious by now to United Airlines' glittering cave and the people rushing through it. The image of trailing and capturing his love had unleashed a torrent of emotions—desire, affection, passion, tenderness. If he caught the next plane and phoned ahead from the plane for a limo, he might be able to beat Moire to her home—or arrive right after her and maybe drag her out of the shower. They would lie in each other's arms within three hours. As they both surely wanted to.

He turned back toward C Concourse.

But, Doctor Murphy, wouldn't it be wrong to go running after a woman just to please your psychiatrist?

As he rushed down the walkway, hurrying to get a seat on the next shuttle, he laughed aloud.

That would be the kind of question he would never dare ask Doctor Murphy.